Gallatin Warfield earned his law degree from the University of Maryland Law School. He is a former Assistant Attorney General in the criminal division of the Maryland Attorney General's office and a former chief felony prosecutor in the Howard County, Maryland, State's Attorney's office.

State V. Justice

Gallatin Warfield

First published in Great Britain in 1993
by HEADLINE BOOK PUBLISHING PLC

First published in paperback in 1993
by HEADLINE BOOK PUBLISHING PLC

A HEADLINE FEATURE paperback

10 9 8 7 6 5 4 3 2

ISBN 0 7472 4064 7

Phototypeset by Intype, London

Printed and bound in Great Britain by
HarperCollins Manufacturing, Glasgow

HEADLINE BOOK PUBLISHING PLC
Headline House
79 Great Titchfield Street
London W1P 7FN

This book is lovingly dedicated
to my wife, Diana

Therefore the sight that is granted to your world penetrates within the Eternal Justice as the eye into the sea; for though from the shore it sees the bottom, in the open sea it does not, and yet the bottom is there but the depth conceals it.

– Dante Alighieri
Inferno, canto XIX, 1.73

PROLOGUE

Appalachian Mountains, Western Maryland
November 27, 1989
5:30 P.M.

The boy was having difficulty breathing. The hand around his throat was no longer gentle. It was rough, and the strength of the grip was increasing. 'Paaa—' He couldn't get out the word. He wanted to call for Papa, but the word hung up. It was clamped off, and now he was really scared. 'Ppp—' He tried to twist his tiny neck, but the hand just got tighter.

This was bad. A bad touch. He wanted it to stop. He wanted to see Anna, and sit close on her lap. He wanted Masha, the pup that Papa gave him for his sixth birthday. He wanted to ride to the park and see the pointy building that reached the clouds. And he wanted Papa to take him home.

Tears began to drip down the man's fingers, and for an instant the grip relaxed. Air rushed into the boy's mouth, but was trapped inside when the clampdown resumed. He could feel his heart beeping the way it did

1

on the plane when the storm hit. And then he saw the man's face.

The doctor had looked that way when his mother went into the tiled room and never came back. And the old gardener, when he carried Masha to the back door and set her cold stiff body on the sill. And it came in his sleep, but Papa was there to pull back the quilt and lift him out, rocking him gently until the ugly face was gone. Papa was always there when he screamed. But now he couldn't even scream.

The knife had a sharp silver blade. It appeared from the back, and the boy had just enough strength to reach out for it with his little white fingers. He was starting to hallucinate from lack of oxygen. 'No!' They were going to cut off Masha's head. 'Please don't kill her!' The small hand brushed the blade, leaving a thin furrow of red across the palm. 'Don't kill Masha!' The knife was closer. 'Don't ki—'

The blade entered the boy's rib cage and pierced his racing heart. His body went limp in the man's arms, and he didn't make a sound. There was no burst of pain. No suffering. He was unconscious from the choking, and had already shut his eyes to blot the image of the execution of his dog.

The man lowered the boy to the ground and extracted the knife. There was a small spot of blood on the boy's chest and a clinging smear on the blade. That was all.

He looked at the inert crumpled form, wrapped the weapon in a handkerchief, and walked away. At the tree line, he turned. In the waning twilight the tall oaks on the far side formed a semicircular backdrop to the grassy clearing. Frosty nights had killed most of the high stalks, and only a few resolute tufts remained, swaying softly in the twilight. Above, the distant rumble of a jet engine was all that could be heard. The man looked up for a moment, then lowered his head in prayer. When the sound had faded into the western sky, he was gone.

He drove around the back roads for hours, twisting and turning through terrain dotted only by the lights of an occasional farmhouse. He tried to find a place to pull off, but the shoulder was too narrow, and the ground too soft to allow the vehicle to park without sinking to the hubcaps. The landmarks, clearly detailed on the map, were useless now, so he couldn't even be sure he was in the right spot. He had to feel his way along the route, led only by the voices in his mind.

A rocky flange suddenly bulged out of the twisting asphalt. He swerved onto its surface and cut the motor. He cranked the window down, and a light breeze flowed in to mix with the warm bubble the heater had raised above his knees. It was quiet. He punched off the lights and listened. The wind twirled silent eddies around the car. He looked toward the darkness, and waited, listening.

The noonday sun of a long-ago summer suddenly swapped places with the night as his thoughts drifted back. 'Down here! It's down here!' The echoes of youth pulled at his brain and, for a moment, sucked out the sorrow. He felt himself crashing toward the sound, leaping ravines and dodging sticker bushes, trying to catch up. 'Hurry! We're gonna leave if you don't get up with us!' He struggled against the bumpy ground, pushing obstacles out of the way, clawing to keep pace with the others . . .

The man got out of the car and felt his way down the embankment. He stumbled once, then switched on a flashlight. The trail had been overgrown for almost a century, but he locked into it as if he knew its every nuance by heart. He walked at a brisk pace, sure now of his footing, led onward by the voices. After fifteen minutes, he was there.

The boards that had been nailed across the entrance to the closed-off pit were rotted out, leaving only skeletal remnants to block the path. Nature had tried to compensate by shooting cables of vine growth over the hole, but they could easily be pulled aside. The man grabbed the network with both hands and pulled. 'Swear! Nobody tell about this! Nobody! Swear!' The man hesitated, remembering, then went in. 'I swear,' he said, as the tunnel closed over his shoulders.

It looked exactly the same. The rocky ceiling. The jagged walls. The deep black pool. It was the same. And it would always be the same. Time could never change it. He had gone on to another life after that summer. A life that was not the same. The world had gone on, too, and it would never be the same, either. But here, nothing ever changed.

He pulled the knife from his pocket and unwrapped its covering. His hand trembled as he held it over the void. There, at the bottom, were the dreams. The secrets. The discoveries. The promises. In this place, or a place like it, he had left his dreams to await their claim by his own child. But now that could not be. Now it was over.

He dropped the knife, and the obsidian liquid ate it up. The circle was complete, and the man knew he would never hear the voices again.

PART I

Discovery

CHAPTER 1

November 28
3:25 A.M.

State's Attorney Gardner Lawson stirred in his bed, trying to fight off the Cayman dream, but it was too late. He was already in the water, a mile from the island, descending, on his way to the undersea wall that protected the shore from a ten-thousand-foot drop into the Atlantic trench. The dream had begun, and now he couldn't come out until the dive had run its course.

In the beginning there was peace, and he found himself floating over coral heads, as glistening umbrellas of air from another diver caressed his face and wiggled like jellyfish on their way towards the light above. He saw silvery tarpons circle in formation, and bat-winged manta rays flap out of the liquid semidarkness, and, everywhere, the unguent peace of the deep. And then he went over the edge.

Suddenly there was movement below. The bubbles of his companion became sporadic, and there was a giant shape in the murk. Gardner tensed. He knew something

9

was wrong as a familiar dread began to cut into the peace.

The diver was pointing to an ominous shadow wedged against the ledge. Gardner saw it and tried to remember . . .

Then he recognized the shipwreck.

The peace was gone now, and the panic had started. The other diver was about to enter the twisted hull. 'No!' Gardner gagged into his mouthpiece. But it was too late. A set of rubber fins undulated into a gap in the freighter's bow, and he was alone.

Pressure 600. Depth 150. He tried to concentrate, but it was too late. He had to get out. The rate-of-ascent rules were gone. Decompression tables, gone. Reasoning ability, gone. The ocean was choking him with its enveloping arms. He had to get out, and the only escape route was a direct shot, straight up . . .

Gardner woke up on the fifth ring. He was still underwater on the first three, almost out on four, and gasping for air on the surface at number five.

'Lawson speaking.' His words were forced.

'Gard?' It was Larry Gray from the county police. 'You okay?'

'Yeah.' He gulped a few calming breaths, trying to acclimate himself to the sudden change of environment. 'What time is it?'

Larry's after-midnight calls always signaled tragedy, and the later they came, it seemed, the more serious the situation.

'Three-thirty.'

'Trouble,' Gardner predicted.

'A bad one.'

Gardner sat up and groped for the bedside light, his dark eyes wincing as its brightness cut away the shadows and allowed him a view of his own face in the gold-leaf mirror across the room. His stomach tightened. 'What happened?' His black hair was mussed, and the silver streaks at the temples seemed to leap out of the glass. His eyes were puffed with sleep. Gardner looked away.

'Child was killed out at Sessy's Woods,' the officer continued. 'Teenagers found the body about one A.M., and phoned it in.'

'Jesus!' Gardner said quietly. 'How?'

'Looks like a knife wound. They're processing the scene now.'

'Suspects?'

'Well, so far, we've only got T. J. Justice. He was seen in the area a couple of days ago.'

'The "Kansas Pedophile"?'

'That's him. Convicted of one child killing. Suspected of others.'

'What do you have on him?'

'Nothing really. He's been staying at the motel up in Hodges. That's close enough to raise suspicion right off the top.'

'What else?'

'Young white boy. Knife. Possible sex assault. That sure sounds like Justice, from what I've heard.'

Gardner breathed hard into the phone. 'How young, Larry?'

The detective could feel the prosecutor tensing for the reply. 'Six years old, Gard—'

'Shit!'

'Looks like he died instantly. No sign of a struggle . . .'

The words did little to blunt the force of the grotesque image battering its way into Gardner's mind. He tried to pull away from the scene, to steady himself on familiar ground. 'Uh, any physical evidence? Witnesses?'

Larry knew what was happening. He and Gardner had fought the criminal wars too long. He knew where the soft spots were, and the sound of the prosecutor's voice told him that the man was struggling to keep his composure. 'We're looking at that right now. So far it looks weak.'

'You want me to come out?' Gardner's speech had assumed a more professional tone. 'I can be there in about forty minutes.'

'Yeah. I think you'd better. There's an extra wrinkle I haven't told you about . . .'

The prosecutor suddenly felt the shadow of an outside force across their path. 'Say it, Larry!' He could sense the silver-haired detective wincing as the command burst out of the other end of the line.

'Okay! . . . This wasn't an ordinary kid. He was Russian. Father attached to the embassy. Some kind of deputy or something.'

The State's Attorney didn't answer. He was trying to assess the implications of what he'd just heard.

'Gard? Did you get that? . . . Gard?'

'Yeah, Larry. I got it. So this means FBI, other federal agencies coming in—'

'They're already here.'

Gardner gasped. 'What?'

'I said they're already here.'

'So fast? How the hell did that happen?'

'I don't know, Gard. They got here the same time we did, and now they're swarming the scene.'

'I'd better get out there!' Gardner said, grabbing for his running suit.

'What do you want me to do in the meantime?' Larry had finally gotten to the point that had prompted the call.

'Just do your thing as always. Investigate. Collect evidence. Look for witnesses. We've got jurisdiction here, not them. They can help all they want to but it's our case until someone says otherwise.'

'Okay.' Larry sounded satisfied, then he hesitated. 'But what about Justice? Do we move on him now?'

That was the toughest question of the night. Gardner had a vague recollection of the criminal's well-publicized history. He had gone free the last time because of a so-called violation of his constitutional rights. If he escaped again because of a legal blunder, the person who gave the order would be a prime candidate for public hanging. 'Shit no! Larry, you'd better nail down some hard evidence first. Just stay loose on him for right now . . . at least till I get out there.'

'You got it. See you shortly.'

'Right.' Gardner hung up as he finished pulling on the jacket top of his nylon suit. The torment of the dream had been replaced by the hideous realities of the prosecutor's waking life. He was forty years old, tall and trim, with a face that some called distinguished, as opposed to handsome in the conventional sense. His

13

outward appearance fit the image of a tough courtroom advocate. Calm. Steady. Unshakable. For the past decade that image had led to multiple terms as the county's elected State's Attorney. He gave no quarter to his opponents, the criminal element and their counselors, and his hard-line stance on sentencing was legendary. But now, at this point in his life and his career, he was beginning to falter. A bitter divorce, severely limited visitation rights with his only child, and a haunting memory of his past were slowly eating away at the polished image. Only his job, and his devotion to it, kept him going. And as always, when the phone rang after midnight, he had to answer the call.

Gardner splashed some water on his face and toweled dry. Then he grabbed his briefcase, tossed a yellow legal pad inside, and ran for the door. His mind was churning with possible scenarios for the days ahead. Some were good, others dismal. It all depended on how soon he could get control of the situation.

3:45 A.M.

The office of the Soviet Affairs Bureau in the State Department Building was quiet. With the advent of *glasnost* and *perestroika* in the Soviet Union, the frenetic pace that had characterized that section in the cold war years had slowed almost to a stop. The midnight shift had been discontinued, and now the individual cubicles and work spaces were dark and deserted. There was no longer a need for constant vigilance, the policymakers said. It was

14

time to begin a stand-down from twenty-four-hour alert.

Although the employees were sent home at a reasonable hour, the plug was not entirely pulled on intelligence-gathering activities. Until the dangers became ancient history, a giant computer in the basement, linked to the National Security Agency in Fort Meade, Maryland, would continue to monitor every Soviet communication flowing into, or out of, Washington, D.C. The unmanned unit systematically logged, decoded, translated, analyzed, and filed the millions of daily bits of information funneled through the satellite network. But the system had not kept pace with the changing times. It was still programmed to generate an alert notice if a transmission triggered a preset list of criteria. When this occurred, the information was immediately routed to the office of the bureau's deputy director.

A few minutes past 1:00 A.M. a flurry of messages was beamed eastward from the Russian embassy. Most of the transmissions clicked into the routine phase of analysis that allowed them to sift into the memory log virtually unnoticed. Then, twenty minutes after the first set of calls went out, a response came in from Moscow. The preset code immediately boosted the computer into a standby alert mode. The translated message simply read: PRIORITY MESSAGE TO FOLLOW. MAXIMUM SECURITY STATUS FOR ALL SECTION FIVE PERSONNEL.

The computer screen showed no outward signs of trouble. There was no klaxon, no alarm. When the message came in, the white letters quietly switched to red, marched into view from the left, and exited to the right. The information was logged.

Within seconds, the sound of the printer in the Soviet bureau deputy director's office was clacking off the empty walls. Then, abruptly, it stopped. The wheels turned, and the paper pushed out the top.

Again, there was a paraphrased translation: SITUATION ACKNOWLEDGED. ALL LEVELS NOTIFIED. SECURE RECORDS. RESTRICT COMMUNICATION. Z. EN ROUTE. All was quiet at the State Department, but elsewhere, something was up.

The road to Sessy's Woods curved from the center of town and ribboned westward toward the mountains. This was the time of year when the tourists came in their greatest numbers, driving the 130 miles from Baltimore or D.C. just to see the transformation of the leaves as they modulated from green to brown before falling to the mossy earth. The annual odyssey was a mixed blessing to the county, bringing a boost of economic activity and, at the same time, a disruption of the hush that filled the valleys the rest of the year.

The woods lay thirty miles to the west of town in a barren, rock-pitted region that buffered the valley from the soaring peaks. Even driving at full speed, at 4:15 A.M., without any traffic to interfere, it took Gardner a full three-quarters of an hour to reach the light show of red bubble lamps splashing intermittently against the trees on the edge of Sessy's Woods. Police cars, ambulances, pickup trucks, and passenger cars were jumbled around the curve of the road that went from the fields into the forest.

The air was cool, and he could see some of the officers

exchanging smoky bursts of conversation as they worked over the scene. Farther back, a dimmer glow illuminated a small white spot on the ground. As Gardner started towards it, Larry Gray stepped out from behind a tree and blocked his path. He was a large man with a smooth handsome face and a striking bush of close-cropped silver hair. 'Gard, you really don't want to go over there,' he said. Gray had known Gardner for a long time, as a colleague, and as a friend. Their relationship had solidified during the hunt for the 'Hooded Jogger' rapist, when Gray had set up a surveillance on a suspect and apprehended him with a knife in City Park, stalking his next victim along a deserted bike path.

Gardner stopped short. He didn't question Larry's comment. He knew there had to be a delineation between the investigation and the presentation of a case in court. The investigator is an essential witness, and if the prosecutor takes a role in the investigation, he could become a material part of the case, and be forced to eliminate himself as trial counsel. Gardner knew this, and held back. He felt much more at ease calling the shots from the antique leather chair in his courthouse office.

'What's the story?' Gardner asked quietly, his breath trailing a brief plume before shredding into frothy wisps.

'Medical examiner is still with the boy. Looks to me like a puncture wound, but you know we can't be sure until the autopsy.'

'Any other physical evidence?'

'We're still looking. Ground's too hard for footprints. No weapons anywhere. The whole scene is real clean.'

'What about the boy? You said he was Russian?'

'Yeah. That's the hard part. See that old lady?' Larry subtly pointed towards the edge of a small group of people standing on the outskirts of the taped-off area where the body still lay. A plumpish Slavic-faced woman, swaddled in black with a babushka covering her head, was staring blankly over the yellow ribbon towards the center. 'That's his grandmother. Seems that they were up here to see the leaves. They spent the night up at Wooley's place near the lake. She called about midnight to report the boy missing, but by the time we could do anything the body had already been found. She's out of it. I mean, it turns out the boy was missing since yesterday afternoon, but she never told anyone until midnight. Out of it.'

'What about the father? Didn't you say he was with the embassy? Where the hell was he?' Gardner felt the flush of anger that always came when he saw the innocent fall prey to savagery. It was the worst part of his job, 'what if'-ing a violent death after the fact. It got so bad sometimes that not even the refuge of a chilled martini could protect him from the attack.

'He was at the embassy, but they tell me he may be on his way up,' Larry said, shaking his head in a way that told Gardner his friend was suffering from the 'what if' syndrome, too. 'Apparently the old lady was afraid to tell Dad about the boy being gone. That's the best I can figure. Must be some sort of culture thing. I don't know.'

Gardner was watching the Russian woman as Larry talked, trying to get a clue from her appearance. He was

18

good at that. Two hundred jury selections had taught him to read people, and he had learned how to interpret every possible inference from the way they carried themselves, talked, or even folded their arms.

The whole story was written in the lines of her face. She had been entrusted with the little boy. He was her jewel, the tiny spark that kept her worn-out heart alive for one more day. She had been his guardian, his teacher, his guiding light. But, somehow, she had let him slip away. Somehow, she had failed. She had hoped that he would come back from the woods where he had run for the hiding game. She had waited. Then she had gone to look, her stiff legs churning the weeds as she called his name, 'Mika!' 'Mika!' But he didn't come back. Her terror mounted, and then it was dark, and she was afraid to call his father. She sat and waited for a gentle tap on the cabin door, but the only sound was the occasional scrape of a tree limb against the dust-fringed windowpane.

'Gard?' Larry had lost the attention of the prosecutor. 'The FBI wants to set up a command post over at the Ramada. That's Agent Smithwick. Remember him? From the practice shoot last year?'

Gray pointed out a dark-haired man in a blue business suit standing behind the Russian grandmother. They were surrounded by other federal men in jackets emblazoned with the initials of their organization. 'Tried to talk to him,' the officer continued, 'but couldn't get close. Too busy, they said.'

Gardner focused on the agent. He was hovering over the Russian woman like a protective hen. There were a

few orders shouted to subordinates, but most of Smithwick's attention was on the old lady, and it was clear
she was off-limits to everyone but himself. 'Did you get
anything from her?' the prosecutor asked.

Gray gave him a 'you've gotta be kidding' look. 'No
way.'

Gardner shrugged his shoulders and turned his back to
the grandmother and her ring of protectors. The officer
turned with him. 'Okay, then,' the prosecutor said, pulling the zipper of his running suit tight to the neck, 'they
set their agenda, so now we set ours.'

Gray shot him a look of concern. 'It's not going to be
that simple, boss.'

Gardner flashed an annoyed expression to his friend.
'Why not?'

'They're hot after Justice . . . even as we speak.'

Shit, Gardner thought. 'How the hell did that
happen?'

'I don't know. That's the first thing they said when
we got out here – "Justice did this . . ." I overheard
Smithwick himself say it.'

Gardner shook his head. 'And so it begins.'

Larry Gray's face assumed an apologetic expression.
'Maybe it's not such a bad thing . . .'

'What do you mean by that?'

'I mean maybe they can nail the son of a bitch before
we can.'

Gardner caught the meaning. 'So *you* agree with
them.'

'Huh?'

'You think Justice did it.'

20

Gray's expression turned sinister. 'Absolutely,' he said.

By 6:20, a slight change in the shadows signaled that night was about to yield its hold over the scene to a fiery autumn dawn. The medical examiners had finished working on the body, and the officers searching the perimeter of the clearing were on a break. The FBI agents had finally taken the worn-out grandmother away in a car, and Gardner felt cold and tired, the way he used to after a hundred-foot dive.

The boy had been carefully placed on a stretcher, his body covered by a dark green army blanket, the face just another small rippling fold in the fabric. Larry Gray returned to his police car for some radio calls, and Gardner stood in the pathway the technicians would use to get to the ambulance.

Larry had told him to stay away because he knew his 'boss' wouldn't really want to see what was under the shroud. He had viewed the dead child, and it was too close a match. It looked too much like the little boy in the frame on Gardner's desk: the prosecutor's seven-year-old son with straight blond hair and a melt-your-heart smile.

Gardner saw the stretcher coming, and stepped back. He would see the pictures in a few days. There was no way to avoid it. It was an important part of case preparation. To convince a jury of the facts, a prosecutor must know the facts. Every gory detail. He must speak with authority. And to do that, he had to lift the veil. There was no way around it.

Gardner nodded to the lead stretcher bearer, and the man stopped. He was one of the new guys down at the volunteer fire company. Early twenties, neatly trimmed mustache, baseball cap. He obviously knew who Gardner was, but the prosecutor couldn't reciprocate and give him a name.

'Rough night,' Gardner said. He was stalling.

'Yeah,' came the reply. It was obvious that he was not going to help delay the inevitable. The attendants set the stretcher down gently and stepped back. Gardner knelt beside the olive drab silhouette of the little boy, hesitating, the way he did on the afterdeck of the *Mindy*, when the sea looked more like crude oil than water, and he was afraid to jump.

He didn't want to do it, but he had to. He peeled away the fold above the face, and looked into the still-widened blue eyes of the child.

'Uhhh!' he gasped. He hadn't expected to see the open eyes. The medical examiners usually took care of those things and closed the lids. The new guy must have forgotten, but figured out the problem, and pushed past Gardner in an effort to correct the situation. 'Sorry, sir, uh, you know how it is . . .'

'It's okay. Don't worry about it.'

But it wasn't okay. Gardner pulled the blanket down to the child's waist, and returned it quickly to the top of his head. He never even looked at the wound.

When Gardner reached the police car, Larry Gray was still talking on the radio. He had extended the curlicued cord to its limit, ironing out the kinks as he leaned across the car's open door. Gardner could see that he was disturbed. 'What do you mean, in custody? Repeat your previous transmission.' The officer turned and gave Gardner a pleading look.

'That is correct, sir.' It was the slightly southern drawled voice of the county dispatcher, Marie Jones. 'The FBI is on the way to pick up T. J. Justice. We just monitored their radio transmission. Thought you might want to know.'

'But he isn't in custody yet. You did say "in custody," but that hasn't happened, correct?'

'Rahht, sir, sorry 'bout the confusion. I figured it would be done by the time I told you, the way they were moving.' Gray didn't need to consult the prosecutor. Gardner's silent nod conveyed his advice. 'Marie, can you give me the freq they're using?' There might still be time to get a calm word in before the feds set the case in stone.

That was the problem in joint-jurisdiction cases. An arrest was an arrest, and the nonarresting jurisdiction always got stuck with the legal niceties that the arresting officers bestowed. If the FBI made an arrest without probable cause, Gardner would end up taking the blame. The court would look to the prosecutor to justify what the officers did in the field. If they got it wrong, Gardner would pay.

Larry had tuned in the FBI frequency, and was desperately trying to raise anyone who would listen.

'This is Captain Gray, county police, any federal agents involved in the two-eleven investigation, please respond . . .'

Silence.

'Captain Gray, county police. This is an urgent call for the FBI personnel handling the Sessy's Woods incident . . .'

He was deviating from standard radio transmission procedures, and Gardner suddenly became nervous. The first thing a good defense attorney did in a major case was subpoena the tapes of radio calls that came in when the investigation began. What better way to look into the collective minds of the police as they sorted their thoughts and began focusing on a suspect. Sometimes the thoughts conflicted as officers shared their mistaken beliefs about the facts over the airwaves. The suspect was a black male in a white car. The suspect was a white male in a black car. The suspect was headed towards Simpson's Mill. The suspect was headed towards Sampson's Hill. The tapes gave the defense attorney a ready arsenal to use as evidence of police incompetence, so, in Gardner's opinion, the less said, the better.

A voice crackled through and broke the silence. 'This is Agent Kranik, Captain. State your business.'

Gardner twitched a smile. Even over the radio the 'federales' always sounded pinstripe-suit professional. He grabbed Larry's arm, and another silent communiqué passed.

'Uh, can you state your position, Agent?' Gray asked. No need to get adversarial. Try to sneak up on him.

'Captain, may I ask what this is in reference to?'

'Uh . . . we need . . .'

Gardner was pinching his arm now. 'Ask for a meeting,' the prosecutor mouthed, still holding on to the elbow like the tiller of a boat.

'Please, Captain, we're in the middle of an operation right now. State your business or get off the air.'

'Have you made an arrest yet?' the officer blurted out.

Gardner winced and turned the arm loose. He had lost control.

'Say what?'

'I asked if you had made an arrest yet.' That was about as direct as it could get.

Gardner could see the tape winding slowly on the spindle as their words flashed out across the fall morning air.

'I said we have an operation in progress. I'm sure you will be thoroughly briefed later.'

'Are you going to answer my question?' Gray persisted.

'I thought I already had,' the agent responded firmly. Then he clicked off the microphone and ended the transmission.

Gardner felt numb as he drove towards town. It was 7:00 A.M., and the sky had lightened in the east. His eyes smarted, and he rubbed them with his hand. The scene at the woods had left him with a dull ache deep in his skull. There had been earlier times when he could take it. When he could push his emotions back and jump on a case with the detached precision that the voters expected. He could see the blood, and the twisted bodies, and not get shaken. He could face those things from an emotional afar, and do the job. But lately, the anguish was getting through the barrier. Lately, when the grisly facts were laid at his feet, he didn't want to look.

The foothills of the Appalachians flanked the road, as Gardner navigated between vistas of rocky crop fields, pastures, and dairy barns. The county was growing in population, especially near town, but the outlying areas were still untouched. Most of the farmhouses were set back against the rising elevations, their salmon brick or weathered clapboard fuzzily visible from Gardner's speeding Chevy four-by-four. Small-town values and attitudes prevailed in this part of the world. There was trust between neighbors, and an appreciation for a life unfettered by big-city concerns. It was a quiet place, where often the whoosh of wind was the only sound. Murders, rapes, and robberies did occur, the same as in the city, but they were rare, and as soon as the clamor died down, the people went back to their uncomplicated lives, and the silence returned.

Gardner rounded a curve and entered the straight-away that led down a ten-mile incline into town. Here the farmhouses were more numerous, the properties smaller than the outlying spreads. Most of them looked silent and morose, still battened down for the night. A few were sending up smoky salutes, pale exhaust from wood stoves rising sharply, then flattening out in grey streaks as they encountered the valley's temperature inversion. There was a sad face on the county today, Gardner thought. He suddenly wanted to talk to someone, but his only company was an endless string of spotted cows lolling against the rusted wire fence that bordered the road, and they didn't seem interested in anything he might want to say.

7:15 A.M.

'What's the matter, Harl?' the waitress at the Four Corners Inn in Elston, West Virginia, asked the weather-beaten man at the counter. 'Didn't get no fish this time?'

The man attempted a smile, but it lacked enough strength to crack his cheek. 'No, goddamn it, didn't get no fish. Got me a goddamn albatross!'

The woman bracketed his plate with her bony elbows. 'What happened? I never seen you like this, 'specially after one'a your lake trips.'

'Never made it to the goddamn lake.'

'Huh?'

'Got hitched up with a son of a bitch at the motel. Decided to drink up ever' goddamned beer 'tween there and the state line.'

'Who was he?'

The man winced. 'J. P. . . . T. P. . . . some goddamn initials. How the hell should I know? Most fucked-up, rat-faced shithead I ever met.'

'You never went out on the boat?'

'Whut' I tell you? We couldn't-a found the goddamn boat if'n we had a map.'

The waitress noticed that her customer hadn't touched his breakfast. 'Not hungry?'

'I was when I come in, but you jes' ruint my appetite.'

'How'd I do that?'

'By remindin' me of the worst goddamn day of my life.'

The waitress jerked her arms off the counter. 'Well, excuse me!'

The man picked up his fork. 'Letta, do me a favor.'

27

She tentatively set her elbows back down. 'What's that?'

'Never let me go back t' Maryland agin.'

She smiled and patted his arm. 'Don't think we have to worry 'bout that, Harl. By the looks of you, you'll be dead 'fore nighttime.'

Dawn had roused the inhabitants of the Potomac River basin in the usual manner. At the first hint of light, the populace began to stir in preparation for the race to the government offices on both sides of the water that divided the District from Virginia. Pentagoners went right, Capitol Hill people turned left, and everyone else scrambled up the middle. That seemed to be the name of the game each day, as the workers jockeyed for position on the roads and in the parking lots around their respective enclaves.

Robert Hamilton had been unprepared for the drill when he first started at the State Department. He had a liberal arts degree and a burning desire to serve his country, but no insight at all when it came to 8:00 A.M. traffic around D.C. The first week he was an hour late every day. He drove his car to work. Then he tried the bus. Next he tried the Metro. Finally it hit him. It didn't matter how he traveled. Unless he got an hour's head start, he was going to be late.

It was 7:30 A.M. and he was ready to roll out of his Georgetown apartment. He was a six-year veteran now, of the city and of the Soviet Affairs Bureau at State. Thirty-two years old, with a 'preppy' style to his dress, the man was, above all, a perfectionist. When his job began, the old attitudes and assumptions were firmly in place. The Soviets were enemies, determined to plow the United States under. They couldn't be trusted. They were to be feared and hated. Then a new leader came in, and things changed. Hamilton's directives likewise began to change. He was still supposed to keep a book on the Soviets' internal activities, but the hard line had eroded.

He switched on the television for company as he normally did while drinking his juice and eating a slab of honeyed toast. Now it was time to turn it off, but as he reached for the power button, a news program flashed RUSSIAN MURDER on the screen behind the anchorperson's head. Hamilton hesitated, then turned up the volume. It was a story about the killing of a Russian embassy dependent in western Maryland. Details were sketchy, the announcer said, but it could be reported that a young Russian boy had been stabbed to death, and that a manhunt was under way for a known suspect. The names could not be released at that time. There was some rapidly edited footage of diplomats leaving the Russian embassy, waving down the cameras, and then the logo switched to a farm subsidy story.

Hamilton turned off the television and sat down at the kitchen table. The story he had just heard worried him. A short time ago, something like that would have set the Russians off like an atomic bomb. He got up and hesitantly walked to the door. In the new regime, there was no telling how they would react. Every day now was new territory, and he sensed that in some way the situation would touch his life. As he left the apartment, the feeling intensified. The race for work had begun, but on this particular morning, Bob Hamilton's heart wasn't in it.

CHAPTER 2

Jennifer Munday was always the first employee to arrive at the State's Attorney's office. Each day the assistant prosecutor awoke at 5:00 A.M., read the paper, did the crossword puzzle, breezed through 'Sunrise Stretch' with Matty Swenson, showered, and had the coffee ready in the office library at least an hour and a half before anyone else came in the door. She was attractive in a businesslike way. Pale skin. Shiny, straight brown hair. Large eyeglasses that shielded a pair of olive eyes.

At 9:15 Jennifer sat in her office and waited for Gardner to arrive. She had heard the news. This was going to be the biggest case any of them had ever seen. She remembered how it was during the Perkins triple-murder trial. Total chaos. Gardner slugging it out day and night with the defense attorney, Kent King. She had only been in the office for two weeks when that one hit, and she had to admit that she wasn't really ready for what happened. All of the legal-theory study sessions, practice seminars, and clinical programs were useless. It was total war, and like nothing she had ever read in a law book. Gardner Lawson and Kent King battled for weeks like

31

gladiators, both inside the courtroom and out, before the jury came in with a guilty verdict against Perkins. Jennifer was only a spectator in that one. As she anxiously awaited her boss, she thought with a mixture of excitement and nervousness that this time she might end up as a participant.

Ten minutes later Gardner flashed past Jennifer's door on the way to his inner sanctum. He had already assumed a hunched position behind the big walnut desk when she entered the room. She was privileged, and didn't need to be announced by Miss Cass, the white-haired secretary who had been with the office as long as anyone could remember.

The prosecutor still had on his running suit, and Jennifer smiled as she recalled the many times they had jogged together up at Rockfield. He was on the phone, so she eased into the North Carolina custom-made chair that sat opposite the black leather work space. The formal documentation of Gardner's career cluttered the wall above his head. 'In all the time I've been practicing, no one has ever asked to see these damn things,' Gardner had snickered when the diplomas and court certifications were unboxed after the office moved into their new modern quarters. 'Guess that means they'll let anybody into court, as long as they wear a tie and speak a halfway intelligent sentence.'

'Okay . . . okay,' Gardner now said into the phone. He was not allowing the irritation that showed on his face to enter his voice. He was good at that, Jennifer thought – keeping his feelings from showing. She had missed the 'bad days' during the divorce. That had been a little before her time. About two years, to be exact. But she had a very clear image of the situation, as conveyed by the office grapevine, and she had her own theory about Gardner and what made him the way he was.

They had spent enough time together for her to notice a difference between his public persona and his true self. The projected image was serious, and at times, almost stiff. A hard-driving prosecution machine, crushing the opposition without mercy. That was the perception a lot of people in the small community had of Gardner, and th t was the way he wanted it. But Jennifer sensed a quiet side, a gentle counterpart that hid behind the ferocious courtroom roar. She saw it in the way he talked about his son. And sometimes, in the way he schooled her on the subtleties of trying a case.

She had driven out to see his old house on Watson Road, shortly after joining the office, to try to get a better understanding of her boss's world. The first glimpse had sent her reeling. A colonial masterpiece on a rise overlooking South Valley, its visual splendor took her by surprise. It wasn't a copy. It was real, well kept and cared for, like a patriarch in the lap of a loving family. Later she ran the chain of title in the musty file room of the courthouse annex, running through generations of Lawsons until she came to the prerevolutionary land grant that transferred the property from the English king to Thaddeus Lawson, Gardner's great-great-great-great-grandfather.

'I'll have to call you back on that. Yes . . . Yes. I will, Steve . . .' Gardner was talking to a court reporter from the *Western Maryland Gazette*. His eyes focused on Jennifer and his expression softened. 'Got to go, Steve. Really . . . No. You know I can't comment on that now. Please, Steve, give me a break. Okay . . . okay. Right. Later . . .' He hung up the receiver.

'These guys never quit. Nine A.M. and they're on the case. Who's the suspect? What are the charges? Can you tell me about the boy's family? Is the case going to cause an international incident? Damn!' Gardner said gravely. 'It would be nice if somebody told *me* the answers.'

Jennifer leaned forward and placed her hands on the desk. She was wearing a navy blue suit with a shirtwaist blouse. Her dark hair was pulled back in the customary ponytail, bangs fringing the top of her glasses like glossy fretwork. 'You look like you had a rough night,' she said softly.

Gardner managed a crooked smile. 'I've had more pleasant experiences . . . I guess you heard . . . looks like we're in for it.' He stared directly into Jennifer's green eyes through her large owllike spectacles.

'It's all over the TV.'

'What are they saying?' Gardner's involvement at the crime scene had shielded him from the reportage on the airwaves.

'Russian boy murdered. Suspect at large. Stuff like that.'

Gardner frowned. 'Did they name Justice?'

Jennifer pulled back from the desk. 'T. J. Justice?'

Gardner nodded. 'Cops think he's the man—'

'News didn't mention who it was,' Jennifer cut in.

'Good!' Gardner replied.

'But they did say the man had a history . . .'

Gardner frowned again.

'What's going on, boss?'

The prosecutor stood up. 'The same thing that always happens in a big case. Grab the first guy who comes to mind, then look for the evidence. They've got nothing on Justice but his past, and the fact he was in the area.' Gardner began to pace as he talked. 'If he killed that little boy, his ass belongs to me!' His voice was rising. 'But the cops have got to do it by the book!'

Jennifer's voice made him stop. 'And they're not doing that?'

'Hell no! Somebody called in the feds before our guys got a chance to put it together. Now they're running their own show, and giving information to the press.' He sat down again. 'Jennifer, the child was six years old. Six years old . . .'

She caught his eyes straying to the gold picture frame on the corner of the desk, then jerking away. 'Okay, what do you want me to do?'

Gardner calmed himself and took a deep breath. 'We've gotta get prepared on the legal side. Get some law together on arresting a suspect even without direct evidence, solely on the basis of his background. There's got to be something, some case law that we can use . . .'

Jennifer was making notes on her pad. 'What else?'

'Get our detectives working out at the scene. Maybe Brownie can come up with something. We need some hard evidence, not just speculation . . .' He noticed Jennifer waiting. 'Uh, I'll take care of that end. You go to the library and hit the books on the arrest issue.'

Jennifer stood up. 'You want me to brush up on my Russian, too?'

Gardner riffled his hair with his fingers. 'God, I forgot about that. We have to deal with those embassy people.' The usual routine in the State's Attorney's office called for extensive consultations with the families of the victims. Explaining procedures. Answering questions. Soothing the pain. 'Uh, I'll have to check on that with the feds. You get to work, and we'll talk later.'

Jennifer left the room as the intercom buzzed. 'FBI on the phone, Mr. Lawson,' Miss Cass said.

The prosecutor muttered an okay and punched the outside-line button. 'Gardner Lawson speaking.'

'Jim Smithwick, Gardner. We went a few rounds with the Uzi last year out at the state police range. Saw you at the woods, but I was tied up. Sorry . . .'

'What the hell's going on, Jim?' The prosecutor's voice sounded slightly irritated.

'What do you mean?'

'I mean who called you guys in?'

There was a pause at the other end, as if the agent had not expected this type of inquiry. 'Who called us?' He was stalling.

'Our people said you got to the scene when they did. I want to know how that happened.'

The pause continued. 'Uh, Gardner, I'm not sure I can answer that. You know we monitor your local transmissions . . .'

'You're not gonna tell me.'

'Not sure I really can. We got notified the same time

you did, and responded. What's the big deal?'

Gardner had an instinctive feeling that something was wrong, but held back. He'd never seen the feds get so involved so fast in a local case, even one with international implications. They usually had to be invited. He decided to table the issue for the moment. 'Okay, just asking, that's all. What's happening with *your* investigation? We tried a radio call at the scene, but didn't get a response.'

Despite his concerns and the snub at the crime scene, Gardner had a lot of respect for the FBI. They had always been there when he needed them for a case, and they didn't complicate the situation with a lot of pecking-order politics like the local police department seemed to do. They were pros, and when it came to presenting testimony in court, Gardner saved them for last, like the headline act in a Las Vegas show. Agent witnesses were like gods to the jury. All you had to do was ask them to recite their curriculum vitae, and when they were through, the defendant was usually convicted. One juror Gardner had postmortemed after a ten-minute-deliberation guilty verdict said it best: 'We all knowed he done it after that agent feller testified. They sure wouldn't-a sent him way out here for nuttin'. You know whut I mean?' Gardner knew exactly.

As Gardner reflected, Smithwick was answering his question. 'Sorry about the flap on the radio. We have a directive on radio silence during an operation. I think Kranik could have been a little more tactful, but he's a transfer from New York. Anyhow, here's the story: Our people got a report on T. J. Justice several weeks ago.

Some citizens had complained about him being in the area, and they wanted us to do a round-the-clock surveillance on him. We checked with Washington to find out how they wanted us to handle it, and they told us to hold off. The idiot still has connections with the ACLU, and their counsel had already stated that they would seek an injunction and punitive damages for harassment if the police followed their client around. Can you believe that? A convicted child killer threatening the cops?'

Gardner winced inwardly. 'Yeah, I can believe it,' he muttered.

But Smithwick was not going to pause for his response. 'The surveillance was put on hold pending a legal opinion from the Justice Department on the privacy rights of convicted felons.'

Gardner's mind began to wander again. He had read about the Justice case in the newspaper, and it was beginning to come back. The man had spent two and a half years in jail awaiting trial on murder charges in Kansas. During that time, he had gone through three new attorneys, four pleas, thirty-five motions, eight postponements, and five prosecutors. The conviction was upheld at the intermediate appellate level. Murder in the first degree. Life without parole. But the state supreme court reversed the case without remand for a retrial, and set him free. Denial of his right to a speedy trial, they said. To Gardner, it was a cruel joke. No defendant ever *wanted* a trial. That's why they twisted and turned so violently to avoid it. But, if they were lucky enough to build up some time, and lay a chunk of it off as the state's responsibility, they could walk free. That's exactly what T. J. had done, and the irony of it made Gardner sick.

'Lawson?' The FBI man realized he had lost his audience.

'Uh, sorry.' The prosecutor snapped back to the present. 'I was thinking about the Kansas case.'

'Hell of a way to let one go, huh?'

'The worst. No wonder the public's faith in the system is shot to hell. Anyway, you were telling me about a surveillance . . .'

'Yeah,' the agent said, resuming his pace. 'They referred the case out and the answer came back no. We couldn't put a man on him. Too much risk of a lawsuit. Then word came in about some investigative reporters on the case. These people were doing the hide-and-seek routine on Justice, and they couldn't care less about being sued, so we decided to keep tabs on them.'

Gardner liked the idea of turning the tables on the press. Letting them see what it felt like to squirm on a microscopic slide.

'Well, that worked fine, until he got to the Hide-Away Motel up in Hodges. He had been run out of town in West Virginia, and wandered into Maryland. Lucky us. He took up residence with the rest of the lowlifes up there.'

Gardner pictured the dilapidated cabins in his mind. 'What happened then?'

'The editors got tired of waiting for him to screw up again, so they pulled the reporters off. We had to back away, too. In the meantime, he slipped away.'

'Well, what was the "operation" they were talking about?'

'The field agent, Walmsley, got some information that he might be coming back to the motel, so they got the REACT team suited up and hit the place, but by the time they got there, he was gone.'

'Had he been back?'

'Not really sure. Desk manager told us that he forgot to turn in his key, and that unit fifteen, the one he had rented, was still vacant. He could have come back. We had to check it out. Anyway, we did get a few items from the room, including a knife. Seems like the right blade size for the wound.'

Gardner's attention flip-flopped again, as legal issues he would have to argue in court became interlaced with Smithwick's words. At least one potential for error had not yet come to fruition: Justice was still at large. Maybe he could get some input before they caught up with him.

'By the way,' Gardner asked, 'what was your probable cause for the "operation"?' So far, he hadn't heard anything.

'Well, I've got to admit it's a little skimpy. Convicted child killer in the area. Same general victim profile. Age and sex, that type of thing. Nothing real specific. But can you imagine the fallout if we didn't go after him? The press would eat us up. That fuckhead has gotten away once. Heaven help the poor bastard who lets him get away again.'

Gardner had been thinking the same thing, only he saw himself, not Smithwick, trying to explain the intricacies of constitutional law to a disbelieving public after the FBI jumped too fast, and dumped him with their handiwork.

'Thanks for the update, Jim. Where do we go from here?'

'We're having a strategy session at the Ramada one-thirty this afternoon. You're welcome to join us.'

'Any Russians gonna be there?'

'Yes, I believe there's a delegation coming up from Washington.'

'Who's running that show?'

Smithwick cleared his throat. 'What do you mean?'

'Who's going to act as liaison to the case, you or us?'

'Oh. We will. Of course.'

As if there was any doubt, Gardner thought. 'So we don't need to be involved on that end?'

'Only in a peripheral way. We'll take care of the protocol, that kind of thing.'

Gardner could feel the slight arrogance of power over the phone. 'And what about the case itself? Who do you see handling that?'

The expected response was, 'You, of course,' but it didn't come.

'We'll have to wait on that one,' Smithwick said.

'I see,' Gardner replied coldly. Then he hung up the phone.

Gardner sat for a moment, bound up in his thoughts; then he raised the phone again and keyed in the number for the county police department. 'Sergeant Brown, please,' he said.

The line buzzed, and a man answered, 'Lab.'

'Brownie, please. It's Gardner Lawson calling.'

'Uh, Mr. Lawson, he ain't here.'

The voice sounded familiar, but Gardner didn't have time for niceties. 'Can you tell me where he is?'

'Out on a case, as far as I know.'

'Can you tell me which case?'

The phone was muffled as the man yelled to someone, then came back to the line. 'Sessy's Woods. The one out in Sessy's Woods.'

'Okay. Thanks.' Gardner put down the phone. That was the best news of the day. Brownie was on the case. Now, at least there was someone in the field he could count on. Someone who knew what in the hell he was doing.

Gardner's mind suddenly focused on Jennifer, hard at work in the library. He smiled. When she joined the office a year ago they were constantly crossing paths there. At first, Gardner made it a joke.

'Are you lost?' he asked. It was common knowledge that trial attorneys never look at law books, they just 'wing it' in court.

'No,' she replied. 'I only came in here for some peace and quiet.'

'Then, what are you doing with the volume of the Maryland Appellate Reports?'

'I'm going to use it as a pillow,' she quipped.

The joke got old in a hurry as Gardner learned that the pillows Jennifer selected usually contained legal lumps that he could lay on defendants with devastating effect. Soon the library rendezvous became routine, and Jennifer's talents for sniffing out prosecution-sided case law became indispensable to the State's Attorney.

One night they were working on motions in a robbery case. Gardner was looking for some law on the issue of 'force.' Jennifer was digging away in the Maryland Law Encyclopedia. It was late, and they were alone.

'Jennifer?' Gardner cleared his throat as he closed his file.

'Yes, boss.' She didn't look up.

'You never really told me why you came out here.'

Her head came up slowly. 'What?'

'I still don't understand why someone with your talent came west. You should be in Annapolis, writing briefs for the Court of Appeals.'

She smiled. 'Are you serious?'

'Uh-huh.'

Jennifer's thoughts flashed to the city. A man's face appeared, and a dull pain nudged the bottom of her stomach.

'You're gonna get stale in the brain department if you stay out here too long,' Gardner said.

Jennifer was still dealing with the face that Gardner had unknowingly dredged up. 'I'll take my chances,' she finally said. Then she lowered her head back to her book, and Gardner knew the subject was closed.

Jennifer rubbed her neck and forced her eyes to refocus. She had gone through six legal treatises in the past hour without finding anything that could justify an arrest on the basis of prior record alone. They all said that you had to have more. There had to be more than suspicion arising out of previous behavior. There had to be a tie-in to the crime itself. Then she saw a headnote about 'signature' cases. In those situations, an offender's unique manner of committing a crime became a calling card that could, in fact, be used as probable cause for arrest.

She dug out a Maryland case citation on that point and pulled the volume. On the third page of the opinion she let out a yell of triumph. There was the answer. An arrest could be based on a criminal's deadly 'signature' if his crimes followed a set pattern. A suspect *could* be taken into custody if the state could show facts establishing the pattern, and if they could place the suspect at or near the crime scene.

She recorded the necessary data, slammed the book shut, and put it back on the shelf. Then she picked up her notes, stapled them together, and placed them in a new file folder she had procured from the supply cabinet. She turned the file to the side and wrote a caption on the flap: STATE V. JUSTICE.

CHAPTER 3

By noon Gardner was starting to feel grungy, so he decided to return home to change clothes. He wanted to look good for the out-of-towners. He knew that when the final verdict was in, he would probably be standing alone under the glare of the cameras trying to justify the result. That was the most frustrating part of practicing law: the fact that the results, the bottom-line results, were always in the hands of others. The judges and jurors held the cards. The lawyers could only try to convince them which to keep and which to throw away. It wasn't like that with doctors and plumbers. They had an opportunity to make hands-on corrections to human problems. They could affect the outcome by direct contact. But not so with lawyers. Their corrections were all done by proxy. They could gloat over a winning verdict, but deep inside there was always doubt as to how much credit they really deserved.

The exterior of unit 1235, Gardner's town house in Marblegate Estates, was a direct opposite of the home that he and Carole had lived in on Watson Road. Neo-urban cookie-cutter construction. Gray-blue siding.

Festooned latticework. It was part of a row that looked squished together like shuffled playing cards.

The only saving grace was what he had done inside. Gardner had rescued as many antiques from the divorce grinder as Carole's lawyer allowed, but that still left him a room short. He had scoured the auctions, and finally the decor was complete. The sterility still lingered in the whitewashed drywall, but the elegance of the furniture gave Gardner some of the peaceful security he had always felt in the warm burnished woodwork of his ancestral home, a brick-faced mansion on a tree-lined rise in the valley, complete with English garden and wooden porches. Filled with the memories of seven generations of Lawsons.

The family had originated in northern Europe, emigrated to Scotland, then, finally, to England in time to join the seafaring caravan to the New World. Gardner's first American ancestor, John Thomas Lawson, had arrived in Annapolis a hundred years before the Revolution. He took up residence near Baltimore, and remained there his entire life. His grandson, Thad, was more adventurous. He traveled west, and when he came upon a lush valley in the shadow of the Appalachian ridge, he halted his journey. He could not imagine that anything beyond the towering peaks could be any closer to paradise than this. The land was petitioned from the provincial governor, the house built, and the Lawson legacy in the mountains of western Maryland was begun. And for the next two centuries, the Lawson family gave its sons and daughters to the county as lawyers, judges, legislators, and community leaders.

Gardner showered and dressed in a dark blue pin-stripe suit, then studied himself in the full-length paw-foot mirror. White shirt with medium starch. Burgundy silk tie, awash with muted amoebas. White line pocket handkerchief. It was his 'jury suit.' His armor. His declaration to the world that he, the prosecutor, was the savior of the people. That he was on the side of good. That he was sworn to do justice. He always went through a ceremony as he dressed. Slowly knotting his tie. Arranging the handkerchief 'just right.' Buttoning the middle button. When he was through, he felt a surge of power that carried him past opening-statement jitters and sustained him through the trial. He hadn't planned to wear the suit today, but now it seemed appropriate. He'd be meeting some big shots from D.C., and maybe a diplomat or two. In that sort of company, the jury suit was the only way to travel.

The meeting was held at 1:30 in the Deerskin Room at the Ramada, in reality part of a single open area, but sectioned off with flexible partitions so the hotel could achieve its advertised status as a 'conference center.'

Gardner saw a few familiar faces. Larry Gray. Agent Smithwick. Pete Tomlinson from the state police. The rest were an assortment of authorities and nationalities he had never seen, but whose appearances he had accurately constructed in his mind on the way over. A large man in a dark serge suit literally stood out above the others. His white hair was shocked back in a severe sweep, and his bulk had stretched the fabric of his coat to bursting point. He looked like a professional wrestler, on his way to a match.

Gardner took a seat in the back of the room. At this point he did not anticipate a speaking part.

Jim Smithwick called the meeting to order. 'Gentlemen, thank you all for coming on such short notice. The purpose of this meeting is to coordinate the investigation of the Anatov child's murder.' This was the first time Gardner had heard the boy's name, and he noticed the burly man wince as the name was spoken. He also noticed a short, plain-faced balding man whispering into the big man's ear as Smithwick spoke, and he assumed it was a translation.

Jim Smithwick's job description as deputy agent of the western Maryland field office of the FBI did not require him to become master of ceremonies for the group. He had simply stepped in to fill the vacuum. When a case with as much potential for disaster as this one came down, there were usually not a lot of volunteers.

'I know that this situation is very, very tragic, and I wish to extend to the family from the bureau, and I am sure from everyone here, our deepest sympathies in this time of grief.' The agent nodded to the big man, and waited for the words to catch up in Russian. Again the man winced, but this time he nodded a solemn acknowledgment to the speaker.

Gardner felt the man's pain. He could always feel it, deep in his chest. A pressure crushing his heart and lungs together, whenever he had to look into the faces of the survivors that vicious killers inevitably left behind.

'Perhaps the best way to begin is for me to introduce everyone, so at least we can see what we have available,' Smithwick continued.

He then went around the room. Four FBI agents, two Alcohol, Tobacco, and Firearms agents, one Justice Department official, two from the State Department, four state police troopers, three county police officers, and of course, the State's Attorney. That did it for the investigators; the only ones left were the Russians.

'We also have with us two representatives from the Soviet Union's embassy security force – Mr. Cherensky, and Mr. Ivanov.' The agent acknowledged two dour-faced companions of the large man and his translator dressed in shapeless dark suits. Then he faced the giant. 'And Deputy Political Minister Valery Zeitzoff.'

The title caught Gardner's attention. It sounded like the man was a major player in the Russian power structure. The other two were security people, but this guy clearly dominated this delegation. Gardner rechecked the group. By now everyone had been identified. The father was not there. He wondered why, then concluded that he was probably overcome with grief.

When Smithwick finally finished the introductions, he faced Larry Gray.

'Jurisdiction over this case lies entirely with the county, in my opinion. This means that the role of the federal agencies is to assist and supplement the county's investigation.'

Gardner was not prepared for this sudden deferral of power. Here was the number-two fed in the district proclaiming to all the world that the 'county' was going to run the show. The FBI had jumped right in at the beginning. No polite deference to the county then. Only radio silence and 'get off the air.' They had even sent in their assault team, and Smithwick implied on the phone that they might be prosecuting the case federally. Now they were changing their tune. Were they back-tracking because they knew something the county didn't? Were they pulling back to save face, leaving the locals behind to face the slaughter?

Gardner's cynicism popped up when he sensed danger. It had made him a master in the courtroom, keeping him alert to the snares that defence attorneys constantly laid in his path. The whole thing sounded too pat. He only hoped he could find what it was before he was too committed to back away.

'At this point, perhaps we can share the information that we have obtained thus far,' Smithwick continued smoothly. He then told the same story he had related to Gardner over the phone, only this time he seemed to emphasize the word 'suspect' when he referred to T. J. Justice.

Gardner twisted around to see if any reporters had sneaked into the room. He had noticed a sound truck from Channel Nine in the parking lot earlier, but no sign of the camera crew. They were probably getting an atmosphere shot from an angle that outlined the crisp profile of the hotel against the craggy rocks of Anderson Mountain.

When the agent finally finished, he turned again to Larry Gray. 'Perhaps Captain Gray can discuss the per-spective from his shop – that is, if he wouldn't mind.'

Put that way, Gardner thought wryly, did Larry really have a choice?

The FBI agent stepped back and cleared a space for

the county police captain to reach the microphone.

Larry approached in a dignified manner, but caught his foot on the cord and almost pulled the small rostrum over. Under other circumstances it would have been amusing, but neither Gardner nor anyone else in the room ventured so much as a smile.

Gardner felt a little like he had at his son's school Thanksgiving pageant the year before. He had followed every word of the palefaced talking turkey with a silent input of body language so the lines would come out right. Even though it was Granville's brief time of glory on the stage, Gardner suffered through every word. He didn't want the boy to forget to say, 'And that is why we celebrate this wonderful feast today . . .'

Now Larry was up there, and the prosecutor knew that he wasn't used to this much attention. He also knew that they hadn't had a chance to plan strategy. He prayed that Larry wouldn't say anything that might raise an expectation they couldn't deliver on later. Gung-ho policemen did it every day. 'Of course we're going to catch the killer, it's just a matter of time.' How often had Gardner heard that repeated on the news? If the case didn't get solved, the comment flapped in the air over police headquarters like a banner.

Gardner preferred the more subtle approach to PR. 'We will do everything in our power to bring the perpetrator to justice.' It was much cleaner that way. No guarantees. No boastful hyperbole. Just a straightforward statement of fact that did not carry the seeds of 'I told you so' destruction.

'The best thing I feel that I can tell you all right

now is that every available officer in my department is working on the case,' Captain Gray announced to the group after regaining his composure.

'The crime scene is still being processed, and we are going to use dog teams and metal detectors to look for more physical evidence. The state police have agreed to let us do some aerial recon with the helicopter they have based at Hagerstown . . . and, uh, the boy's body is being taken to the office of the chief medical examiner in Baltimore, uh, for autopsy.'

The big man put his face down when the translation of that last part came through.

'We are pursuing T. J. Justice as a possible suspect in the case, based upon the fact that he has committed similar crimes in the past. We do have a knife that was obtained at his motel room, and the crime lab is going to check it for latent prints before we send it back to the FBI lab in D.C.'

Mr. Zeitzoff still had his head lowered.

'Uh, and we do have one more thing . . . a possible witness to the crime.'

The Russian suddenly looked up. So did Gardner. No one had mentioned a witness before. Gardner looked at Larry, as if to say, 'Hey, remember me? Your legal adviser, the guy you're supposed to keep informed?' But he was too far back to make good eye contact.

'Sorry some of you are just hearing about this for the first time,' Larry continued, looking in the prosecutor's direction but not directly at him. 'I got a call on my way over here. Seems there was a camper up there last night. It's too early to say how much he saw, but I've got a man interviewing him right now.'

God, I hope it's not Officer Barnes, Gardner thought. The last time he did an interrogation in a murder, the report he turned in ended up losing the case for the state.

By two o'clock Larry Gray had concluded his report by saying, 'I would like to assure everyone that my people will put forth the very best effort possible to see that this case is solved.'

Gardner felt relieved that his friend had adopted the noncommittal approach. Not too much said in the high-expectation department.

After Larry had returned to his seat, Smithwick resumed his position at the podium. He then looked around the room to see if anyone else wanted to make a statement. His eyes swept past Gardner, then stopped and came back. 'Would the State's Attorney care to add anything?' he asked in a tone that hinted this was only a courtesy, not an essential part of the program.

Gardner was caught slightly unprepared. He didn't have any remarks ready. But he had learned a long time ago never to turn down a chance to say a few words no matter what the occasion.

He rose dramatically and walked to the dais, carefully watching for the microphone cord. He then checked his coat button, grasped the podium by its sides, and began to speak.

'Ladies and gentlemen, my name is Gardner Lawson, and I am the State's Attorney of this county,' he began, just as he had in a hundred opening statements. 'It will be my responsibility to take the case to trial after a suspect has been caught and formally charged.' He glanced at Smithwick as if to say, 'If that's okay with you.' 'But in the meantime, we have to be sure that the legal requirements for arrest have been met.' He looked at the Russians, and slowed his delivery for the translation to catch up. This speech was really for their benefit, he had decided. The law enforcement people didn't need it; they were already in the business. He was sure that the delegation at the meeting didn't have a clue as to how the American 'system' worked. This lesson was for them.

'Uh, for those of you unfamiliar with our legal system, let me say that anyone who is charged with a crime has a long list of rights that the state, our government, must respect.' He waited for the soft drone of the translator to die down. 'We can't just grab someone off the street and throw him into prison. We have to have some evidence first. Something to show that he "probably" committed the crime.' Again, he paused for the whispered tones of the translator in the background. 'Even then, we may have a problem. If he asks for a lawyer, we cannot question him. Or, if we make a slight error in the arrest, or in a search, the judge may not let us use the evidence we find.' He could see a look of dismay cross the delegates' faces as the Russian words drifted in. 'That's a reality in our system of justice. We have to follow constitutional procedures. If we don't, a guilty man can be set free.' The dismay was still there. 'We don't like it, but we have to live with it,' Gardner continued. 'I am telling you this to prepare you for the days ahead . . . so you won't be shocked if we have some rulings that go against us.' He looked directly into the eyes of Zeitzoff, and received a cold, almost hostile return stare. The reaction jolted his train of thought. He decided to end right there. 'So, uh, please bear with us. I pledge that my office will do everything possible to see that justice is done.'

Gardner returned to his seat and sat down. He then checked to see if Smithwick was annoyed at the direction his remarks had taken. He didn't seem to be, but he didn't ask anyone else to speak, and appeared to be ready to end the meeting. 'Thank you all for coming . . .' was all he got out before the big Russian and his interpreter stood up.

'Mr. Zeitzoff would like to say something,' the bald man said, half to the agent and half to the crowd.

'Of course,' Smithwick muttered, a little embarrassed that he had slighted a foreign dignitary. 'Please come up, sir.'

The belated invitation was unnecessary. The Russians were already in position, so the FBI agent sat down.

Zeitzoff did not have the type of voice that Gardner expected. It was so soft that he had to strain to hear it, and he spoke in a rhythmic cadence that made the interplay of his words sound almost poetic.

The interpreter lagged a sentence or two behind, then caught up with a burst of lightly accented English. 'The deputy minister wishes to thank all of you for the work you are doing. He says that these are very dark times for the Anatov family. First a wife. Now a son. The United States was going to be like a holiday for them, but it has turned into tragedy.'

Suddenly the interpreter switched from a 'he says' point of view to a first-person translation. 'Please, I beg you to find this man . . . this Justice, and put him to trial. No family should have to endure this butchery. We always say that such things never happen in the Soviet Union. We are not used to the killing of children. Please catch this evil person so that little Mika can rest for eternity in the arms of his mother. Thank you. Thank you.'

The two men then walked down the center aisle, collected the Russian security officers, and headed for the door.

It was obvious that the meeting was over. 'We stand adjourned,' Smithwick said, leaning into the microphone from the side.

Gardner and Larry Gray left the building through the cocktail lounge. They didn't want to encounter the media people they were sure had staked out the main entrance. By now the word had spread that a network-level story was brewing. No doubt some big-name news stars were already booked in at BWI or Washington National Airport. At this point, neither the prosecutor nor the police captain was ready for that kind of attention.

'Well, what do you think?' Larry said when they reached the parking lot behind the hotel.

'About what?' Gardner responded, looking over the officer's shoulder for any sign of a minicam.

'About the Russians. What do you think?'

Gardner could still visualize the face of the gentle-voiced giant, Zeitzoff. His first impression had been empathetic. He had thought the man was the dead boy's father. He had felt the pain. But now he wasn't so sure how to feel. He had tried to explain that the case had not yet been solved. That things had to go by the book. But that didn't seem to matter to Zeitzoff. 'Find Justice and put him to trial.' A simple request. Gardner could still sense something wrong.

'I don't know, Larry,' he finally answered. 'Did you see that guy's face?'

'Huh?'

'The big guy, Zeitzoff. Minister, whatever. Jesus, that guy's a live one. Last time I saw eyes like that was Banzak, after he killed the old lady.'

Gray touched the prosecutor's arm. 'You okay, Gard?'

Gardner pulled away. 'Yeah. Fine. Didn't you notice something strange about him?'

'He's big as a house . . .'

'No. It's something else, I can't put my finger on it, but there's something weird going on here. FBI's in, then they're out. Nobody knows how they got in so fast. And then, just as fast, they back off. And the Russians – right out of Central Casting, those guys.'

'Gard, I think you'd better go get some rest. You sound paranoid.' Larry touched his friend's arm again, and this time Gardner let it stay.

'Yeah. Maybe I do, but I can't help it. Something's out there . . .'

Larry opened his police car door. 'Take care, now.'

As Gray started to enter, Gardner held his arm and added, 'Oh, by the way. Thanks a lot for telling me about the witness. What the hell's the story on that?'

The officer sighed. 'Sorry, Gard. Nothing much to report now. We only have a preliminary from the field. Should get a follow-up tomorrow when we bring him in.'

'You don't sound hopeful.'

Gray gave a shrug. 'Don't hold your breath. It's another Charlie Barnes special.'

Gardner groaned. 'I knew it!'

'We'll see, okay?' Larry said softly. Then he closed the door and drove away.

As Gardner watched him leave, the eyes of Zeitzoff appeared again in his mind. He could feel the Russian silently imploring him to 'put Justice to trial,' and threatening some unknown consequence if he failed.

It was 3:00 P.M. by the time Jennifer broke for a late lunch at Russel's Deli across the street from the courthouse. She usually brown-bagged it and ate at her desk. Tuna sandwich. Hard-boiled egg. Skim milk. The health food of the month. 'That stuff is going to kill you one day,' Gardner often teased as she delicately munched her homemade meal, always careful to keep the sandwich safely clasped in a nitch of wax paper while she ate. This habit didn't escape the prosecutor's sarcasm either. Occasionally he referred to her as Ms. Tablemanners. It was all in good fun, and Jennifer never minded the kidding. In fact, she sometimes felt slighted when he rushed past her on his way out of the office and didn't say a word.

Today she sat on a red linoleum-topped stool at the

counter, indulging in a BLT and a chocolate milk shake. Russel's was a turn-of-the-century-style eatery that had seen service in the 1800s. It occupied the ground-floor corner of the old Horner Mercantile Building on Court Avenue. The plate-glass window was etched in gold letters spelling out the name that everyone in town had grown up associating with the best chocolate milk shakes on earth. Ted Russel was dead now, but his daughter Ida had kept the family tradition alive by learning the secret of the shakes. She was a bulky woman who seemed to glide back and forth behind the counter as she dispensed the chocolatey glop to her regular customers.

'Sad thing, that little boy,' Ida said as the final cold inch of shake was being sucked ever so slowly through Jennifer's plastic straw.

'Them Russians don't deserve that. No sir. Seem like the world just fallin' apart on us, an' ain't nuthin' or nobody kin do nuthin' about it. What do you think they should do to him, when they kitch him? Cut off his privates?' Ida was just rolling along in conversation without any expectation of a response. That was her way. Whenever you were ready, you just jumped in – that is, if you wanted to. It was your option. Otherwise, you could pay your check and leave. It made no difference to Ida.

Jennifer didn't want to go back to the office yet, so she jumped in. 'Now, Ida, this is not the Dark Ages. You know they don't do that sort of thing anymore.'

'Shore as hell seem like it is. Damn perverts all over the place, messin' with little kids, an' 'em doctors sayin' they just sick an' we got to put 'em in the hospital an' not in jail. What kind a world we got, Miss State's Attorney? You gonna answer me that?'

Jennifer looked at the proprietor and shook her head. In law school, everything had been theoretical. The victims were only blurry sketches in a law book. But in the world of criminal prosecution, the bodies were tangible, the horror, a reality. In that sense, at least, the Dark Ages were still here. She wanted to say something reassuring, but at the moment her mind was blank.

'I don't know, Ida. I just don't know . . .' was the best she could manage before she paid her check and left.

Later that afternoon, Sgt. Joe Brown pulled his van off the road at Sessy's Woods, making sure not to overrun the crisscross of tire tracks that had been left there the night before. He had visited the scene earlier but had been called back to the station for a briefing by Captain Gray after a meeting at the Ramada. Now, as the shadows of the trees edged into the clearing, he had the woods all to himself.

The black officer was a legend at the department. His body was solid, with a hint of a paunch in the midsection, his arms were muscled and his shoulders broad. His eyes always danced gleefully when he spoke, and everyone in the county affectionately referred to him as 'Brownie.' But, despite his jolly demeanor, as a laboratory technician and detective, he was all business. Once he homed in on a clue, most criminal suspects were doomed. 'The man just don't know when to quit,' his lab partner, Sam Jenkins, often said with a shameless expression of awe.

Brownie assembled his gear at the sliding door of the mobile lab. From what Larry Gray had said, it was going to be up to the county to nail this one down; the feds were backing off. The reasons were not explained, but that was just fine with Brownie. He was a loner in the investigation department. Did his best work with nobody else around to bother him. And now he was facing the woods. Somewhere out there, he thought, between the trees, or in the high grass, was a key to the case. A tiny fragment of the killer's identity. And he was determined to find it.

CHAPTER 4

The fall line of the mountains to the west of town was backlit by the dimming late afternoon sun. Shadows elongated, and the air began its autumn cool-down as darkness approached. Gardner wanted to see his son, so he headed out to the Watson Road house. It wasn't his 'appointed time,' and Carole had hassled him about coming over, but he had insisted, and she had finally agreed. Gardner needed to know that Granville was okay. He had to see the boy face-to-face. A phone call wouldn't do it this time. 'Hi, Daddy . . . Fine . . . I'm fine, Dad . . . School was okay . . . I love you, too, 'bye,' was the usual two-minute version of fatherhood that Gardner had available to him on weekdays. It was all the court had let him have, considering that Carole had emphasized the spousal noninterference clause of the separation agreement over and over at the hearing. 'How can I be left alone to live my life in peace if this man is calling the house every five minutes?' she demanded of the judge. 'But, Your Honor, how can my client check on the welfare of his child unless he is allowed to call?' Gardner's counsel responded. They finally resolved it by compromise. Two minutes or less each day were permitted, except in the case of an emergency. Gardner was sure that Carole stood behind the boy with a timer. He never got an extra second.

Granville had been born in Gardner's mind long before he was conceived in the four-poster bed his great-uncle had made in the shop below the Watson Road house. Gardner couldn't explain it, but he had a vision of a fair-haired boy running to greet him at the end of the lane. The features were handsome. The body lithe. And inside, a high-voltage spark of Lawson spirit, catapulting him through the air into the waiting arms of his father.

He had resolved always to be 'there' for the child-to-be. To bait the hooks, and throw the balls, and teach, and train, and laugh, and cheer.

But there was a problem. An unexpected shadow across the image in the vision. As hard as they had tried, nothing happened. Carole couldn't conceive.

For two years, the monthly wait ended in failure, and they both cycled into an emotional chasm each time the confirmation appeared. Recriminations sometimes flew, but there was mostly sadness.

Then one day, almost unexpectedly, Gardner received a phone call at the office. They were in the old building, and the chief prosecutor was sharing space with three chatty assistants. He tried to quiet the din, but still couldn't hear. 'Please!' he hollered. 'It's my wife!' There was an immediate hush; then, when the others saw the expression on his face, the silence erupted into a standing ovation.

But the happiness was short-lived. Carole miscarried

in her third month, and the agony of expectations began again. There were two more years of fruitless attempts, and then, finally, it 'took.'

The pregnancy hit Gardner harder than it did Carole. He became overprotective, overanxious, and overbearing. Every pain, every physical twinge signaled disaster, and the father-to-be panicked accordingly. Midnight calls to the doctor became routine, and after seven months, everyone in supporting roles for the great event had become accustomed to Gardner's behavior and showed him considerable tolerance and understanding.

On the third of July, after an endless heat wave and two false alarms, Granville Alcott Lawson was presented to the world. He was physically perfect, but a touch of jaundice kept him from being released from the hospital with his mother.

For the next two days Gardner sat in a darkened hospital ward with his son. The child was in an ultraviolet incubator, his face masked against the rays that would burn the disease out of his tiny body. From time to time a nurse came in with a feeding bottle, but most of the time they were alone. Gardner sat patiently, watching the arms and legs bunching together and releasing in spasms of life.

Occasionally one of the boy's hands popped through a round access hole in the incubator. Gardner touched the wrinkled fingers, and felt a strong firm grip around the tip of his own finger. He left it there for a long time, until the grip relaxed. He was suffused with joy. There was no need to talk. It was as if they had known each other for a long, long time.

* * *

Driving Watson Road was an experience that Gardner approached with dread. Each time he entered the serpentine gateway to the past, his stomach knotted up, and his mind dissolved into a delirium of conflicting images. Carole on horseback. Granville arcing high on the swing. The snow-filled lane adrift in February. Carole's face when he found her letter to Kent King tucked away in the mothballed comforter. It was unincriminating enough, on the surface. A request for the name of a good divorce lawyer. But there was a hint of guilt, and she wouldn't answer when he asked her what 'thanks for the other day' meant.

During the legal battles over their separation, his emotions had swung back and forth between love and hate, frequently propelled by anger. 'The fact that you're a prosecutor doesn't mean a damn thing in family court,' Roger Winston, his lawyer, had said. 'In fact, it may just be used against you. The court knows what kind of attention you can give a young child, and, if you'll pardon my saying so, it ain't much.' That advice had led to his decision not to seek custody. 'It would be a losing battle, anyway,' Roger told him. The first of many, it turned out, as Carole won a hefty support award and the right to live exclusively in Gardner's family home for the next five years.

Gardner parked in front of the porch, went up, and knocked on the door. Carole opened it immediately. She looked coldly elegant in a black cotton jumpsuit. 'Granny! Your father is here!' she called. Gardner winced. He hated that nickname. The kids in school are going to tear him up if they ever hear it, he thought to himself, locking his ex-wife in a defiant stare-down that let her know exactly how he felt.

Gardner and Carole had grown up in social groups that had frequent contacts with each other. Her peers, from the Baltimore suburbs, and his, from the hill country, often intermingled at debutante parties, school functions, and summers at the beach, but somehow Gardner and Carole never quite met. His 'career track' led from Watson Road to a prep school in Hagerstown, then to college in the Northeast, and back to the University of Maryland Law School. In between, he endured a stint as a lieutenant in the post-Vietnam marines. As he moved from one phase of his life to another, he was always alone. There were women, on a short-term basis, but he was looking for a female bolt of lightning, and until the day twelve years ago that he leaned against a horse-ring fence in the Greenspring Valley and saw Carole for the first time, there hadn't even been a flash.

The sight of a slim girl with dark hair cantering in the ring took him by surprise. He was there to meet a male friend who lived nearby. They were supposed to go to a baseball game later. He watched her move around the circle, rocking in time to the hoofbeats, steady and anchored to the saddle. Hands fixed in place above the mane, knees locked, her only moving parts, it seemed, were her deep chestnut tresses, which flew up and down in rhythm with the horse's gait.

'Who is that?' Gardner asked his friend, his eyes glued to the rider.

'Carole Andrews. She was at Bethany last year.'

Gardner tried to picture the same form in a bathing suit, but the image wouldn't come. The scene in the ring blocked everything out.

Finally she dismounted.

The intro was short and sweet. The friend decided to head for the barn, and the novice lawyer and rider were left to themselves.

'You looked good out there,' Gardner said. Her close-up was striking.

'Thanks.' Her voice was delicate, but carried a reserve that Gardner knew could control a horse or a man.

'I hear you were at the beach last summer.'

'Uh-huh.' She looked him in the eye, and advanced the forerunner of a smile to the corners of her full lips.

'What's so funny?'

The smile had emerged, and a healthy grin spread from white teeth to hazel eyes. 'You don't remember me, do you?'

Gardner was caught by surprise. 'Uh . . .'

'The Beach Club. Tequila shooters. Red dress . . .'

'We met?' He had drawn a blank on all three hints.

'Not exactly.' She gave a throaty chuckle. 'My date drove you back to the Dunes after you won the drinking contest.'

The dim recollection of a smoky bar, a screaming crowd, and a dozen face-down glasses began to take hold.

'Oh no,' Gardner groaned sheepishly. 'One of my greater performances.'

She smiled and touched his arm. Her fingers were slender, her nails clear. 'I thought you did just fine,' she replied. At that moment, for the first time ever, Gardner felt the searing thrust of a lightning bolt as it entered his heart.

But times had changed, and now she used the door almost as a shield. 'I hear there was some trouble out at Sessy's,' Carole said in a matter-of-fact tone. 'You going to be involved in that?'

Gardner didn't answer. He was there for his son, not small talk. He shrugged his shoulders. 'We'll see,' he said, as a blond-haired boy shot through the opening and leapt into his arms.

The little boy looked pale. 'How're ya doin', Gran?' Gardner asked, cuddling his son.

The boy was slow to answer, so Gardner tenderly touched his shoulder and turned him to the side.

Granville kept his eyes cast down, and then gradually raised them up to meet his father's. He was obviously sad, not the usual bouncing ball of energy he became on alternate weekends at the town house.

'Hey, what's the matter, son, feeling sick to your tummy?' Gardner asked quietly. The boy had a tendency to get stomach-aches. Most likely a reaction to the 'healthy' diet that Carole had him on, his father thought.

'Uh, no, Dad. I feel okay,' Granville said, his voice faltering slightly. His eyes dropped down again.

'Hey, this is your dad here. Aren't you glad to see me?' This time Gardner pressed his fingers against the delicate ripples of the boy's backbone.

'Yeah, Dad . . . It's just . . .' Granville was faltering again. Suddenly he looked up and said, 'Dad, is someone coming to get me?'

'What?' Gardner's voice was louder than he wanted

it to be. 'Son, what are you talking about?' The prosecutor had picked up a very subtle emphasis on the word 'get,' and it alarmed him. 'Please, tell Dad what's wrong.'

'Mom said that a man was after me, and that I had to be careful.'

Gardner didn't need to hear another word from his son. He knew immediately what had happened. God-damn that bitch! he screamed to himself. She's doing it again! There's a killer on the loose in the area, so she has to have a heart-to-heart talk with her seven-year-old son. She has about as much tact as a bulldozer when it comes to talking to children. Gardner fumed.

'There's nothing to worry about, Gran, nobody is going to get you,' Gardner said in a reassuring tone, his arm slung over the boy's shoulders. 'Just remember those things we talked about. You know, don't go anywhere with a person you don't know. Don't talk to strangers. Tell someone if a stranger asks you to go with him. The safety rules.'

'But Mom said—' the boy broke in.

'Forget that, son!' Gardner snapped back. 'Just follow the rules and you'll be fine, I promise . . . Okay?' Gardner hugged his son as tightly as he possibly could without doing any damage to the fragile bones. He pressed his chin against the boy's soft hair, inhaling the scent of innocence that clung to every strand. Just then he noticed that Carole had pulled the hall curtain all the way back. That was the signal that his time was up.

As he swung the car out of the driveway, Gardner decided not to go directly home. He needed time to cool the anger that Carole, once again, had poured over him like molten metal. He was forced to admit to himself the real reason for his visit. He, too, was worried about Justice, and he wanted to make sure that his son was safe. Perhaps he was overreacting.

Gardner headed aimlessly west, away from town. His thoughts alternated between Granville and the case as he fumed silently and pressed the accelerator pedal.

He suddenly found himself on the side road that led to Sessy's Woods. There had been no intention to return to the scene of the crime when he left the house, but unconsciously he had been drawn back. The road, known for its blind curves, was especially hazardous in the darkness of this early fall evening. Many cars had run off the road out there. Gardner tried to keep alert as he jerked his vehicle around the hairpin turns.

Just then, a set of headlights leapt out of a deep dip in the roadbed. Gardner was startled, and almost blinded by the high beams that refused to dim. He had to swerve abruptly to keep from meeting head-on at the crest of the hill, as the oncoming blur drifted across the center line.

'Damn!' he muttered aloud, as the cars sliced past each other with less than a foot of clearance between them. This bastard doesn't know the road, Gardner thought as he tried to make out the features of the person in the driver's seat. The conditions were too poor to make a decent ID of the driver, but he did catch a glimpse of the passenger in the backseat. A large white male with slicked-back silver hair. Zeitzoff. The Russian giant. Gardner squinted, trying to clear the lingering afterglare of the lights. 'Son of a bitch better watch where he's going,' he said to himself. Then he wondered what had brought the Russian back to the crime scene.

There was one person at the clearing, and Gardner knew who it was as soon as he saw the tan mobile crime lab. Brownie.

The inconvenience of nightfall had not even slowed him up, the prosecutor was sure, remembering the time the officer spent a week in old lady Brewster's house before finding the tiny clue that cracked the case. She had been brutally murdered, but he hadn't been able to turn up a thing for the first six days. No weapon. No latent fingerprints. Nothing in the trash, or even the traps in the sink and toilet. He had picked the house clean, and it appeared that the criminal had escaped without leaving a single remnant of his presence. The lieutenant told him to call off the search, but Brownie went back after duty hours and vacuumed the rug in the lady's bathroom. Then he put every piece of lint and every strand of hair under the crime lab microscope. After several tedious hours, he found something unusual: a hair that was dyed a garish shade of purple. The arrest of Peter Banzak, an itinerant punk-rock musician, followed soon after, and his conviction and life sentence soon after that. Brownie was amazing. And he never gave up.

'How's it goin'?' Gardner said loudly, before he reached a spot of light bouncing across the tree trunks. He knew it wasn't a good idea to startle someone in the woods, especially when he was carrying a side arm.

'That sounds like Mr. Lawson,' came the chuckling

response. 'What the hell you doin' out here? Who's watchin' them deadbeats back at the office?'

'Office is closed,' Gardner replied, stopping so his shoe tips barely inched into the light. 'Find anything?'

'I tell you, man, I got a bad feeling about this one.'

'Nothing, huh?' Gardner sighed.

'This is worse than Banzak. Not a goddamn thing out here. No weapon. No footprints. No fuzz balls. No nuthin'. Almost like the boy just dropped out'a the sky.'

'That's what you thought when you started Banzak,' Gardner said quietly. 'You got yourself all worked up, but it came out okay in the end.'

'The hell it did!'

'What do you mean? He got convicted.'

'Yeah, but no death penalty. After what he put that woman through . . . like to drop the pellets on the scumsucker myself.'

Brownie's one weakness was showing, and Gardner was attuned because he suffered the same malady. 'Loss of objectivity in the face of distress.' It could be a trial attorney's undoing if he let it get out of control. And for a police officer, it could make him either overlook something important, or think he saw something that was not really there.

Gardner decided to change the conversation. 'You about ready to call it a night?' He turned and took a step towards the parked vehicles. 'Come back when you're fresh?'

'Yeah,' Brownie said tiredly. 'Not gettin' much done just walkin' around.'

He joined the prosecutor, and shone his light on the

ground in front of them. After three steps, he stopped.

'What's wrong?' Gardner asked.

'Thought I saw something. Shiny flash of something,' Brownie said. The officer then took another step forward, and squatted in the brown grass.

Gardner bent down beside him. 'Whattaya got?' he asked. His hushed tone would have been suitable for an operating room.

'Take a look at this,' Brownie said as he lifted a small object from under a rotted leaf with an index card he had removed from his pocket. He was careful not to touch it with his bare fingers. 'Looks like one of them decorations that the girls like to sew on their sweaters.' The flashlight illuminated a bright blue glass chip.

'Could be,' Gardner replied. 'Do you think it has anything to do with this case?'

'Well, look at it. Still shiny. No woods gunk on it. Had to be dropped here in the last couple days.'

That might be important, they both knew. It could be a tie-in to the killer, or to a witness. But then again, it could have been dropped by one of the high schoolers who found the body.

'Better hold on to it, just in case,' Brownie said.

Gardner had a sudden vision of it being placed carefully into a large box full of lint, hair, and disposal scrapings.

When they reached the van, Brownie pulled out a plastic evidence bag, labeled it, and sealed the small sequin inside.

''Bout time to hit the road,' he said, climbing into the cab.

Gardner knew his departure was only temporary. He

would be back tomorrow. And as for himself, it had been a day that began and ended at the same spot. A long one. Now it was time for him to head home, too.

Gardner was settling in behind the wheel, when an afterthought hit him. The door was still open, so he jumped out and flagged down the van before Brownie had time to get away.

The officer rolled the window down, and turned his ear.

'By the way, I meant to ask you before,' the prosecutor said. 'What were the Russians doing out here earlier tonight?'

Brownie crinkled his face. 'I never saw no Russians,' he replied before nodding good-bye and driving off into the night.

Gardner slumped into his wingback chair after he got home from the woods. A few minutes of TV for relaxation. That was the idea. Mindless entertainment to block the images trying to seize control of his brain. He tried to pay attention to the sitcom plot, but it was too nonsensical to follow, so he put his head back and closed his eyes. By 11:30 he had nodded off.

He woke up just as the news anchorman said, 'And I guess we'll be hearing more about that on tomorrow's edition of "Late Report." ' The room was gloomily dark, except for reflections being cast by the screen on the oriental rug in front of the television. Gardner couldn't seem to focus. He was disoriented.

Just then the telephone rang. He picked it up on the second ring.

'Lawson speaking,' he answered half groggily.

'Me again, boss.' It was Larry Gray. 'Just thought I should let you know they've arrested T. J. Justice.'

CHAPTER 5

It was 8:30 A.M., and Bob Hamilton was already at his desk at the State Department. His premonition of the day before had come true. Early that same afternoon he had been called into his supervisor's office and given a new assignment. They wanted him to 'keep an eye' on the murder case in western Maryland. The one involving the Anatov child. The one he had seen on TV.

His speciality in the department was military and political activities inside the Soviet Union. He didn't know a damn thing about law, but he had learned over the years never to turn down an assignment. The men at the top had a subtle way of sending signals to the bureaucracy climbers sweating their way up from the obscurity of the basement. Sometimes the tasks they assigned carried a message. 'You're going places, so we're giving you a boost. A high-profile job that will stick out on your résumé like a gold-crested eagle.' At other times, the assignment simply said, 'Clean the stables, slob. You're going to be out of sight for a while.' The only problem was how to interpret what they were saying, so Hamilton had decided long ago to take them all, and worry about the meaning later.

He had arrived early to get a head start on the project, and when he reached his desk he was surprised to find a briefing file already there. He leaned back in his chair for a moment and looked at the Washington Monument peeking over the marble façade of the building across the street. Then he snapped forward and tore into the file.

It had been prepared by an unknown official even lower than Hamilton. The basic facts were outlined and supplemented with press clippings and intelligence reports on the main characters. Some were FBI-generated, others came from the Maryland State Police Headquarters Unit. Two were encased in the familiar blue-and-silver folders of the CIA. They were both marked TOP SECRET. AUTHORIZED PERSONNEL ONLY. Hamilton smiled and picked up the first report. He had a sudden vision of gold wings embossed on the cover of his own personnel dossier.

The title page read: VALERY ZEITZOFF, KGB, AGENT HISTORY, OPERATIONAL DATA, ASSESSMENT OF CAPABILITIES. Hamilton skimmed through the first few pages of the man's background. Born in Kiev before the Second World War. Parents lost to the Nazis. Raised in a home for war orphans in Moscow. Leader of Communist Party Youth Organization in his early teens. Member of military intelligence for the Soviet army with extensive duty as an adviser in Latin America, Cuba, and Southeast Asia.

Hamilton flipped a few more pages and learned that Zeitzoff had worked with every Soviet high-roller since the war. Khrushchev. Brezhnev. Andropov. Chernenko, Gorbachev. His official title identified him as a 'security officer.' 'Zeitzoff has fulfilled a role as jack-of-all-trades in every Soviet "administration" in the last quarter century,' the report stated. 'He has been associated with several covert operations that have resulted in the deaths of agents and foreign nationals allied with the U.S. In addition, he is suspected of carrying out several "hits" on behalf of top-level leadership within the shifting power structure of the Soviet Politburo.'

Bob Hamilton was suddenly hooked. What on earth was a cold war horse doing in the middle of an American crime scene? The new leaders were friendly and open, but this guy was definitely back alley, a throwback to the bad old days. Something major was happening here. And the appearance of Zeitzoff was not a good sign. He flipped to the end of the CIA report to find the connection. Nothing there except the 'Assessment of Capabilities.' He returned to the briefing file, and found it. 'Soviet Activities in Western Maryland.' The Russians had developed a fondness for a small resort area at the base of the Appalachians, the outline stated. It was used for embassy personnel to R and R, and in the past, for meetings between agents. The murder of the Anatov child had taken place near the resort, and after the crime was committed, several security officers from the Soviet embassy had visited the area, including Zeitzoff. A suspect had been identified by American authorities within hours of the killing, but the Russians had begun conducting their own secret investigation.

Hamilton stopped reading. He picked up a notepad

and wrote the word SECRET. Then he resumed. 'The conclusions of the department concerning these activities may be based upon either of two distinct assumptions. First, the information gathering may be a legitimate exercise of the right-to-know that attends the family of a crime victim. The other assumption is that the clandestine nature of the operations reveals another motive: possible interference with, or circumvention of, the American criminal justice system.'

It was time to see how the CIA assessed the potential of Mr. Zeitzoff. Hamilton flipped to the back page. 'The experience level of this officer makes him particularly dangerous. His ability to transcend changes of leadership without removal from power attests to his adaptability. He should be considered a lethal threat if put in a position where force may be used.' The young State Department officer whistled and shook his head. As he did so, several photographs spilled out of the file, and Hamilton suddenly found himself staring into the face of Zeitzoff. He literally towered over the party secretary and the other familiar Soviet leaders in the picture. The shock of thick white hair made him look particularly sinister. Hamilton paused over the scene. 'You're one person I hope I *never* get to meet,' he said with an ironic laugh. Then he put the photo aside and went on to another folder.

The warden had decided to put T. J. Justice in the south wing of the detention center annex. This location provided the best security and would enable them to monitor him around the clock with closed-circuit TV.

They couldn't do that in the old jail, and besides, this might give the county some good publicity on its upgraded physical plant, the warden thought. Ever since T.J. had been brought in early that morning, the switchboard had been burning up with inquiries. The news media. The FBI. The State Department. They all wanted to know the same thing: What is the status of the prisoner? The problem was a matter of jurisdiction. The detention center was simply a holding facility. They didn't control any proceedings. Feed him, bathe him, and put him to sleep. That was their only responsibility. As to the status of the prisoner, the callers were all told the same thing: 'Sorry, you will have to speak to the State's Attorney about that.'

Gardner sat in the warden's office and watched T. J. Justice on the small black-and-white screen. 'Would you look at that bastard. He's smiling. Actually smiling,' he said to Warden Phillips in a voice that barely revealed the disgust he felt. 'I wonder what he's thinking about.' The prosecutor was imagining the same look on the man's face as he thrust the knife into the little boy. 'Murder is just like breathing to this son of a bitch.' Gardner wanted to get him by the throat and cut off his air until the grotesque, toothless smile went away.

The warden seemed to read his thoughts. 'We can't forget that he is entitled to due process of law,' he said sarcastically.

'Well, he's certainly availed himself of it up till now,' Gardner replied. The cloak of the Constitution had been used as a shield between Justice and his accusers at every conceivable turn, and although he looked like the village

81

idiot, he knew his 'rights' like a professor of criminal procedure. He'd probably picked it up in prison. Somewhere along the line, a jailhouse lawyer had schooled him in how to beat the system, and he'd taken to it like a natural. He knew that if the police picked him up for questioning, they must Mirandize before beginning. He knew that he had an 'expectation of privacy' in his personal possessions, and that he didn't have to consent to a search. And he knew that if he said the magic words, the police were obligated to stop all questioning until his attorney arrived.

T.J.'s expertise had been used the previous night at the Pennsylvania border, when an alert state trooper thought the passenger in a pickup truck looked a little like the image of the man in the fax that county police had distributed in connection with a child murder. The trooper had encountered the truck at Tommie's Last Chance Gas 'n' Go.

'Sir, would you mind identifying yourself?' he had asked the man sitting in the right seat of the vehicle while the driver was pumping gas. The man had not flinched in the slightest.

'Justice is my name, but my friends call me T.J.' That was all it took. The trooper asked him to step out of the truck, and placed him under arrest. There was no struggle. There were no questions from the man, no protestations of innocence. He had allowed himself to be frisked and handcuffed as if it happened every day. The trooper then seated him in the rear of his tan cruiser, and read him his rights. Did he understand those rights? Did he need any of them repeated? Did he wish to speak to a lawyer prior to questioning? The man had grunted yes to the first. No to the second. And, as to the last, he said, 'I would like an opportunity to speak with counsel before you ask me any questions.' That response took the trooper by surprise. 'Damnedest thing I ever heard from a guy who looked like that,' he told his colleagues later. 'Sounded like a fuckin' law book.'

T.J. sat down on his cell bunk and lit a cigarette. The morning feeding of the prisoners was complete, and he was locked again in the small detention center cubicle. His bony fingers pushed the glowing tip around in a semicircle, sprinkling flakes of ash across the wrinkled grey trousers he was wearing. They hadn't issued him the standard denim uniform yet. 'After the lineup,' one of the guards had said. He could see his warped reflection in the polished stainless steel square mounted above the triangular sink. A gaunt pale face with close-set brown eyes and thinning blackish hair. Back again, he thought, back behind bars. The sights, sounds, and smells of prison were familiar, and not altogether unpleasant. By now it was second nature for him to sit in a cell with only his thoughts for company. He had done it in Kansas, and several other places before that. And he had always found a way out.

T.J. studied himself in the shiny metal, turning slightly from side to side so his image was distorted the way it used to be in the carnival mirror. The display of twisted faces amused him, and he smiled a cracked-lip smirk that bared a set of reddened gums and a few crooked teeth. He had enjoyed working at the carnival. That had been a time before all the trouble started. The people had treated him okay, and he got to move around a lot. But the best thing was that he got to get away from the old man.

The prisoner shifted again on his bunk and made another face. In no time, he'd have himself a lawyer, and things would start happening. He'd be okay until then, but once he got hooked up with counsel, it'd only be a matter of time till they cut him loose.

The warden interrupted Gardner's thoughts. 'Public defender called just before you got here,' the warden said. 'They're sending somebody over for the lineup.'

Gardner nodded absently. 'Okay.'

'Man. Sure got your hands full with this one,' the warden continued, 'but I've got a question. How the hell could the Russian boy have been kidnapped? Didn't they have any security on him?'

Gardner shook his head. 'No. Apparently not. They don't need that kind of thing anymore. We're all friends now. No guards necessary. Not here . . . Welcome to America, guys, land of the free, home of the brave, with truth, liberty, and T. J. Justice for all—'

The telephone on the warden's desk suddenly rang, cutting off Gardner's soliloquy.

'Hello, Warden Phillips here. Uh, yes . . . he's in my office . . . would you like to speak with him?' The warden gave Gardner a gently scolding look and handed him the phone. It was obviously not business.

'Where were you last night?' a shrill feminine voice said as soon as Gardner put the receiver to his ear. It was Elaine Tower, his so-called girlfriend.

Damn, Gardner thought as his private life suddenly encroached on the case. Why did I ask Miss Cass to forward my calls?

'I called you ten times, but there was no answer. Mind telling me where you were?'

Elaine was what some people around the courthouse jokingly called a 'groupie.' She had served on a jury during a time when Gardner's marriage wounds were still aching, and he was drifting aimlessly alone. A post-trial conversation in the corridor led to lunch, and later a dinner or two, and finally to a sort of relationship. Emotionally, his heart wasn't in it, but she was a sexy redhead who knew how to ease the pain with the contours of her body, so he stayed with it, despite her increasing possessiveness.

Gardner's answer was firm. 'I was on a case. The Russian thing.'

'Well, we were supposed to get together . . .'

'Sorry. Uh, listen, Elaine. This isn't a good time. Maybe we can talk later . . .'

Her silence signaled anger and disappointment.

'Elaine?'

'Okay! Call me if you have any *free* time.' Then she hung up.

Gardner gave the warden a sheepish look and handed him the phone. 'Got any dinner plans, Phil? It looks like mine have been cancelled.'

The warden gently laid the phone back on its cradle. 'No problem. Happens to me all the time.' Then he smiled.

The line buzzed again almost immediately. 'For you again,' the warden said, handing the phone back. This time it was official. 'Gard, it's Larry. Do you want to speak to the witness before the lineup? We have him down in the visitors' area.' They had brought the eye-witness in for a confrontation with Justice.

'Don't know, Larry. Are you going to give him the usual briefing?' Gardner was again faced with the possibility of becoming part of the investigation, rather than the power behind it. If he instructed the witness, his instructions might become an issue at the trial, and he could be forced to take the stand.

'Why don't you meet me in the shift commander's office,' Gardner suggested, 'and we'll discuss it, okay?' He needed a few minutes to get Elaine's interruption off his mind so that he could fully concentrate on the case.

Larry Gray looked as though he had been up all night. His beard was the same color as his hair, and the stubble had really started to sprout after two days of inattention. Gardner unconsciously shook his hand when they met in the alcove of the chief correctional officer's area just beyond the shift commander's office.

'What's the deal on the witness?' he asked as he released his friend's firm grip. The details had been allowed to slide to the back burner as other developments in the prosecutor's public and private life took over.

Larry Gray had been very hopeful when the call first came in. A young man had stopped by the woods when he saw the string of police cars. He had been camping the night before, and was on his way home. He asked what happened, and when they told him a child had been murdered, he started acting crazy, running around screaming, 'I knew it! I knew it! I saw the man! I saw the man!' One of the field officers assured Captain Gray that the witness could make a positive identification. It was only later that he found out that the officer who took the original report was Charlie Barnes, the police department's resident screwup.

'I'm not sure he's going to hack it,' the captain replied. 'He's scared shitless, and his mother isn't helping matters any.' Gardner could see the teenaged boy through the Plexiglas partition. He had a blank, pimple-dotted face and spiky blond hair. He was talking to a woman who looked so much like him she never needed to be announced as his mother.

'What does he know?' The State's Attorney was still studying the two people on the other side of the window as he spoke. He wondered if a jury would buy the testimony from such a pathetic witness.

'He thinks he saw a man with a child heading into Sessy's,' Larry responded.

'Thinks?'

'Well, he's not really sure enough to swear an oath.'

'That's going to make him real helpful in court. How on earth did we get to the brink of a lineup with that kind of garbage?' Gardner tried not to sound as if he was issuing a reprimand, but he was surprised at Larry.

'He says that if he ever sees the person again, that he may be able to identify him. He was on a camping trip with some kids out of North Wellwood. They sent him back to get some supplies . . . case of Coke and some doughnuts. Anyway, he had just passed the turn when he saw – excuse me – *thinks* he saw a man and a child walking the dirt trail into the woods. That's about it. He can't describe the clothing. Can't describe age, race, or distinguishing features, but he insists that he would recognize the man face-to-face.'

'Larry, please tell me there's more,' Gardner said wearily.

'That's about it, boss. Sorry.'

Gardner walked into the room where the witness was being sequestered. He knew instinctively what he would find. Billie Harris was just like a thousand other witnesses he had seen over the years. Scared. Confused. Pushed and pulled by family members and 'outside influences.' He looked weak at best. But if Gardner yanked the plug on the lineup all hell would break loose in the press. Someone in the department would leak it, and the headline would read: STATE'S ATTORNEY REFUSES TO ALLOW EYEWITNESS IDENTIFICATION. The defense team would then leap into action, knowing that the witness could only be a 'dud' if the prosecution was afraid to let him go one-on-one with the defendant. They would send out their investigator and get the witness to sign a statement verifying that his observations at the woods in no way implicated their client. Gardner considered his options and made a decision. For now it was best to stay on the sidelines and let the procedure run its course. It was too late to do anything else.

Patty Glasboro, a humorless stalwart of the public defender's office, was brought to the adjoining room in the visitors' area to preview the proposed setup. When she saw the group, she reacted. 'This is not going to do,' she said. 'You have too much of a contrast in your people. You have to change it.'

Gardner chuckled inwardly, surprised that she even knew which of the lined-up men was her 'client.' Must have seen his picture in the papers, he surmised, knowing that she had never even been in his presence until two seconds ago.

'Shift number two to the four position, and pull number five out and find a substitute,' she declared.

Even Gardner had to admit that the thin mustache on the fifth man tended to set him off from the rest of the group. He nodded okay to Larry, who was looking to him for a clue as to how to handle the complaint. He turned to one of the correctional officers lurking by the back wall.

'Is there any other alteration you would care to make before we start?' Larry asked the public defender. Up to now the whole thing had seemed like a trite domestic scene where the demanding wife has forced her husband to rearrange the living room furniture six times before she's satisfied.

'As far as the array is concerned,' Patty replied, 'it's probably as good as it's going to get.'

The six men now in position were enough alike in appearance to avoid a charge of 'unfair suggestiveness,' which can occur when the accused is so different-looking from the others that he attracts a greater amount of attention than they do. That was not the case here, with six middle-aged white men wearing tan shirts. There was a slight variation in height, weight, and hair color, but otherwise they were all on the same wavelength. The only distinction that Gardner could see was the attractiveness quotient. None of the fill-ins was going to be competing in a male beauty pageant anytime soon, yet T. J. Justice still stood out. He was the ugliest one in the group.

The men were given their final instructions by Larry Gray. March forward on command, stand still, and turn only when the order was given. No sudden movements allowed. Did they all understand? The last-minute fill-in had a question. What was this all about? His lawyer had not advised him about any new charges. Don't worry, he was told, you're not the one in the hot seat. When that comment was uttered, every eye in the room suddenly turned on Justice. T.J. gave them a look that would melt concrete. Gardner smiled. 'Keep it up, you bastard,' he said to himself before leaving to join the witness in the other room.

'Time to get this thing rolling,' Larry Gray announced at 10:15. 'I think it would be best if counsel would sit over there, and the witness comes up here by me.' Gardner saw immediately that Larry knew exactly what was going on with Patty. He was setting up the room so as to place himself between Billie and the PD, creating a buffer against her possible attempts at inquisition during the procedure.

Patty acquiesced without argument, realizing that she was outflanked, and that they were not going to let her get a cheap shot at the witness.

Just then a man poked his head through the alcove

door. He was dark-eyed and graying, dressed in a silk suit, carrying a burgundy leather briefcase. When Gardner saw him, he stiffened. 'What the hell are you doing here, King?'

The man pulled himself up to full height and smiled. 'Just wanna make sure you're playing fair with Miss Patty. Knowing you, you probably got this thing rigged.'

Gardner stood up, and Larry Gray moved toward the door. 'You got business here?' the officer asked.

Kent King looked at the prosecutor. 'Where *he's* involved, it's always my business.'

Gardner took a step in his direction, and Larry moved between them as if to block. 'This is a private showing, King,' the prosecutor said. 'You need a ticket to get in.'

'Says who?' the intruder asked defiantly.

'Says me!' Larry Gray answered. 'Unless your appearance is entered in this case, you can get the hell out.'

King looked at Patty Glasboro for support, but she just shook her head. It was her case, and she wasn't about to share it with anyone, not even the wild man of the private defense bar.

Larry reached out to close the door on him, but King blocked his arm. 'Don't make any mistakes in there,' he said, again looking at Gardner. 'I'll be watching . . .' Then he turned and allowed the door to slam behind him.

'Thanks for the warning,' Gardner said, then added 'asshole' under his breath.

Larry tried to regain the group's attention after the interruption. Gardner was a bit steamed, but he calmed himself and focused back on the lineup. The rest of the group had hardly noticed that anything was wrong.

'Okay, okay,' Larry said. 'Let's get on with it. We've got a lot of people here who need to finish this up and get on with their business.' He looked at Gardner and Patty, then turned to Billie and began his memorized litany in a loud monotone.

'In a few moments a group of six men will be brought into the next room. The light in here will be turned off, so no one will be able to see you. The men will stand and face this window; then they will turn to the side so you can see their profiles. They will each carry a number, which designates the position that each occupies. You are being asked to look carefully at each man. If you recognize anyone, please refer to him by number. You can have as much time as you need, but please understand that I will not be permitted to tell you anything about any of the men until the procedure is over. Do you understand what we are going to do?'

Billie nodded yes.

'Do you have any questions before we begin?'

Billie hesitated, then shook his head no.

'Is the man Billie saw going to be one of them?' Neva Harris asked, tapping the police captain familiarly on the shoulder.

Gardner winced. He didn't want to look at Patty for fear of showing his concern.

'Ma'am, all I can say is that we have a group of men here for your son to look at. Who exactly is or is not in the group I am not allowed to discuss at this point.'

Gardner eased up. Larry had given the right answer. The police were under strict orders not to tell a witness that the suspect was actually in a given lineup. That knowledge might influence him to make a choice even if he was not really sure. It was better to let the witness react naturally from memory, rather than from the subtle pressure of believing that he 'had' to pick out the 'right' person.

'Well, if he ain't here, why did you bring us down here this morning?' Billie's mother persisted.

'Again, ma'am, there are things I can and other things I cannot tell you,' Larry repeated patiently. 'You'll simply have to take my word that that is the way it has to be. We can discuss the whole thing more fully later, but not now.'

Couldn't have said it better myself, Gardner thought, as Mrs. Harris pushed back in her seat and crossed her arms.

The light was turned off, and Gardner could see a couple of correctional officers scurrying to the side like TV technical people suddenly caught off guard by the camera. He was glad it was dark. Patty would not be able to observe the thin beading of perspiration beginning to pop out along his hairline. This was going to be the moment of truth. Either a resounding victory or a devastating defeat, all in a matter of seconds. Either way, he would be the one held accountable. The 'state's case' was the 'state's case.' It didn't matter to the public that the state had different arms that did not always work in concert.

'They're coming in now,' Larry said solemnly. Gardner found himself holding his breath as the grotesque procession came into view on the other side of the glass.

They had decided to switch numbers after Gardner had left the room. Larry Gray was not comfortable having Justice in the first slot, so he moved him to number four. This took the prosecutor by surprise. The first man through was Ralph Purdy from the fire department, a fill-in they often used in this sort of situation. 'Always glad to help my friends at the police,' the lean West Virginian said whenever they asked him.

Gardner got his bearings after the line stopped moving. He fixated on number four. He couldn't help it; besides, in the dark it didn't make any difference. He wasn't going to tip off Billie. The gaunt face of Justice seemed to be focused on the room, his eyes like dull glass chips washed up on a seashore. He sees us, Gardner thought, shifting uncomfortably in his chair.

'I think that's him,' Billie Harris said in a hushed voice.

Gardner tensed.

'Now, take your time,' Larry instructed. 'Don't say anything until you're sure.'

Billie waited a moment before he spoke again. Then he calmly picked out number six, Sgt. Louis Stern, the homeliest officer on the second squad.

Dallas Stubbins did not like his cellmate. He smelled like a weasel, and was as friendly as a snake, but the son of a bitch just might be his ticket out. 'Be nice to Mr. Justice,' the shift officer had said. 'He needs all the friends he can get.' Dallas was not stupid. He had done hundreds of nighttime B and Es on construction sites before he accidentally tripped off an alarm and found himself staring into a pump-action shotgun. That was three months ago, and the public defender's office had not been able to get his bond reduced. The only chance to get back on the street was to cut a deal. And the best shot at that was to get T. J. Justice to tell him something he could use as a bargaining chip.

'These county boys ain't worth shit,' Dallas began, lapsing into a forced drawl.

Justice lay on the top bunk, slowly sucking the life out of a Marlboro, its tip glowing in the midnight darkness.

'They got all the 'quipment, but they're dumber than the butt end of a mule.'

T.J. didn't look over. He remained fixed to the mattress, leg crossed at the knee, arm cocked into a feeding position, cigarette pinched tightly between his fingers.

'D.C., man. They really know how to jack you up down there . . . You ever been locked up in D.C.?'

Justice blew a long, slow plume of smoke from the side of his mouth without letting go of the tip.

'I got the piss knocked out of me by six nigger guards down there, 'bout four years ago. Them bastards definitely do not like us. No sir. You look like me an' you when you go in, but by 'time they done, got so many goddamn bruises, you look like one of them.' Dallas was flailing, trying to find something that T.J. could relate to. Trying to get something going. 'Had a guy down there killed six people. This sucker popped off his wife, his mother-in-law, and his four kids. Shiiiiiit, they tried to shear his nuts off in the shower room the first day he got locked up.'

Justice put his leg down flat, but otherwise didn't

change position. Dead ash lined his chest just below the chin. His eyes held steady in an unbroken staring contest with the ceiling. 'Whut they do to him?' he said without moving anything but his jaw.

Dallas felt the strike, but knew he shouldn't jerk the line too fast.

'Sons of bitches caught him up against a pipe, and damn near got a wire under his balls before the fire alarm got punched.' Justice stayed frozen in place, but Dallas knew he was listening. It was time to pull a little on the hook. 'See this here?' The B and E defendant raised his shirt and pointed to a long lightning-bolt scar that extended from above his left nipple to the underside of his bicep. 'Two hundred stitches,' he announced. 'That's what the nigger screws done to me.'

Justice turned his head very slightly to the left as Dallas pushed his chest against the cold metal frame of the bunk. His eyes were inches from the pinkish trail of the scar. 'Got me with a riot baton. Almost ripped my goddamn arm off.'

'Thought you said they was tryin' to hurt the other fella,' T.J. grunted, rolling his head back to its previous position. 'Whut they git you for?'

''Cuz I'm the one that hit the alarm,' Dallas said proudly.

Assistant Medical Examiner Peter Stinson looked out of the window at the Baltimore skyline. The seasonal retreat of the sun marked its route daily by adding another pane of flaming glass to the southern tier of the office tower across the street. The distraction delayed him for a moment as he contemplated the shimmery copper reflection and thought about the world of light that existed above the refrigerated basement where his 'patients' lay on their metal slabs. A new one had come in yesterday morning, and he was in no rush to get to it. Young kid, the officer accompanying the body had said. A priority case. It was 3:15 as the sun lit up another southerly square, and a lone sea gull drifted across the angled shaft. Behind, the deep blue November sky filled in gaps between the buildings. The city trembled with life. Just a few seconds more, the doctor thought, as he absorbed the scene, inoculating himself against the chill that spread across the floor whenever the body-storage compartment doors were opened. The cool air always seemed to linger about trouser-cuff level and never dissipated until the autopsy was over. He didn't like that feeling, and it seemed that no matter how much they fiddled with the thermostat, it never went away.

The telephone rang. 'Medical examiner's office,' Dr. Stinson answered. It was Dr. Herrmann, the acting chief medical examiner. 'Pete, I understand you have a case from western Maryland. What is your timetable on processing it?' The acting chief was on extended leave, caring for a terminally ill wife, but was still trying to 'run' the office.

'Just about to get to it, sir,' Stinson replied.

'Well, this one needs some special attention,' Herrmann said. 'I got a call from the governor's office this morning. The Russians want us to turn the boy over to them almost immediately. They are planning to send the body back to Moscow for burial, and they do not want to wait.'

'No problem, Dr. Herrmann.' The assistant ME

looked out of the window again. The rush hour was tuning up early, and exhaust haze had begun blurring the skyline. 'We can have it finished by this evening, and they can come by for a pickup first thing tomorrow,' he said.

'Good. That sounds fine. Oh, there is one more thing . . .' Dr. Herrmann had saved the kicker for last. 'They do not want the body dissected.'

'What?' Stinson croaked.

'The Russians want the boy back in one piece. They do not want us cutting on him.'

'Well, how do you expect me to do the autopsy, then?'

'I have a lot of confidence in you, Peter. I'm sure you will think of something. Be creative, but get him back in their hands no later than noon tomorrow. Understood?'

'Yeah, I think so,' Dr. Stinson replied, but he was not being truthful. How on earth could an autopsy be performed without going inside the body? There was no such procedure. He sighed. 'I'll take care of it, Doc. Don't you worry,' Stinson said before hanging up.

He took another look at the outside world, then stood up. 'Be creative,' he said sarcastically to himself as he opened the door that led to the stairwell. 'What the hell does that mean?' He was still pondering the question halfway down the steps, when he felt the bite of the freezer draft on his ankles.

Gardner sat in the back booth of Paul's Place, slowly twirling his martini glass so that the olive rolled around the rim. This was the second of his customary evening 'whiteys,' and it was only eight o'clock. The first had gone down fast. But this one was a sipper, and the nerve cables in his neck were already sputtering into numbness as he wobbled the conical glass around in his hand.

Another night in the cradle of the Appalachians, Gardner thought to himself. What a life. The regulars were riding their usual positions at the bar, their voices blending with the low-volume country ballads on the jukebox in a pleasant whisper of sound. And the predatory singles, out for the night, were tentatively edging around the reserved seats.

For the State's Attorney, Paul's was like a satellite office. A familiar site where he could transact business or wind down after court. Some detractors referred to it derisively as 'Lawson's Place,' but, Gardner thought, if they really knew how many winning jury arguments had been conceived there, or how much the place contributed to the county prosecutor's mental health, they might have reconsidered their comments.

'Heard about the case.' Gardner pulled out of his reverie as big Paul pushed his gargantuan belly against the tabletop of the booth. The proprietor was an integral part of the establishment. Always there. Always attentive. Always respectful to the private lives of his loyal customers.

'God-awful,' Gardner replied, shaking his head. 'One of the worst . . .'

Paul had endured the breakup days with Gardner as his closest confidant. Night after night in the back booth, he listened as the prosecutor replayed and second-guessed the events that led to the fall. He never judged, just listened and advised, and that put him high on

Gardner's list of special people.

'What happened with that witness?' Paul continued. Word traveled like chain lightning in the back streets of the town. By now everyone knew about the disaster at the police station, and opinions about the consequences were already being voiced. 'Gonna have to let Justice go?'

Gardner looked up at his friend. This always happened. The lay person's misperception of the facts. 'Hell no!' he growled. 'There was no ID, no goddamn ID. That's all that happened. He didn't eliminate Justice.'

Paul was used to Gardner's tirades. He had taken many an afternoon off and seen him in action in court. The gut-wrenching style of argument that Gardner employed was effective as hell. It was forceful and righteous, and shot through with sincere belief. Most juries didn't have a chance to resist. They went with the flow, and voted conviction.

'So who dropped the ball?' Paul asked. There was obviously a reason for the screwup.

Gardner grimaced. 'Cops. Rushed it. Had the whole thing arranged before they told me . . .'

Paul nodded. He knew the routine by heart.

'The Harris kid should have been screened out in the field,' Gardner went on. 'Nailed down as to lighting, distance, descriptive detail . . . should have taken his number, given him a "will call," and sent him home. But no. They had to set him in for a face-to-face, and hand the defense a fuckin' free shot before we even got the investigation off the ground.' Gardner guzzled the remainder of his drink and ate the olive.

'Another?' Paul reached for the glass, and the prosecutor signaled okay with a snap of his head. Only Paul knew how to make Gardner's special martini: Tanqueray gin. Four drops of dry white vermouth. Three washed pitted olives. Frozen glass. No oil slick. The other bartenders all deferred to Paul whenever Gardner ordered it, but they joked to each other that that drink alone had enabled the owner to put in a new club basement. The recipe was one more confidential connection between the two men.

The drink was delivered, and Paul hesitated at the booth, ready for any further comments from his regular customer.

'This guy's an animal, Paul,' Gardner said. 'Goddamn mad dog . . .'

Paul wasn't sure who the 'guy' was, so he tried a name: 'Justice?'

Gardner nodded. 'Uh-huh. Likes to kill little boys . . .'

They had talked about Granville so much in the last two years that Paul felt like an honorary parent. Gardner's life centered on the child, and during some of their late-night sessions, Paul saw how deep the feelings ran. The grief of separation was overwhelming, and often Gardner got so choked up he couldn't talk. The same look was in his eyes tonight. 'It's okay, man,' Paul said. 'You're gonna get him.'

Gardner took a major swig of his drink. 'We've got to . . .'

'Excuse me,' a female voice suddenly called out from behind Paul's bulky form. It was Elaine. She had learned from numerous tries that she could probably find him in the back booth at Paul's if he didn't answer his phone.

Paul moved aside, and she slid into the seat next to Gardner. 'Hope I'm not interrupting anything.'

Paul shrugged and smiled. He knew exactly how Elaine fitted into the prosecutor's life. And he knew that the kind of heart-to-heart talks that he had with Gardner was not a part of it. The big man pushed away from the table, and left Gardner alone with Elaine.

She immediately leaned close and whispered in his ear. 'Wanna play tonight?' The words tickled softly, and he felt her nails bite into the muscles of his inner thigh.

Gardner pulled back so he could focus on her face. 'What did you have in mind?' She had fixed her hair in a stylish upsweep that he found exotic. That was her mood cue, her subtle way of communicating her short-term agenda. Tonight it said sex.

'I'll show you when we get back to my place,' she said sultrily. Then she smiled, and gave him a naughty wink.

Gardner's martinis had worn him down, and at that moment he couldn't resist. The day had been a disaster. He needed a break. 'Okay,' Gardner said weakly. Then he let her take his arm and lead him out of the bar.

Jennifer was dead tired. It was 11:30 and the night was moonless. The dim headlights on her Toyota barely stretched far enough to keep the car from overrunning into the deep darkness ahead. Gardner had suggested earlier in the day that there were a few things out in the 'field' that needed some attention. He didn't come right out and ask her to do anything. That was not how he worked. His method was a lot more subtle. 'You know, the people up at the motel in Hodges are going to be key witnesses in this case. We'd better get them lined up for an interview.' That wasn't exactly a direct order, but Jennifer saw it as her cue to volunteer.

'I can take care of that, boss,' she told him, knowing that she still had tomorrow's docket to prepare and a plea pending before Judge Danforth.

'Great,' he had responded. There was so little hesitation in his voice that it was obvious he wanted her to do it all along. She didn't mind the extra work. In fact, the task was already on the 'to do' list in the case file she had put together.

'By the way,' Gardner had added as she hustled past his door on the way to court, 'while you're out there, see if you can swing by the Ramada and check on the Russians. Keep it low key. Not too obvious. Are they still there? What have they been doing for the past few days? That sort of stuff. Talk to Sally Foster in the office if she's available. We don't need any surprises from those guys. We have enough from the usual sources.' Again, Jennifer said okay, and again she was a half-step ahead of her boss's request. 'Follow up on activities of outside investigators' she had written in notes the day before.

Her mind came back to the road, and she blinked behind her glasses, fighting the urge to close her eyes completely for a millisecond of rest. A late afternoon in court had set back her schedule, and now she was paying the price. A little air might help, she thought, rolling the window open a notch so the tang of fall could blow a few more minutes of alertness into her sagging brain. No traffic, as usual. Not in this area. The entire sector was pockmarked and sliced up with abandoned coal mines and access roads. A century ago the place had been teeming with miners and coal cars, but now it was completely deserted, and the only hint of what had been was the ROAD CLOSED signs on the many overgrown pathways into the woods.

A Robert Frost poem suddenly drifted into her mind: '. . . the loneliness includes me unawares . . .' The cool air was working, waking her up as it whiffled her bangs. The car jumped over a slight hump in the road, and the jolt reinforced her mood. The county wasn't much to some people. Rocks, trees, and bumpy fields thrown against a mountain. A town with two movie theaters and a courthouse. A bunch of slow-talking hicks. Jennifer smiled. Others might complain and pack their bags to leave, but to her it was home.

Just then she passed the sign for Rockfield, and smiled again. This time her thoughts focused on her 'boss.' She was approaching the spot where the two of them had spent many a late afternoon walking out their frustrations along a four-mile course.

The 'jogging club' had started as one of Gardner's tongue-in-cheek challenges. Jennifer had only been in the office for a few weeks when she used the word 'faddist' to describe the chief prosecutor's obsessive need to run.

'Bet you couldn't even make it from here to the corner,' he had laughed in response. 'If you're gonna criticize, you're gonna have to be qualified.'

Jennifer was too new to see the point. 'I only suggested that your running may be motivated more by social than physical needs,' she said defensively.

Gardner smiled. 'And I said you couldn't go half a mile, no matter what your motivation.'

Jennifer suddenly realized where the joke was heading. 'Do you want to test that theory?' she asked.

Gardner laughed. 'You bet!'

One day in late April the challenge was met, and the State's Attorney's two-member jogging club was born. The rain had left puddles in the indentations of Gardner's personalized course through Rockfield Park. He made no effort to avoid them. In fact, it seemed he was going out of his way to hit each and every one, and every time he did it, Jennifer got splashed.

She hung in there, obstacles and all. Arms pumping as their strides matched, bangs flopping over her sweatband, breath snorting in even bursts. The sunlight had just faded behind the ridge line, and the air was beginning to pick up the scent of dusk.

Gardner was starting to strain. He had been acclimated to the routine for years, but it had never come easy, and towards the finish he always had to push. He glanced at his companion.

'How're ya doin'?' he gasped.

Jennifer maintained her pace. 'Okay.'

'Wanna slow down?'

She kept her eyes to the front. 'Do you?'

Gardner could tell that the joke was over. She had proven herself, and there was no need for further testing.

'Just ease off a little,' he said, clicking the speed down a notch. Jennifer slowed as he did and noticed a large wet pool in her path. Her feet hit with accentuated force, and Gardner got drenched. 'Hey!' he yelled.

Jennifer continued forward. 'Sorry!' she hollered back.

They looked at each other in the failing light. Steam rose from their heads, and their skin was flushed. Jennifer smiled.

'So you think you might like to try it again?' Gardner asked.

Her smile lingered. 'Any time, sir.'

They walked the remainder of the course, cooling down and talking strategy on an upcoming case. As darkness closed out the scene, the first meeting of the jogging club was adjourned.

The road suddenly departed from the woods at Wyler's Crossing, and Jennifer's mind returned to the present. The intersection consisted of a weathered brown frame general store and a closed-up gas station. At this time of night nothing was moving. Jennifer hesitated at the stop sign, then pulled into the short gravel lot in front of the store. She drove up to the telephone booth and got out. There was nothing to report from the field. That's what she wanted to tell Gardner. Nobody had much to say on any of her assigned topics. The witnesses were duds, and nobody knew anything about the Russians. It could probably wait until tomorrow, but she wanted to hear his voice, to see if he was okay. The last few days had been tough on him, and she was concerned.

The phone rang ten times. Jennifer hung up and tried again. This time she let it go for twenty. 'Must not be home,' she mumbled to herself as she got back into the car. On the drive to her apartment, she didn't come up with a single line of poetry. Her mood had changed, and she wasn't really sure why.

Gardner lay awake in the bed, unable to sleep. He could feel Elaine's smooth legs locked into position behind his knees, her nails barely touching the point where his chest tapered into his abdomen. He could feel her jaw pressing sharply into his shoulder blade, and the even cadence of her breasts lower down on his back, and he knew that she didn't have the same problem. He had dozed off earlier, after she had put him through several hours of their 'special game.' The exhaustion had taken over after the last round, and his recollection of the final moments was hazy. Elaine had assumed control, he could remember that much, her face contorted into a lewd caricature of passion, her voice pitching down into a throaty breathless murmur, urging, threatening, animating images of lust that ate up the walls and flung them both into a spinning dimension of heat, light, paralyzing shocks of pleasure, and finally, darkness.

The room was still partially lit by Elaine's pink dressing-table lamp, and the bedside clock read 2:45 A.M.

'I want to see everything,' she had told him brazenly the first time. That was one of the things that kept him going. She was not the least bit inhibited in anything, especially when it came to sex. No psychoanalysis. No 'defining the parameters of permissible activity.' No guilt-ridden second thoughts. She had opened the inner lining of her subconscious to him, and was not at all embarrassed when a bizarre wild-eyed creature came charging out. He enjoyed that part. A lot. It was the rest of the package that gave him trouble.

Elaine's Elvis painting covered the entire south wall of the bedroom. Gardner had teased her about it at first, but backed off when he saw how serious she was about her 'hero.' He even had to stop using 'pill-popping psychopath' to describe the 'king.' She was a country music aficionado. And of course, in that realm, there was but one icon. Gardner listened occasionally, when the mood struck, but his tastes shaded more to urban rock. That was one of many differences in their personalities, but it didn't seem to matter in bed. She always allowed him to switch off his mind when they were having sex. No judges. No grand juries. No toothless criminals staring at him. No Carole. Only blue eyes, red hair, sharp fingernails, and 'special games.'

The repetitive dream had awakened him. He remembered that now, as he studied the droopy lines of Elvis's face. They were on the *Mindy*. One of the days when the clouds looked like they had been shot out of a whipped cream can. The sea was calm, and the water was so clear that the stern ladder seemed to be suspended in air. He had helped Carole on with her scuba tank, and now she was helping him on with his. She handed him the regulator, then reached around the other side and grabbed the hose, pulling it against his neck. He couldn't breathe. 'Please! . . . Pl . . .' he was trying to say before he opened his eyes and realized where he was.

His thoughts jumped for a moment to the day it started. The day Carole took the bait and committed herself to take the plunge. Gardner and Carole had been in the family room as 'The Undersea World of Jacques Cousteau' began. Granville was three years old, talking in sentences, and telling Dad he wanted to be a 'diber.' The camera panned the rippling surface, split the screen with water and air, then canted downwards into a school of dolphins. Gardner noticed that Carole had put down her book. She was not a TV watcher per se. She sat in front of the set, but seldom raised her eyes above page level. This time she was actually watching.

'Spectacular, isn't it?' Gardner said.

'Pectakalar,' Granville mimicked.

Carole didn't answer. She closed her book.

'And now, Claude will attempt to make contact,' Jacques said softly, his French twang diplomatically soothing relations between man and mammal.

'Eeeee,' a dolphin voice intoned.

'Zeee!' said Granville.

Carole was honed in on the swirling mass of sleek bodies encircling Claude. The blue-green background set off the swift grey torpedoes in a three-dimensional pattern. Gardner looked at Carole. She was enveloped by dolphins.

'What are you thinking?' he asked. For years he had been trying to get her in scuba gear, but she always begged off. Now he sensed an opening.

'Looks super, doesn't it?' he argued.

She was still watching the underwater ballet.

'Well?'

She kept silent, her eyes swimming with the school. Gardner smiled. For the first time, she hadn't said no.

He tried to get back to sleep, but it was impossible in Elaine's bed. He needed to go home. Slowly he eased out, and got his clothes together. The spell was wearing off. Pinpricks of reality were penetrating the perimeter of their private world. He looked at Elaine. Except for her hair exploding from beneath the rumpled covers, her features were invisible. He slowly tiptoed towards the door, opened it, and, without looking back, descended the stairs. By the time he got to his car the magic was gone, and all that was left in its place was the startling cold of the night.

CHAPTER 6

At 8:45 the next morning, Sgt. Joe Brown cautiously parked his lab van on the parking lot of the Hodges Hide-Away Motel. It was like going into enemy territory, an enclave of thugs and slime balls whose guest register could be swapped for the police wanted list at any time without changing a single entry. The place looked the part. Individual 'cabins' flung across a seedy-looking stand of pines. Weathered gray siding shedding its color in flecks and curls, rusty window screens peppered with holes, shingles sliding off the rooftops. In fifty years the place had probably never seen a paintbrush or a hammer, Brownie surmised as he mounted the rotting steps to the 'office' and rang the night bell.

'Yeah? What you want?' Grandma Hodges was working the desk. She was as frail as a twig. Thick glasses, hair pulled into a poor imitation of a bun, razor-thin shoulders draped in faded polka dots. She looked like an open invitation for a scam, but Brownie knew otherwise.

'Police, Ms. Hodges,' he announced, checking to see if her hands were beneath the counter where the family .357 magnum was kept.

111

'Again? Ain't you people ever satisfied?' the old lady squawked. Her right hand stayed out of sight below the level of the scratched-up Formica top. Brownie knew that the gun was pointed directly at him.

'Now, Ms. Hodges, you know you don't got to be 'fraid of me,' he said softly, getting in close enough for her lenses to take effect. 'We just want to take another look-see in the cabin you rented to Justice. Just a little look around, that's all.'

She pulled her right hand out of its hiding place and reached across the counter. 'What the hell is goin' on, Mr. Brown?' Grandma Hodges asked, grabbing a handful of the officer's uniform sleeve. 'Must'a been twenty people out here snoopin' around already. Goddamn foreigners, FBI, state cops, even had a lady from the DA's here late last night. What in the name of tarnation is all them people lookin' for?' She still had Brownie in her grasp, but he didn't try to pull away.

'Remember the time with the shootin',' he said, 'when we had to take all them tests 'cause the prosecutor needed to find out what happened?' She nodded. The glasses made her crinkled eyes as big as half dollars. 'Well, maybe there's a clue hiding in the room they can use at his trial.'

'Ain't nothing left. Them others done took it all. I told 'em and told 'em.' She finally let go of his sleeve. 'Anyway, I done had the room cleaned. Ain't nothing there now, even if there was before.'

Brownie liked the old lady's spirit. He had done the lab work the time she had almost cut a would-be robber in two with her magnum. Three shots. Three bullet holes in the dead body. The problem was that two were in the man's chest and one was in his back. The State's Attorney said that it was a possible manslaughter if the shot in the back came first. That would have meant that the robbery was over, and there would no longer have been an imminent danger justifying the use of deadly force. Brownie had tested the gun, and found that the first two rounds were copper, and the third was lead. Microscopic filings on the shell casings in the cylinder established that fact, so when the autopsy turned up a lead slug in the man's back, Ms. Hodges's shooting was ruled self-defense. 'The first two shots spun the suspect around as the third was being fired,' the close-out report said. Exactly what Grandma had told them in the beginning.

'How 'bout lettin' me have a look, anyway?' Brownie said. 'Never can tell what might have slipped through the cracks that nobody saw.'

'My lands, it's a wonder we don't shut this place down and let all you policemens just move in.'

'Come on, Ms. Hodges, we were there when you needed us. Can you just let me have a little peek? I'll be quiet as a mouse. You'll see.'

'Maw? What's the problem?' It was Buster Hodges, the old lady's grandson. He was a twenty-year-old who looked forty. Baggy eyes. Yellowish pockmarked skin. Unwashed and uncombed hair. 'He givin' you trouble?' The inflection on 'he' carried with it the sting of a racial slur.

'Just some police business,' Brownie answered in his official-duties voice. 'Need to get a look at the room

Justice was in.' The grandson had elbowed up to the counter. Brownie stepped back. He didn't want this idiot to start fiddling with the family piece.

'Look, county cop, you got a search warrant?' Buster demanded in a nasty tone. The old lady had yielded her authority and now stood silently while the men faced off against each other.

'I don't need a warrant to look in the room. This is a consent search. All I need is your okay.' Brownie was paraphrasing the constitutional law handbook. Leased premises that have been vacated no longer carry a legitimate expectation of privacy for the lessor. Any evidence or contraband found after the lessor has terminated his lease may be seized if permission to enter has been granted by the landlord.

'Please, just give me a chance to look at the room, and I'll be on my way,' the officer said, dropping the confrontational edge off of his words.

'What do you think, Maw?' Buster was starting to back down also. The old lady held the swing vote.

'I'd say it was okay, 'long as he don't do what the other fella done,' Grandma Hodges said.

'What was that?' Brownie asked.

'Shoot, he like to tore the stuffin' out of the mattress. Had to patch it up myself. You can look around but don't bust anything up, you hear?'

'Yes, ma'am. I'll be careful. Uh, Ms. Hodges, which one done that, uh, with the mattress? Which police officer?'

'One them foreign cops. Big guy. White hair. Messed the place up bad, but did give me a little money to pay for what he done.'

'Did he say what he was looking for?'

'Didn't speak no English. Jus' give me fifty dollars and left. Took me darn near 'hour to sew the thing up.'

Brownie furrowed his brow. Russians digging into mattresses didn't sound good. What the hell were they after?

'Did you see if he found anything?' the officer asked.

The old lady pursed her lips. ''Course not!' she huffed. 'I don't butt into nobody's business!'

Brownie touched her arm gently. 'I know that, Ms. Hodges. Thank you for your help. Now, can I see the unit?'

She pointed the way, and the officer thanked her again. Then he put his hands on his hips and walked over to T. J. Justice's last known address.

Unit 15 was as beaten up as the others. It sat at the end of the line of cabins, almost invisible from the road because of trees. The front porch sagged to the left, its underpinnings slowly giving way to the water that rushed out of the encircling swale each time it rained. Brownie inserted the key and pushed open the door. The air inside the room carried with it all the ambience of a mildewed basement. The metal frame bed was made up. The bedspread matched the curtains: faded pea-green polyester, spotted with stains that darkened the fabric to its original color. The rug was a rag-type weave direct from Workshop of the Blind. Brownie completed his initial survey. Ms. Hodges was right. Nothing here. At least nothing on the surface. Then he smiled. It was time to go to work.

'Every human being leaves a trail,' Brownie's professor of forensic science had said. 'Most of the time it just blows away with the wind, but sometimes it sticks itself to something and stays there until a keen-eyed cop sees it and pulls it off.' The words became the student's motto, later the rookie police officer's philosophy, and later still, the veteran lab technician's claim to fame. He could see what others couldn't: invisible flotsam bobbing in the wakes of people who had long ago sailed past the horizon. The place had been picked over, old lady Hodges said. State police, FBI, Russian agents. Brownie was troubled. He could understand that kind of attention to a crime scene, but not to a place that had been occupied by the suspect. Fingerprints, hair samples, fibers, anything that might have come off of Justice and stuck to the room, none of it was worth a damn. So what if it showed that he had been in the room? Everyone already knew that. They needed to find something from the victim. A clue trailing in his wake that made the connection to Justice. But, Brownie thought, the boy had never been to the room. He was killed in the solitude of Sessy's Woods. Blood pattern. Position of the body. And there was the time of death. MEs judged it at plus or minus eight hours from the time the boy's body was found. Figuring in the grandmother's estimate of dusk for his abduction, there was no way in hell for Justice to have gotten from Hodges to Wooley's, then back to Hodges and then all the way to Sessy's. No. Mika Anatov was murdered in the woods. The only way there could be anything off the boy in unit 15 was if T. J. had been stupid enough to come back here.

'Whut you lookin' for, man?' A voice through the open cabin door. Brownie raised his right hand to belt level, next to the nine-millimeter automatic strapped in its holster. He turned around. The bright sunrise haloed the figure of a fat man standing on the porch. A plaid bandanna was tied to his head. The rest of him was washed-out denim.

'This is a police matter,' Brownie replied, moving to angle the shadow of the porch overhang across the pumpkin-shaped head.

'Yeah? Well, you better hurry up, 'cuz they jus' rented me this room.'

Brownie unsnapped the trigger guard with a casual flick of his thumb. This was why he didn't like it out here. Too many mug-shot faces. 'Well, if it ain't a small world,' he said. 'What you been up to, Meatball? Just get out of the slam for the fiftieth time?' It was Willard Junking. Part-time motorcycle repairman, full-time trouble-maker.

'You got it, county boy. Never want to leave me alone, do you, sons a bitches?' Brownie stood still. The 'b' word coming from the fat man didn't bother him. They had tangled before, and Brownie always won, usually without a punch. The Meatball was one big mouth. 'As if his body didn't advertise that fact,' Gardner Lawson once said.

'What we get you for this time, Meat?' Brownie asked, putting a little extra zing into the word 'we.'

'Fuckin' DWI on my hog.'

'Yeah? What's that now? Number six?' Brownie couldn't resist a smirk.

'Laugh all you want to, sn'm bitch. I got me a good lawyer this time, an' he's gonna stuff them charges right up yo' mutherfuckin' black butt. Fact, he's already started. Got my bond dropped to personal recog.'

Brownie stopped smiling. He didn't have anything else to say, and he already had a good idea who Meatball was talking about.

'Step down from the porch, please,' Brownie said firmly. His right hand still lingered near the side arm, thumb tucked in behind his belt.

'Take it easy, now,' Meatball replied, feeling for the leading edge without taking his eyes off the police officer's midsection.

'You're gonna have to give me some privacy,' Brownie continued, grasping the edge of the flimsy plywood door and giving it a boost toward the frame.

The fat man eased his bulk fully into the sunlight as the door swung in an agonizingly slow arc. 'You got it, mutherfucker,' Meatball said defiantly. 'But don't plant no bugs in there, or you'll be pissin' sideways when Mr. King gets done hogtyin' yo' puny little dick.' The last word slipped in as the door tapped against the jamb.

'Well, he gonna have a hell of a time with this baby,' the officer chimed back in a mock ghetto drawl. Then he grabbed his crotch like a bowling ball and did an emphatic 'bump' toward the door, just for emphasis.

'Dumb fuck almost got me forgettin' things,' Brownie said to himself, pivoting his attention back to the shabby cubicle. Everyone must have assumed that T. J. actually returned to the cabin the night of the killing. That could be the only reason they invested so much time and effort tearing the place apart. No one found a pinprick's worth of evidence relating to the boy, that was obvious.

Brownie never expected that they would. It didn't seem possible that either Justice or the Russian child could have trailed wakes across the bleakness of Hodges either directly or indirectly after the snatch. Brownie could not have cared less about that angle. He was looking for something else.

His training at the department was always being upgraded. New investigation techniques, new equipment, new interrogation procedures. One program stood out from the others. The name of the course was 'Criminal Profiling, a Study in the Habit Patterns of Serial Offenders.' Brownie had been sent to D.C. for three weeks. FBI headquarters. Sheraton Hotel. Fourteenth Street. 'Best damn upgrade program I ever took,' he had chuckled to Sam Jenkins in the lab when he returned. After a while, the whole department knew about the 'fox' he met in Georgetown and their brief but satisfying 'overnight romance,' but there was another dividend of the trip. He had really learned something.

Signature criminals like Justice all had one thing in common: they secretly documented their crimes. Some preferred photographs. Others, audio- or videotapes. Some even took cuttings of hair, personal belongings, or even body parts. Their methods differed, but their obsession was the same. Keep a reminder, so they could relive the 'high' of their crimes. From the background bio the officer had read on T. J. Justice, it was clear that he fell right in line with the syndrome. His methods varied, and his records were crude, but he always played the game.

'Compulsive behavior. Compulsive behavior,'

Brownie chanted to himself as his eyes swept back and forth across the room like the probing dish of an ultra-sensitive radar. Up. Across. Down. A step forwards, then up, across, and down. 'Where the hell would he put it?' he whispered through his teeth. Then, instinctively, he looked straight up. 'Them clues and things, they all float down,' Brownie said, 'but a hidin' spot, now that's another story.' He reached up and began probing between the slats of the false ceiling. On tiptoe he followed the pattern all the way to the wall, slipped around the edge, and tiptoed all the way back. Dust particles and dried-up insect wings skirted his finger, uncannily choosing his face and hair as landing spots on their way to the floor. 'Uhhh!' He spat out the remains of a mummified bee. Suddenly Brownie's finger hit something. He stopped. The bee was still auto-rotating silently downward. He reached up with the other hand and pulled it out. Four pages of school-type note paper, folded over. He lifted the flap. 'Got you, sucker!' Brownie declared. On the first page was a drawing of a snake. It was coiled around the neck of a tiny stick-figure boy.

Brownie checked the other three pages. More of same. Crude, graphic scrawlings of a snake choking the life out of a small child. The records of a crime, kept in the normal course of business by a psychopath. Just as predicted.

Gardner was alone in his office, at work on the Justice file, trying to assemble the pieces into a coherent picture he could present to the grand jury. He had been at it for hours, and now the shadows of the late-afternoon sun had replaced the brightness at his window. He looked down into the courtyard where a news reporter was set up for a report. It was Krysta Collins, one of the national network regulars. She was attractive in a sultry way. Dark hair and eyes that conjured images of Spain. Gardner could imagine what she was saying. 'The world stands aghast at the horror of this senseless crime,' he mumbled aloud. He watched her for a few moments as she false-started several times, and had to repeat. Then he went back to the file.

It seemed like only moments, but it had to be longer. When Gardner looked out of the window again, the shadows were almost horizontal and the reporter was gone. He flipped open his mahogany cigar case and pulled out a Royal Jamaican, putting it to his lips. Slowly he spun it around, inserted it into his mouth, and wet it down. Then he leaned back in his chair and lit up. As he blew a smoky ring towards the ceiling and leaned back in his chair, his private line buzzed.

'The Federal Express package is here, sir,' Miss Cass said over the speaker. 'Do you want me to bring it in?'

'Yes, if you would, please,' Gardner intercomed back.

'And I have Mrs. Lawson on line one, Miss Tower on line two, and Jennifer waiting to see you . . .'

Silence.

'Uh, Mr. Lawson, any instructions?'

Gardner blew a long, steady mouthful of smoke while he considered his options. He hated having Carole referred to as 'Mrs.' Lawson. It was technically correct, even in a divorce situation, but it carried such a connotation of ownership and privilege that he had considered instructing people to use another title. The alternatives, unfortunately, were just as bad. 'Your ex-wife.' 'The mother of your child.' Or, simply, 'Carole.' None worked. It was less hassle to go back to the original.

'Tell Mrs. Lawson I'll call back,' Gardner finally responded.

'Yes, sir. Uh, what about Miss uh . . .'

'Please give Jennifer the package and have her wait a sec. I'll take the other call.'

'Fine, Mr. G.'

Gardner punched the button to number two. 'What's up, Elaine?'

'How come you snuck out on me again?' she said, her voice sounding slightly hurt. She was calling from the clothing store where she worked.

Gardner could hear the burble of the shop customers in the background. They were probably listening. 'You know about my back. That water bed of yours gets it messed up.'

'Well, you never complain when we're doin' it.' Gardner grimaced. The shop noise suddenly seemed to hush into silence.

'Elaine, we can discuss that another time. I've got some major problems on my hands right now.'

'More important than me?'

'Uh, different.' Gardner was getting what Big Paul called the 'love dividend.' First they let you have it, then they submitted vouchers for payment. Up to now Elaine hadn't done much of that, but lately she seemed to be dunning him every chance she got.

'You working with Jennifer Munday?' Her mood abruptly swung to jealousy as the whirling passion of last night 'poofed' and disappeared.

'Please, Elaine, we'll talk about it later.'

'Yeah? When?'

'The next time I see you.'

'Yeah? When is that going to be?'

'When I can. Okay? Right now I have to get back to work.' Her hesitation told him that his responses had scored a hit.

'Uh, okay. Call me later?'

'I will.'

'Promise?'

'I promise.'

'Okay. Love you. 'Bye.'

'Okay.' Gardner hung up the phone. 'Send Jennifer in please,' he said wearily into the squawk box.

'On her way, Mr. Lawson,' his secretary replied. 'By the way, Mrs. Lawson said there was a matter she needed to discuss.' Gardner groaned. He couldn't wait to hear what that was.

The door opened, and Jennifer breezed in. 'Didn't take long getting here,' she said, claiming her customary seat. She had switched the grey frames for tortoiseshells. Her hair was slightly different also. The ponytail had been pulled to the side. This made the thick blunt end brush casually across her shoulder each time she turned her head.

'Feels pretty hefty,' Gardner said as he took the envelope from his assistant's slender hand. 'Guess they do a more thorough job on these things out there.' He slit the seam and pulled out a tan folder. There was a label on the cover: PRESENTENCE INVESTIGATION REPORT ON THOMAS JACOB JUSTICE, KANSAS DEPARTMENT OF PAROLE AND PROBATION.

Inside, attached to the first page, was a letter. 'Hope you can do more with Justice than we could,' it began. 'Keep the heat on him, and don't be shocked if you get a few surprises along the way. You never know what he is going to do next. Good luck. We're all pulling for you.' It was signed *Bill Howard, District Prosecutor, Linden City, Kansas*.

'They're wishing us luck,' Gardner said when he finished skimming the letter.

Jennifer did not respond, so Gardner looked up. Her face registered concern. 'You haven't told me yet,' she said.

'Told you what?' Gardner replied.

'Whether I'm officially on the case.'

Gardner's mind jumped to the Staggers case. Jennifer's first jury trial. He had sat sidesaddle on that one, a silent co-counsel, whispering instructions, advising, but not involving himself in the action. She had goofed on a few evidentiary points, and her voice had trailed off occasionally in her arguments to the jury, but it was otherwise a credible debut. Staggers was convicted of robbery, and received a jail sentence. After that, Gardner turned her loose on most of the minor felonies, and she scored a win every time. She was ready for advancement.

'Well?' Jennifer was still waiting for an answer.

'You're in,' Gardner said. 'Official second gun.'

Jennifer smiled, but it quickly faded. 'Have you really looked at this thing?' Her tone sounded skeptical as she emphasized 'looked.'

'What do you mean?'

'I've been evaluating the evidence, and from what I see so far, we've got some holes.'

Gardner leaned forward and stared into her eyes. 'I thought you knew better than that . . .'

'What?'

'Goddamn it, Jennifer, you don't back into a case!' His voice was rising. 'Don't start off crying about what you don't have. How many times have we gone over that? Accentuate the positive evidence, don't bitch about the things the cops didn't find.'

Jennifer picked up on the last phrase. 'Which is about everything we need for conviction,' she said resolutely.

Gardner's eyes squinted with anger. 'We're gonna convict the son of a bitch. We've got enough. Just have to put it to the jury. But you better get your attitude adjusted if you want to tag along.'

Jennifer knew she had gone far enough. 'No problem,' she said with a smile, but the doubts still tugged on the inside. The evidence she had seen was skimpy at best. It was all circumstantial, and there was nothing to tie Justice directly to the crime scene.

Gardner softened his expression. 'Good. If it's any consolation, I'm not giving up on the field work. Brownie's still looking, and I'm gonna see if we can get a rent-a-cop from the department for the duration of the case. Okay, so much for that. Now, what have you got on prior crimes?'

Jennifer plopped a file on the desk. 'Every Maryland case is right here. If we can establish a unique pattern, the Kansas stuff can come in.'

'Okay. Great. I'll go over that later. In the meantime, can you do me a favor?'

Jennifer nodded.

'I'm gonna take a while with this PSI. Can you rough draft me a set of charges on Justice?'

She nodded again.

'Thanks. Give me first-degree murder, felony murder, kidnapping, sex offenses, lesser includeds.'

'Drafts?'

'Yeah. Just do it rough. We'll hammer out the final version next week, before grand jury day. By then we should have all of the evidence lined up.'

Jennifer stood to leave. 'I'll have it on your desk tomorrow morning.'

'Thanks,' Gardner replied. 'Uh, Jen . . .'

She hesitated.

'Sorry I got huffy, but we gotta work together, and it's better if we're pulling in the same direction.'

Jennifer smiled again. 'I'm with you, boss.'

'Thanks. We'll catch up later.'

She left the room, her perfume faintly lingering in the air, and Gardner immersed himself in the PSI file.

The presentence investigation report had originally been developed as a tool to assist judges in their sentencing decisions. A compendium of the defendant's life that would enable the court to evaluate his inner soul. Everything was covered. The crime from the state's point of view. His version of what happened. His personal history. Family background. Marital situation. Employment. Prior offenses. Incarceration and probation history. Driving record. Medical and psychiatric treatment. It was all there.

Sometimes the crime was like a single smudge on an otherwise clean parchment. No priors. Good job. Stable family. Positive prospects for the future. They were candidates for leniency: frail humans who crossed the line in a moment of weakness, but would probably never err again. And then there were the others whose PSIs read like horror stories. Page after page of transgression. Page after page of misplaced trust. 'I can forecast the sentence by the weight of the probation report,' Betty Stevens in the clerk's office boasted. After ten years of predictions, Gardner had to admit she was usually right.

Gardner flipped to the Crime section of the report.

The six-year-old boy was abducted from a playground. His mother had left him there while she went shopping at a grocery store across the street. The body was found in a wooded area three miles away. There had been no attempt to conceal it. There was evidence of anal penetration and ligature strangulation. The cause of death was a single knife wound to the chest . . .

He read on.

. . . the defendant's clothing contained dried blood, which was matched and typed as coming from the victim. The knife was also recovered. It was a

127

hunter's buck knife with a five-inch blade . . .

Gardner stopped. The scene was sickeningly familiar. He scribbled a red asterisk in the margin with his felt-tip pen and continued to the end of the page. Then he turned to the Defendant's Version. 'On advice of counsel, Mr. Justice declined to make any statement to this agent,' was all that it said.

Gardner studied the report carefully, reading and rereading each page. 'Find out everything you possibly can about the defendant, and start to build your theme,' Gardner told his assistants. 'Get into his brain, and learn his habits. Then lay out your pattern. If you do it properly, he'll slither right in during the trial.' Of course it went without saying that you had to know what to look for.

He turned to the Prior Offense section. Six pages of entries laid out a criminal career of progressively more serious crimes. Vagrancy, alcohol offenses, and indecent exposure began the list. Then there was a gap of four years without an arrest. When the entries resumed, he had graduated to the big time. Three successive arrests on suspicion of child abuse and murder in three different jurisdictions, followed by three releases for insufficient evidence. The final entry was the Kansas case. Arrest, prosecution, conviction, appeal, and release.

Gardner flipped the page with disgust, and focused on the Family Background section.

Thomas Jacob Justice was the youngest of four children born to Zachariah and Manda Justice. He grew up in Sneadville, Tennessee, where his father worked in the meat-processing plant. His mother died when he was eight years old, and he ran away from home when he was twelve. Prior to that time there were several unconfirmed abuse complaints filed against his father, claiming that he beat T. J., but the cases were not pursued.

Gardner groaned inwardly. He could see the writing on the wall: 'Another abused child gone bad.' 'He's not a criminal, he's just sick.' 'He needs help, not a prison cell.' There would be the usual roundup of psychiatric apologists. There would be the endless cycles of tests and evaluations. There would be the agonizing image of the little hillbilly boy incessantly bullied and savaged by his old man. And there would be a group of twelve flesh-and-blood citizens pondering it all in their hearts, unable to sift out the emotion and leave the cold reality of a dead six-year-old behind.

Gardner spent another hour and a half on the report, probing the internal workings of Justice. He learned that T. J. had never returned home after he ran away. He drifted across the country, working, stealing, panhandling, and skirmishing with police. For long periods of time he was out of sight, so much so that there were no records of any kind to establish where he was or what he was doing. The longest he ever stayed in one place was two years, and on that occasion he was in a Texas prison serving a sentence for 'flashing' a child in a schoolyard. And there was a period when he worked with a traveling carnival, cleaning the reptile cages in the sideshow exhibit. Other than that, the man's life was a mystery, chronicled only by his bouts with the authorities in almost every state in the Union.

Gardner turned to the last page of the report, where the agent who prepared it wrote his recommendation: 'It is respectfully recommended that this Honorable Court impose the maximum sentence prescribed by law.'

'No kidding,' Gardner said aloud. He had seen enough. Justice was a human saw blade cutting his way across the country. He had to be stopped. Just then his thoughts were interrupted by the telephone blinker. It was flashing an incoming call, and nobody was picking it up. Official business ceased at 4:30, and apparently no one had hung around. Gardner sat in the silent late-afternoon gloaming of his office waiting for the light to go out. He didn't want any more conversations. The winking continued. Finally, out of frustration, he pushed the button and picked up the phone. 'Lawson speaking.'

'Listen, you bastard, I'm really getting tired of your shit.' Gardner recognized the whiny voice immediately. It was Sandy Harmon, the public defender.

'What are you bent out of shape about this time, Sandy?' Gardner asked wearily. His tone was a lot more subdued than his caller's.

'Tried to pull it again.'

'What?'

'Tried to bust the lawyer-client privilege again.'

'Did what?' Gardner had no idea what the man was talking about.

'That stunt at the jail. Trying to get something out of my client. You made a mistake this time. Your stoolie

was already a client, so you know what that means?'
Gardner was still in the dark, but a vague realization of
what had happened was starting to come through.

'Spell it out, Sandy. What the hell is going on?'
Gardner was really strung out by now.

'We represent Dallas Stubbins, and we represent T.
J. Justice. It appears that one of these men has some
nasty things to say about the other in a court of law.
Now, the rules say that to represent them both would
be a conflict of interest, so to make it okay, we're gonna
have to panel out one of the cases. Can you guess which
case? And to whom?'

Gardner saw the picture as clearly as the crisp lines
of a custom-tailored silk suit. Some yo-yo in the jail had
decided to appoint himself a secret spy for the police.
He had gotten something on Justice, and now the public
defender had an excuse to get rid of the case.

'Well?' Sandy was still waiting for a reply, but Gardner's silence told him that it wasn't really necessary. He
was certain that the State's Attorney had gotten the
message that from this moment on, T. J. Justice would
be represented by private defense attorney Kent King.

PART II

Order of Battle

CHAPTER 7

In age and body type, defense attorney Kent King was much like Gardner Lawson. Fortyish and fit, tall, and striking enough in appearance to fool some naive female jurors from time to time. But his tastes were more flashy. He wore a gold ring on his little finger and a Rolex watch. His suit was Italian silk, with a muted bluish sheen, and a red floral pattern was splashed across his tie. The office itself was 'modern' in decor. Scandinavian furniture, track lighting, and abstract art all spelled 'money.'

'I'm sorry about that,' he said firmly on the telephone in his law office. 'I am now your attorney, and you do not have a choice in the matter.' He ran his fingers through the drooping salt-and-pepper forelock that tickled the wrinkle in his brow. 'I'm sending my investigator over to see you. After that I'll come by and we'll discuss your defense. In the meantime, keep your mouth shut. Do not talk to anybody. Is that clear?'

'Uh-huh.' T. J. Justice was beginning to understand what the guys in the jail had told him about King. 'Mean kick-ass son of a bitch,' a scar-faced thug from the west wing had said. Everyone else agreed. He was the hottest ticket in town, a fence-buster, and now he was assigned to T. J.

'One more thing,' King continued. 'When my man gets there, you tell him everything. I mean everything. If I catch you lying, you're history. Is that clear?'

'Yup.'

'Good. Now, I got things to do. I'll see you later.' He hung up without saying good-bye, and leaned back in his swivel chair. They just kept coming. An endless stream of clients, flowing into his office like the polluted current from an industrial waste pipe. There had been a lot more volume back in the city, but nothing had really changed after the move west. There was still plenty of business, and from time to time a 'gimmee' like the Justice case. What a present. Wrapped and delivered by the PD's office. A high-visibility case with plenty of free publicity, and a bonus to boot. Another shot at Gardner Lawson.

This was going to be fun, he thought, jotting down some notes on his pad. The preliminary report sent over by the public defender was promising. No eyewitnesses. No confessions. No hard evidence. All they had was some vague assertions about his past, and it wouldn't take long to blow that theory to hell.

'Monique, get me Lawson on the phone,' King barked into the black speaker on his desk.

'Right away, Kent,' the smooth, sultry voice that only a 'Monique' could possess purred back. There was a click-over, brief pause, secretary-to-secretary prelim, and then the voice of the county State's Attorney came on the line.

'Lawson speaking.'

'It's Kent. How're ya doin'?'

There was a short delay before the prosecutor answered. 'Reasonably well, and yourself?' The words were impeccably proper, but the tone was icy. It was obvious that the sins of the past had never been forgiven. And now it was starting again.

Here was the behind-the-scenes struggle that the public never saw. Intense psychological warfare with no rules, no ethics. Gardner had lived it over and over with the slick out-of-towner who had settled in the county three years before. 'I'm gonna teach you boys a few things about trying cases,' King had declared at the bar association meeting that had been specially convened to consider his application for admission.

'Is he kidding?' Tom Proctor had whispered to Gardner, after the statement had been uttered. The prosecutor had hesitated. He knew of King's reputation in Baltimore. An animal loose in the courtroom. And he had some other negative feelings about the newcomer to their lives, which had nothing whatsoever to do with the law. Feelings he thought best to keep to himself.

The way King postured when he talked, with his back so straight it left his jacket in a convex curve, and the way he strutted with his hand in the shallow pocket of the double-breasted topcoat had become his trademark. Whenever Gardner pictured him, it was in that stance. A peacock on parade. Showy and affected. And deadly as a cobra.

'When are you planning to take Justice to the grand jury?' King wasn't wasting any time.

'You know the schedule,' Gardner said smoothly.

'Does that mean you're going in with it next Tuesday?' The normal routine called for the grand jury to meet every other week. Whatever was pending during the interim period had to wait until the appointed day, unless it was so complex that it needed more time to prepare for presentation.

'It will go in when it's ready,' Gardner said as he fiddled with a paper clip.

'Next week?'

'When it's ready.' Gardner knew by experience never to commit himself with King. He was not to be trusted with anything. Not even a harmless piece of information.

'Well, that answer isn't going to do,' King snapped. 'We've got some preindictment matters to get out of the way first.'

'Such as?' Gardner had a good idea what they were. Motion to record grand jury testimony. Motion to appear personally before the grand jury. Motion for appropriate relief, setting out some novel legal theory tailor-made to start the case off with an explosion.

'Oh, a couple of things that might make you reconsider presenting the case at all,' King said airily.

'Yeah? Do you mind telling me what they might be?'

'You going to give me the date?'

'No.'

'Well, then, I guess it'll just have to be a surprise.' The smug confidence in King's voice gave the words the impact of a death threat.

'So, what's the point of your call, then, Kent? You knew I wasn't going to tell you anything.'

'Oh, old buddy, lighten up. Just wanted to find out if

you'd been scuba diving lately.' There was a snippet of laughter in the air as King hung up.

Gardner began to perspire as an old memory bubbled to the surface. Diving was a bug that bit him as a boy. The mystery of the deep had lured him and drew him from a lonely single-child existence into a world of endless dimension and possibility. He read every book he could find on the subject. Watched 'Sea Hunt' with awe, and subscribed to *Skin Diver* magazine. He had a mask, snorkel, and fins, and play-acted elaborate scuba scenarios in the neighbor's swimming pool.

But he never submerged more than a few feet, and he never had a tank on his back until he was eighteen. To celebrate his birthday, the family took a trip to Barbados, and Gardner convinced his father to pay for a 'resort course.' Three hours in the pool and two ocean dives with tank, regulator, and instructor.

Gardner ate it up. He had some trouble at first, keeping his breathing rate down, but soon he was gliding into the depths, absorbing the sights that until now had only been secondhand reproductions.

The first ocean dive was to thirty-five feet. They saw spiny lobsters, a school of angel fish, a sea turtle, and two barracuda. Visibility seemed unlimited. The water was warm, and Gardner relaxed in the flow. In no time the air was low, and they had to surface.

On the second dive, something happened. Gardner drifted away from the group, following a coral formation that splintered into rifts and gullies. He was exploring and was so caught up in the delirium of the sea that he forgot his depth, his air supply, and his direction. He felt a cold chill, as an overhang blocked the penetrating sun rays. He looked down. The ocean floor was gone. He had strayed off the edge of the reef into deep water. The only thing below him now was an azure chasm. He gasped into the regulator and turned his head. He was alone. At that moment, it wasn't fun anymore. The mermaid's face had turned ugly. Gardner was suddenly uncomfortable. He was buried under a hundred feet of water, locked inside the sea like an insect embedded in amber. He couldn't catch his breath. He couldn't think. He was trapped.

Terror penetrated his heart like injected serum. There were several erratic beats and a paralysis of his limbs.

In an instant, it passed. Gardner steadied his breathing and made for the surface, popping up a hundred yards from the boat. The instructor had a few harsh words, but by the time the boat was docked they were laughing. Any dive you could walk away from was a good dive, he said.

Later that night, Gardner had recounted the exploits to his parents. He went on and on about the fish, and the coral, and the weightlessness. He described the colors and the soft caresses of the sea fans. He proudly accepted the titles 'scuba diver' and 'aquanaut.' The only thing he neglected to tell was his flirtation with panic, and the more he went on about the positive things, the less important that episode seemed. Years later he had forgotten all about it.

As Gardner reflected and braced himself for the inevitable assault, King was moving ahead with his plan.

'Send Bruno in, please,' he told Monique on the inter-com. A moment later, Bruno Calvano entered the room. He was a private investigator who had worked for King in the city, and had followed him to the mountains. A wide-shouldered man with a swarthy complexion, Calvano looked out of place in his new environment. He was urban to the core, but his allegiance to King pulled on him harder than the streets of Baltimore.

'What's the word?' he asked his employer, as he lounged into a chair in front of the desk.

King smiled and focused on the bridge of Bruno's nose, where his thick eyebrows joined together.

'New case. Justice. That Russian deal . . .'

'We got it?'

King bounced his chin in a nod. 'Uh huh. I want you to work him up asap. The usual checklist.'

'Okay.'

'And pull the Lawson file.'

Calvano smiled. 'Drew him again, huh?'

King handed a note across his desk. 'I believe we will once again have the honor . . .'

The investigator looked at the note and whistled. 'Man, you got some shit here!'

'Just check it out for me, Bruno,' King said impatiently. 'Especially that land deal Lawson's fronting for. Talk to the insiders and put together a paper trail . . . and update our file on his tax returns. We're running a year behind.'

Calvano grunted an okay and left the room. Soon after, King followed, passing his bleached-blond sec-retary without a word and exiting the front door.

Outside, he put on his wide-rimmed European shades
and walked to a dark red Jaguar parked next to
Monique's Corvette. He then removed his jacket and
carefully placed it on the passenger seat. Finally he
gunned the engine and wheeled out of the town house
office complex, turning at the end of the block onto the
street that led out to Watson Road.

Bob Hamilton drove out Sixteenth Street and parked
two blocks above the Soviet embassy. The day was cool
enough to warrant an overgarment, so he selected his
tan trench coat. It seemed appropriate, under the circumstances. There was a normal midmorning glut of
traffic on the sunlit street. Some last-minute stragglers
on the way to work. He proceeded down the sidewalk
at a brisk pace, ignoring the impressive façades of the
northerly habitations on Embassy Row. He'd checked
in at his office earlier, then signed out for an hour. That
would be enough time to meet with his contact, then
return. The phones were still being monitored on both
sides, so this had to be done in person.

He flashed his State Department ID at the gate and
was allowed entry into the compound. It was huge. An
overpowering structure reflecting the stodginess of the
previous era of iron curtains and cement tank barriers.
He was ushered into the reception area, which was dominated by a glass partition dividing the insiders from the
visitors.

'Valeri Yenkoff, please,' he told the moon-faced lady
through the small porthole. He had met Yenkoff two
years before, at a reception. The man was on the lower

rungs of the ladder in his own foreign office, and the similarity of their plights made them instant comrades. They had met often in a social context and occasionally shared insights on nonclassified political issues on the tables in their respective shops. He might be able to smooth out some of the wrinkles in Hamilton's Justice file.

'I am sorry, sir,' the receptionist said, after conferring with someone on the telephone. 'Mr. Yenkoff is not available.'

Hamilton could sense a deeper meaning in her words. 'Can you tell me when I would be able to see him?'

The woman did not hesitate with her response. 'That will not be possible.'

Again, the response seemed pat. 'May I leave him a message, then?'

'I'm sorry, sir,' she repeated. 'He's been reassigned.'

Hamilton was stunned. He hadn't heard anything about a transfer, not a word. Something was definitely amiss. He thanked the woman, and she summoned an escort to lead him to the gate.

On the drive back to State, Hamilton pondered what had just happened. He had been cut off from Valeri. A planned, deliberate act that smacked of the old days. No *glasnost* handshake today, just a cold shoulder. Why? What was so damned important that they had to revert to the transparent game playing of the hard-assed regimes? First they brought in Zeitzoff, and now they were backtracking again. There was one thing he was sure of: The Justice case held the key. And, as he pulled into the underground lot beside the department, he made a solemn resolution to himself. One way or another, he was going to find it.

'How about driving up to police headquarters with me?' Gardner asked Jennifer as he raced by her desk at 4:30, his blue wool overcoat buttoned all the way up. The staff secretaries were queued at the door, poised to escape when the sweep second hand on the clock hit the apex and the workday officially ended. 'Never linger in front of the State's Attorney's office at four-thirty,' the jokesters in the clerk's office chided. 'You're liable to get trampled.' Gardner usually sneered when he heard them say that. How the hell should they know? During working hours, the clerks buzzed around in their open-bay cubicles like drones in a hive, but one second either side of an officially authorized pay period, and the place was as deserted as an ancient tomb.

'Let's go, boss,' she said crisply, trying not to show how pleased she was to be included as she slung her bag over her shoulder, grabbed her briefcase, and dashed towards the coat closet.

Gardner drove up the steep hill that led to county police headquarters. Jennifer noticed that he was unusually quiet. 'How're ya doin'?' she asked, trying to catch the corner of his eye to see if his mood was reflected there.

'I'm okay,' he replied. It was his 'jury voice,' the one that always shielded any revelation of his emotional state.

'King hassling you?'

'What? Uh, no. He's just warming up. No big deal.'

'I heard he called.'

'Yeah. Tickling my feet to see how I'll react. Same old story.'

'Are you ever going to tell me about it?'

Gardner eased to a stop at the corner before making a right into the headquarters parking lot. He turned and gave Jennifer a slight smile. 'About what?'

'You and King. You know. The *thing* between you two?'

'Jennifer . . .' Gardner sounded slightly irritated.

'Well, since I am in this case now, don't you think I should know the whole story? I mean, he may come after me next, and I'd like to be prepared.'

Gardner pulled into the deputy chief's reserved parking space and shut off the engine. He turned again to face his associate prosecutor. 'You don't have a thing to worry about,' he said with a jury smile. 'It's me he's after. Only me.'

'Does that mean you're not going to tell me about it?'

'Not now.'

'Ever?'

'Maybe. If it becomes important. Right now it's not.'

Jennifer could see that this was a dead end. The rumors of a deep, dark secret about the relationship between Gardner and King had been buzzing ever since she joined the office. It was just assumed that there was a source for the animosity that emanated between the two men whenever they came into contact, but no one seemed to know what it was. There had to be an explanation for the dog-eat-dog ruthlessness that erupted inside and outside the courtroom as Gardner and King repeatedly faced off over a case.

'Here to see Chief Rawlings,' Gardner announced through the inch-thick glass enclosure that housed the duty officer as they arrived at the headquarters. The county police had a total force of eighty-five officers. Of these, twenty were in supervisory positions, and the rest were 'line' cops. There was a strict protocol in the hierarchy of the department. Each level paid deference to the next-highest rank. And everyone in the organization knelt down to the chief. The job of duty officer usually went to a walking wounded on the force, an officer who was recovering from an injury or illness, but who could still function at a desk. Gardner suddenly realized that the blurred face on the other side was the infamous Charlie Barnes. He had obviously screwed up again and been relegated to doorman.

'Push the door, mmm . . . Mr. Lawson. Buzzer is broken.' The electric lock customarily gave off a rattling buzz when the duty officer hit the release on the console behind the glass. This time the latch had to be lifted manually. The door swung silently open and allowed the two prosecuting attorneys to enter the narrow maze on the other side.

'Thanks for seeing us, Chief,' Gardner said as they were ushered into a secluded office at the end of the second-floor corridor. The walls were hung with certificates and photographs, all attesting to Rawlings's longevity with the department. He stood up as they entered. His hair was totally white and neatly trimmed, and his face was ruddy, but he looked as though he could still take down a felon in the field.

'You know Miss Munday, of course,' Gardner continued. 'She's working with me on the case.'

''Course I do. Good to see ya, Miss Jenny.'

The chief smiled a broad, tooth-filled grin in the direction of the State's Attorney's assistant. She mumbled a hello under her breath and pulled her chair over to align it with Gardner's in front of the chief's desk.

'What do you want to talk about?' the chief asked, leaning forward on his desk so that the gold braid on his uniform sleeves drooped onto the calendar mat.

'We need some help.'

'Help?'

'Coordination between my office and the department.'

'I don't understand what you mean. We've got our job, and you've got yours.'

'I know that, Chief, but this time it's different. There are forces at work here we're not used to . . .'

The chief had stopped smiling. He could see where the prosecutor was leading.

'You going to bring up that business about an investigator again?' he asked, stiffening his jaw the way he always did when addressing the ball on the ninth tee at the Fair Hills Country Club.

'Yes I am,' Gardner said firmly. 'We have a lot more police work that needs to be done. Crime scene reconstruction, witness interviews, forensics . . .' He gripped the arms of his chair as the words tumbled out.

'That old song and dance has already been played to the county council, and they didn't buy it,' the chief drawled. He was referring to Gardner's annual request to fund an investigator for the State's Attorney's office. They always turned it down, citing the expense, and Gardner was left to beg the police for a 'loaner' detective.

'Don't lecture me on politics, Paul,' Gardner shot back. 'The council doesn't have a clue about what it takes to put together a case. We saw that at the last budget hearing. I've had about as much of "let the police do the investigating" as I can swallow. You've got to let me have someone.' Gardner locked the chief in a stare-down, knowing that the veteran officer jealously guarded his power base and would not yield the least tiny chip without a fight.

'Gardner, why can't we go the usual route? You submit your request. We run it through channels, and you get the things done that you want. Hell, we've been handling it that way for years.'

'I need more flexibility with this one,' the prosecutor responded. 'The sand is shifting, and I can't wait for your commanders to decide when they are going to send someone over. The open cases are backed up now. When the "extra duty" is assigned, it's in addition to the work they already have. I don't need that. I've got to have someone who can concentrate on this case and not worry about getting his butt chewed for not turning in some B and E report.'

'Are you asking me to assign one of my men to your office full-time?'

'Yes, but just until this case is past the trial stage.'

'Hell, that could be months.'

'Paul, I really need it. What do you say?'

'No way.' The chief had long ago conceded the stare-down contest. He now had his head lowered. This was a sign to Gardner that vanity had once again won over common sense. He decided to keep going.

'Why not?' he asked calmly, relaxing his grip on the chair, and folding his hands across one knee.

'We can't spare anyone. You yourself said we're back-logged. How can I justify cutting a full-timer out of the schedule?'

'Because if you don't, Justice is liable to walk just like he did out west.'

The chief looked up again. His decision had been made, and he wasn't going to change it. 'Well, I guess that's a chance we will just have to take. You've got your killer, now go prosecute him. Anything else we need to discuss?'

Gardner sat quietly before answering. The frustration of giving in to a tin god felt like a splash of acid in his face. He wanted to grab the blue-suited icon and shove a 'request for temporary duty assignment' in his mouth, but he knew the temperament of the man, and he knew that things would only get worse if he pressed the point. After a calming pause, he responded. 'What do you know about the Russian situation? The feds don't seem to care what they're doing around here, but they still have guys playing hide-and-seek in the woods . . .'

'We have that under control.'

'You do? How?'

'We've got some people on it.'

Gardner suppressed the urge to scream. They couldn't

spare him a single investigator, but they had people out tailing Russians.

'Well, what are they doing?' he finally asked.

'We'll let you know when we find out,' the chief answered pompously, rising suddenly and walking over to the coatrack. 'I'm going to have to take off. Call me in a day or two and I'll let you know what we've got. Nice seeing you, Ms. Munday.' He barely had the bulky blue coat in place before tapping Gardner's hand and leading them out the door.

'That guy is a real jerk,' Jennifer said as they drove back down the hill. 'He doesn't have the sense of an oyster.'

'He's from the old school. Worked his way up from the patrol beat when the county had three people to cover the entire west end. Knows that he's in for the run to retirement, and that no one has the guts to push him out,' Gardner replied. 'I knew what he was going to say.'

'Excuse me for asking, boss, but why did we just go through that humiliating exercise if you knew the answer?' Jennifer turned her gaze on Gardner.

'I wanted to check out something.'

Jennifer waited for a follow-up to the last comment. When it didn't come, she prodded, 'What?'

'I guess you don't know about old Chief Rawlings's favorite pastime, do you?' Gardner turned on his headlights as darkness enveloped the road.

The possibilities seemed intriguing to Jennifer. Hammering nails with his head. Target practice with his toes. Some inane activity guaranteed to bore any marginally intelligent person to death. 'You got me,' she replied. 'What is it?'

'Golf.'

Jennifer smiled. That one was high up on her list. 'He plays golf. So what's the deal?' She was entering the discussion with Gardner in the usual manner. He teased with clues before delivering the punch line.

'He likes to play golf with a certain group.'

She was still behind. The clues were not making sense. 'So?'

'Every golfer likes to play with his cronies, and among that group is a well-known defense attorney.'

She caught up in a burst of speed. 'King!'

'None other. His foursome partner every Thursday.'

Jennifer was on the verge of taking the lead. 'Are you suggesting that he's got something going with that maniac?'

'Not at all, but it's nice to see where the loyalties lie. I thought I'd push Paul a little. See if he'd cut us a break. The fact that he didn't shows me where we stand.'

Jennifer was holding her own next to the boss. The conversation could have ended there with the conclusion as clear to Jennifer as it was to Gardner, but she decided to ask the final question. 'Well, Mr. G., where do we stand?'

Gardner took his right hand off the wheel and patted her arm. 'On our own, Miss Munday,' he said somberly. 'On our own.'

When they reached the office lot, Gardner dropped Jennifer off at her car, then drove the South Street route to the detention center. The wintering sky had absorbed all traces of daylight. Pole lamps around the austere compound were trying to compensate, but they only accentuated the darkness beyond the fringes of their circular beams. The mountains, so close in the daytime, were now only a shadowy black-on-black overlay in the distance, underscored by a string of shimmering silver spots. New houses dotting the lower ridge. Gardner saw that the warden's car was still there, so he pulled in next to it. The air had a sharpness that he hadn't noticed earlier, so he hitched up his collar and headed for the front gate.

'Good evening, Warden Phillips,' Gardner said as he peeked around the partition that separated the clerical area from the assistant superintendent's office. The facility was designed to look like a commercial office, but it still carried the unmistakable feel of a jail. The warden was sitting at one of the computer terminals, punching up green letters on the monitor.

'Well, well, if it isn't our county State's Attorney. How's it going, Gardner?'

'Okay, I guess. You busy?'

'Not too busy to talk to you,' the warden replied. 'What's up?'

Gardner's cheeks pinched tight. 'I want you to tell me how you happened to hook up Stubbins with Justice.'

The warden frowned. 'We had to put them together while we got T. J.'s cell wired with the TV monitor,' he said solemnly. 'One night, and that was all that little creep needed to get himself so tight with ole T. J. you'd'a thought they were married.'

'Don't your records show representation? Putting two PD-ers in the same cell is not good business.' Gardner was discussing, not arguing. He knew that Warden Phillips was not responsible for bringing King into the case. He also knew that getting one inmate to 'rat' on another sometimes worked out just fine.

'We did it in such a rush that the PD angle just slipped by,' the warden said. 'But why complain? You got yourself a statement, didn't you?'

Gardner nodded. 'Yeah. I guess we did.'

He had read over the report about twenty times. Stubbins had asked Justice what it was like to kill a child. The response from T. J. was sickening. 'It don't feel good at first, but somethin' happens when the blood comes out, and they start shakin' around . . . You got to try it sometime.' What about the Russian kid? the cellmate had asked T. J. How did that feel? According to the account, there was no answer to the question, only a smile on T. J.'s face as he squeezed his pillow with both hands in imitation of the real thing.

'But I'm not sure we can even get the damn thing in,' Gardner continued, knowing the painful gauntlet he was going to have to run between King and the court, just to get the so-called statement into evidence.

'What can you tell me about Stubbins?'

'Other than the fact he is a thief and a liar, nothing.'

'Liar?' Gardner's ears perked at the word.

'Have you seen his intake report?'

'No. Not yet.'

'The son of a bitch gave us a string of false IDs when he checked into this cross-bar hotel,' Warden Phillips said with disgust. 'It took us three days just to find out who in the hell he was.'

'You got that documented?'

'It's in the report.'

Gardner could see Kent King gloating when he got his hands on that destructive piece of paper. It would be flaunted so many times in court that half the jury would have it committed to memory before the state had a chance to argue its side.

'Where is the report now?' the prosecutor asked. 'Have you given it to anyone?'

'Not that I know of.'

'Okay. Don't release any documents from here, unless either I specifically authorize it or you receive a court order.'

'No problem.' The warden nodded and winked.

'And as long as we're on the subject, what have you told your troops about making statements?'

'Well, we had a reporter in here the other day who wanted to do a background report on Justice. Asked to interview some of the people.'

'What did you say?'

'Come on now! Gardner, give me some credit.'

'You said no.'

'Bingo!'

'Did you issue any sort of directive on talking?'

'You've been on me for a long time about putting things in writing.'

Gardner smiled. His advice on written records was well known in the county. To prove a fact, it was always important to have a written record. 'No writing, no fact' was the shorthand version. But policies and directives were different. If a person could be advised on how to act and obeyed the advice, why record it?

A written record could fall into the wrong hands. Sometimes with disastrous results. WARDEN TRAMPLES FIRST AMENDMENT RIGHTS OF GUARDS, the headline would scream above a verbatim reproduction of his 'leaked' confidential memo ordering detention center employees not to talk, as every correctional officer in the place clamored to sell his own version of a day in the life of a child killer. It was better to skip the memo and deliver the order verbally.

'You said something about it?' Gardner asked.

'Yep.'

'What do you think?'

Now the warden was smiling. 'I think they got the message.'

Gardner was through with his interrogation. The detention center was not going to spawn any media stars in the near future, he was sure. 'Keep me posted if you get another interview request. You know that Calvano sometimes uses reporters as a cover.' They both had seen King's henchman and investigator Bruno Calvano skirt the edges of law and ethics to get a statement.

The warden nodded emphatically. 'I'll be on the phone to you before they even get in the gate.'

'Thanks, Phil, you're the best.'

The warden stood up and shook Gardner's hand. 'The feeling is mutual,' he said sincerely. 'By the way, how're things at home?'

Gardner frowned. 'Super,' he replied without much enthusiasm.

'Well, you know you can call me anytime. Maybe we could have dinner.'

'Sure. Thanks. See you later.'

After Gardner left, the warden reached under the flap of his desk mat and pulled out an embossed calling card. On the flip side was a scribbled set of numbers. He picked up his telephone and dialed. It rang four times before a female voice said, 'Hello?' He hesitated. 'Hello?' the voice said again. He hung up the phone. It felt as though the State's Attorney was still in the room, watching him. He turned over the card and looked at the name: Krysta Collins, CNA News. On the way out the door, he ran the card through the paper shredder.

Bruno Calvano had old Mrs. Hodges cornered against the back wall of the motel office. The clock above said 8:30 P.M. 'All I need is answers,' he said, 'not a bunch of questions from you.' His hair was lubed and greased in a wave of frozen comb tracks, and a black leather jacket sleeve rode up on his thick forearm as he leaned into the cracked plywood, blocking her avenue of escape to the family room in back.

'Why do you want to know?' she asked defiantly, unintimidated by his dark appearance and manner.

'I told you, that's confidential police business.'

'Well, I done talked to them before.'

'I know, ma'am, but we have to get it one more time for the record.' Calvano dropped his arm and pulled out a notepad. 'Now, what time did Justice check out on the twenty-seventh?'

'Don't remember.'

'Don't you have a register book that shows that?'

'Yup.'

'Mind pulling it out for me?'

The old lady made a move toward the counter, and Calvano backed up just enough to grant her access. She looked over his shoulder, but he didn't flinch. He knew no one was behind him.

'This was turned over to the police before. They kept the pages that was in the book. Jes' left me these here copies.'

Calvano picked up the dry-rotting ledger book. Mid-November was gone. In its place was a folded sheaf of photocopies. On the November 27 page was a jumble of barely legible entries. Near the bottom of the page was the notation, *Unit 15. Clear. 1:00 P.M. R.H.*

'Is that you, R.H.?' he asked.

'Could be. Then, my grandson done got the same initials as me.'

Calvano stiffened. 'Well, who wrote this, you or your grandson?'

'Uh, let me look.' She pressed the page up to her face and goggle-eyed it through her filthy glasses. 'Cain't really tell.'

'What did you tell the "other" policemen? They asked you who wrote it, didn't they?'

'Don't remember,' she muttered.

The last response brought a smile to the man's lips. A classic witness, he thought to himself, noting down and underscoring 'memory' in his book. 'Can you tell me, then, when you last saw Mr. Justice on the premises?'

'Sure kin.'

'Well? When did you last see T. J. Justice?'

'He was gittin' in a car over there, on t'other side of the road.' She was pointing past Calvano's shoulder again, but he still didn't turn around.

'And that was about the same time he checked out?'

'I guess so.'

The swarthy interrogator had been making notations throughout the conversation. He took a brief pause, ripped off a page, and wrote something out in meticulous longhand. 'Ma'am, I've got a statement here that summarizes what you have told me. I would like to read it to you and then have you sign it for me. Okay?'

'They told me never to sign nuthin'.'

'Who told you that?'

'Lady from the district attorney's office. The pretty one.'

'Oh, you must be talking about Jennifer Munday. It's okay. We work together.'

Mrs. Hodges looked at Calvano the way she would have ogled a used car in a cut-rate lot. There was just enough 'official' chrome on the man to make him believable.

'You work with her?' she asked suspiciously.

'Sure do. We've had about four or five cases together.'

'So she says I kin put my name down?'

'Absolutely.' Calvano tried to smile.

'Well, giv' it to me, then.'

'Fine, let me read it to you. "Statement of Reena Hodges. This is my recollection of the events on November 27. At approximately 1:00 P.M. on that date, T. J.

158

Justice, a tenant occupying cabin 15 of the Hide-Away Motel, came to the office and gave notification that he would be vacating the premises. He paid his account in full with cash, then went across the road, where he got into a vehicle and left the area. Signed, R. Hodges." '

Calvano handed her his pen and directed her hand into signing the bottom of the paper. 'That ought to do it, ma'am,' he said. The voice signaled an end to her captivity.

'You say hello to that Jennifer,' Grandma said at the back of his jacket as it did a fast fade toward the door.

'Sure will,' Calvano snorted over his shoulder, adding under his breath, 'you bet I will.'

In the dim light of the console, the investigator reviewed his take. A photocopied page of the motel register. A cabin key. And a signed witness statement. He reread the words, chuckling to himself when he reached the part just before the wobbled signature. 'At no time after he checked out did Mr. Justice ever return to the Hide-Away Motel,' he said aloud.

'You're welcome, Mr. King. Why yes, I do believe that the nice lady will make a terrific witness.' A brief sniggling laugh later, Calvano was out of the potholed lot and on to his next assignment.

'Gramm, why was you talking to him?' Roberto 'Buster' Hodges asked as he came through the door and his withered relative sank into her torn, broken-spring easy chair.

'Same thing as before,' she sighed.

'That Justice stink?'

'Yep.'

'Well, whut you tell him?'

'Nuthin'.'

'You sure 'bout that?'

'Them cops already done heard it all.'

'Cops? Did he say he was a cop?' Buster snorted.

Grandma nodded. 'Said he was a detective, workin' on the case.'

'Well, you done got took,' Buster laughed. 'He's as big of a cop as I am.'

Grandma looked surprised, then laughed along with her grandson. 'It don't make no different whut he was,' she wheezed. 'The truth is the truth, and that's all this ole lady ever speaks to anyone.'

At 11:00 A.M. the next morning, T. J. Justice and Kent King stared at each other across the table in the visitors' meeting room of the detention center. The walls were soundproof, and the steel door shut them off from the rest of the institution and the world. They were alone. The conversation had reached an impasse.

King had been interrogating him for two hours, getting a feel for his strengths and weaknesses. He demanded a full rundown on his client's background, to see whether or not an insanity defense might fly, and a minute-by-minute account of Justice's activities on the days surrounding the murder. So far it was one step up and two steps back on every point. T. J. was either holding back, or he had some major cognitive problems in his twisted brain. King had to find out, so he told T. J. he would be set up for a psychological evaluation.

'Don't need no doctors!' the thin-faced inmate declared, giving his attorney a defiant glare that most

160

men who knew King would never even consider.

'What you feel you need, and what's best for your defense, are two different things,' the lawyer replied succinctly.

'Well, I done seen them back in Kansas, an' they never done me no good.'

'You mean they didn't tell the court to let you go?'

'All they done was ask questions. They stuck some wires on me.'

'So you don't like doctors. That's too damn bad.'

T. J. glared again. 'For you.'

This had gone as far as King was willing to let it go. He reached across the table and grasped Justice by the throat. The grip against his stubbled Adam's apple was strong enough to momentarily cut off the airflow. 'Listen, you son of a bitch, we're gonna get one thing straight between us here and now. Me lawyer. You client. Me say you go see doctor, you bend over and spread-um till doctor say you can pull up your pants! You got that?'

T. J. had not expected this kind of treatment. He had always been the darling of the defense bar. 'Mr. Justice' this. 'Mr. Justice' that. Syrupy-sweet female public defenders. ACLU flunkies. This lawyer had the strength of a bull hidden in the sleeve of his gray silk suit. He tried to answer, but all that came out was 'Uhhh!'

'What?' King asked. The grip eased up slightly, then released.

'Okay!' T. J. rubbed his neck and stared at his attorney like a child who has just given in reluctantly to parental authority.

'That's better. You and me are going to get along fine

as long as you understand just who in the hell I am,' King said.

The blank look on T. J.'s face made a follow-up mandatory. 'I'm the guy who's going to make the prosecuting attorney curse the day he was born,' King said with a confident grin.

T.J. eased off the hostility. He recollected the other prisoners talking about what a 'hot shit' Mr. 'Kent' was. Now he could see what they meant.

'To repeat what I said before, I want you to work with Dr. Fender on your psychological history. We have to get you diagnosed, and we have to see if you have any neurological brain damage.'

T.J. just nodded. His own opinion of the medicos was not going to cause any more problems.

'The date will have to be approved by the court, so we'll have to wait a bit for the actual testing. In the meantime, I do not want you to talk to anyone but me or Mr. Calvano about the case. Is that clear?'

T.J. nodded again. He and King had already discussed the Stubbins situation. He had explained how he knew better than to brag about a case. Squealers were everywhere. He knew that. 'Never said nuthin' to the feller,' T.J. told his attorney. 'Son a bitch is lyin'.' That's when King smiled and nodded, as if it didn't matter anyway.

'All right then, a few more little details need clearing up before they take you back to your cell.' The meeting was back on track. Lawyer directing. Client following directions. 'I want you to tell me about the car you got into after you left the motel.'

'Wuz blue, I think. Blue or black.'

'What make?'

'Not sure. Wuz one them big old cars.'

'American?'

'Mr. King, I don't know cars. Never did learn drivin'. Hell, I cain't tell a Mazarato from a Toyona.'

'Okay. Take it easy. Can you describe the car?'

'Big. Like I tole you. Long front part, where they keep the motor.'

'Okay. How many doors?'

'Huh?'

'How many doors? Two or four?'

'Hell. I never done counted.'

King was analyzing his client's testifying abilities as they talked. At that moment, Justice was pushing down the bottom number of a one-to-ten scale. 'All right, let's try something else. Tell me about the driver,' the defense attorney said, shifting gears.

'White guy. Old.'

'Anything else? Did he tell you his name?'

'Uh, think he sed Charlie . . . or Marley . . . sumpthin' like 'at.'

'Anyone else in the car?'

Justice squinted and scratched his head. 'Nope. Don't think so.'

King resisted the urge to whack his client's head for some more recollection. This was common among criminals. Their lack of brain power was usually to blame, but sometimes they couldn't remember because the scene never happened. 'T.J., I'm going to need more information in order to find that guy. Do you understand that? We've got a possible alibi here.'

'Goddamn it! I'm tellin' you what I know. Not gonna make it up.'

'Fine. Are you willing to go on the box for me?'

'Huh?'

'Polygraph. Lie detector. Will you take it?'

T.J. was confused by his lawyer's change of tone. He was asking, not ordering. 'Why I gotta do that?'

'You don't gotta take it, but I gotta know you're not lying to me.'

'I ain't lying.'

'Then prove it!'

T.J. had been polygraphed before. He had come up deceptive every time. Now he was afraid of the machine. 'Ain't gonna agree,' he said with a touch of the same defiance he had shown earlier.

'Fine. From this point on I'm going to take everything you tell me as the absolute truth. Lie to me all you want. That's up to you, but I'm going to base my defense on what you tell me. If you're deceitful, it won't make a damn bit of difference to me, because I'll be cruising around in my Jaguar, and you'll be burning in hell.'

T.J. sat quietly for a moment. 'You want me to do that box thing?'

'You going to lie to me?'

The men stared into each other's eyes defiantly. Then, as if they both recognized something, the tension was broken. 'It was a blue over white 'sixty-nine Ford, and the man was Harley Smith,' T.J. said softly.

At 3:00 that afternoon, Gardner, Jennifer, and Sgt. Pete Early were leaning over the large round table in the conference room. A jumble of yellow legal papers, photographs, and stapled reports lay between them. A cigar butt still smoldered in the ashtray, and all three looked frazzled.

They were in the process of finalizing the charges for presentation to the grand jury. Under the system, the state outlined the facts to the twenty-six-member jury and presented a set of formal charges to them. If the jurors were satisfied that the facts established a probability that the defendant committed the crime, the foreman signed the indictment, and the defendant was formally charged. There was no live testimony, no defense, no point of view other than the state's, and the proceedings were secret. The trick was to get them to charge as many crimes as the prosecution could conceivably prove. If the grand jury declined to sign off on a particular charge, the state was prevented from taking it to court.

'Goddamn medical examiner picked a great time to get lazy,' Gardner said. 'No report. No photos. No conclusions.'

'They explained that,' Jennifer responded. 'It will be here by next Friday.'

'Great. Grand jury meets Tuesday. In the meantime we can just take their word for the extent of injuries.'

'They did give it to us over the phone.'

'How nice of them,' Gardner sneered. 'Reading their notes to the State's Attorney. Do you know how many revisions they usually make before the final product? And what about the approval? They have to get what's-his-name, uh, Dr. Herrmann to sign off on the damn thing, and he's not even there half the time. We've got to move on this indictment now. We can't wait.'

Sergeant Early was listening, trying to determine how much trouble he was going to get from the grand jurors when he presented the facts to them. 'What does the autopsy report say?' some well-informed juror might ask. Umm, he'd have to look to Gardner for that answer. Much too technical for a mere police officer. 'Boss,' he said, picking up the written summary of Jennifer's phone call to the medical examiner's office, 'can we use this? I mean, can we charge with this as a basis?'

Gardner took the paper from his grand jury presentment officer. 'We have to. The more we wait, the more time King has to mess us up. We're gonna have to accept their summary, and charge accordingly.' He looked over the notes, then perused the charges that Jennifer had drafted. 'Where are the sex offenses?'

Jennifer frowned. 'I pulled them out.'

'Why?' Gardner asked with disbelief.

'Because there's no evidence of anal injury,' Jennifer said. 'It's in the notes. I had the ME go over it with me twice. "No apparent sexual injury" . . .'

The chief prosecutor's face lined with concern. 'We can charge a sex offense without physical evidence,' he said sternly. 'There's not always a mark . . . the lack of injury doesn't mean there was no attack. We see that all the time.'

Jennifer was caught off guard. She had tried to play it safe and go only with the charges they had hard evidence for, but her boss didn't like it. 'But what about King?' she said defensively. 'Isn't this one of his pet issues?' It was common knowledge that if you charged an offense against one of King's clients, you had damn well better be able to put some evidence on the table. King was a master at filing civil suits against prosecutors for alleged misconduct, and a charge without evidence to support it would lay that weapon right into his hands.

'Screw King,' Gardner said gruffly. 'We can't let him intimidate us into backing off a key charge. Anyway, we need it to qualify Justice for the death penalty.' Under Maryland law, a killing warranted the death penalty only if it occurred during the commission of certain enumerated felonies. Forcible sex offenses qualified, but unless they were formally charged, the state could not seek execution as a sentence.

'We've always got kidnapping,' Jennifer reminded him. That crime also qualified for death.

'Yeah,' Gardner came back. 'But on the facts, where's the element of force? What if the jury decides the boy went willingly?' There was no evidence of forceful abduction. No witnesses. No drag marks. No signs of a struggle. 'If they don't buy the kidnapping, we lose the death predicate . . . No,' Gardner continued, 'we need the sex charge. That's what this son of a bitch is all about. He sodomizes little boys, and then he kills them . . .' There was a faraway look on the prosecutor's face for a moment; then he came back. 'We've got a dead child. A knife wound. A knife. A bloody shirt. A well-known pedophile without a credible alibi. An incriminating statement, and some weirdo drawings that clearly symbolize the murder. What the hell else do we need?'

Jennifer had lapsed into silence as she remembered Gardner's admonition to her to 'pull together.' She still had some major concerns about the proof, but at this point, she bit her tongue. She didn't want to be taken off the case, and she was afraid that too much devil's advocate might do her in. Her wanting to stay had nothing to do with her career. She recognized that now. It was something else, not so professional. She wanted to be with Gardner. She was beginning to feel tingles around her heart whenever they were together. She hadn't analyzed it thoroughly, but she knew something was starting to build. And she wanted to stay close to him until she figured it out.

'So you've decided on the charges,' Jennifer said.

Sergeant Early had already retreated to the sidelines, realizing that his input was irrelevant.

Gardner was not paying attention, so he didn't answer. He was focused on a crime scene photo lying on the table. The fine blond hair of Mikhail Anatov was fanned out against the withering grass. His eyes were open, and the pale face seemed to be locked in a cry for help. Gardner felt a flutter in his heart, as he thought of Granville running down the steps of the old house, eyes bright, hair flying, alive and well.

Gardner looked up. 'Uh, what, Jennifer?'

'The charges?'

Gardner picked up the photo, slid it into the file, and snapped the cover shut with a violent flick of his wrist. 'First-degree murder. Kidnapping. First-, second-, and third-degree sex offense, weapons charges, intent to seek the death penalty. The whole goddamn ball of wax.'

The police officer nodded agreement, but Jennifer reached over and gently placed her hand on his shoulder. 'Are you sure?' she said quietly.

Gardner's jaw tightened. 'Positive! From now on, we do not stop.'

Jennifer wanted to say something about caution, but the words died in her throat. If she was going to stay with the team, she couldn't keep second-guessing the captain.

Gardner's attention was still focused on some internal vision of the future. 'We keep pushing, and we do not stop . . . not until Justice is in the gas chamber.'

As Charlie Barnes swung his take-home police cruiser around a curve close to midnight, his headlight beams caught the tail end of a white car that was barely visible behind the closed-up service station. That was enough to make him stop to investigate. Suspicious vehicle. Possible B and E in progress. Criminal trespass. The officer was off duty, on the way home from the station, but that didn't matter. He was a twenty-four-hour man. Always ready and willing to bust crime. The 'able' part had dogged him from rookie days. 'The officer has a high degree of potential,' his rating report said. 'His enthusiasm, however, sometimes overtakes his skill level. Keep on extra supervisory status until further notice.' That hurt. They obviously didn't like an officer who could think for himself; at least that's the way he read it.

Barnes flicked on his side-mounted search beam and took a cautious turn around the back of the building. The scene was quiet, not unusual for the small filling station that split the fork between Watson Road and

Randall Lane. No other businesses within two miles of the place, and the few houses in the area were hidden by undulations in the rocky earth. Sessy's Woods lay another fifteen miles west.

The officer stopped behind the car, and brushed it up and down with the cylindrical shaft of light. No sign of life. He slid over to the back door. Secure and locked . . . same with the windows. No forced entry.

He backed up and pulled parallel, then got out with his hand-held flashlight. Following procedure, he touched the hood. It was still warm. Barnes tensed and unsnapped the flap on his side arm holster.

'Something wrong, Officer?' The voice almost caused Barnes to discharge the weapon. He whipped around, and encountered a stoop-shouldered form slowly emerging from the darkness.

'Just hold it there,' Barnes ordered.

'Needed to use the phone,' the voice said weakly.

'Okay. Step forward. Slowly.'

The face came into the light, and Barnes lowered his gun.

'Didn't mean to startle you. Just stopped to make a call in the booth over there.' The quavering hand motioned toward an unlit expanse beyond the silent pumps. The face looked nonthreatening. Pasty and beaded with sweat. Middle-aged salesman features. No obvious criminal intent.

'Just doing my job, sir,' Barnes said, holstering his weapon and standing aside so the man could walk to his car.

The man said nothing.

'You okay, sir?' Barnes asked.

The man nodded his head yes, then entered his unlocked car, turned over the engine, and drove away.

Barnes sat in his cruiser and readied the notepad for his shorthand report. *White Chevrolet parked at Gaston's 11:45 P.M. No occupant visible.* He repeated his notations as he wrote, *Investigation commenced. No entry determined. Occupant found using phone. Questioned and released.* Barnes stopped suddenly. He had forgotten something. Something he usually put up at the top. 'Shit,' he said aloud, making two more entries in his own version of shorthand. *Ohio registration. Slight damage to rear fender.* Then he slammed down the pad on the seat. 'Shit, you're slipping, Charles!' he snorted at himself. He had missed something that he'd never forgotten before – the license number.

CHAPTER 8

'What do you have to say about that, Mr. Lawson?'
Judge Ellsworth Simmons asked from the midsized
bench of courtroom 4. At 10:30 on the morning of
December 7, the small nonjury hearing room was
thronged with spectators – press and TV people, mostly
– filling the two rows of benches and lining the wall in
back. No one wanted to miss the opening volley,
especially on Pearl Harbor Day when they could draw
clever analogies between the bombs of 1941 and the
verbal shrapnel fired from the mouths of the legal
adversaries.

'Your Honor, Mr. King has made a request to transcribe the testimony of witnesses in the upcoming grand
jury session,' Gardner began. 'He knows full well that
the only testimony offered there is going to be from the
grand jury presentment officer. We do not intend to call
that witness at trial, so the whole point of transcribing
the session becomes moot.' Gardner was dressed in his
jury suit, brushed and combed and ready for business.

'Doesn't the law of this state make the decision to
transcribe or not to transcribe a matter solely within the
discretion of the trial court?'

'Yes, Your Honor.'

'So I get the last word on whether or not to allow it.'

'Correct, Your Honor.'

Kent King had done exactly what Gardner had anticipated, led off with a barrage of complex motions, and the first one on the agenda was his request for a transcript of the grand jury proceedings. Because of the secret nature of the process, the state never kept any record of what was said. In fact, the grand jury room did not even have recording facilities. The only rationale for such a request was to impeach a witness whose trial testimony differed from what he told the grand jury. If the witness wasn't actually called in the case, the tedious business of transcribing the testimony became a colossal waste of time.

The elderly judge switched his gaze to Kent King. 'Well, Mr. Defense Attorney, you heard the prosecutor say he's not going to use the witness at trial. The only reason to transcribe in the first place is so you can use inconsistencies in grand jury testimony and trial testimony to cross-examine the witness. If they're not going to call the man to the stand, I'm inclined to agree with the state's position.'

King blasted to his feet in an instant. His blue-gray silk outfit glinted as he spoke. He was scrubbed up too, preened for the fight ahead. 'What about inconsistencies in the underlying theory of the case, Your Honor?'

Judge Simmons lowered his head slightly so he could stare across the top of his pince-nez half glasses. 'What do you mean, Counsel?'

'I mean, Your Honor, that I have the right to know

if the state proceeds on one theory in the grand jury room and another in court. A variation between the two would give me grounds to attack the sufficiency of the indictment itself.'

Now Gardner was back on his feet. 'Your Honor, Mr. King is trying to confuse the court by combining two separate and distinct legal principles. The law permitting transcription is limited only to the issue of impeachment testimony. It has nothing whatsoever to do with the viability of the charge —'

'Uh, excuse me, Your Honor,' King cut in. 'Wasn't it my turn to talk?'

'Yes, Mr. King. Uh, please sit down, Mr. Lawson.' Gardner stood fast for a moment, then sat down without losing any outward sign of composure.

'He's trying to get in the back door,' Jennifer whispered, cupping her hand subtly around her lips. She was dressed in a fitted charcoal gabardine suit and a crisp ivory silk shirt. A single strand of pearls and matching button earrings completed the outfit. The prosecutor nodded agreement, writing *He'll grant it* on his legal pad. This was the agonizing reality of the courtroom. The law could be 100 percent on your side, and the judge could still rule against you. He would follow the precedents as *he* saw them, right or wrong; he had that discretion. It all depended on which lawyer was more persuasive, not who was legally correct.

'Anyway, Your Honor, as I was saying,' King continued, 'if they establish one set of facts before the grand jury and a different set of facts in court, the entire premise of the charge is invalid. The proof offered must comport with the proof alleged, and the only way to know is to transcribe the testimony.'

The judge had assumed his pensive look. It was usually a prelude to giving in on a point he really didn't understand. Gardner saw King lower respectfully to his seat, so he shot back up before Judge Simmons had a chance to utter his ruling. 'Your Honor, as an officer of the court, I can assure you that there will be no variation in proof. We are prepared to offer the court an "in camera" summary of grand jury testimony to keep and refer to at trial, but we must vehemently oppose any intrusion into the secrecy of the grand jury proceedings. Mr. King has misstated the law. He is on a fishing expedition into territory that has been restricted from his interference by the Court of Appeals. They said so in the *Hawkins* case . . . He has no legal right to know what goes on inside the grand jury room unless a witness who appears there also testifies at the trial . . .'

'Your Honor' – King was arched in his familiar pose – 'counsel's whining is giving me a headache. Can you please ask him to modify his tone?'

A ripple of nervous laughter ran through the packed gallery. Everyone focused on Gardner, who now stood in a stance mockingly similar to defense counsel's. 'I am surprised that Mr. King is so sensitive,' he said coolly. 'Perhaps we should take a recess until he feels better.'

'Gentlemen!' Judge Simmons rattled to life in a forceful attempt to regain control of his court. Gardner's comment had touched off a few chortles of its own, and the after-buzz at the back of the room was causing the court reporter some clear irritation as she lifted one earpiece of her headphones and motioned the judge to hush the crowd.

'Ladies and gentlemen. These proceedings are recorded. Please keep your voices down, or the sheriff will escort you out . . . Now, gentlemen, let's proceed, and with more light and less heat.'

Gardner and King were both standing at their tables. The din had quieted, replaced by an expectant silence. All were awaiting the next move.

'Sorry, Your Honor, I apologize if I offended the court,' King said. Then he turned to Gardner. 'I believe my brother counsel had the floor, so I respectfully yield.'

Gardner didn't say thank you. The sarcasm was too thick.

'I'll conclude by reiterating the state's position. There is no legitimate reason to order transcription. The defense is not entitled to breach grand jury secrecy on a whim. Where is Mr. King's . . . ?' The judge was not even looking at him. A bad sign. He'd already made up his mind, and Gardner knew his words were floating into a meaningless record. He stopped in midsentence. 'Your Honor, we'll submit without further argument.'

When King started to rise for his rebuttal, Judge Simmons waved him back down. That confirmed Gardner's intuition.

'Gentlemen, I have made my decision,' the judge announced. 'In the interest of justice, I believe the transcript should be made. The state's assurances that their witness won't testify are not sufficient here. The defendant is entitled to be prepared in the event the prosecution changes its mind.'

Gardner glanced at King. There was a triumphant smirk on his face, and he made sure his adversary saw it. The prosecutor smiled coldly, then turned back to the bench. Round one to King.

'Next item,' the judge continued. 'Motion for bond restriction.' He looked to the defense attorney. 'What are you looking for, Mr. King?'

The defense attorney popped to his feet. 'Like to have Your Honor consider dropping the bond to something my man can afford.'

Judge Simmons picked up the court file. 'He's on five hundred thousand, full amount, now . . .' That meant that Justice would have to post a half million dollars to get out of jail pending trial. He turned to Gardner. 'What's your position, State?'

The prosecutor rose. 'The man's got no fixed address. The charges are extremely serious, and we need to be sure that he's not going to run . . . Remain the same, Your Honor.'

'Mr. Justice has never failed to appear for trial, Your Honor,' King cut in. 'That's the only criterion that should be considered . . . the only criterion.' He shifted his eyes toward Gardner as if to imply that the prosecutor's bond request was punitive.

'If Mr. King's so sure his man's going to show up,' Gardner retorted, 'maybe he should put up the money himself.'

The gallery reacted with a scattering of snickers, but Judge Simmons quickly restored order. 'Stick to the issues, gentlemen!' The attorneys heeled to the judge's voice. 'Now, I'm going to ask again, what bond do you think is appropriate, Mr. King?'

'My client is destitute, Your Honor,' King said solemnly. 'Any monetary amount would be too much.'

'So you want me to let him out on his own recognizance?' The judge looked incredulous.

King didn't answer immediately. He made the court wait, testing the judge's patience. 'Every defendant is entitled to a reasonable bond,' he said finally. 'In Mr. Justice's case, five hundred thousand is preposterous.'

Judge Simmons glared down at the defense attorney. '*I* set that bond originally!'

'Then why don't *you* change it?' King said flippantly.

Gardner sighed internally. This was it: the patented King defense strategy. Shotgun-blast motions and issues in rapid succession. Alternate sweet and sour dispositions. Shoot and shoot until scoring a hit, then retreat. Make the court and the prosecutor lose their concentration. Manufacture opponents' mistakes.

'Thank you, Mr. King, for the suggestion, but I decline,' the judge said coldly. 'The bond will remain the same.'

The round went to Gardner by default. King couldn't have cared less about getting his client out on bond. The real meaning of the motion was in its delivery, a message to the prosecutor and the court that they would have to work for every inch they traveled on the long road of the case.

And it went on that way for hours, as King jumped from one legal issue to another, dragging them out in his irritating style, interspersing witty jibes between persuasive blocks of oratory. And Gardner stayed with him all the way, responding and countering each inventive argument and personal barb his opponent came up with.

Finally, at the end of the day, it was over. The scorecard on winning motions read: King 3, Lawson 3. A draw on the legal issues. As to the baiting contest, the reaction of the crowd was the only gauge, and from varying decibels of their response, that appeared to be a dead heat.

After court was adjourned, Jennifer and Gardner walked wearily back to the office, pushing through a throng of reporters and well-wishers, politely declining comment. The notations on Gardner's legal pad had summarized the successes and failures of the day:

MOTION TO RECORD GRAND JURY TESTIMONY – GRANTED

MOTION TO REDUCE BOND – DENIED

MOTION TO DISQUALIFY GRAND JURY FOR PRETRIAL PUB-
LICITY TAINT – DENIED

MOTION TO PERMIT PRIVATE MENTAL AND PHYSICAL
EXAMINATION OF DEFENDANT – GRANTED

MOTION TO PRODUCE POLICE COMMUNICATIONS TAPES
AND LOG – GRANTED

MOTION TO CHALLENGE JURISDICTION OF COURT –
DENIED

'So how do you like it so far?' Gardner asked his assistant as he unlocked the State's Attorney's office door. As usual, after quitting time the employees were long gone.

'He's incredible,' Jennifer said, unloading an armful of law books on her desk.

Gardner smiled a weary grin. 'The first time up close is a real treat . . .'

'It's amazing how he can do it,' she continued. 'Hour after hour of spewing that garbage, and he never seems to get tired.'

Gardner took a book off the top of the pile. 'He's just getting started . . . wait till he hits stride.'

The assistant shook her head as her boss turned toward his office. 'Why don't you take off,' he said. 'I've got a couple of cases I want to look over.'

Jennifer walked to the door as he dropped into his chair. 'Can't I help?' she asked.

Gardner's face was lined with fatigue. 'No. You've had enough of this BS for one day.' When she hesitated he added, 'That's an order. You're through for today. See you bright and early tomorrow.' Then he opened the book.

Jennifer stood quietly for a moment, hoping he would reconsider. When he didn't look up, she closed the door, gathered her things, and left. On the way down the stairs she scolded herself for not grabbing him by the arm and dragging him over to Paul's for some dinner and an opening-day drink.

The phone interrupted Gardner's concentration. It was his private line. The one that didn't go through the switchboard. He picked it up.

'Gardner Lawson.'

'You can't have Granny this weekend,' Carole said flatly.

For weeks he had told Granville that they would go

shopping for Christmas presents the next time the boy came over. They would visit all of the toy stores, and Gardner would make a list of the things that his son wanted, so he could send it to Santa. This was to be a special time, and it was only three days away. 'Don't do this, Carole,' Gardner said firmly, his eyes closed.

'I have him scheduled for a counseling session on Saturday. He can't miss it.'

'Counseling?' He sat up and tightened his hand around a letter opener. 'What for?'

'He's been having nightmares.'

Gardner seethed with anger, but he kept it in. 'How long has this been going on?'

'About a week.'

'He never said anything when I talked to him. In fact, he sounded fine. Let me talk to him.'

'Can't come to the phone. He's eating his dinner.'

Carole was using her hit-and-run tactics.

'Let me talk to him now. Please, Carole.'

'Sorry.'

'Okay. I want to talk to him after he's eaten.'

'He's going to bed.'

The situation was obvious. Carole was back on the warpath, and Gardner had a sudden intuition that some outside force was causing it.

'Tell my son I'll be picking him up Friday.'

'No. Because you won't be.' The line clicked, and she was gone.

Gardner put the phone down slowly. Carole's words still throbbed in his ear. 'Can't see your son.' It was the worst thing anyone could say to him. Other attacks he could handle, but this one left him weak and vulnerable. He sat forward and put his face in his hands. This was bad timing. He had enough other problems. He didn't need this. For a moment his mind relaxed back to a happier day. The grand ceremony that had gotten them started, the ironic beginning that overflowed with hope and naive expectations.

The wedding was staged in the garden behind the Watson Road house. Late-spring showers had softened the earth, and the bulbs that Gardner's mother had planted many years earlier burst their seams and shot red tulips and yellow daffodils into the bright warming sun.

The crowd was a curious mix. Her group hailed from Baltimore and the country clubs that ringed the city. His group was no less titled, but a rural patina of multiple generations had coated over the abrasiveness that still lingered in their urban counterparts.

Carole's side gazed on the setting with skeptical eyes when no one was looking, but bubbled over with enthusiasm whenever a Gardner supporter approached.

'What a lovely couple,' they said out loud.

But inside they thought, 'She's going to die of boredom way out here.'

Gardner picked up on the less-than-enthusiastic vibrations, but he didn't care. He was happy. Carole came from a stiff-lipped world of social structure and harsh judgments, but she wasn't like that. Not at all. She did a super imitation of her aunt Lilly that mocked the blueblood scene to the core. She bought him cigars.

She got mud on her L. L. Bean boots and didn't clean it off. She loved the old house below the mountains. And she loved him.

The trellis at the end of a curving stone walkway had been converted into an altar. There were cut flowers filling the spaces in the lattice-work, radiating a splendor that competed with the earthbound blooms. White ladder-back chairs were arranged in wedges on either side, so the bride and groom's friends could be clearly delineated. The air was still, except for an occasional breeze that whooshed the pine needles in tall trees overhead and blended the sound with violin music drifting down from the porch. The day was perfect, and as Gardner waited for a slim figure in white lace to join him under the crown of color, he projected a lifetime of similar days, and squeezed back some moisture in his eye.

'Do you take this man . . . ?'

Her eyes sparkled. She giggled, 'I do.'

'Do you take this woman . . . ?'

He hesitated, for effect. She giggled again.

'I do!' he yelled.

The crowd twittered. Louder, it seemed, from his side.

'You may kiss the bride . . .'

Gardner scooped Carole into a movie clinch and bent her over backward.

She giggled again, then thrust her tongue into his mouth.

Her side sat in stony silence.

His side stirred, then clapped.

By the time Gardner got her back to her feet, both

sides were cheering. It was obvious to everyone that the two had a world of their own, and no one on the outside could ever break in.

Returning to the present, he sighed and his eyes drifted down to the day's scorecard, the outline of motions lying on his desk. Suddenly a thought hit and tied back in with Carole's telephone call. He opened his directory, raised the phone again, and dialed Kent King's number.

There was a recorded message, but he didn't speak. He went back to the directory and pulled out a second number.

'Yeah?' The voice on the other end was rough, but familiar.

'Let me speak to him,' Gardner demanded.

There was a pause, then another voice came on the line. 'King.'

'Congratulations on your performance today.'

'Really? I was disappointed.'

'I'll bet you were. I called to ask you a personal question. My son is having bad dreams. You happen to know anything about that?'

There was silence on the other end. Gardner could see King's mind grinding out an interpretation. The accusation had never been made formal because there was never any proof, but it was clearly understood that Gardner held King responsible for his marriage breakup. King had counseled Carole when things began to go wrong at home, and they had spent time together in Baltimore, but the reality of a relationship between them had always been hidden. Not even a private detective could come up with anything. So there was never an overt charge or public scene. The antagonism bubbled beneath the surface, and while both men knew the cause, only one of them knew the truth.

'Uh, sorry,' King said coolly. 'Can't say that I am familiar with that situation.'

'Are you sure?' Carole was one thing. His son was another. If King had somehow induced Carole to cut off visitation, Gardner wanted him to know he would pay dearly for the interference.

'I told you no. What more do you want?'

Gardner knew that his point was made. 'Maybe we should keep it that way,' he said. His voice delivered the slicing edge of a threat. 'I'll see you in court.'

'Hope your kid feels better.' King almost sounded sincere.

'So do I. For your sake.'

The line went dead, and Gardner leaned back again. This was going to be World War III. No sanctuaries. No safe houses. Everything fair game. That was the way King had set it up. Now, at least, Granville had been declared off limits. If the battle strayed off in that direction again, Gardner thought, things could get very bloody.

On December 8, at 4:00 P.M., Gardner walked out of the grand jury room with the signed indictment. He was visibly disappointed. The grand jury had been in session for over four hours, deliberating the charges of the Justice case. Sergeant Early had gone over the facts, and Gardner had explained the law, but the jurors had gotten squirrelly and balked at endorsing the full list the State's Attorney had given them.

They had gotten hung up over the sex offenses. Gardner had cited case after case of sexual abuse without physical injury to the victim, but they weren't buying it. 'How can we charge a crime without evidence to support it?' was the refrain from the jurors in the back row. It was soon picked up by the rest of the panel, and no matter how hard Gardner pushed, they stood fast. The medical examiner's verbal report had done them in, and the intrusion of the court reporter didn't help either. It inhibited Gardner from trying to ram the charge through, knowing that Kent King would receive a play-by-play of his every move in the sanctity of the grand jury room.

The reporters were waiting in the hallway, and in a flash the court clerk had supplied them all with copies of the indictment. 'Mr. Lawson! Mr. Lawson!' They were all vying for his attention as he mounted the court-house steps to take their questions. Jennifer had been sent back to the office to check the day's messages, so he stood before the press alone.

'I'd like to make a brief statement before I answer any questions,' Gardner began, quieting the crowd. 'As you can all see, the county grand jury has returned an indictment against T. J. Justice charging him with first-degree murder, kidnapping, assault, battery, and malicious stabbing.' He put his hands in his pockets and hunched his shoulders against the brisk late-afternoon air. The sky was still bright with the afterglow of the sun, now hidden behind the ridge, and there was an occasional rattle of dry leaves in the wind. 'The role of the grand jury,' he continued, 'has nothing to do with deciding guilt or innocence. They decide only what a defendant is to be charged with, *not* what he is guilty of . . .' A car horn beeped in the distance, as if to add emphasis. 'Please remember that. These are only charges . . .'

'What about sex?' a young reporter hollered. 'They didn't charge a sex crime.'

Gardner looked annoyed. 'What's your question?'

The crowd stirred restlessly. 'What happened to the sex offenses?' another reporter called out before the young one could speak.

'They declined to indict,' Gardner said simply.

'Why?' several spoke at once.

The prosecutor assumed his courtroom face. 'That's privileged. The rationale for charging or not charging is secret, not subject to public release.'

'But wasn't it recorded?' someone yelled. The implication was clear: recording it destroyed the privilege.

'It's still private,' Gardner replied, 'and can only be used for a limited purpose by the defense . . .' As he spoke, he realized it would not be long before King leaked the transcript to the entire press corps. And then they would see that twenty-six people refused to endorse the theory that Mikhail Anatov was sodomized before he was killed.

'I can't comment on why charges were or were not brought,' Gardner continued. 'Any other questions?'

'Are you still seeking the death penalty?' This time it was Steve Greene from the *Gazette*.

'Absolutely,' Gardner said. 'The kidnapping charge enables us to file, and we fully intend to go all the way with it . . .'

'Are you disappointed with the indictment?' a faceless back-row journalist yelled.

That one was loaded. A yes would show early weakness in the case, and a no would be illogical. He was stuck. 'We are very satisfied to be proceeding on the charges we have,' he said, avoiding the answer.

Then, amid a volley of additional questions, he turned and retreated to the State's Attorney's office. The inquiries had hit a nerve, and if he stayed, it could only get worse.

A short time later, after the siege of Gardner, the press thronged Kent King in his office. He was a lot more ready to talk, they found, and was especially vocal on the grand jury's failure to bring in the sex counts of the indictment. 'They never did have anything,' he pontificated. 'Lawson knew there was no evidence on a sex charge, but he tried to get it in anyway. He acted in bad faith, just like he always does. Just like he's going to do in this farce of a trial. You'll see. This is just the beginning . . .' The media ate it up, lavishing their accounts of the day with the defense attorney's volatile quotes, playing up the innuendo that Gardner Lawson was less than honorable in his intent, and portraying Kent King as the guardian of fair play.

As they were leaving, King motioned reporter Steve Greene to stay behind. They went into the inner office, and King shut the door.

'What's up?' Greene asked. At thirty-five, he was overweight and a sloppy dresser, but his face was boyish.

'Thought you might want a scoop,' King replied.

The reporter's ears picked up. The infighting was intense in the story business. It always helped to have an edge over the competitors. 'What've you got?'

King handed him a file folder. 'Some facts concerning the private business interests of the State's Attorney,' he said innocently.

Greene thumbed through the file. 'Is this authentic?' he asked without looking up.

'Why don't you check it out for yourself,' King said.

The reporter kept reading, then closed the file and smiled. 'I think I may be able to do something with this,' he said. 'Thanks.'

As he walked toward the door, King stopped him. 'You can't take that,' he said, removing the file from Greene's hands.

The reporter looked surprised. 'Well, why did you show it to me, then?'

King stared at him with disbelief. 'You're the investigative genius. I'm sure you can figure it out.'

Greene hesitated, then smiled and nodded. 'I got a tip from a concerned citizen . . .'

King continued to usher the man toward the exit. 'You do whatever you think is right.'

The reporter tried to thank him again, but the attorney quickly shunted him aside. 'Don't call me,' King said sternly. 'I don't know a goddamn thing about it.' Then he shut the office door and threw the bolt.

December 10
12:00 Noon

The Fat Cow was an ideal place to meet Brownie, Gardner thought. Police officers stopped there for lunch, and it was a hangout for court personnel as well. The fact that they had to drive to the edge of town to get their barbecue did not matter. There was always a line at the 'place orders here' counter. He timed it so Brownie could slip in ahead of him in line. 'How're ya doin', Sergeant?' he said as if they had not prearranged the encounter.

'Okay, boss. Saw the papers. Too bad about the grand jury.'

Gardner smiled stoically. 'We tried. At least they came in with the kidnap charge.'

'Yeah. That ought to make T. J. squirm a little.'

'I sure hope so. He's had it his way so far.'

They placed their orders, and slipped into a booth to await the delivery. Gardner made a subtle sweep of the area with his eyes. He could see that Brownie was doing the same. There was no one within earshot of their conversation, so Gardner began, 'Thanks for coming, Brownie, I appreciate it.'

'You ask. I comply. Try to, anyway.'

'I know. That's the reason I called.'

The officer tilted his head. He had no idea what this was all about. Gardner continued, 'I guess you heard that I met with the chief.'

Brownie nodded.

'He's being tight-assed with his personnel roster.

Won't assign me anyone, at least not the way I want. Wants me to use channels.'

Brownie knew the story, thanks to the department scuttlebutt. His intuition began to fill the space ahead of Gardner's words. 'You gotta have your own man,' he cut in.

'Exactly.'

'An' just maybe you done found him.' The officer's white teeth suddenly burst through his lips in a wide smile.

'Orders up!' the counter jockey called, juggling two paper platters of tin-foiled sandwiches.

'I'll get it,' Brownie volunteered, sliding out of his seat. Gardner saw him speak briefly to a young uniformed officer at the counter before he returned with the food.

'Who was that?' the prosecutor asked. He knew most of the men on the force, but this one was not familiar.

'Name's Paul Jackson. He's a transfer from the Eastern Shore.'

'Recent?'

''Bout a month ago. Seems like he's okay . . . for a white guy.'

Gardner had to laugh. Brownie was easing the tension the way he knew best, and humor at that point was just what the State's Attorney needed. The prosecutor's smile slowly faded. 'I want you to do some work for me,' he said between bites of his sandwich.

'I got that part already,' Brownie replied, attacking his barbecue with ferocious precision, fat dripping onto his fingers.

'This is not going to be the normal stuff.'

'Keep talking.' Brownie was giving him the 'lab technician' stare. Total attention. Absolute commitment. The sandwich was almost history.

'You may have some career trouble if anyone finds out.'

Brownie didn't flinch. 'Couldn't be any more than I got now.'

'It could mean suspension or even expulsion.'

'Look, you need me to help you, right?'

Gardner nodded yes.

'That's all you got to say. I'm a big boy. I can do for myself. Now, what you need done?'

'I've issued a formal request to the department for the services of Larry Gray,' Gardner began. 'That should give you cover for the things I want you to do. Larry can take care of the witness background checks, report gathering, evidence coordination, the routine stuff. He can file his reports on the work he's doing so he can get credit with the chief . . .'

Brownie could sense what was coming.

'King is going to try to get his hands on every report in the file.'

'So you want my work undocumented,' Brownie cut in.

Gardner smiled. 'Exactly. If it's not official, King can't get it. No reports. No memos. No other individuals involved.'

'No sweat,' the officer said.

'Okay, now to specifics. I've got two – actually three – problems. The first two are related to the case. The other is personal. First, as you know, there's some very strange Russian behaviour going on in the county. The chief says they're keeping an eye on it, but I need my own "eyes." See what you can find out, but be discreet. *Very* discreet.'

Brownie gave Gardner a 'you don't gotta tell me that' look.

'And while you're at it,' the prosecutor continued, 'check out what happened with the autopsy. For some reason, they didn't do a normal postmortem on the boy . . . some BS about releasing the body to the family. I don't buy it. Check it out, maybe there's a connection with what's going on out here.'

Brownie nodded agreement.

'Okay. Next, Calvano is on the loose again. I've got to get a track on who he's talked to, what he's told them.' He pulled a piece of paper from his coat pocket and pushed it across the table. 'This is a list of our major witnesses. See if you can pick up his trail.'

'Want me to tell them anything?'

'No. Just find out what they told Calvano. And find out who he's misrepresenting himself as these days.'

'No notes?'

Gardner pondered his previous directive. 'Uh, if you have to, use a code, but keep anything you write down out of sight.'

Brownie nodded again, and waited for his last assignment. When Gardner didn't speak, the officer began to sense a conflict in the prosecutor's mind. He waited a moment longer, then asked, 'You got something else for me?'

'Huh?' Gardner seemed to be daydreaming.

'You said you had three things. I only heard two.'

'Brownie, I changed my mind,' Gardner said slowly. 'I think we'd better leave it at that.'

'Look. You want a man for a job, you get the whole man. Now give it to me.'

'I told you it's personal. The situation is bad enough with you working on a case behind the chief's back. At least we can say it was for the public good. I don't think we can justify anything beyond that if it comes out.'

Brownie looked Gardner in the eye with a steady affirmation of longtime trust. 'You got yourself a King-sized headache, right?'

The prosecutor didn't answer.

'What if I was to do a little undercover work because I was afraid that some unscrupulous person was trying to hurt a friend of mine?'

Gardner still remained silent.

'Nobody's done tole me to do it.' He was lapsing into ghettoese for effect. 'But I jus' done it on my own? Now who they goin' to blame for that?'

Gardner suppressed a smile. Brownie was a classic.

'You know I can't ask you to do that,' he said sincerely.

'I know that. An' you ain't askin'. I'm volunteerin' on my own.'

The two men looked at each other, and as their eyes locked, an understanding was sealed. Brownie would keep an eye on Kent King.

They got up together and headed for the door, nodding hellos to several newly arrived officers and court clerks. Gardner walked Brownie to his police van. When they got there, he extended his hand. 'This means a lot to me,' he said.

Brownie responded with a bone-crusher. 'You don't got to say a thing.' He released the grip and swung up into the elevated seat. 'After all, you is now a man of distinction.'

Gardner looked puzzled.

'You is the onliest State's Attorney in the whole damn state who gots himself his own private spook.'

'Your man has the brain of a genius and the sensitivity of a stone,' Dr. Rolf Fender told Kent King. They were conferring in the psychiatrist's office on the second floor of the Appalachian Medical Building early the next afternoon. There was a pile of testing reports stacked haphazardly on the doctor's untidy desk, and a jumble of outdated medical journals and patient files on the floor. The dingy walls were spotted with faded documents in lopsided frames.

'You gave him the full series?' King asked.

'Of course.'

'And he was cooperative?'

'Not at first, but we got that straightened out.'

'Yeah? How?' the attorney pressed.

The old man smiled, flashing a silver tooth. 'I told him that you were watching the procedure behind my two-way mirror.'

Now King smiled. 'He bought it?'

'Sat right down. Went through everything without a whimper.'

'Okay. Give me the verdict.'

The psychiatrist picked up one of the test sheets. 'IQ one forty-five. No organic brain dysfunction. Extreme antisocial personality disorder. Passive-aggressive personality traits. No overt psychosis. And . . .' He turned the page. 'Fixated pedophilia.'

King whistled. 'Our boy seems to be carrying a lot of explosive material in his ugly little head. Did you get to the specifics of the crime?'

'No. He says he doesn't remember.'

'He went the same route with me. What do you think? Is it bullshit?'

The doctor thumbed through a few more pages. 'I tried to run the voice stress analyzer on him. Figured he might relax a little if he didn't know what it was, so I told him it was a machine to measure brain activity. It went fine until I pushed him about not remembering. Then he clammed up. Wouldn't say anything else as long as the equipment was running.'

'Did you get a reading?'

'Only a partial. It looks like he means it.'

'Means what?'

'That he doesn't remember. At least that was the way the first response came out, but without a confirmatory test, I can't be sure.'

King took the paper from the doctor's hand. The wavering data lines stopped suddenly midpage, interrupted when Justice refused to continue the test. They had to extend all the way to the border to complete the cycle.

'Mind if I use your copier?' the lawyer asked, rising

to his feet and shoving a pile of papers off the ancient copy machine in the corner. When he returned he put the copy on Dr. Fender's desk and pulled a pen from its wobbly wooden holder. A few strokes later he was done.

'What do you say now, Doctor?' King asked, handing over the page. Thanks to the defense attorney, the lines had completed their journey from start to finish, rendering a completed document.

'I'd say the man was telling the truth,' the doctor replied with a diabolical grin.

It was Sunday lunchtime. Gardner and Granville sat by the fountain in the Marble Mountain Mall. Two weeks until Christmas and the mall was mobbed. Typically American, it contained all of the national chain stores and a few localized versions that filled similar hangarlike enclosures from coast to coast. And of course the holiday decorations were out in force.

The boy was eating a strawberry ice cream cone, and dribbles of pink wetness were threatening to drip from his chin onto the new sweater they had just bought.

Gardner reached over and wiped it with a tissue. 'Careful, son, don't want to mess this up before Mom sees it.'

The boy's eyes widened in acknowledgment, but he was too much into the ice cream to answer. Gardner tried to relax as he watched his son eat, but the scene with Carole had left him tight in the chest and neck. He had driven out unannounced and confronted her as she and the boy were getting out of the car. 'Dad's here to take you Christmas shopping,' he had declared before

Carole had a chance to spirit 'Granny' into the sanctity of the house. The tactic had worked. Granville ran into his arms with a whoop of joy, and Carole knew she had been outflanked. 'Never let your child witness dissension between parents,' they had been told by the family therapist the court had appointed to represent the interests of their son. Carole let him go without a fight, but gave him a warning that sailed over her son's head. 'Enjoy yourself today. You never know what's going to happen tomorrow.'

'Dad?' Granville had finished his cone, and was now rubbernecking at the Sunday afternoon crowd.

Gardner was still mulling Carole's remark. The soft tug on his sleeve brought him out of it. 'Huh?' he answered.

'Who's that man, Daddy? He keeps staring.'

The passersby interfered with a direct view across the indoor courtyard. Gardner squinted at a long figure slouched against a stone window on the other side. He recognized the face immediately. It was Bruno Calvano.

'It's a man I know from work,' he said quietly.

'He looks scary.'

'Aww. He's not that bad. Just looks mean.' Gardner was returning Calvano's looks, letting him know that he had been 'made' by a seven-year-old. Finally the message got through, and the man pushed away from the glass and swaggered down the shop-lined corridor. 'See? He went away.' They stood up and, hand in hand, headed in the other direction, toward the toy-and-hobby store that the boy loved to visit every time he came to the mall.

Before entering, Granville had to stop at the window

display. The dresser had created a wonderland of fabulous gadgets. Trains winding through mystical papier-mâché valleys. Robots and mechanical animals doing push-ups and spins. Miniature roller coasters rocketing noisily up and down their tracks. The boy was taking it all in, stopping briefly at each new device before going on to the next. Then he stopped and stayed put. Granville was fixated on a display, mesmerized by its haunting scene. 'I want that one, Dad,' he said, pointing to a frogman trailing silver bubbles from the bottom of a giant water tank.

When Gardner had finally convinced Carole to take a scuba course, he assumed that he was over the hump. She would love it, and that, combined with his enthusiasm, would make for some exciting adventures as they glided hand in hand through the aquatic netherland.

It had been a long time between dives for Gardner. Although he had meant to resume what he had started in Barbados, the chance never came, and it was not until he was midway through his life, with a law career, a wife, and a child, that the opportunity came again.

They took the PADI (Professional Association of Diving Instructors) course at the 'Y' in Newbury. It seemed ironic that a landlocked valley with no divable water for hundreds of miles would offer such a sport, but twenty eager candidates showed up, among them Gardner and Carole.

The 'land school' came first. Atmospheric pressure. Physiological considerations. Equipment nomenclature.

They breezed through that phase in two weeks. Next

came the pool work. It began with mask and snorkel, and went on to tank dives to eight feet.

Gardner was surprised at how well Carole took to it. She nailed the book work cold, and her pool exercises were singled out by the instructor as the right way to do things.

Gardner, on the other hand, was not faring so well. He had trouble with his breathing rhythm. He was experiencing a choking sensation whenever he descended, and a slight anxiety whenever he reached the bottom.

Despite his feelings, Gardner pressed on. Carole was getting into it in a big way, and the look on her face as she ended each dive told him to swallow his fears and play the role he had played since they met: the swaggering hero braving the dangers of the world, there when she needed him, always by her side.

After six weeks, it was time for the final checkout. They were required to jump into the pool with all diving gear off, then sink to the bottom of the pool, put everything on, and swim to the surface.

As usual, Carole excelled. She had the equipment assembled in record time, and staged a triumphant ascent amid the accolades of the group.

Then it was Gardner's turn. He hit the water with a galumphine splash and somersaulted to the bottom. He was totally disoriented. He couldn't see. He couldn't breathe, and he couldn't locate his regulator. He almost gave up, but the knowledge that everyone was watching spurred him to fight the fear and hang on.

By some miracle, he finished the test. His time for

completion was longer than anyone else's, but it wasn't fatal. Finesse didn't count. Out of the original twenty, ten graduated and received their 'certification' cards. Gardner and Carole were now equally qualified to explore the wonders of the deep and, thanks to Gardner's insistence, carry the joy of their relationship into reaches yet unknown.

Their lives were super, back then. They worked hard and played hard, Gardner as a lawyer, Carole as a mother. They did their jobs in the daytime, then shared hours of comparing notes and nuzzling across the pillow. It seemed as if the ups and downs of the barren days were behind them, as if it would be smooth sailing from then on. Carole had even started riding again, and on occasion trotted beside her husband as he trail-jogged in the silent pathways of the hills above the house. But then they went to Cayman . . .

Carole's descent was marked by a fine mist of bubbles, which tickled Gardner's chin as he followed. The dark outline of the *Mindy* soon became an ill-defined smear at the surface, and then disappeared. Ahead lay the drop-off to the midnight depths of the Atlantic trench, a shading of blues as stark as the transition between earth's atmosphere and interplanetary space. Directly below, the island's shelf stretched tentatively toward the gorge, its solid coral floor a comfort to those who approached the limits of the wall and dared the challenge of what lay beyond.

Carole and Gardner were alone. The guide stayed with the boat, and as scuba rules required, the two divers were coupled as 'buddies,' alert to each other's position, condition, and safety.

Thirty years earlier, a hurricane had spun a four-hundred-foot freighter into its spiraling web, split its hull, and launched it into the oblivion of the trench. But the currents forced it back toward shore and it crashed on the edge of the wall and hung up between two coral mountains, its stern jammed into the solid extension of Cayman, and its bow hanging out over a black hole bored into the heart of the sea a billion years before.

Carole, in her newfound exuberance, finned down toward the dark mass slowly taking shape in the waning light. Gardner fell behind. He pushed himself to keep up, but the gap didn't diminish. He kicked harder. His breath came in ragged bursts. Then he looked over the edge.

The nightmare realization of where he was suddenly hit. The Barbados twinge of fear, the checkout dive panic, the nervous discomforts of thirty other dives. They were nothing compared to this. He had stepped off the Empire State Building, and only then understood he was afraid of heights.

Carole was about to enter the wreck. He tried to cry out, but the scream was swallowed in the crushing density of the water. He tried to relax, to get it under control, but it was too late. The vertigo had set in . . .

Carole ducked into the hatchway on level three. She shone her light down the murky hallway and saw the stairs they had located in the wreck diagram. Without looking back, she swam to the stairs and turned the corner. When she reached the shadowy expanse of the hold, she realized she was alone. And it was then, when the kicked-up muck obscured her way out, that her own personal version of Gardner's nightmare hit.

The guide went over the side of the *Mindy* when Gardner came up alone. He didn't ask questions. Gardner's distress told him something was wrong, and he hardly paused on the way down.

He found Carole in the wreck, frantically weaving herself deeper into the maze of the ship, almost out of air. He got her stabilized, and established a buddy-breathing pattern on the way up.

In twenty minutes the incident was over. Gardner and Carole were safe on deck, toweled off and secure. Gardner tried to explain, but she didn't want to listen. Her eyes brimmed with betrayal. Gardner put his hand on her shoulder, but she brushed it off. 'I want to go home,' she said in a shaky voice. The trust had been torn, their world split from within. And on the way back to the island, Gardner saw a storm in the distance and felt a sharp pain in his heart when a lightning bolt jolted into the vastness of the darkened sea and vanished beneath the waves.

'Dad?'

Gardner snapped out of his reverie. 'Yes, son?'

'Are you gonna get it for me?' He was still thinking about the frogman.

Gardner took his hand and led him away from the store. 'Did you ask Santa?'

'Uh-huh.'

'Well, why don't we wait till Christmas to find out.'

'Okay, Dad.'

Father and son continued walking hand in hand past the decorative façades of the shop. They had to hurry. Carole was waiting for the boy to be returned.

At 11:30 that night, Bob Hamilton sat at the kitchen table of his apartment. Normally he would be sleeping by this hour, but tonight he had work to do. 'We need an update on the Justice case,' the bureau deputy had said last Friday afternoon. 'Have an oral summary ready first thing Monday.'

He had been scraping information together all weekend, after finally resolving the Yenkoff situation. His friend had called the apartment on Saturday morning, responding to a series of messages that Hamilton had left at his known hangouts around town. He knew nothing about Hamilton's visit to the embassy, just as suspected. No, he was not being transferred, but yes, there was definitely a freeze on information leaving the compound. When he said he didn't know why, Hamilton believed him. He was too low on the totem pole to see the workings of the inner chamber. His sincere disavowal of any knowledge about Justice sealed the conclusion that Yenkoff was a dead end on the issue, and they agreed that it was not career-wise for the Russian to get involved.

The upshot was simple. Hamilton would have to put the puzzle together another way, and the best starting point, he decided, was to assemble and study everything he had so far. Now his table was piled with data, and he was going through it scientifically, piece by piece, getting ready for his talk on Monday, and trying to figure out what the hell was going on.

One of the stacks was designated as his 'media' resource. Press clippings. Transcribed TV broadcasts. News releases. Wire service summaries. He separated it into two smaller segments: 'Background' and 'Court.' He subdivided it again into 'Russian' and 'Justice,' then carefully reviewed the contents of each category, sipping on a cup of black coffee as he read. Finally he stopped. There was a problem.

By now he was an expert on the criminal history of T. J. Justice. He could recite the man's prior record verbatim, and he knew every bizarre idiosyncrasy of his modus operandi. But the most troubling factor involved the boy's father. Ever since the murder he had been totally invisible, almost as if he ceased to exist. There was no explanation for this anywhere. The clippings, news reports, and summaries were all silent on that point. Not one of them mentioned anything about the father except his name: Anatoly Anatov.

The gap in coverage had bothered Hamilton so much, he had sent for a CIA file on Anatov to see if it contained any clues. All he got back was a one-paragraph biography and a note of explanation: 'We are unable to provide further information at this time. Complete file temporarily unavailable. Will forward when returned from off-site utilization.' Yenkoff had never even met the man, so there was no information there. And the brief bio didn't help either. He seemed to be a typical bureaucrat with average credentials. Electrical engineering degree. Military Air Defense Command staff. Diplomatic mission liaison, North Korea. D. C. embassy political adviser. Nothing jumped out as significant, but Hamilton was filled with a growing sense of uneasiness. The Russians were handling the situation strangely in every aspect of their involvement. The father was obviously incommunicado. And the latest word on the defendant was that he somehow forgot his primary urge: a sex attack on the young victim.

That fact had dominated the media reports ever since the indictment came down: NO SEX CHARGES AGAINST JUSTICE. He had read that some legal experts differed on the significance. If there was no proof it happened, some said, then it didn't happen. Others disagreed. You can touch an object and not leave a fingerprint, and you can rape and not cause a wound. An absence of proof is *not* exculpatory, they retorted. He still could be guilty even if there was no sexual injury.

Nevertheless, it was troubling. The keystone of Justice's perverted structure seemed to be missing. That, coupled with the appearance of Zeitzoff, the lockout at the embassy, and the disinformation campaign raised his suspicions to an even higher level. There was something else here, beneath the surface . . .

He picked up his notepad and wrote out the skeleton of his talk. Case status report. Charges. Trial date. Names of parties on both sides of the prosecution. Anticipated evidence. Current Soviet field operations in western Maryland. And the possible international-relations impact of a non-guilty verdict. Then he tore off the page and continued on the next sheet. At the top he wrote: *Private File Only. Not for Department*

Release. He made some notes, stopped for a few minutes, then made some more. Finally he reached the bottom, finishing up with a set of single words: CRIME. LOCATION. ACCUSED. FATHER. SECRET. He looked at the list, then added one more: KILLER?

It was midnight, and Gardner could not sleep. Elaine was lost in slumber beside him, but all he could do was stare at Elvis, and hope that the night would render him unconscious with its melodic throb of wind and rain against the roof. The pain of letting Granville's hand slip back into his mother's was almost unbearable this time. Not even Elaine's wild-woman routine could make it go away.

He thought ahead to Christmas. To Granville running down the curving staircase to get his presents under the ten-foot tree in the front hall. He imagined the boy's face, lit with the reflections of the twinkling lights and shiny new toys. A twinge of sorrow seized his heart as he saw himself alone with his own stubby tree back at the apartment. And then sharing a drink with Elaine at a bar before going home to the emptiness.

Gardner looked at Elvis again, as the shadows of a single candle played back and forth across the puppy-dog eyes of the 'King.' Suddenly an involuntary name association surfaced. The melancholy mood and Christmas scene vanished with a pop. In their place was a glowering image of Kent King.

Gardner's mind leapt to the case, as he restlessly churned out strategies and countermoves he might need for the trial. Before long, the sound of the wind buffeting the shutters outside of Elaine's window began to soothe his brain. The thoughts of court slowed, and Gardner closed his eyes. Christmas would soon pass. And then the fireworks could begin.

The shall [illegible] at [illegible] be [illegible] a [illegible]
[illegible] The [illegible] in [illegible] and [illegible]
[illegible] the [illegible] Christmas could soon pass, but from
the [illegible] s could be[illegible]

CHAPTER 9

Jennifer's holiday decorations were still on the wall of her office, but the glint of the tinsel had hardly been noticed. The days had accelerated their pace after the Justice indictment came down, and Christmas seemed to be gone in a hiccup. Now the pretrial tidal wave of motions had hit, and Jennifer was struggling to keep herself and her boss afloat.

King's motions strategy replicated his moves in the courtroom. Throw out every argument imaginable, and hope that something sticks in the judge's craw. That was the design, but there was an added fringe benefit: The press got copies of the pleadings. That meant that the accusations of state misconduct would go out to the public and place the entire proceeding under a cloud of suspicion and innuendo. One particular issue, the Stubbins episode, was almost tailor-made for King, and he hammered again and again on the assertion that it was a setup from start to finish. Gardner Lawson arranged for the two men to be put together, King maintained. There was a secret deal with Stubbins to exchange his freedom for an unauthorized interrogation of Justice. It was a flagrant violation of T. J.'s right to counsel during questioning and his right to be informed that a statement could be used against him. It was illegal, unethical, immoral, and a total outrage to all that is civilized. Of course, the accusations were untrue, but they looked damn good in print. And Gardner Lawson had to answer the charges, or his silence would be deemed an admission.

On the arrest, search and seizure, prior crimes, and a dozen other issues, King always kept coming back to the same shopworn theme: The state was railroading an innocent man, and Gardner Lawson was driving the locomotive.

'It's an endurance contest,' Gardner had told Jennifer when they conferenced the pleading. 'He's gonna keep chugging along until we give up.' That got Jennifer's attention. She could see creases in the boss's face that she hadn't noticed before, and his door seemed to be shut a lot more than usual. She was worried about him. She wanted to do something to help, but she wasn't sure what. She considered a hug, but suppressed the urge. Gardner never used the term 'give up.' With that in mind, she poured her emotions into a counterattack, ripping off an 'Answer to Motions' that made King's monster look almost sophomoric. This was therapeutic. It aided the case, and put her thoughts back into perspective where she did not have to deal with feelings for Gardner she could not quite understand.

The phone buzzer cut into Jennifer's review of her work. She glanced at the clock, then at the window. The gray winter morning had not yet cracked a single beam of sunlight. No one should be calling this early, she thought, letting the blinker flash on and off without picking it up. It didn't stop. 'Hello. State's Attorney's office,' she finally said.

'I thought you might be there.' It was Gardner.

Jennifer's face heated slightly. 'Uh, yes, sir. On the job.'

'Mind telling me what the hell you're doing in the office at five A.M.?'

'I'm the early bird, you know that . . .'

'Jennifer!' His voice was playfully gruff. 'Are you working on those damn motions?'

She didn't answer.

'What did I tell you yesterday?' He now sounded like a supervisor. 'I said we'd split them down the middle. Remember?' She remained silent. 'But when I went to get my half of the file, it was gone.'

'Okay,' she finally answered. 'I'm guilty, Counselor.'

'Look.' He was back to a normal tone. 'When I said I'd do it, I wasn't kidding. I want you to stop right now and hold it for me.'

Jennifer hesitated, then answered, 'It's too late.'

'What?'

'I'm done.'

Gardner smiled to himself. She was a workhorse. A classic blend of intelligence and stamina. He couldn't fault her for that. In fact, it was hard to fault her for anything. 'All right,' he said, 'I guess I'll just have to dock your pay for disobeying orders.'

She laughed. 'I don't think you'll be disappointed. I followed your suggestion to lay out the facts against the law on each issue King raised . . .'

'And?'

'And when you get past the smoke, it's easy to see there's nothing behind it.'

'What about the arrest?'

'No problem. I've got six cases on point. He's dead on that one.'

'And the Stubbins fiasco?'

'Covered. There's no proof that anyone from our offices contacted him at any time prior to the statement. In fact, jail records show he had no visitors, phone calls, or letters from the time T. J. was arrested until they were put in the cell together. King's version is all hype.'

Gardner smiled again. 'Sounds really good, Jen.'

'So you're not mad?'

'No. Of course not,' he said, 'but I will be if you don't take a break. Why don't you leave the pleading on my desk and take some comp time? Go jog, or something.'

'I'll think about it,' she replied.

'Okay,' he said. 'You do that.' But when Gardner hung up, he knew she'd still be at the office when he arrived, and that she'd stay at her post for the rest of the day.

Russel's Deli was deserted. The professional day crowd had retreated to the countryside, and only a few 'townies' were left at the counter. Gardner sat in a booth midway between the door and the kitchen. That position provided him the best angle on the TV, which was wedged in an alcove above the soft-drink cooler. The

6:30 evening news was about to come on, and rumor had it that a major story on the case would be aired on the national broadcast.

Gardner fiddled with a half-eaten grilled cheese sandwich and swizzled the dregs of his milk shake. The commercials had run, and the announcer was listing the array of natural and human disasters that would follow in the next half hour. He concluded his set of 'teasers' with, 'And finally tonight, an exclusive interview with accused child killer, T. J. Justice.'

Gardner gasped and dropped his sandwich. This was a surprise. They must have slipped it past Phil at the jail. No one had told him about it. A 'story' about the case was all they said. Not a word about an interview with Justice.

The next few minutes were agony. A train wreck. A fire. African political unrest. At last the scene cut to Krysta Collins standing in front of the courthouse, dressed in a fur-collared leather jacket, telling everyone that 'we are truly fortunate to have an opportunity to speak to the man accused of murdering the Russian child.' Then there was a cut to the dull gray walls of the detention center visiting area and the repulsive angular features of T. J. Justice.

'Do you know why you are here?' Krysta asked. Her voice had a mellow quality, as though she were interviewing some corporate CEO.

'No, ma'am,' T. J. said.

'Gimme a break!' Gardner groaned aloud. He could imagine King out of sight in the wings, directing the action.

'Well, have they told you what you are accused of, Mr. Justice?'

'No, ma'am.'

Gardner clenched his fists as T. J. continued. 'My lawyer told me that they done said I killed a young boy.'

'Well, did you?'

The camera pulled in for a close-up, but T. J. kept his eyes down, as if he was afraid of the lens.

'No, ma'am,' he said quietly.

Gardner took a deep breath. 'Goddamnit! Why don't you just give the mike to King and let him do the interview?'

'How do you feel being accused of a crime you didn't commit?' Krysta asked over Gardner's sidebar comment.

T. J. suddenly looked up and stared directly into the recorder. 'Uh, not too good. They got me locked up in a cell by myself. Can't talk to nobody. Ain't got no TV. No radio . . .'

'No little boys to play with,' Gardner cut in sarcastically.

'My lawyer said that's wrong. I got rights. They can't keep a man punished for no reason.'

'What do you plan to do about it?' Krysta inquired.

T. J. half smiled, as if he knew something that no one else did. 'My lawyer says we have to wait for the trial. Then you'll find out.'

The interview terminated with a return to the courthouse setting. 'John, the mood of the defense is one of optimism, as you can see. They feel that the trial will vindicate Mr. Justice, and that he will be set free. As to how that will be accomplished, they aren't saying. Back to you in New York.'

'Ooooeee! Your ole boy sure does enjoy bein' on TV,' Walt Smathers said to Gardner as he craned his neck around in the adjoining booth.

'He's not my boy, Walter,' Gardner replied. 'He's Kent King's. Body and soul.'

'Well, whoever he is, he's gonna put this town on the map once and for all.'

Gardner shook his head. The interview was a brilliant maneuver, although going to the press carried a risk. The client could actually incriminate himself. That, unfortunately, hadn't happened this time, and never would as long as King was calling the shots. Gardner was more worried about the motive. Did King really have something, or was he pulling a bluff the way he did in the Stumper trial when he intimidated a young assistant into pleading to a lesser charge? The threat of a 'surprise witness' did it that time, and when Gardner tried to confirm his existence later, he was told the man had 'left town.' All they had was a signed statement that Calvano had miraculously obtained at the eleventh hour.

'What do you think about the TV story?' Gardner asked Walt, tapping him on the shoulder to get his attention.

'What 'say?'

'What's your feeling about the case, now that you saw tonight's news?' Gardner was experimenting in his legal laboratory. How it played on Main Street often repeated in court. Jurors were human. They got impressions locked into their psyches just like regular citizens.

'Looks like trouble,' Walt said.

'What do you mean?'

'They're gonna fight you all the way.'

'We always get a fight.'

'Mebbe. But they got sumpthin' they're not tellin', and I'd say it ain't gonna do you a bit of good.'

Gardner looked at the side of the retired farmer's face. Tiny broken blood vessels had reddened the skin into mottled contusions. Thick glasses and a greasy baseball hat completed his rural fashion statement. On looks alone, he would make an ideal juror. 'But what do you think about Justice? How did he come across?' he pressed stubbornly.

'Uh, dunno, really . . .'

'Walt. If you had to decide the case just on what you saw tonight, what would you say?'

'Gee. That's a tough one. Guess I'd have to say no.'

'No what?'

'No deal. Seem like the boy just might be tellin' the truth.'

Gardner muttered a thanks and turned back to his crumbling grilled cheese. The lab work was complete, and the results were not good. Score a well-executed flanking maneuver for King.

January 24 was listed as Brownie's day off on the departmental manning roster, but at three o'clock that afternoon, he had an appointment at the medical examiner's office in Baltimore. He was fitting in the undercover work for Gardner whenever he could. After hours, between shifts, any time he was able to block out between his official duties.

He'd come up blank on the Russians. Everyone he talked to either put him off, or didn't know. The report files at the station didn't reveal anything about a 'shadowing' operation, and the computer followed suit. Brownie concluded that the chief was blowing smoke at Gardner when he said they had the situation under control. The police didn't have a clue as to what the Russians were up to. And if they did, it was going to be damn hard to root out.

Calvano was easier. He left a trail as wide as an interstate and made no attempt to be discreet. He was back to his ploy of impersonating an officer. All of the witnesses on Gardner's list had a similar response: 'That big cop? Yeah, I talked to him. Wanted to know what I saw . . .' Although a few picked up on it and refused, others were deceived into making a written statement and entrusting the only copy to Calvano.

And now it was down to the city for a one-on-one with the medical examiner. He had made the appointment to see Dr. Stinson on the pretext of reviewing the autopsy report.

'But we sent that in weeks ago,' the doctor had said, trying to put him off.

'Need a few minutes of time to sort the thing out,' Brownie had fired back. 'You have to admit it's a little more unusual than the average slice and dice.'

That stopped the doctor cold. 'Okay. I guess we'd better talk about it, then.' By the sound of his voice, Brownie knew he had him. It was as if the man was ashamed of something he had done.

Brownie pulled into the parking lot of the medical examiner's complex adjacent to University Hospital.

The snowfall of last week was now blackened gutter lining, and the mound of ice scrapings in the center of the asphalt was peppered with gritty exhaust holes. He got out of his car and walked toward the building. A splattering of melting salt had left a mark like high tide across the filthy façade. The city looks like hell in the winter, Brownie thought, as he pushed through the revolving glass door that led to the heated offices above the freezer bins.

Stinson was dressed in his white apron with attached hospital ID. Brownie was in civilian clothes.

'Come on now, Doc,' he persisted. 'The autopsy was not normal, and we want to know why.'

The doctor, cordial but noncommittal, continued his previous spiel. 'The examination was conducted under fully sanctioned medical procedures. Every aspect conformed to the book – uh, of course with the obvious limitation . . .'

'Yeah. What about that? You guys usually whip out the saw.'

Stinson's face darkened. 'Couldn't do it this time.'

'Couldn't or wouldn't?' Brownie sensed an inroad to the truth.

'Officer, if your superior gave you an order, would you follow it?'

Brownie had to think about that one. Considering the ironies of his own double life, a 'no' might be appropriate. But he opted to give the accepted response. 'Uh-huh.'

Stinson gave him a 'You've got the answer' look. 'Well?'

'So you were ordered not to cut up the kid,' Brownie said. 'By whom?'

'Chief ME . . . above that, I can't say.'

The officer shifted in his metal chair. 'So he got ordered too?'

The assistant ME nodded. 'I think so.'

'You think or you know?' Brownie clicked into his interrogation mode.

Stinson stared at him without answering, but his eyes gave the answer: I know.

'Okay, okay,' Brownie chuckled. 'I get the picture. Now, let me switch to something else. Does the autopsy as performed leave any room for error? I mean, were you able to fill in all the blanks?'

The doctor nodded. 'I will testify under oath as to its accuracy.'

Brownie shook his head. 'Doc, that's not what I asked.'

Stinson looked confused.

'Is there any chance something slipped by because you didn't open the boy up?'

Now the question made sense. The doctor frowned. 'It's a possibility, of course, but with the X rays, the tissue and blood samples, the probes and the other tests, I'd say we came pretty close.'

'But still,' Brownie asserted, 'something could have been missed 'cause of the way the thing went down.'

The doctor nodded again. 'It's a possibility, but I don't think so. I tried to compensate for the limitations by putting in extra effort on the procedures I did. I'll stand by my work . . .'

Brownie thanked him and left the building. It had been an interesting interview. The only thing that troubled him was the nagging gut feeling that he had just taken down a confession.

On the morning of January 25, Gardner Lawson and Kent King had a rendezvous at the property room of the county police department. It was required in criminal cases for the state to preview its physical evidence prior to trial, so there wouldn't be any surprises when the objects were trotted out in front of the jury.

The two men arrived simultaneously, and it didn't take long for the action to begin.

'Just show me the exhibits, and cut the bullshit,' Kent King said to Gardner at the entrance to the fenced-off property room.

'You don't like having your pet gorilla's methods criticized?' Gardner drawled, leaning against the gray wall.

'I'm not here to listen to paranoid delusions,' King snapped. 'I just want my due under the discovery order.'

King shoved a copy of the 'State's Response to Defendant's Request for Discovery' at Gardner's midsection. The prosecutor ignored it. The words were indelibly inscribed in his brain: 'Upon due notice to the State's Attorney's office, the defendant will be accorded an opportunity to inspect any and all physical evidence in the state's possession that is intended to be introduced at trial.'

'You'd better get Calvano under control,' Gardner warned, ignoring King's attempt to change the subject. 'His misrepresentations are borderline obstruction of justice, and he just might find himself on the receiving end of an indictment if he keeps it up.'

The defense attorney pulled himself up to his straight-backed courtroom stance. 'You got any evidence?'

'On that?'

'Yeah. What is it?' King snorted.

Gardner faced him square on, then broke out in a wide, ironic smile. 'I guess it'll just have to be a surprise,' he quoted.

King was not amused. 'Shithead,' he muttered under his breath. 'Let's get to the junk on my man – that is, if you have any.'

Sgt. Oakley Dover presided over the property room like a pharaoh, sending his two rookie 'helpers' scurrying in the compartmented catacombs while he sat at the metal gate and decided what, and who, should be allowed in and out. He was a character of irrepressible humor, and a person impossible to dislike.

'Well, if it ain't the Bobbsey Twins, Heckle and Jeckle,' he joked as the two dark-suited lawyers entered the off-limits area inside the screen.

Gardner grinned and patted him on the back playfully.

King scowled. 'If this man has a twin, please find him, and put him out of our misery.' Then he laughed. The space was too confined for hand-to-hand combat. Adapt to the circumstances. That was King. And like a chameleon, his color could switch in an instant.

'Here for the Justice evidence, right?' Oakley asked.

Gardner nodded, and King stood immobile. This was the prosecutor's show, and the defense attorney was yielding the stage.

'Paco, get me L-nine-twenty-five, please,' the sergeant shouted to a shadowy figure lurking behind the first tier of floor-to-ceiling metal racks stacked high with boxes and folders. Oakley was a legend in the department. There were over ten thousand items stored in the property room at any given time, and he always knew exactly where to find anything that was asked for. Amazingly, he never needed to look at the log before he called out the number.

Gardner was shocked when he saw the cardboard box. It seemed so small, as if the state's entire case had been miniaturized. 'It's not the quantity of your evidence, but the quality, that makes or breaks a case,' he always said. But, on the other hand, juries liked 'stuff,' and the more items you could pile on the counsel table the better.

King whistled, and Gardner knew why. He didn't even have to say, 'And that's it?'

Two steak knives. A shirt. Four sets of crime scene photographs, two black-and-white, two color. An aerial photo. A crime scene diagram. Tennis shoes. Brownie's glass chip, and the drawings. 'What the hell is this?' King said, picking up the plastic bag containing the primitive artwork.

Gardner unfastened the seal and spread the papers out on Oakley's desk. 'Wow!' the sergeant exclaimed, as he pushed for a better view behind Gardner's right shoulder. 'An artist he ain't!' The four pages each depicted a progression of the same scene. A little boy being stalked, playing with, and finally being strangled by a snake. The last one was the most gruesome. The victim's eyes had been Xed out, and his tongue dangled from his mouth. There was no question that he was dead.

'You are kidding with this one, right?' King asked.

Gardner scooped them up, careful not to get his hands dirty from the fingerprinting dust that still clung to the edges.

'Kidding? I think not.'

'You know this shit isn't admissible. Read the *Sanders* case. Drawings and photographs cannot be admitted to prove state of mind. Case is right on point. And besides, there's no way you can tie it to my client.'

'I'm familiar with *Sanders*,' Gardner said airily, picking up the box and feeling around the folded-under flaps. 'We're not going on the same theory of admissibility . . . and this should answer your other question.' Gardner pulled a small white card from the box and threw it on the table. It was a latent fingerprint. 'Compliments of the artist,' he said.

King turned the card over and read the documentation that had been placed on it after the print had been compared to a known set.

In the space marked ID? it said YES. And in the space marked NAME? it said T. J. JUSTICE.

'Big deal,' King said nonchalantly. 'You still haven't got a prayer of getting this piece of crap into evidence.'

'We'll see,' snarled Gardner. 'You just might have to eat your fuckin' words.'

The rest of the inspection session was hurried. King's momentum changed, and the defense attorney seemed to be anxious to leave. He eyeballed the knife and the shirt, ran through the photos and chart, and barely even glanced at Brownie's 'chip' before tossing it casually into the box. 'I was pretty sure before, but now I'm certain,' he said to Gardner as he got to the door of the 'cage.'

'What's that?'

'You ain't got shit.'

King didn't wait for a reply before he bolted, so Gardner decided to try to get the last word in the parking lot. As he hustled past the checkpoint, Oakley grabbed his arm. 'How many shirts were in that box?'

'One. Why?'

The sergeant looked upset. 'Uh-oh! I was afraid of that.' He turned his head toward the back. 'Paco, you forgot to bring the other box!'

'You have a visitor,' Miss Cass told Gardner as he returned from the clerk's office at 4:00 P.M. 'Thought it would be best if I put her in your office.' Gardner's neck muscles tightened. 'Her' could be any of a number of unwanted guests at the workplace. Ex-wife. Clingy girlfriend. Disgruntled crime victim. He wasn't in the mood for any of them. There were motions to get ready for, and he didn't need any tangential tugs at his concentration. 'Anyone we know?' he asked.

'Not personally,' his secretary replied, 'but I hope you won't be upset that I let her in.'

Gardner opened the door, and Krysta Collins jerked up out of her seat. She looked as if she had just walked off the news set. Her red wool suit clung tightly to her well-shaped body, and her hair and makeup were camera-ready.

'Mr. Lawson?' She extended her hand. 'I'm sorry to

226

sneak up on you this way, but there's something . . .'
She didn't finish her sentence. The prosecutor was staring, and it stopped her short. 'Did I make a mistake?'
she asked. 'This doesn't look like a good time.'

Gardner grabbed her hand and squeezed firmly.
'Sorry,' he said. 'I can't give any interviews right now,
got too much work to do.'

She frowned. 'I was hoping we could at least talk
about setting something up. Can you give me a minute
to state my case?'

Gardner motioned her into Jennifer's customary
chair. 'Okay, I guess we can manage that.' He did not
want to appear rude. 'What did you have in mind?'

She smiled sweetly in a cat-and-canary way. 'I want
to do an indepth report on you. Your behind-the-scenes
life. The personal side. Inside the head of a real-live
county prosecutor.'

Gardner cringed internally. There was always an angle
with the media, and it was not beyond the realm of
reason that this was a setup engineered by Kent King.
'Uh, sorry, Miss Collins, I never do those kinds of
interviews . . . I just stick with the public record.' Unlike
some other people, he wanted to add.

She didn't blink. 'It might help your image,' she
replied.

'Are you saying it's bad?' Gardner retorted, trying to
draw her out.

Krysta smiled. 'Well, let's just say it could use a little
polishing.'

She seemed sincere, but Gardner still didn't trust her.
'Can't do it,' he repeated. 'I don't play those games.

You'll have to go back and tell your buddy I refused.'

She seemed genuinely confused. 'Buddy?'

Gardner gave her his 'lying witness' stare, the one that said: You know damn well who I'm talking about.

'I'm sorry, Mr. Lawson, but I don't understand.'

'How did you manage to set up that Justice interview? You didn't just march into the jail . . .'

'Ohhh . . .' Her eyes widened as the innuendo finally hit. 'You think I'm working with Mr. King.'

Gardner did not answer.

'I'm an independent reporter, Mr. Lawson. I go where the story is, and I don't compromise my objectivity.'

'How did you get the Justice interview?' he repeated.

'That's privileged.'

'Did you have to promise anything to King to get it?'

This time she remained silent.

'Uh-huh,' Gardner said sarcastically, 'very objective.'

She seemed to redden slightly, but otherwise kept her on-air cool. 'Don't make accusations, Mr. Lawson, it doesn't become you.'

Gardner stood up. 'That's my job, Miss Collins. I do it every day.'

She acknowledged his signal and stood up also, but as she prepared to leave, Gardner touched her arm. 'By the way,' he said, 'did you happen to get any outtakes on the Justice interview?'

'I don't have to answer that,' she replied.

'I'll ask it again. Was there more to the tape than you broadcast?'

She looked him directly in the eye. 'I can't tell you.'

'I could get a summons to find out.'

'And the network legal department would fight it to the death.'

Neither was going to give in, and neither was going to get anything. It was a standoff.

Gardner smiled politely. 'You know where to reach me if you change your mind,' he said.

Krysta handed him her card. 'That works both ways,' she replied. Then she did an about-face and marched out the door.

CHAPTER 10

The formal motions in *State v. Justice* were scheduled on February 2 at 10:00 A.M. This was the phase of the prosecution where all of the pretrial objections raised by Kent King and the countermotions filed by Gardner would be aired and decided. It was crucial to the state that most of the defense attorney's arguments be shot down here. If any of them got through, the case against the defendant would be severely damaged. And it was important also that the court endorse the prosecutor's peremptory requests for a ruling on the admissibility of its own evidence. Gardner and Jennifer had worked late into the prior night putting the finishing touches on the arguments, and now the courtroom was being called to order.

'All rise,' the bailiff announced. 'Hear ye, hear ye, hear ye, anyone having business in the circuit court, please come forward, the Honorable Ellsworth Simmons presiding.'

The rumbling of the gallery halted as His Honor sat down. A full complement of press and interested citizens. No vacant seats.

'Gentlemen, what have we this morning?' Jennifer was glossed over without so much as a look acknowledging her existence.

'Motions, Your Honor,' Gardner answered.

King stood silently, staring up at the bench. Beside him, T. J. Justice doodled on a yellow legal pad.

'Well?' Judge Simmons said impatiently.

'They're his motions, Your Honor, all but two, that is,' the prosecutor replied. 'I assume that the burden of going forward has not changed, and that the proponent of a motion carries the responsibility of starting off.'

King still stood with his back arched, silently eyeballing the bench.

T. J. was lost in his note paper.

'Well, somebody do something!' the judge roared. A ripple of amusement ruffled the crowd like a sudden breeze through a stand of corn. Then it was quiet.

'I was deferring the first word to the prosecutor, Your Honor,' King said in a deep baritone. 'It's always so enlightening.'

Judge Simmons slammed down the gavel so fast, the court reporter almost fell off her chair. 'Listen, you two,' he screamed. 'We're here to conduct legal business, not a personal feud. Do you hear me!' He pointed the handle of the gavel first at King, then at Gardner. From floor level it almost looked like the barrel of a gun.

'Of course, Your Honor,' King said. 'I'm prepared to go forward with my motions at this time or to stand fast while the state presents theirs. What would the court's pleasure be?'

Judge Simmons had been disarmed without a struggle.

He looked at Gardner. 'Why don't we hear from the state first.' He picked up the file. 'Motion *in limine* to determine admissibility of evidence. What's it all about, Mr. Lawson?'

Gardner was as much of an expert at switching gears as his opponent. He had been prepared to defend the defense suppression motions first, then attack with his own, but King's psychological maneuvering had turned it around. Now he had to lead.

'We have some evidence that we want to introduce at trial,' he began smoothly, 'and we believe that a ruling on admissibility in advance will greatly streamline the proceedings and save the court valuable time. First, as has been set out in our motion, we wish to offer proof of "Prior Crimes" of the defendant to establish his identity as the perpetrator of the offenses in this case; and second, we wish to present to the jury some drawings that the defendant made . . .'

Every eye in the courtroom suddenly jumped to T. J. For a second he kept doodling, then he stopped, and folded the top sheet over.

'It is the state's position that these two evidentiary items are admissible under state law, and that such evidence would, in conjunction with other proof, establish the guilt of the defendant.'

'Very well,' the judge said. 'Call your first witness.'

Gardner fiddled with a cuff link. 'Uh, Your Honor, we do not have any witnesses.'

'No witnesses?'

'No, sir, just legal argument on the points set forth in the motion, which we filed previously.' Gardner could tell by the murmur behind his back that the crowd sensed weakness. 'He didn't call any witnesses on his motion,' some rookie reporter would phone in to the city desk. As if that made any difference. Legal and technical arguments never needed any formal 'proof' of facts. They were self-contained. The law did the rest. Either the law applied or it didn't. Argument had to carry the day, not live testimony.

'Okay,' Judge Simmons said. 'Before the state argues its position, does the defense wish to be heard?'

King stood up. 'Why don't you ask him how a signature "sex offender" profile can possibly be admissible in a case where there's not even a single sex offense charged?'

The judge looked at Gardner, while King continued standing, as if to say: It's me and Simmons against you, pal.

'What about that, Mr. Lawson?'

'There are enough additional similarities to make a compelling case for admissibility, Your Honor.'

'But you concede that the sex crime aspect is not one of them?'

Gardner had been afraid of this. Getting derailed before he had a chance to make his pitch. 'We concede nothing, sir. A sex crime can be perpetrated without producing any physical evidence.'

Judge Simmons looked at King, and Gardner suddenly felt as if the double-team signal had just been given. 'Your Honor' – King's baritone was tinged with sarcasm – 'ask him how sex crime evidence is relevant without a sex crime charge.'

The judge was about to speak when Gardner responded, 'Can we do without the ventriloquy from counsel?'

The gavel slammed, and the State's Attorney found himself staring down the handle again. 'Mr. Lawson, I'll decide who speaks in this courtroom and when. I warned you. One more comment like that and I'll consider it an act of contempt. Now, what about Mr. King's question? How on earth can you put evidence of a sex crime profile into a case without the underlying prerequisite of a charged sex offense? It's not relevant.'

Gardner could sense King smirking. 'We're not seeking to put in any evidence of sex crimes,' he said. 'Only the other similarities. The abduction. The characteristics of the victim. The weapon. The wound. Those aspects are identical. We would delete any reference to sexual activity.'

'He can't do that, Your Honor,' King butted in.

The judge looked at the defense attorney, then picked up the theme. 'Mr. King's got a point. You want to put in the man's alleged signature, but you want to leave out a few letters. Well you can't do it. All or nothing. That's the way I see it. Sorry, Mr. Lawson, I'm going to deny the motion. No proof of prior crimes will be allowed.'

Gardner felt a wave of heat rise from his collar to his cheeks. He glared at King for a moment, then turned to the court. 'Very well, Your Honor,' he said. Then, keeping his backbone rigid, he sat down.

Judge Simmons called a short recess and left the bench.

The crowd stirred and stretched, and King quietly slipped past the reporters into the hall. Gardner and Jennifer remained seated at the trial table.

'Are you okay?' Jennifer asked.

Gardner was staring straight ahead, not having moved since the ruling.

'Yeah,' he replied, easing back in the chair and turning toward her. 'Just a flesh wound, but I think I'll make it.'

Jennifer saw the resolve slowly returning to Gardner's face. The calm, assured expression she was used to. He had been kicked hard, but now he was up, dusting himself off, ready to fight again. She felt a surge of admiration that stirred her deeper, secret feelings, but she kept it inside. This wasn't the time for sentiment. They had work to do.

'It can still come in,' Gardner said suddenly. 'If T. J. screws up on direct examination and opens the door, we can still get the prior crimes evidence to the jury.'

Jennifer frowned. 'Do you really think King's gonna let him?'

Gardner glanced over her shoulder as the defense attorney threaded his way through the gallery crowd, swaggering as usual. 'If we play our cards right, he may not have a choice.'

Just then the clerk came in and announced Judge Simmons. And the proceedings resumed.

'All right, gentlemen,' the judge said, 'What's next?'

He looked at King, and King looked at Gardner. 'He's got another motion, Your Honor.'

The prosecutor stood up. 'You want me to move to the second item?'

'That would be nice,' Simmons said sarcastically.

Gardner plunged right back into the flow as if the prior ruling hadn't happened. 'We have four drawings that we are going to offer into evidence at trial,' he began. 'These drawings can be unequivocally tied to the defendant. They were found in the motel room where he was staying at the time of the murder.'

King leaned back and looked up at the ceiling.

'There is no question that he is the artist—' Gardner continued.

'What's the relevance?' Simmons interrupted.

King nodded a 'ditto' toward the bench.

'The relevance is the similarity of the drawings to the crime, Your Honor.' Gardner walked to the bench and handed a set of plastic-covered sheets to the judge. King had nonchalantly waved them off when he was given the courtesy of a first look.

'These drawings clearly show the murder of a child,' Gardner said.

The judge's eyes widened slightly when he saw the drawings, but he did not speak. Finally he looked up. 'You got any law on this point?'

'We have cited several authorities in our written motion, Your Honor,' Gardner replied.

'But not *Sanders*,' King said suddenly, shifting lazily to his feet.

'*Sanders*?' The judge had obviously not read the defense's answer to Gardner's motion.

'It doesn't apply,' Gardner argued.

'Right on point, Judge,' King came back.

'Okay!' Simmons said loudly. 'Mr. Lawson, why don't you tell me why it *doesn't* apply.'

King caught the signal and sat down.

'Because we're not offering the drawings under the *Sanders* theory of admissibility. We're not trying to show "state of mind." We're saying it's actually a confession . . .'

The courtroom suddenly fell into a deeper hush than already existed. Judge Simmons blinked. 'A confession?'

'That's correct, Judge,' Gardner said. 'A written confession. Admissible under the rules of evidence governing confessions. We intend to present psychological testimony that this man had a need to divulge his crime, and that this was his way of acting it out . . .'

The judge gave the prosecutor an 'I've got to think about that one for a while' look. 'Okay, okay . . . Mr. King? What have you got to say about that?'

'One word, Judge, only one word: *Sanders*. It's the only precedent for this kind of evidence, and it says the drawings can't come in. This confession nonsense has no legal basis anywhere . . .'

The judge rubbed his forehead and closed his eyes. 'All right, then,' he said slowly. 'I'm gonna table this one for now. I'll read *Sanders* and the state's citations in chambers, and then, when we're done with the other motions, I'll give you my ruling.'

Gardner and King exchanged glances, then smugly resumed their seats.

By 4:00 P.M. the crowd had thinned to a row and a half of hardcore watchers. The rest had fled to meet deadlines and evening newscast time slots. The day had continued with the biting repartee between Gardner, King, and the court that had commenced with the opening gun. There had been several short recesses and one prolonged break when King had been called away for an important phone call. And now everyone awaited the judge's return from chambers to announce his ruling on the three remaining undecided issues: Gardner's *in limine* motion on the admissibility of the drawings, and Kent King's motions to suppress the knife and the testimony of Dallas Stubbins.

Gardner and Jennifer were whispering quietly at the state's counsel table, King was reading a report, and T. J. Justice was dozing when the judge mounted the bench. They put their distractions aside as the judge adjusted his glasses, shuffled several pieces of paper, and prepared to speak.

'Ladies and gentlemen,' he began, 'after considerable deliberation in chambers, I am prepared to rule on the motions still outstanding. Is there anything more from counsel before I announce my decision?'

Gardner sat still, but King stood up. 'We withdraw our motions, Your Honor.'

'What?' Judge Simmons looked dumbfounded.

'I said the defense withdraws the motions. The court need not rule.'

Gardner, Jennifer, and everyone in the courtroom sat in shocked silence. 'When did you make that determination, Mr. King?' the judge said in an irritated tone. 'You could have saved us all a lot of trouble.'

'Sorry, Your Honor,' King replied. 'The situation changed, so we modified our position accordingly.' He looked at Gardner, then back at the judge. The prosecutor ignored his stare.

'Okay then,' Simmons said. 'All that's left is the state's

in limine motion to admit the drawings.' He put down one set of papers and picked up another. 'I have looked this over, and frankly, I have real doubts as to whether the jury should see them. But giving some consideration to the state, I am going to defer ruling until the evidence is actually offered at trial. Perhaps by then Mr. Lawson can show some extraordinary circumstances as to why they can come in.'

Jennifer looked at Gardner, expecting a smile, but his face was blank.

'All right,' the judge continued, 'that concludes business for today. Counsel is reminded of the chambers conference with Judge Danforth on March nine. If there's nothing further, we stand adjourned.'

Jennifer poked Gardner's arm as the judge left the courtroom. 'What's the matter?' she asked.

'I don't know,' Gardner said absently, his vacant expression still in place. He looked over at King. The defense attorney was indulging himself in a self-satisfied grin, waving good-bye to his client as the deputies took him away.

Gardner finally turned to his assistant. 'I've never seen him do that,' he said solemnly.

Jennifer squinched 'Do what?' with her eyes.

'Walk away from a winner,' Gardner answered. 'Simmons was on a roll. I'll bet he was planning to knock out the statement, or even the knife, but King cashed it in . . .'

Jennifer squeezed his arm. 'So why worry? We got what we wanted.'

Gardner sighed. 'Yeah. Thanks to him.' He watched

King leave the courtroom with a jaunty gait, acting as if he'd won the lottery. After what had just happened, it simply didn't add up.

Bright sunlight had transformed Bob Hamilton's office into a warm nook away from the winter wind. The newspaper on his desk lay open to the JUSTICE MOTIONS LEAVE STATE IN LIMBO headline. The story had already been carefully clipped and filed. The headline was destined for a separate folder. Hamilton leaned back in his chair and took a splash of heated rays across his face. He needed to relax. The more he got into the case, the weirder it became. There were too many loose ends. Too many odd discrepancies.

A memo lay next to the chopped-up newspaper. Hamilton reread it for the fourth time. It had seemed like the best way to do the job. Get a closer look.

To: Thomas Quinton, Deputy Director, Soviet Affairs Bureau. Please accept this as a request for one week temporary leave to attend legal proceedings in the *State v. Justice* case. Due to the nature of the reporting assignment, it would be appropriate to have the opportunity to obtain firsthand information at the source, rather than to rely on second-party reports. In addition, personal interviews with the participants would allow a more accurate assessment of the international implications of the case to be made.

Respectfully submitted, Robert Hamilton, ASDO

Below the signature line was the handwritten reply:

Request denied. You are instructed to refrain from any contact with persons connected to the case, directly, through telephone or mail, or intermediaries. Your assignment is limited to the gathering of data from existing sources only, and the evaluation of that data. You are not, repeat, not to become personally involved.

It was initialed T. Q., DD.

'Don't become involved,' Hamilton said out loud, still basking in the sun. 'Maybe I already am.' He snapped forward into a cool shadow. The transition made the skin on his face tingle. He picked up the phone and dialed the number to CIA central records.

'Two-four-six-three.' A male voice.

'Constance, please.'

'This official?'

'Yes. Internal. Twelve-twelve. State Department.'

There was a split-second pause, then a soft female voice: 'Yes?'

'Con? Bob.'

'Hi.'

'Got a quickie. What's the status of the Anatov file?'

'Hold on, let me check.' The muted clatter of computer keys came over the line. 'Still out.'

'Still?'

'Uh-huh.'

'Can you tell me who's got it and when it's due back? I've had it on request for a long time.'

'Sorry.'

'You know and can't tell me? Or you don't know.'

'Just, sorry.' It was as if she wanted to say more, but couldn't.

'Okay, 'bye.' Hamilton sighed and hung up. His stomach knotted as he assessed the situation. Someone was holding the file out of circulation, and this added more pieces to the puzzle. Who had it? Why were they keeping it under wraps? And why didn't they want to be identified? He shoved the paperwork aside and tried to work on another project. But the questions continued to batter his brain. Finally, he gave up. Until this thing was solved, it appeared, the rest of his life would be on hold.

It was ten o'clock at night, and Gardner's undercover operative was on the move. His target: Kent King.

'Damn!' Brownie exclaimed. 'Sucker done it again!' The road ahead was clear. No sign of a Jaguar taillight anywhere. For the third time in a row, the defense attorney had slipped away into the darkness, and the officer didn't have a clue as to where he had gone. Brownie had swept by all of the possible destinations the last time it had happened, even out as far as Watson Road, but the man had vanished, and that didn't sit well at all. It was almost as if he was trying to elude a tail.

Brownie pulled to the shoulder of Farm Lane and shut off his engine. 'Gotta think,' he said to himself. 'Car? No problem.' He was using his brother-in-law's black Trans-Am. About as unofficial as you could get. 'Outfit? Uh-uh.' Blue denim ensemble. 'What the hell could it be? Man ain't got that much sense. No way he know 'bout me. No way.' He didn't have a chance to continue the soliloquy. A car brushed by so fast that the shock wave rocked Brownie against the door.

'Shit!' He had to make a decision. Off duty. Unauthorized undercover. No uniform. No dome light. The only thing he had was his badge, but that was enough to make a stop. Brownie started the engine and peeled out onto the road. 'Mutherfucker gonna kill somebody,' he muttered as two red dots accelerated away in the distance.

The dots danced and swayed as the road twisted toward the hills. Brownie was hitting ninety, but they weren't getting any bigger. In fact, they seemed to be shrinking. The rail crossing at Timberview should slow him up, the officer thought; at least it should get him in close enough to read the tag. That might be the best he could do before they reached the high country and the trails went everywhere.

Brownie crammed the accelerator, and the Trans-Am leapt the tracks. The dots were bigger, and the outline of a tail end appeared. BFR–945. He was close enough to make out the license, but couldn't see the driver. The tachometer read six thousand RPM, and a sudden image of his brother-in-law loomed up, screaming for him to slow down. By the time his concentration returned, the dots were shrinking again. Brownie eased off the pedal and watched them disappear over a steep hillock that elevated the road above windshield level. He had enough ammo to take out the driver without risking his in-law's precious baby. No need to press it. The

Timberview Exxon sign shone on the right-hand side, and Brownie swung in and jumped out of the car.

A call to the COMM shop should do the trick, he thought. Without a radio in the car, he'd have to use the land line. 'Uh, let me speak to Stevenson, please,' Brownie said into the pay phone.

'Stevenson.'

'Brownie. Listen, Steve, got time to run a tag for me?'

'Shoot.'

'Maryland BFR-nine-four-five.'

'Hold on . . .'

Brownie drummed his fingers against the booth while he waited.

'Okay. Got it. Rental vehicle listed to Midstate Leasing. And . . . wait a minute . . . wait a minute . . . Well, what do you know?'

'What's the problem?' Brownie heard the snap of recognition in his colleague's voice.

'Shit, man, we must've got four calls on this car already,' Stevenson said. 'You're wasting your time. Guy's got some kind of diplomatic immunity.'

Brownie groaned. 'Got any more data than that?'

'Just a note in the COMM file. "Stay clear." That's about it.'

Brownie said thanks and hung up. He'd thought the Russians had moved on. Maybe he was wrong.

February was Gardner's least favorite month. It was the coldest twenty-eight days of the year, a time when the wind off the ridge cut into the thickest layers of clothing like a scythe. The days were still miserably short, and the pale sun often hid behind the dark clouds that preceded the latest subzero frontal system roaring down from Canada. With the Justice case hanging fire, he couldn't even fit in a ski afternoon at Waddington. And then there was Valentine's Day to be dealt with.

To Gardner, the prospect of doing something with Elaine on the fourteenth did not seem particularly appealing. Romance was supposed to be spontaneous, not served up at the behest of, and on the timetable of, card companies and candy manufacturers. Elaine had caught him by surprise and set up a dinner date at the Timberlodge Inn. He knew that if he didn't go along with it, he'd pay the price in aggravation, so he accepted. He even ordered flowers. But Elaine was disappointed. She was expecting something more expensive from him, perhaps even some jewelry, and when it didn't appear, she showed her distress.

The meal progressed in awkward silence, as Gardner found himself unable to penetrate the zone of hurt his second-class gift had created. He finally got her to loosen up in the car, on the way back to town, by using the case as an excuse. It was eating him up, timewise, he said. But the real truth was now taking shape in his mind: He was tiring of Elaine's company.

She was almost back to normal when they arrived at her apartment, and she whispered a few naughty suggestions in his ear as to how they could make up. Gardner struggled to keep up the charade of an embrace in the hallway, but his thoughts fixated on the emptiness of their relationship. He was on the verge of saying good night, when a familiar surge of heat took over, and he went inside. He was certain now that his days with Elaine were numbered. The only problem was, in the middle of February, with the wind shaking the scrubby pines on the lip of the ridge, he had no place else to go.

PART III

Under Oath

CHAPTER 11

March 9
10:45 A.M.

Gardner and Kent King lounged in armchairs across from Judge Danforth's giant mahogany desk. They were relaxed. Legs crossed. Elbows hanging over the tufted armrests. No animosity or conflict apparent on the surface.

'You fellas know that I've gotten the trial assignment on this case,' Judge Danforth told the two attorneys in his spacious walnut-paneled chambers.

'Thanks for the warning,' King said with a laugh. 'By the way, Dan, have you heard the one about the golf-crazy judge?'

Danforth shook his head, an anticipatory smile barely upturning the corners of his thin lips. Gardner yawned.

'Well, it seems that this old judge was such a nut on the game that he carried his clubs with him everywhere, even into court.' The two listeners kept silent, but the judge's smile was becoming more pronounced with each word. Gardner suppressed another yawn. 'Well, one day this babe comes into court. I mean a babe.' He caressed a set of gigantic imaginary breasts. 'Anyhow, she keeps eyeing the old geezer up and finally she raises her hand and asks to approach the bench. When she gets up there, she says to the judge, "Excuse me, sir, but I couldn't help noticing that you have something under your robe. Would you mind telling me what it is?" The judge just looks at her, and finally says, "Ma'am, if you must know, it's my favorite putter." "Great," she says, "now all you need is some balls, and we can have a twosome." '

Danforth broke into a guffaw, and even Gardner couldn't suppress a smile. The joke was a hit, but how could it miss? On the far wall was a collection of golfing trophies and memorabilia that announced to everyone who entered the true love of Judge 'Digger' Danforth's life.

'I'm surprised you hadn't heard that one before,' Gardner said, 'considering how much time you two waste together at Fair Hills.'

'Gardner, don't get nasty,' the judge said. 'I'm gonna get you out there one of these days . . .'

'Not a chance.'

'Yeah,' King interjected. 'Too common a sport for his blood.' Everyone was still smiling, as if politeness was the order of the day.

'Okay,' the judge said. 'We might as well get started and lay down the ground rules for the trial, what say?'

'Let's roll,' Gardner replied, pulling some papers from his briefcase.

'Not too fast,' the defense attorney replied. 'There have been some recent developments that have to be discussed first.'

'Got a problem, Kent?' Danforth asked.

'Yeah, Dan. It's called "missing evidence." '

The judge looked at Gardner. 'What's he talking about?'

The State's Attorney shifted in the plushness of his chair. 'Er, there was some misplaced evidence, Judge, but it's been found, and counsel has been given an opportunity to inspect it. There's no problem.'

King's face suddenly flashed an exaggerated expression of skepticism that he often played to the jury. 'Misplaced evidence? Give me a fuckin' break!'

Judge Danforth closed his eyes and leaned back in his chair. 'What did he do this time, Kent?' There was a weary tone of 'here we go again' in his voice.

'Gave me a look-see at the evidence,' King said, 'but held out his ace . . .'

'What?' The judge opened his eyes and leaned forward.

'It wasn't intentional,' Gardner said.

'I say again,' King responded, 'give me a fuckin' break!'

'Okay! Okay!' Danforth interrupted. 'Somebody tell me what happened!'

'He—' the defense attorney began, but the judge held up his hand.

'I want to hear it from you.' He pointed at Gardner.

'We showed him the evidence, but it wasn't all there at the time,' Gardner said. 'The property guys had missed the box with a bloodstained shirt seized from the defendant.'

Danforth's face suddenly mirrored the skepticism of King. 'Misplaced?' he repeated slowly.

Gardner nodded. 'They found it immediately, but Kent had already left. We called and gave him the information, then set him up for another look. That's it.'

King turned to the judge. 'Nothin' to it, right, Dan? Only the key to the whole damn case . . .'

Danforth looked at Gardner. 'That does sound serious.'

Gardner took a deep breath. 'It was not intentional! Anyway, he's seen it now, and we've given him the FBI analysis report on the bloodstain. What the hell else does he want?'

Danforth's gaze returned to King. 'Well?'

'I haven't had a chance to evaluate it,' the attorney said smoothly. 'That's going to take time.'

'Are you talking postponement?' The judge pinched his brow.

'That's about the size of it,' King said.

'We'd object!' Gardner responded. 'He doesn't need any more time. That's just an excuse.'

Judge Danforth rubbed his cheek the way he did in court when he was tired of listening to arguments. 'Okay, why don't we put that aside for now, and we can come back to it. What other preliminaries are there?'

King hesitated, so Gardner filled the void. 'Two things, Judge. We have yet to hear from Mr. King as to whether he's going to raise a psychological defence, or whether he's going to present any alibi witnesses at trial. We've filed discovery requests on these points, but he has not answered.'

Danforth looked at the defense attorney.

'Got the alibi witness right here,' King said, jotting a name on a piece of paper and passing it over to the prosecutor. 'And on the psychological thing, the state's just gonna have to wait on that one.'

The floor went back to Gardner. 'Is he going to assert a psychological defence or not? That's all we want to know.'

'You haven't filed an insanity plea, right?' the judge inquired of King.

'Correct.'

'So what's the problem?'

The golfing partners both looked at Gardner.

'I know he's loaded with psychological studies,' the prosecutor said to the judge. 'If he's going to use any of that stuff to try for a "diminished capacity" defense, I'm entitled to see it.'

'By what authority?' King shot back.

'I'm talking to him. Do you mind?' The State's Attorney looked annoyed. 'The use of any expert testimony, psychological or otherwise, requires a pretrial disclosure. So far I haven't seen shit.'

'You haven't? I thought you lived in it,' King said nastily.

'Okay, okay!' The judge restored order. 'Do you have any psychological reports?' he asked the defense counsel.

'Yes.'

'And have you shown them to the state?'

'No.'

'Well, do you intend to?'

'I haven't decided yet. We may not go the psychological route at all, and in that case he's not entitled to any of the material.'

'Well, when do you plan to make that determination?'

This time it was Gardner who interrupted.

The judge answered for King. 'He doesn't have to reveal his defense before trial. You know that. I suppose we'll all find out in due course, which leads us back to the operative question: to postpone or not to postpone. How much time do you need, Kent?'

'Sixty days.'

'Bullshit!' Gardner exclaimed.

The judge glared at him, then looked at King. 'Thirty days. No more.' Then his eyes shot towards the door and both men knew the meeting was over.

March 14 was a typical early spring day. Blustery. Low off-white clouds snug against the mountains. Trees still at the bud stage. The snow was almost gone now, and only a few spotty strips remained, filling shadowy crevasses and ravines where the sun never reached. The landscape had a grayish tint to it, as if this year the green would not come, and the rest of the year would be spent in a colorless haze.

Gardner's mood reflected the weather. He had been conserving his inner strength for the trial, but the postponement had sapped it in an instant. That was a common disease among trial attorneys. There was always a letdown when a big trial didn't go off as scheduled. Mind and body were ready for action, but the battle had been delayed. And now he had to cope with the wait and fill the days with meaning until court resumed.

Gardner had taken Jennifer to Paul's for a working lunch. He had been quiet on the way over, and ordered a special martini as soon as he sat down.

'How 'bout a glass of wine?' He looked at Jennifer guiltily after ordering his own drink.

She was dressed in a black wool suit and her hair was pulled back tightly at the temples and ponytailed in back. She smiled politely. 'Soda, please.'

'God, Jennifer, are you ever going to loosen up?' Gardner sounded almost angry that she wasn't going to have alcohol.

She looked into his dark eyes. 'You want me to have a drink?'

'One time wouldn't kill you . . .'

She continued her gaze, then glanced down uncomfortably when he didn't break eye contact. 'Maybe I don't like it.'

'Fine. But maybe just once you could have a taste.'

Jennifer stuck with her soda, and during the meal Gardner went on to his second, then third martini. They were there to discuss strategy, but not a word about that subject was uttered. Gardner began with a tirade about T.J.'s history, and how he should have been stopped by now. Then he picked up the King-Danforth golf connection and made dire predictions about the judge's rulings at trial. Then he went into a detailed description of how to make a 'special' martini. It was obvious to Jennifer that he was struggling against postponement depression. She listened patiently, nodding and responding with one-word answers, but he wasn't about to come out of it.

'Jen, are you ever gonna have children?' he asked suddenly.

The unexpected track switch startled her. 'Uh, that's

kind of personal, don't you think?' She blushed a very pale shade of pink.

Gardner was clumsily groping for topics. 'You dating anyone?'

She blushed a deeper hue.

'Christ, no wonder you're so tight all the time. You do nothing but work. That's definitely not healthy . . .'

Jennifer knew it was the martinis talking, so she silently forgave him. 'I like my work. Is that such a crime?' She was trying to shift him away from the obvious question: Why wasn't she dating? That was one inquiry she could not answer truthfully. She *was* interested in someone, more and more each day, but it was obvious that the person she cared for was not ready to reciprocate the feeling.

Gardner looked as if he was going to continue, so she interrupted. 'I do think I'll have the drink after all,' she said.

Gardner's chin dropped with surprise.

'Tequila shooter, please, Paul!' she yelled over at the bar.

Gardner still hadn't said anything when the drink arrived.

Jennifer went through the routine like a professional. Salt on the wrist, swallow in one gulp, chew the lemon. In an instant the glass was face-down on the table.

Jennifer looked at the State's Attorney, an expression of triumph on her face.

For the first time today, he was smiling.

Gardner's mood swing was short-lived. Despite the postponement, the days seemed to accelerate their pace towards the trial date like a brakeless train, and that meant no time for self-indulgence. He had to get back to work.

With three days to go, Gardner and Jennifer were still at it. 'Gotta work through the weekend,' he told his assistant as they conferenced in his office. The case blueprint was laid out on his big walnut desk. Witness list. Physical evidence log. Legal issues. Jury roster. The plan of attack, meticulously assembled after months of effort. It was almost done, but not quite.

'We have to get the order of witnesses finalized and voir dire prepared,' he continued. 'That's going to put us well into Saturday, and probably Sunday too.' Then, suddenly, he realized what that meant. It was Granville's time with Dad. Prearranged and preordained, circled in red on Gardner's calendar.

'Can you change it?' Jennifer asked when she saw his finger tapping his son's name, lovingly written into the alternate weekend blocks. She was vaguely aware that his ex-wife was as flexible as a slab of granite.

'I'll try,' Gardner said, picking up the phone and dialing.

'Hello?' There was a touch of ice in Carole's voice, warning the unwary that the reason for the call better be good.

'It's me.'

'Granny's at school.' The ice thickened.

'I know. Listen, I need to ask a favor. Can we switch visitation the next weekend, and then pick up the schedule again? I'll do two in a row—'

'Why?' She cut off the request midsentence.

'Uh, Justice case goes to trial Monday. I need some time—'

'Not my problem,' she cut in again.

'Christ, Carole, can you give me a break?'

Jennifer looked down.

'What for? What on earth for? What break did you give me?'

Gardner's blood surged with a mixture of rage and shame. 'Never gonna give it up, are you?' he said with a tremor. 'Gonna carry it forever . . .'

'Go to hell!' she screamed, then slammed down the phone.

Gardner slowly eased the receiver into its cradle and looked at Jennifer. She had heard it all, and was trying to manage a sympathetic smile.

'She wasn't always like that,' he said.

The assistant waited for a follow-up, but he leaned back in his chair and shut his eyes. The pain on his face was too deep to hide. Jennifer decided that he wanted to be alone, so she rose and quietly left the room.

Gardner lapsed into a reverie as he tried to loosen the noose that Carole's words had tied around his throat. 'It wasn't always like that,' he repeated silently to himself.

It was a year after they were married, and he had just been elected State's Attorney. The cases were piling up, and as much as he tried to delegate, he found himself trying all of the major felonies. The Shepherd ax-murder case kept him at work day and night. Carole was usually asleep when he got home, and he tried not to disturb her when he left in the early morning.

Then, after three weeks of trial, the jury went out at six o'clock in the evening. When they were still out at nine, he called home, but there was no answer. He was alone in his office, waiting for the clerk to call with the verdict. Suddenly there was a knock on the door.

It was Carole. Dressed in an evening gown, carrying a picnic basket and a bottle of wine. 'Mind if I join you?' she said in a sultry voice.

Together they laughed, ate, and drank, as the jury deliberated. The call came well after midnight. Shepherd had been found guilty on all counts. Carole was ecstatic, and they celebrated some more. And then before going home, they made love on the oriental rug.

Gardner opened his eyes and leaned forward. The past was long gone. He had a lot of work to do, and somehow, even with Granville underfoot, he'd find a way. He pushed the intercom button. 'Miss Cass, please send Jennifer back in.' His voice was firm. He was going to nail T. J. Justice, and *nobody*, not Carole, not King, not even Digger Danforth, was going to stop him.

Jury selection began at 10:15 on the morning of April 11. Gardner and Jennifer had completed their work on schedule, plying Granville with coloring books and Lego blocks as they toiled away at the office, taking breaks for snacks and, later, a suitable-for-kids movie. And now, the high ceiling of the stately paneled courtroom number 1 echoed with the voice from the bench, and the case against T. J. Justice was launched.

One hundred prospective jurors had been called for duty, and they filled every spectator seat in the gallery, the jury box, the aisle, and even the extra sheriff's-deputy chairs. The press and the public were forced to stand in the hall, assured by the bailiff that they could come in as jurors were excused and seats were freed up. Reluctantly they agreed, and wound up clustering against the outer door, pushing forward expectantly whenever it opened.

Inside, the selection procedure had begun with the judge asking the voir dire questions he had been given by the defense and state. The object was to smoke out opinions and beliefs of potential jurors that were not apparent on the surface. That would help the lawyers decide which candidates were the most predisposed to their own particular point of view. It was a very effective method. And it didn't take long to get a reading.

'Has any member of the jury panel ever been the victim of a crime?' Judge Danforth asked the sea of blank faces in the expansive gallery. Immediately forty hands went up.

'All right. Please line up at the rail, give your name and panel number to the bailiff, and come forward one at a time as you are called. Counsel please approach the bench.'

'What about the defendant?' Kent King asked, standing behind T. J. Justice like a chaperon at a prom.

'Does he wish to participate?' the judge asked.

King whispered to his client, then pulled back the chair so he could stand. 'Yes, Your Honor. He definitely wants to be part of the selection process.'

'Very well. Come forward.'

The potential jurors were still queuing when the attorneys got into place at the base of the elevated platform. The idea was to have them each give their answer privately at the bench, so they wouldn't inadvertently 'school' each other in what to say. Gardner and Jennifer took the right side, King and Justice went left. The space in the middle was reserved for the juror.

'Okay,' Danforth whispered, 'before they start, let's get the routine straight. I'll question first. Then, alternating between jurors, state and defense will have a chance to interrogate. Understood?' Both sides acknowledged in the affirmative.

'Panel two, juror six. Mr. Swanson, Your Honor,' Bailiff John Toms announced.

'Yes, Mr. Swanson.'

The man hesitantly stepped into the gap between the state and defense. He was fat and balding. Mid-forties, wheezing heavily as he breathed. 'Got robbed.'

'You were robbed?'

'Yup.'

'And when was that, sir?'

''Bout four years ago.'

Gardner could see Justice peeking over King's shoulder, trying to get a better look at the man.

'Now, sir, would that experience in any way impair your ability to render a fair and impartial judgment in this case?'

'Huh?'

'Let me rephrase that. Would you hold what happened to you four years ago against the defendant in this case? Uh, be less able to decide guilt or innocence on the evidence presented here in court just because you got robbed?'

'Wuz hit pretty good.'

'Well, would that have any effect on your ability to serve as a juror on this case?'

The man raised his eyes in thought, then answered, 'Don't think so, Judge.'

'Well, do you have any doubt? Any doubt at all?'

The man's eyes went up again, then dropped. 'Nope.'

'You're sure?'

'I can be fair, Judge.'

Danforth put a check mark on the roster. 'Okay. Counsel?'

The judge looked towards the defense side first.

'Kent King, Mr. Swanson. How are you today?' They shook hands, and Gardner very subtly shook his head. King was out to sell, and face-to-face there were few who could get the job done better.

'Say you got robbed?'

Swanson nodded.

'Were the robbers white or black?'

'White boys.'

'Uh-huh. How many were there?'

'Two.'

'Did they get caught?'

'Yep, but didn't either one get no jail time.'

'Uh-huh. You dislike criminals, then, I take it? Don't have much use for 'em?'

'No.'

'What about a person accused of a crime? Do you think that just because he's charged, he must be guilty?'

'Object, Your Honor,' Gardner broke in. 'He's making an argument.'

King looked as if he had been slapped in the face, but the prosecutor knew it was just for show. Every eye in the courtroom was watching, and the outward appearance of righteousness carried a premium.

'This is voir dire, Mr. Lawson,' Judge Danforth said firmly. 'I think he can ask the question.'

'Questioning and arguing are two different things, Judge,' Gardner replied. 'At this stage, especially—'

'I said he can proceed. Now let's get on with it.' His eyes told Gardner not to utter another word.

'Thank you, Your Honor,' King said unctuously. 'Now, Mr. Swanson, are you going to hold it against Mr. Justice simply because the state decided to charge him with a crime?'

There was some hesitation, then he answered, 'Nope. Won't do that.'

'Can I have your word on it?'

Gardner glared at the judge as if to say, 'Pleeeeease!'

'Okay, Mr. King, I think you've gone as far as you can go with this line. Any more questions?'

King shook the juror's hand again and stepped back. It was now Gardner's turn to sell. 'Mr. Swanson, how were you treated by the police and prosecutors during the robbery case? Were you satisfied with their performance?'

Again, hesitation. Then he turned to face the State's Attorney directly. 'Well, no, sir, I wasn't.'

Gardner saw King flash a brief smile in the background. He smelled blood.

'Uh, what was the problem?'

'Didn't do a thing. Never got me no money back. Never paid no medical bills. Never done nuthin' to them boys.'

'So how do you feel towards the prosecution in this case?'

'Not too good, I reckon.'

After the juror returned to the fold, Gardner addressed the court. 'Move to strike for cause, Your Honor.'

'On what grounds?'

'Man's got a vendetta against the state.'

The judge looked at King, but spoke before the defense attorney could respond. 'Said he could be fair. That's all the law requires, and that's good enough for me. Use one of your peremptories if you don't like him. For now he is a qualified juror. Motion to strike for cause denied.'

The voir dire questioning went on for two more tedious days. There were endless lineups at the bench, and endless interrogations by the judge, prosecutor, and defense attorney as the potential jurors bared their inner souls and revealed their congenital biases. During this stage all of the hot topics were covered. How much pretrial publicity had they seen or heard? Were they related to anyone who had been prosecuted before? Would they believe the word of a police officer over that of an ordinary citizen witness? And the court's follow-up question always held the barbed hook:

Despite their prejudice, would they still be able to render a fair and impartial verdict in the case against T. J. Justice?

Those who couldn't agree they could be fair were immediately stricken for 'cause.' And those who said they could were left in the pool from which the final twelve would be chosen. Their fate lay in the hands of Gardner and King, each of whom was armed with notes taken during voir dire. Notes that clearly delineated the inner leanings of the prospective juror, enabling the choosers to maneuver their favorite candidates into the box.

So, after two days, the massive group had been reduced to seventy-five, the reporters and watchers had returned, and the lawyers were deep into the final selection process. At 1:30 P.M. it was coming down to the wire. They had been culling all morning, and now there were two strikes left for the state and four for the defense. They had started with ten 'peremptory challenges' for the state and twenty for the defense. Each could excuse as many jurors as they had 'strikes.' But when they were used up, the next juror in line had to be taken. This left the holder of the last strike with the advantage.

'Is the jury as now constituted acceptable to the defense?' the judge inquired. The box was full. If King said yes, the selection process would be over, and both sides would be stuck as is.

Gardner knew that the defense had to act. He had managed to seat two 'ringers' in the last go-round. By luck, the roster listed several hard-line law-and-order types in a row. A farmer, a schoolteacher, and an insurance salesman. All had families and all had looked at Justice as if he were a piece of rancid meat. King bounced the farmer immediately, but let the other two take seats in the box. Gardner waited, dividing his attention between the number six and eight positions. They were destined to be vacated, he was sure. 'Ask juror six to be excused, Your Honor.' The teacher got up and pushed her way out of the enclosure. 'And number eight.'

Gardner scanned the next two names on the list. One plus, and one minus. The plus was first. Son of a security guard. College educated. Worked in a bank. *Robbery victim* the note said.

'Acceptable to the state,' Gardner announced.

'Strike,' said King.

The next candidate hailed from Eastern Europe. First-generation immigrant when the 'iron curtain' was studded with barbed wire spikes. Proud U.S. citizen now. *Russian hater?* Gardner had noted. 'Strike, if Your Honor pleases,' he said.

One strike left on each side, and a couple of middle-of-the-roaders coming up. Either would be okay in a pinch, Gardner thought, but nothing to brag about. Two spaces ahead, on the other hand, was a real bell-ringer. Former military man. Wife. Family. Grandkids. Dog. He even looked like a foreman. The State's Attorney checked seat number one, the foreman's slot. Swanson, the man with a chip on his shoulder against the state, was still there. He had been allowed into the box as a ploy. Gardner had no intention whatsoever of letting him stay there.

'Both acceptable to the state, Your Honor,' Gardner told the court. All eyes focused on the defense attorney as he evaluated the choices. 'Accep—' He stopped and leaned over his client. The two whispered back and forth; then King rose to his usual arched stance.

'Strike number two,' he said, looking at Justice, who nodded.

'Very well. That exhausts the defendant's peremptory strikes. Take seat number six. The next juror come forward, please.' Gardner couldn't believe it. He had one strike left and a clear field ahead. He let the next juror take seat eight unchallenged. King sat in silence. Without strikes, he wasn't even asked.

'Is the jury acceptable to the state?'

'Strike juror one, Your Honor.' Mr. Swanson looked surprised, as if he didn't expect removal. A few moments later, Gardner watched the ex-staff sergeant settle into the foreman's seat. 'You fucked up, pal,' he whispered. But inside he worried. How could King have made such a mistake?

Bruno Calvano pushed a thick manila file across King's desk at 11:15 that night. 'You're all set,' he told his employer. 'Statements. Documents. Evidence breakdown. Head reports. All in there. You got enough shit here to blast that wimp all the way to hell.'

'Thanks for putting it together, Bruno.'

'No problem. You always take care of me. No reason I can't return the favor. You headin' out again?'

'Uh-huh.' King looked distracted.

'She must be sumthin'.' Bruno had his own idea of where his boss was going.

'What?'

'That bitch you're tied up with. Must be some kinda hot.'

'Oh. Yeah.' King stood up and put on his overcoat.

'Got any more stuff for me?' Calvano looked like a big dog begging a bone.

'You done with Lawson yet?'

'Not quite. Almost.'

'Finish that up, and I'll give you another assignment. Meanwhile, stand by in case something comes up at trial.'

'Right.'

King walked towards the door.

'So you're not going to tell me,' the investigator said.

'About?'

'Who the bitch is.'

King stood in the doorway and didn't answer, obviously off in thought. Finally he turned. 'Let's just say that my liaison is with a person who shall now and forever remain anonymous.'

Calvano whistled as the attorney pushed out into the night. Opening day was tomorrow. The man really should be conserving his energy.

CHAPTER 12

April 15
10:03 A.M.

'Go to the jury, Mr. Lawson,' Judge Danforth said ceremoniously. It was showtime. The first step in a ten-thousand-mile journey. The smoking fastball to the lead-off batter. The gallery was full to overflowing, and the tension in the air was palpable. The major players shifted nervously in their seats. This was it.

'The case is either won or lost at opening statement,' Gardner always schooled his students. 'When you get up there, remember, they're on the other side of the fence. The presumption of innocence already has the defendant acquitted. You've got to make them climb over. Make them *want* to convict. Make them commit themselves emotionally. Grab 'em and don't let 'em go . . .'

The prosecutor rose slowly and walked to the podium in front of the jury box. Jurors and spectators waited restlessly. All was quiet. Gardner unbuttoned his blue pinstripe jury suit and grasped the rails of the wooden stand.

'Ladies and gentlemen of the jury, my name is Gardner Lawson. I'm the State's Attorney in this county, and as such it is my duty to present evidence against the defendant in this case.' He turned towards the prosecution table. 'With me is Assistant State's Attorney Jennifer Munday. She will also be involved in the presentation of evidence and is duty bound, as I am, to represent the interests of the state of Maryland against criminal wrongdoers.'

Jennifer looked towards the box. She was wearing a navy wool blazer, white silk shirt, and a slim grey flannel skirt that grazed her knees. Her expression was pure business. Serious. Determined. Perfect, Gardner thought. He then turned to the other side, and a very subtle tone change in his voice occurred. 'Kent King is the defense attorney. His duty is to vigorously represent his client and see to it that he is accorded every benefit of our legal system.' The eyes in the enclosure all swung to King. He nodded professionally, discharging a double dose of charm. The subliminal message of Gardner's words didn't escape him: 'King knows the man is guilty, but he's got to see to it that he gets a fair trial. That's his job.'

'And sitting next to counsel is the *defendant*.' Gardner inflected a bitter twang on the word, like introducing a plague virus. The jurors shifted their attention one seat. T.J. glowered back. Right on cue. There was a pause while everyone waited for the prosecutor to ascribe some 'duty' to Justice, but he said nothing. The silence conveyed the point.

'Judge R. Ford Danforth is the presiding judicial officer at this trial,' Gardner continued. 'It will be his duty to keep order in the courtroom, rule on questions of the admissibility of evidence, and eventually to pronounce sentence.' The judge sat stone-faced, unwilling to let his expression endorse any particular point of view.

'Excuse me, Your Honor.' It was King.

'Counsel?'

'Mr. Lawson said—'

'May we approach the bench, Your Honor?' Gardner cut him off. He didn't want the defense to get in a free open-court shot.

The judge beckoned them forward and the attorneys walked up to the tall platform. Justice tagged along behind King and tucked in on the other side.

'This is opening statement. What's the problem?' Danforth demanded. He was looking at both lawyers.

'You don't pronounce sentence unless the man is guilty,' King said.

'So?' The judge was slow in seeing the point.

'So the State's Attorney left out one little prerequisite that has to be met before you have a chance to do your *duty*, as he puts it.'

A light came on in Danforth's eyes, and he glared at Gardner as if to say, 'How dare you do that?'

'Come on, Judge, everyone knows that a person must be convicted before a court can sentence. It's self-evident. Counsel is just trying to harass me.'

The judge looked at King, then back at Gardner. 'We're not even two minutes into the trial, gentlemen, and you've started. Is this the way it's going to be right down the line?'

The prosecutor and defense attorney locked each other in a stare-down.

'Okay, okay,' the judge said in a frustrated voice. 'I'll straighten this out. Let's return to work.' He waved the assembly away with the back of his hand. 'Ladies and gentlemen of the jury,' he announced. 'I know it's probably obvious, but one thing that counsel said needs some clarification. My sentencing responsibility occurs only if and when you, as jurors, find the defendant guilty beyond a reasonable doubt. Is that understood?' Every person on the jury nodded. The point was clearly self-evident.

'Now we come to you,' Gardner continued. The ease of his resumption conveyed the failure of the defense's attempt to break his rhythm. 'You, ladies and gentlemen, are the judges in this case. You have taken an oath here today to "well and truly try and a true deliverance give based upon the law and the evidence." That was your oath. Do you remember it? Do you understand the significance of the function you are performing?' He paused for effect, running the two lines of faces from start to finish, contacting everyone, eyeball to eyeball.

'You are sitting in hallowed ground. A place reserved for citizens who perform the greatest service our society can ask. You and only you stand between the government and an individual accused of a crime. Without your approval, the state cannot act. Without your consent, the defendant cannot be subjected to punishment. If you believe that a man has been unjustly accused, you, as a group, can stand up to the state and say, "Stop!" ' The word rang out like a shot, and Gardner backed it up with a whack to the podium. ' "No, State, you may not deprive this person of his liberty . . . we will not permit it." ' He paused for a moment.

'*But*, your power is a two-edged blade,' he resumed. 'Not only do you stand between an accused and his accusers, you also stand between victims and the criminals who would do them harm. You and you alone hold the sword of retribution. You and you alone can stand up and say, "Stop!" ' He whacked the podium louder than before. ' "We will not permit you to hurt our brothers, our sisters, our fathers, our mothers . . ." ' He paused, assuring that his audience was with him before adding, ' " . . . our children." '

'Object,' King said matter-of-factly.

'Approach,' the judge responded, noticing that Gardner was already halfway there.

'What is it this time?'

'Argument, Your Honor. Melodramatic at that. Almost had me crying.'

Danforth looked at the prosecutor. 'Response?'

'Does it really need one, Judge? I haven't even gotten to the good part yet.'

'Okay. Listen to me, both of you. We can do this the hard way or the easy way. Cut each other some slack now, or I'm gonna keep this thing in court till midnight every night so we can finish the trial by the end of the year.'

'Are you suggesting that I waive legitimate objections on behalf of my client simply to accommodate the court's schedule?' King asked, pushing up to the microphone so that every word could be clearly recorded by the tape machine.

The judge looked at him as if to say, 'Wait till I get

you out on the golf course, you bastard!' but he hesitated and dropped his voice. 'No. I'm not saying that at all. I'm just asking for a little common courtesy between brothers at the bar.'

King stifled a smirk. 'So what about my objection? You gonna rule?'

The judge hunched his shoulders. 'Yeah. Overruled!'

'Thank you, Your Honor,' Gardner said, returning to the podium.

'Thank you, Judge,' King echoed.

'Continue, Counsel.'

'Very well, Your Honor,' Gardner replied. 'As I was saying, ladies and gentlemen, you hold a double-edged sword . . . The power is yours to exercise as you, in your collective wisdom, see fit. You may, of course, choose to exercise it against the state. That is your prerogative. But on the other hand, you may choose to act as vindicators of the victims in our society. In this role you can stand up to those who wreak suffering on our fellow human beings and end their reign of terror with but a single word.' He paused again, before bringing down the hammer. 'Guilty.'

'Objection.'

Judge Danforth didn't even call the lawyers up this time. He thought for a split second, then answered, 'Overruled.'

Jennifer's legal pad was crisscrossed with check marks. She had a copy of Gardner's opening statement outline, and as each point was covered, she lined it out. When he got into the evidence against T.J., she stopped. Gardner was mesmerizing the jury with the mass of proof he had against the defendant, and she didn't want to miss a word. The jurors were riveted to the prosecutor as he spoke of the knife and the bloody shirt, flight from the scene, and the Stubbins confession. And each item was punctuated by an invitation to look at the scowling defendant who, it appeared, was Gardner's best exhibit of all. King had tried to interrupt eight times, but Gardner pressed on undaunted. And now, almost an hour after beginning, he was on a roll to the finish. By the time he was nearing the close, Jennifer was convinced. Her earlier doubts had dissipated under the relentless force of Gardner's presentation. There was no question about it. Justice was guilty as hell.

'You will conclude the undeniable, when you retire to deliberate the verdict. There will be no doubt. None at all. What happened that night in Sessy's Woods will be burned into your collective consciousness, and you will rise in unison against it. With but a single word you will condemn the killer of Mikhail Anatov. You will stand shoulder to shoulder before the innocent and issue a rebuke to the defendant for all the world to hear. A single word. Vindication for a dead child, and hope for children everywhere.' He looked at Justice, T.J. scowled back. 'Guilty!'

'Object,' King said.

Danforth shook his head. 'Overruled. Are you ready for your opening statement, Mr. King?'

By now Gardner had returned to his chair. When he got there, Jennifer touched his arm. *SUPER!!* she had written across the top of her pad in large capital letters.

Gardner whispered thanks, and thumbed through his own notes to expose a blank page. If King was in usual form, this should take about two hours and give them an idea where his defense was going. Until now, it was still a mystery.

King rose and walked to the podium. 'Reserve opening, Your Honor,' he said softly, then walked back to his table and sat down.

King had suddenly changed the scenario drastically, and Gardner needed a few moments to think. He requested a recess. What the hell was King up to? He was as attuned to the importance of a dynamite opening as the prosecutor, and his normal follow-up to the state's words often left the jury gasping for breath. To hold back was unusual, to say the least. Whatever the reason, it was cause for alarm. The case had to begin in the blind, without a clue as to how the defense was going to strike back.

'Call your first witness, Mr. Lawson,' Judge Danforth said with a hint of impatience after denying Gardner's request for a recess. He was ready to move, and the trial would proceed, ready or not.

'Very well, Your Honor, the state calls Timothy Anderson to the stand.' Gardner had no choice. The case was rolling, and his momentary confusion couldn't slow it down.

The gallery stirred, and faces turned towards the rear of the courtroom. The bailiff poked his head out for a moment, then pushed the door inwards to allow a tall, thin teenager through. He had a crew cut and wore a sweater with the word PERFECTION stenciled on the front. The young man shyly threaded his way down the narrow passage between the pews, finally arriving at the swinging gate that separated the inner circle from the spectator section. Gardner ushered the witness into the lawyers' arena and then up to the elevated stand. The boy started to sit, but the prosecutor waved him up with his hand, motioning him to look at the clerk standing opposite, ready to administer the oath.

'Do you swear or affirm, under penalties of perjury, that the testimony you shall give is the truth, the whole truth, and nothing but the truth?'

The witness nodded nervously.

'You have to speak into the microphone,' the judge said.

'Uh, yes, I swear.'

'State your name and address for the record.'

'Timothy Samuel Anderson. Uh, do I got to say where I live?' The boy was scared, and when Gardner had interviewed him for trial, he was told, 'You don't have to give your exact address, just say "Rocky Valley." That's good enough.' He had obviously forgotten.

'Your Honor, may he simply recite the area where he resides?' Gardner said, attempting a rescue.

King stood up. 'No good, Your Honor.' T.J. was staring at the witness, and the boy could feel it. The message coming across was, 'Tell me where you live, you little shit, and I'm gonna stop by some day and pay you back for testifyin' against me.'

The judge looked at the witness. 'State your full address, please.'

'But, Your Honor,' Gardner pleaded.

King twitched a smile and sat down.

'Uh, nine-five-three-two Weddington Way, Rocky Valley, Maryland two-one-one-five-seven.'

T.J. hung on every word, as if he was recording the information in his brain for future reference.

The judge motioned with his hand, and the witness sat down, but he was clearly shaken. He chanced a few nervous glances at Justice. The defendant was still staring. His eyes conveyed a threat: 'One word, and you're dead.'

'You may examine, Counsel,' the judge said.

'Timothy, I'm going to ask you some questions,' Gardner began, 'and I want you to look at the jury when you give the answers.' He had to get the witness away from T.J.'s 'evil eye.' 'Do you understand? The jurors are the only ones in this courtroom who really need to hear every word you say, so speak and look directly at them, okay?'

The witness nodded unconvincingly, still canted at an angle that allowed him to see the defendant.

Gardner rose and approached the stand, grasping the boy by the shoulders and turning him to face the jury directly. 'There, that's better,' he said. T.J.'s access was totally cut off. 'Now, let's get started. Can you tell the ladies and gentlemen how old you are?'

'Seventeen.'

'And where do you go to school?'

'North County High.'

'And what grade are you in?'

'Senior.' He was settling down. The voice was smoothing out.

'And what are you studying?'

'Objection,' King interrupted. 'It's all well and good that we have an aspiring student here, but his academic record is hardly relevant.'

'Background, Your Honor,' Gardner replied quickly.

'Well, let's dispense with that and get to the foreground,' Judge Danforth said.

Several jurors giggled. Gardner stood silently at the table, then leaned down to Jennifer. 'Dan's giving us the cut-rate version,' he whispered. 'Better warn the others to be ready to get right to it.'

'Let's go, State,' the judge prompted.

'Thank you, Your Honor. Now, Timothy, I wish to direct your attention to the evening of November twenty-seventh. Can you tell the ladies and gentlemen of the jury where you were and what you were doing, say, about eleven o'clock?'

The witness looked blank. Not enough warm-up. 'Uh, you mean the night it happened?'

They had been over the testimony five times. There was only one important date. Gardner fought the urge to yell: 'Of course, the night it happened, jerk, did we ever talk about any other night?' But all he said was, 'Yes.'

'Well, me, Sue, Rimmy, and Kathy took a drive out Sessy's.'

'Can you be more specific about the people you went with?'

'Uh-huh. Sue Tredway, Rimmy Martin, Kathy Bendix.'

'And these are fellow students?'

'Leading, Your Honor,' King chimed in.

Gardner was leading, but on such a trivial point, it hardly made a difference. He was just trying to keep the ball rolling before the witness got lockjaw and forgot everything they had discussed.

'Don't lead, Mr. Lawson,' Judge Danforth said.

'Yes, Your Honor . . . Tim, can you tell the jury who these people are that you just named?'

'Uh, students.'

'And where do they go to school?'

'This again?' King was back on his feet.

'The witness can answer,' Danforth replied.

'Same as me. North County.'

'Now, Tim, tell us, why did you drive out to Sessy's Woods?'

'Just drivin' around.'

'And that is something you and your friends do often?'

'Once'nawhile.'

'And on this particular occasion, what were your intentions?'

'Same as usual. Go out Sessy's. Sit. Talk. Come back home.'

'Okay. Now, on the evening of November twenty-seventh, did you go directly out to Sessy's?'

King popped up. 'Objection. Leading again.'

'Okay,' Gardner replied. 'Can you describe your route of travel that evening?' The judge nodded, thanking the prosecutor silently for correcting his ways.

'Met out at Rimmy's. Drove Watson Road to Taylorsville Pike, then took the mine road down Sessy's.'

'Any stops?'

'Got some subs at the Fat Cow. That was it.'

'Okay. Now can you tell the jury what time you arrived at the woods?'

''Bout eleven forty-five.'

'How can you be sure?'

'Got a clock in my van; anyway, had to check the time on account's the girls.'

'Why was that?'

'Curfew. Both had to be home twelve-thirty.'

'Uh-huh.' Gardner had wanted the witness relaxed before they hit the meat of the testimony. Now he seemed ready. 'Tim, please tell the ladies and gentlemen of the jury what, if anything, unusual happened while you were out at Sessy's Woods that night.'

Suddenly Tim's face went taut. 'We found a body . . .'

'Please back up for a moment,' Gardner said. The witness was overrunning himself. 'Did any of you enter the woods?'

'Object. Leading.' King again.

The judge looked at Gardner, waiting for him to correct. 'Ask another question,' he finally directed.

'Tell the jury how you happened to find a body.' It was the best Gardner could come up with. He looked over at King. No objection visible in the breach.

'I, uh, had to go to the bathroom, so I walked into the woods, and that's when I found it.'

'And what time was that?'

'After midnight. Not exactly sure, it got crazy after that.'

'Can you describe the scene as you first saw it? Tell the jurors exactly what you saw.'

The face went taut again. 'Thought someone lost a

jacket at first. Just looked like a piece of cloth on the ground . . .'

'And?'

King rose to his feet. ' "And" isn't much of a question, Judge.'

'And, what else did you see?' Gardner added.

'Saw his hands and feet . . . then saw the blood . . .'

Gardner picked up a two-foot-by-two-foot color blowup photograph and walked it over to King's table. The defense attorney turned away from the jury so that he and his client could examine it, then he stood up. 'May we approach the bench, Your Honor?'

Danforth looked at the clock. 'Let's break for lunch,' he said, ignoring King's request. 'Reconvene at two P.M.'

One of the jurors was late returning from lunch, and Judge Danforth had already taken the bench. 'Told 'em all to be back here one forty-five, Your Honor,' the bailiff said.

The judge glared down from his perch. 'We can't hold up the world for an extra piece of pie,' he declared angrily, 'you make sure it doesn't happen again.'

The elderly bailiff looked back sheepishly, embarrassed that he had become the momentary center of attention. 'Yes, sir, Your Honor,' he replied.

'We had a request on the floor before lunch, Judge,' King said. 'Don't need the jury for that.'

'Approach the bench.'

The two sides marched up to assume the positions they had staked out earlier. On the way, King stopped off at the clerk's station and picked up the giant photograph. 'We'd object to this, Your Honor. Clearly

284

inflammatory,' he said, hefting the wide cardboard-backed picture onto the deck for the judge to view.

'We haven't offered it yet,' Gardner argued. 'He's premature in his objection.'

Danforth glanced at the photo, then looked at the defense counsel. 'He's right. This hasn't even been marked.'

'Just trying to save the court some time, Judge,' King replied. 'You know, and I know, and he knows that I'm gonna object when he tries to get this abomination into evidence, so why wait?'

The judge looked at Gardner as if to say, 'Let's get it over with.'

'The photograph is admissible under the *Roberts and Johnson* case holdings, Your Honor,' the prosecutor responded, 'discretionary with you to let even the most gruesome crime scene in . . .'

Danforth was studying the photo, not listening. He had to push it away at arm's length for proper focus. The ripples in his brow spelled trouble. 'Counsel,' he said in Gardner's direction. 'Don't you have anything smaller?'

Gardner tightened his jaw. Here we go, he thought, first act in the King and Danny Show. 'Uh, Judge, size isn't a relevant factor in admissibility, content is . . . All the cases say that.'

King picked up the baton that the court just handed him. 'It's too big. Way too big. Inflammatory. Prejudicial . . .'

The judge had already made up his mind. 'Get something a little smaller,' he said.

Gardner paused before answering. 'What are you

saying, Your Honor? You're not going to let me use this?'

Danforth put on his 'I've ruled, and that's it' face. 'That's about the size of it,' he said.

Gardner cringed inwardly at the pun. King smirked, and the judge sat there staring, not even realizing that he had just dropped an ironic joke on the state.

'Juror's here, Your Honor,' the bailiff said with a sigh of relief at 2:15.

The teams were still at the bench. 'Okay, let's get back to work,' Judge Danforth announced, pushing the blowup at the prosecutors.

Gardner touched Jennifer's arm. 'Tell Larry to dig out the originals, and get them here pronto,' he said. 'Colour and black-and-white.' Jennifer nodded and rushed out. The clock was running.

Twenty minutes later Jennifer returned breathlessly, holding an envelope, and after two tries, Gardner had succeeded in getting the court to allow him to show a photo of the victim to the witness. Unfortunately, it was no comparison of the blowup. A small, drab, colorless picture, but it conveyed the point. 'Yup, that's the boy,' the witness said, choking back the horror of remembrance. The drama was just right, and the jury got caught up in it. Gardner noticed a couple of the women on the panel starting to mist at the eyes.

Now it was King's turn to cross-examine. 'Say you went out there to sit and talk?' King stood by the jury box, one hand backward on the rail, the other tucked into his lapel.

'Yes, sir.' Gardner had schooled him to be polite in the face of the cross.

'And how long did it take you to get out there?'

''Bout twenty, twenty-five minutes.'

'Uh-huh. And you drove?'

'Yes, sir.'

'Uh-huh. And who paid for the gas?'

'Object,' Gardner said. 'What possible relevance could that have?'

King gave the judge a tart look. 'I'll demonstrate that forthwith, Your Honor.'

'Please do,' Danforth invited, implying that the objection would be sustained if he didn't. 'Answer the question, Mr. Anderson.'

'Uh, what was it? Forgot,' the boy stammered.

'Who paid for the gas?' King repeated.

'Me.'

'Uh-huh. You got a job, Mr. Anderson?'

'Part-time.'

'Uh-huh. How much do you make?'

Gardner stood up. 'Judge . . .' this was going nowhere.

Danforth shifted to the defense counsel. 'Is this your "demonstration," Mr. King?'

'Couple more questions, Judge. Cross-examination. Remember?'

'Two more. That's it.'

'Right. Thank you, sir. Now, Mr. Anderson, please tell the jury how much money you make.'

'Twenty-five a week.'

'Uh-huh. So you're not exactly raking in the bucks.'

'Nope.'

This was it. The final question. 'So tell the jury why it is that a young man of your limited means drives such a long distance away from home, expending precious personal resources, at such a late hour in the evening, on a school night, just to sit and talk?'

'Objection,' Gardner huffed, springing to his feet. 'Argumentative. Compounded. Assumption of unproven facts, and totally irrelevant.'

The judge pondered for a second, then looked at the prosecutor. 'He may answer.'

Gardner didn't need to be told why. Attacks on credibility are fair cross-examination game.

The witness looked confused. 'Why did we go? Is that the question?'

King turned to the jury. 'Tell these nice people why you really went out to Sessy's Woods that night, and this time tell the truth.'

Gardner's objection almost blew the earphones off the court reporter. 'Your Honor!' His voice cracked with righteous indignation, and his look of disdain speared King like the thrust of a blade.

'Approach,' Danforth ordered. He could tell that this was going to be messy, and he wanted to spare the jury.

King picked up a piece of paper from T.J. and strutted up to the bench. His client stayed behind.

'Gentlemen?' The judge turned to Gardner.

'Unfair question, Judge. He hasn't laid any foundation to establish that this witness is not telling the truth.'

Danforth turned to King for a response.

'This should fill in that gap,' the defense attorney said smugly, handing the judge a piece of paper.

'Would you mind if I look at that?' Gardner asked.

Protocol required a courtesy stop at opposing counsel for all exhibits. The judge nodded agreement and passed the paper to the State's Attorney without reading it.

Gardner recognized the handwriting immediately. Calvano's. Damn this kid! He said he hadn't made any statements or signed any documents. Told that to Brownie and to him, but here it was, STATEMENT OF TIMOTHY ANDERSON, delivered, sealed, and signed.

'Object to this, Your Honor,' the prosecutor said, returning the paper. A moment passed while the judge perused the statement.

'Grounds, Counsel?'

'It was procured under false pretenses, Judge.'

'Is that the standard?' Danforth was at it again.

'What do you mean, Your Honor?' Gardner asked, fearing a response he was almost sure would come.

'Does it really matter how it was obtained? I mean, isn't authenticity the only issue?'

That was the route Gardner knew could get it into evidence, and the judge was parked right in the middle.

'You're right, Judge,' King tagged along, 'just ask the witness if that's his signature.'

'Object. Object. Object,' the State's Attorney said.

The judge leaned over the bench and showed the paper to the witness.

'Did you sign that?' he whispered.

The boy's eyes flew down the page and landed on a barely legible scrawl at the bottom.

'Uh-huh,' he answered in a hushed voice.

The judge took the statement back and handed it to defense counsel. 'Proceed, Counsel,' he said.

Gardner walked back to his seat. 'He sandbagged us,' Jennifer hissed in his ear.

The prosecutor nodded. It really didn't matter who

'he' was. The judge, the defense attorney, and the witness all qualified.

'Maybe this will enable you to answer my question,' King said, handing Timothy his newly unearthed statement. It took about thirty seconds for him to complete the page. Finally, he looked up.

'Well, tell the jury why you went out to the woods that night,' King said impatiently.

'Do some smoke,' the witness said weakly, holding his head down.

'And what do you mean by smoke?' King boomed out.

The witness looked up. 'Drugs. Okay? . . . Do some drugs.'

King smiled, and turned to the jury. The message was beaming from his face. The state's witness is a liar and a drug addict. Expect more of the same.

'Did you see the paper?' Jennifer asked. Her face was drawn, her shirt wrinkled, and she didn't look professional anymore. It was 6:30 that evening, and as she looked at her boss seated at his desk, he didn't look so hot either.

Gardner could tell that something else was in the wind, other than the backslide they had just experienced getting the case launched against T. J. Justice. 'Bad news?' he asked.

She nodded listlessly and passed the county late edition across his desk.

JUSTICE CASE BEGINS AMID CONTROVERSY, the bold-faced headline announced. PROSECUTOR'S FINANCES QUESTIONED

subheaded the article. Gardner groaned. 'You bastard!'
He picked up the paper and began to read aloud:
' "County Prosecutor Gardner Lawson, who today
opened the state's case against accused child murderer
T. J. Justice, may have his hands full before it's over.
Sources have confided to the *News* that Mr. Lawson is
involved in a real estate deal currently under investigation by the Maryland Attorney General's office. It
seems that the State's Attorney has been spending a
significant amount of time at work on projects unrelated
to the taxpayer-funded job he was elected to do." '
Gardner stopped reading and looked over the top of the
page. Jennifer sat in her chair, waiting. She could see
the pain glazed on his face.

'Hatchet job,' she said gloomily, before Gardner
ducked back in.

' "It is alleged that Mr. Lawson has been using his
power and influence as a county official to win approval
for the development of Back River Canyon, a major
planned community project in the west end that he owns
in partnership. When contacted about this, Mr. Lawson
declared, 'All work on BRC was done on my own time,
and every step in the process is a matter of public documentation and public record.' Not so, sources close to
the investigation say. 'Mr. Lawson has attempted to
circumvent the system by unfairly influencing the
members of the Planning and Zoning Commission,' an
un-named source is quoted as telling the
investigators . . ." ' Gardner stopped again. 'Unnamed
source. Unnamed source . . . Source, thy name is King.'

He put the paper down and looked at Jennifer. 'How

do you feel, working for a criminal?' he said. The 'deal' involved a piece of land that he owned with three other people. They were trying to get it developed, and Gardner made some phone calls and filed some applications. His participation had been minimal and aboveboard every step of the way, but *someone* had filed a complaint and fed the story to the news media.

She smiled. 'Oh, I think I can manage to suppress my feelings.' The humor was just a salve, coating the surface. She knew the injury went deeper, and that no nursing from her could heal it. 'What now?' she asked.

'Nothing. Business as usual. Just press on.'

'What about the investigation?'

'They haven't called me to testify yet. When they deliver a summons, I'll worry about it.' Gardner could feel Jennifer's eyes probing into him through her glasses. 'You know I didn't do what they say,' he said softly.

She broke eye contact, and looked down.

'Jennifer?'

Her eyes came back to his. 'I know . . .'

'You're not just saying that to make me feel better?'

Jennifer shook her head. 'I'd *never* do that.'

Gardner smiled thinly. 'Okay. Let's forget it then . . .'

'And in the meantime we do nothing?' she asked.

'We?'

A blush hinted across her cheeks. 'You're not alone in this.'

Gardner switched to his 'boss' look. 'Yes, I am. You stay out of it.'

Jennifer leaned forward. 'Why?'

'Because I don't know how far he's going to take

this one. Dropping accusations is one thing. If he gets someone to commit perjury, that's another. And if you're involved, you could get hurt.'

'Oh,' Jennifer said mockingly. 'I didn't know you cared.'

Gardner looked into her eyes again and didn't say a word, as his mind flashed back to last year's office ski trip and the third 'run' of the night session. He and Jennifer had been paired in the lift, and decided to ski the trails together. They had taken a narrow cross-cut path that intersected Mogul Alley halfway down and connected with Lover's Lane, an intermediate-level course winding in and out of the woods.

The trees were plastered with artificial snow. Most of the guide lights had been turned out, and the bumps and berms were filled with solid ridges of ice. This made every turn an adventure, and evoked whoops and hollers from the two skiers as they side-slipped across the frozen obstacles, gaining speed along the way, threading in and out of the whitened darkness.

When they reached the other trail, Gardner plowed to a stop at the side of the narrow entrance. He had beaten Jennifer to the finish, but only by a few seconds. As he turned awkwardly to greet her, a dark figure hurtled the final rise and cut an airborne trajectory toward the prosecutor. Gardner tried to get out of the way but his skis twisted, and he was locked in place. Wham! The object hit, and Gardner went down. The other skier's momentum carried him ten feet further, but he went down too.

Jennifer arrived as Gardner struggled to get up.

'Son of a bitch out of control . . .' He was fuming, his hot words burning against the cold. 'You're gonna hurt somebody,' he yelled downslope.

Jennifer tried to help him up, but he was too tangled. 'Try to roll over this way,' she instructed.

Gardner wasn't paying attention. He was still trying to communicate with the other skier. 'Did you hear me?' he yelled.

By this time the dark one had arisen and dusted off. 'Don't yell at me, Grandpa.' His teenage face now complemented the nasal 'fuck-you' implication of his words.

Gardner wasn't ready to quit. 'You'd better get yourself under control, or—'

The kid was ready to resume his banzai charge down the trail. 'Or what?' His arrogance almost exceeded his hostility.

'Or both he and I will kick your impertinent little butt,' Jennifer cut in.

Gardner and the kid flashed identical expressions of shock. Neither had a comeback. The teenager shrugged and pushed off on his poles. Gardner raised his arm and allowed Jennifer to pull him up. 'A skier *and* a fighter?' he said. 'What on earth have I hired?'

This time Jennifer smiled. 'A damn good prosecutor, sir.'

Gardner nodded agreement, and they picked up their previous pace, weaving the trail downwards towards the lodge, where Elaine waited impatiently for her man to return from the cold.

CHAPTER 13

Bob Hamilton had told his secretary that he would be
out the rest of the morning. The newspaper still lay on
his desk, the Justice first-day article exposed. It hadn't
been cut out yet, but a portion had been heavily outlined
in red:

> On another aspect of the case, the Soviet embassy
> issued a surprise news release late yesterday declar-
> ing satisfaction with the manner in which the case
> is being handled by the county. Until now, the Sov-
> iets had remained silent, refusing to comment on
> the case at all. The brief statement read, 'The Soviet
> people wish to express to the United States govern-
> ment and the state of Maryland their hope for the
> prompt resolution of the criminal action against T.
> J. Justice, the killer of a young Soviet citizen. They
> have confidence in the process by which this man
> will be judged, and extend to those involved in
> presenting the case in court their deepest
> appreciation.'

In the margin Hamilton had inked an exclamation mark.

And now he was on another secret mission. This time within the walls of his own government.

The Senate Foreign Relations Committee maintained its own private data bank in the basement of the building where the senators' private offices were housed. As with most sensitive areas, it was off-limits to outsiders. Only those attached to the legislative committee could have access. Executive branchers were the same as anyone else; unless they were specifically cleared, they couldn't get in.

'I'm taking a hell of a risk, letting you do this,' Dean Knight told his former college roommate as he keyed the combination door lock to the archive room. 'If we get caught, my butt is as good as out.'

Hamilton patted his friend on the back. 'Don't worry, this shouldn't take long. Anyhow, I still have my pass.'

'That's no good down here. Look.' Knight flipped up his ID badge. In the order was a set of numbers, some of which were inked in. 'Two-six-five is data processing. No mark, no entry. Your pass isn't going to hack it, so don't even bother to pull it out.'

The seal was vented, and the door swung back. Both men slipped inside. The room was dark. 'This is not always active,' the legislative aide said. 'When committee is out of session it's usually quiet, unless some senator gets a wild hair and wants some data. Now, what was the info? Russian attachés?'

'Uh-huh.'

Knight led to a set of hooded consoles in the back of the room. They looked like square-headed beasts in the semidarkness. The young aide pulled the cover off of one and sat down in front. In a few seconds he had the machine on and whirring.

'Gotta let it warm up,' he said in a hushed voice. 'What the hell is this all about? You going to tell me?'

'Just a little private research.'

'On a legal case?'

'Yeah. Told you. *State v. Justice*. You know.'

'Haven't been following it . . . what's the deal?'

'Just need some info on the dead boy's father. That's all.'

Knight had turned back to the screen. 'Okay. It's up. Name?'

'Anatoly Anatov.'

'Assignment?'

'Embassy staff. D.C.'

'Okay. Let's see what we have.'

The screen went blank for a moment, then filled with figures, paging through lines and numbers for twenty seconds before finally stopping. 'Well, well, well,' Knight said.

Hamilton stared over his shoulder, trying to make some sense of the repetitious notation on the screen. 'FIAI,' followed by a date.

'What is it, Dean?' he asked. The initials didn't make any sense. Page after page of the same thing.

'It seems you aren't the only one.'

'Huh? What do you mean?'

'Someone else was sure interested in finding out about your man. Look.' He reversed the feed and paged back through the entries. They were all identical, except the dates. 'Started about a year and a half ago and stopped last August.'

'What does it stand for, Dean?'

'Oh, sorry. Thought you knew. FIAI – Freedom of Information Act Inquiry. Some citizen was trying to get committee documentation on your guy. Kept repeating the request, according to this, so they must not have sent him anything.'

'Can you tell what he was after?'

Knight keyed in for a directory, but the screen kept coming up blank. 'Wait a minute,' he said, going back to the main menu, then switching pathways. After a few more keystrokes, a new page of information appeared.

Hamilton didn't have time to scan it before his friend spoke.

'Uh-oh. I was afraid of that.' The central column of letters was now in sharp focus: INFORMATION DELETED. Over and over from top to bottom.

'So what do you have on Anatov?' the State Department officer asked.

'Nothing. Not a fucking thing,' the legislative aide replied.

Suddenly he jerked his head around, as if a thought had yanked him by the ear. 'Hold on. Hold on!' He hit some more keys, and a single entry materialized: N–25–445.

Knight jumped up and walked to the other side of the room. Hamilton followed, and soon the two men entered a shadowy room of file cabinets. Above the narrow corridor was a suspended letter N.

The lead man stopped in front of a cabinet at the end

of the line and pulled a drawer. 'Okay, okay, okay . . .'
He was leafing through files. 'All right!' he suddenly
said, pulling a thin grey folder from the pack and slap-
ping it on top of the cabinet. The light from a ceiling-
height slit window illuminated the contents as it was
opened.

'What the hell?' Knight spoke first, but Hamilton was
close behind.

'Dean?'

There were two pages stapled together. Photocopies.
The first page was an envelope. Addressed to the Soviet
Embassy, Washington, D.C. The second page was
apparently the contents. A single sheet of paper with
the numbers 21:24 typed again and again from the top
of the page to the bottom.

'Don't ask, because I don't know,' Knight finally said.

'Can I get a copy?' his friend responded.

'Are you nuts?' Question was met with question.

'We've come this far. Please?' The look on Bob Hamilton's face drew on a longtime balance sheet of favors.
It was hard to say who was ahead at this point, but it
didn't matter. Neither of them ever kept score.

'Okay. Let's do it and get the hell out of here.'

'Great. You're the best, Deaner.' Knight ran copies
on the small desktop while Hamilton pondered the discovery. The letter meant something, he was sure. It was
very bizarre: 21:24 over and over, filling the page. It
was addressed to the embassy in mid-November, less
than a week before the murder. And it was somehow
connected to Anatov.

3:10 P.M.

'Just tell what you saw, Officer,' Judge Danforth instructed, 'not what someone told you. Objection sustained.'

'Thank you, Your Honor,' Kent King said, standing for a moment longer than necessary to get his point across, looking at Gardner the way he had all day, as if to say to the jury, 'What else did you expect from a jerk who's more interested in his own wealth than he is in the truth?'

Gardner had fought back from the morning bell, totally ignoring King's jibes and innuendos. Business as usual. Calm, cool, and steady at the helm. 'Okay, Officer Christian, you know that you cannot say what another person told you. That would be hearsay. Just tell the ladies and gentlemen of the jury what you observed, all right?'

The policeman nodded.

'Fine. Now describe the body of the child as you first encountered it. Where was it? How was it situated? What, if any, injuries did it have?'

'Object.' King was up again. 'Your Honor, most law school students can ask a better question than that.'

The judge was tired of refereeing the free-for-all between counsel.

'Come up here,' he ordered sternly.

The attorneys marched up in dignified formation, brandishing self-confidence in the face of imminent public castigation.

'I've had enough of you,' he said angrily, looking at

the prosecutor. King started to smirk, but the judge turned on him like a snarling dog. 'And you too! Can't we go for a full minute without dragging each other through the mud?'

Gardner stared back at the judge with a 'but he started it' expression. 'It would have been nice if the defense had stipulated to the chain of custody of the body, Your Honor,' he said. 'I'm sure things would be running a lot smoother . . .'

King had 'don't bet on it' chiseled into his face, but he stayed silent.

'How about that, Mr. King?' the judge echoed. 'Chain of custody is always a stipulation. Why are you being so stubborn?'

Customary trial etiquette required the defense to agree that the body found at the scene was the same one autopsied, and that there had been no tampering on the way to the morgue. It was a technical point that required many witnesses and long hours of proof. Most defense attorneys never pressed the issue.

'Is it being stubborn to insist that your client receive all his rights under the law?' King fired back.

'No, of course not,' Danforth said in a conciliatory tone, 'but the chain is just a pro forma requirement. You could bend a little, give us all a break.'

King was wondering how his own objection had put him in the hot seat. It was supposed to be reserved for the prosecutor, but a switch had been pulled. 'What about my objection?' he finally ployed.

'We're talking about stipulations now,' Danforth replied. 'Are we going to have to hear from every single person who touched the body?'

King pondered the situation, then turned and whispered something to his client. There was a brief exchange of whispers before he turned back. ''Fraid so, Judge,' he said with a shrug, implying: 'I want to stipulate, but my client says no.'

'Very well, then,' the judge said with a sigh. 'Objection overruled. Proceed, gentlemen.'

Gardner and King turned simultaneously and stood face-to-face. 'You heard the man,' the prosecutor said. 'Please get out of my way, so we can *proceed*.'

At 5:30 they were still at it. Thanks to King, the painfully slow transfer of the dead child had to be chronicled from Sessy's Woods all the way to the medical examiner's office in Baltimore. 'To ensure that there were no post-mortem wounds inflicted on the body,' the theory went.

King had insisted that Gardner lay out the chain in its entirety, and the prosecutor had no choice. Without it the pathologist would not be permitted to tell the jury the little boy's 'cause of death.' To get there he had to put the ME's assistant on the stand. The one who had forgotten to close the boy's eyes.

'So what did you do after you placed the body in the van?' King asked. He was on cross-examination, standing back at the rail, posturing as usual.

'Got up with the driver.'

'Uh-huh. And who stayed back with the body?'

'No one.'

'No one stayed with the body?' King's intonation implied shock.

'No, sir. Wasn't nothing to be done . . . he was dead.'

Gardner scanned the jury for a sign of levity as a nervous chuckle surfaced somewhere in the gallery behind him. They all remained stonily immobile, as if they were hearing the eulogy of a loved one instead of the witness's testimony.

'So the body was out of your sight for a considerable period of time,' King continued.

'Just during the trip.'

'Uh-huh. And how long was that?'

The witness looked towards the ceiling, calculating the time frame with jerks of his head. 'About two, two and a half hours, I'd say.'

'And during that time the body was unattended.'

'Right.'

'So you can't really say that nothing happened to it during that time, can you?'

Gardner started to object, but stopped when he saw the foreman roll his eyes in disgust.

'Would've been real difficult, in a moving vehicle,' the ME said.

Two more front-row jurors mirrored the foreman's expression, and gave King a look that screamed, 'Satisfied now, creep?' Gardner smiled inwardly, and stayed put. The defense attorney was doing just fine. No need to interrupt.

'So you went direct from the woods to the ME's office.'

'Yep.'

' "Yes," sounds better,' Judge Danforth corrected from the bench.

'Uh, yes. Sorry, Your Honor,' the witness replied.

'Didn't make any stops?'

'Nope. Uh . . . no, sir.'

'Sure about that?'

King walked back to his table and picked up a piece of paper, then headed for the witness stand. When he got adjacent to Gardner he paused. 'Did you make any stops on the way to Baltimore, yes or no?'

'Don't think so.'

King handed Gardner the piece of paper. It was the communications log for November 28. 'Stop: Frederick Truck-Inn 8:40 A.M.–9.20 A.M.,' it said. The ME had taken a breakfast break on the way to Baltimore. The body was unattended for over forty minutes. In anyone's language the meaning was the same. The chain had been broken. And someone inside the investigation had helped break it.

Larry Gray and Officer Charlie Barnes sat in the State's Attorney's conference room waiting for Gardner. It was 9:00 P.M. and the harsh overhead light contrasted with the blackness beyond the windows.

'Is he upset with me?' the younger policeman asked.

'Not really . . . he's under a lot of pressure,' the senior man replied. 'I thought you knew better than to cooperate with King.'

'I didn't tell that investigator anything.'

'Are you certain about that?'

'Yeah, I'm certain.'

'Okay. Why don't we go over it, to be sure. What did he ask you?'

Barnes took a deep breath. 'Wanted to know about the kid. Billie Harris. Asked to see my report.'

'Did you show it to him?'

'No, sir.'

'You're certain?'

Barnes pulled in another chestful of air. 'Positive.'

'Okay. What else did he want to know?'

'Asked about the duty schedule. What squad was on nights. Who was off, stuff like that.'

'And did you answer?'

The young officer suddenly looked guilty, as if in retrospect something that seemed right at the time turned out to be a mistake.

'You did give information,' Larry Gray said, in response to his own question.

'But it wasn't about the case,' Barnes argued, 'only personnel stuff.'

Larry tried to hold back his anger, but two years of dealing with the department's problem child had pushed him to the limit. 'You idiot! Don't you know he set you up?' he snapped.

Barnes sat in silence, used to the woodshed his superiors constantly dragged him to.

'You didn't, by any chance, show him any personnel paperwork, did you?'

The young officer shook his head. 'No. Absolutely not.'

Gray's eyes revealed no hint of forgiveness. 'Okay. Exactly what did you tell him?'

Barnes fidgeted with a pencil. 'Who on my squad was working crime scene, and who was on patrol.'

'What else?'

'Also wanted to know who was off duty.'

'And you told him, I presume?'

'Uh-huh.'

Larry stopped the interrogation and opened a file. After scanning the contents, he flipped it shut. 'Did you bring your notes from the twenty-seventh and twenty-eighth?'

'Got 'em right here. Brought the whole week.'

'Good. Now let's go through them.'

Barnes started to unfold a sheaf of notepaper, then stopped. 'Why take notes, sir? I mean, what's so important about my notes?'

Larry's subsided anger gushed up again. 'Because the State's Attorney doesn't want any more goddamn surprises!' he said. 'He's got to know what you gave them so he can be ready for it.'

Gardner walked in suddenly, as Barnes was laying out his notes on the conference table. He did not look well. His eyes were glazed, and his shoulders were bent as though he were dragging Anderson Mountain around on his back. He mumbled a hello and slid into a chair next to Larry Gray.

'Sorry,' Barnes said.

The State's Attorney knew Calvano had hoodwinked the young officer. King had all but bragged about it when the witness lineup for the next few days was revealed to the judge after court.

'Barnes?' the defense attorney had mocked. 'He's your witness? Gee, I thought he was mine.'

'That's not necessary,' Gardner said softly in answer

306

to the officer's apology. 'Water over the Weston Dam. What we need now is some damage control . . . in advance.'

'I'm still sorry,' Barnes said. 'It won't happen again.'

The notes were arranged by date. November 24 through November 30.

Gardner picked up a page. 'What is all this stuff, Charlie?'

The officer took the paper from the prosecutor's hand. 'Observations,' he replied after deciphering the messy, illogical scramble of letters and numbers on the lined sheet.

'Observations?'

'Uh-huh. What I see on patrol that catches my attention.'

'So these aren't notes from specific calls.'

'No, sir. Not these. Here's a set of interview notes.' Barnes handed Gardner another page. They both looked the same.

'How can you tell one from the other?' the State's Attorney inquired.

'Just the way it's written. Here, look.' The officer indicated a notation. STPD FR UNATT VH 2320 OH 143-CAS MNCS R NSA. 'That's an observation.'

'You mind translating?' Gardner asked.

'Sure. Stopped for unattended vehicle. Eleven-twenty P.M. Ohio tag one-four-three-CAS. Minecastle Road. No sign of activity.'

'What was that all about?'

'Nothing. Just a parked car in the boonies. Sometimes they're abandoned, so we have to get a tow. I note 'em and if they're still there a couple of days later, call it in . . . see? Didn't even have to follow it up.' He pointed to another entry. 0015 MNCS VH CLR. 'By quarter past midnight, the car was gone, so that was the end of that.'

'Charlie, who have you shown these to?'

Larry silently dared the young officer to name someone.

'Nobody, sir. I promise.'

'What's on your mind, Gard?' Gray asked thoughtfully.

'Look what he's got here. A virtual play-by-play of county activities on the night of the murder. If King gets this, he'll have everyone who stopped to take a piss within fifty miles of the crime scene branded as a suspect.' Gardner looked at Barnes.

'What do you want me to do?' the officer asked.

'King probably has a lot of information already. Calvano may be a jerk, but he's a pretty good investigator. Do me a favor. Tonight, before you go to bed, translate all of your notes into plain English for me, and leave it with my secretary first thing tomorrow.'

'Yes, sir.'

'And Charlie, not a word to anyone. I mean it.'

Barnes nodded. 'Yes, sir. Don't worry.' The hour of redemption was at hand.

The police officers left, and Gardner tidied his desk, preparing to shut down for the night. It had been a long day, and tomorrow promised to be even longer.

As he was about to turn off the light, his phone rang.

Gardner picked it up hurriedly, anticipating another problem.

'Working late again?' It was Elaine.

'Uh, yeah,' Gardner said flatly. 'Trial's still rolling on.'

There was a brief pause. 'You working alone?'

The emphasis on *alone* implied an accusation.

'Yeah,' Gardner said, 'as a matter of fact, I am.' His voice was irritated.

'Don't get huffy. I just wanted to know if you could use some company.'

Gardner's mind flashed an image of Elaine twisting sensuously in a rumpled bed, then jumped forward to a cold, empty aftermath. 'Uh, don't think so. Not tonight . . .'

'You got *other* plans?' The accusatory tone was back.

'No! I can't do it. That's all,' he said flatly.

'Okay!'

'One of these days, Elaine, we've got to talk,' Gardner said solemnly.

'Jeez! You sound so serious!' Elaine responded. 'Why don't you call *me* when you're in a better mood.' Then she hung up before Gardner could answer, as if she anticipated an imminent kiss-off and didn't want to hear it.

As he left the darkened office, Gardner's mind went back to the case. He had strategy to plan and tactical decisions to make. And there was no place in those thoughts for Elaine.

At 11:45 Charlie Barnes was still pecking out his

translation on the small manual typewriter his mother had given to him in high school. It was slow going. Hard to believe how many 'pop-ups' there were out there, he mused to himself. Little things that ordinary citizens missed, but that a 'trained observer' noted in passing, just in case they became important later. License tags. Hitchhiker identifications. The number of crates stacked on the porch of Jenson's Grocery. You never knew when the information might come in handy.

'OH one-four-three-CAS,' he said out loud when he came to the 'example' he had shown to the prosecutor earlier. 'One-four-three-CAS,' he repeated. Something about the combination of numbers and letters suddenly seemed familiar. There were so many tag notations in his book that they all ran together. One was as nondescript as any other. But for some reason, this was different, and the out-of-state plate didn't explain it. Pennsylvania, West Virginia, and Ohio tags saturated the area on a daily basis. He had as many of them peppering his notes as he did Marylanders. No. There was some other reason that this particular tag rang a bell in his brain. The problem was, he couldn't quite get it into focus.

Just then there was a tap at the door to his apartment. Barnes glanced at the clock and got up. 'Yeah?' he said through the crack.

'Open up, Charlie,' a deep voice replied.

The officer peeked through the spy-hole. 'Shit,' he said to himself. It was Calvano.

'Let me in, Officer Barnes, we've got to talk.'

'It's too late. Got to do it another time.'

'You were out all night, pal. Sorry for the inconvenience, but this has got to be done now.'

'Can't.'

There was a brief silence on the other side, then Calvano spoke again. 'Listen to me, Barnes, if you want to keep your job, you better open this goddamn door.'

That one came out of left field. 'What do you mean?' the officer said.

'It means that I have a videotape of you doing some pretty interesting things during duty hours.'

Barnes froze. He was as straight as any guy on the force, but he was human. The snooze breaks and occasional drop-bys at his girlfriend's were all part of a normal ten-hour shift. Hell, everybody did it.

But, the officer thought, everybody wasn't Charlie Barnes, permanent occupant of the department K–9 facility. They'd jump at the chance to dismiss him for dereliction of duty. He glanced at the notes.

'Well?' Calvano growled. 'We gonna talk? Maybe you can convince me to erase what I got, that is, if you have something to trade.'

Barnes tried to think. The prosecutor said that King probably already had most of the information. That could be the explanation if some of the material started coming out in court. What other choice did he really have? Police work was his life. He couldn't exist without it. 'Okay, okay,' he said sadly. Then, without making any attempt to hide the papers on the table, he turned the lock and slowly opened the door.

April 19
10:05 A.M.

'Call your next witness, Mr. Lawson.' There was a touch of relief in Judge Danforth's voice. At last, some testimony of substance, it seemed to say. Three days of monotony, tracking the dead child's slow progress toward the cold stainless steel slab in the ME's basement was enough. Now it was time to get on with the show.

'Call Agent Harvey, Your Honor.' Gardner had exchanged his blue pinstripes for charcoal gray, signaling that today there would be a fresh start.

'State your name and duty station for the record, please,' the clerk said in her usual monotone.

All eyes turned to the witness. 'Peter Harvey. Special agent, FBI, currently assigned to the western Maryland branch, Special Weapons REACT team.' He looked the part. Blue eyes, razor-cut hair, and a body like a steel robot.

'You may examine, Counsel,' the judge said. He had an expression of resignation on his face as if he had finally accepted the fact that his courtroom had turned into a pit bull arena, and there wasn't a damn thing he could do about it.

'Thank you, Judge,' Gardner replied, rising from his table and walking over to King's favorite spot against the rail. 'Please tell the jury the meaning of REACT, Agent Harvey.'

'It's an acronym for Rapid Emergency and Counter-Terrorism.'

'And how long have you been a member?'

'I've been with the bureau for seven years, and with the team for two.'

'Uh-huh.' Gardner even sounded like King, arching his back in the same irritating manner as his opponent. 'And how long have you been assigned to the western Maryland area?'

'Four years.'

'We'll stipulate that this witness is an FBI agent with several years' experience, Your Honor,' King said, snapping to his feet. 'Do we have to hear his whole life story?'

Gardner looked at the defense attorney, then at the judge.

Danforth was obviously counting to ten.

'We'll accept the stipulation, if that will help,' the prosecutor said. 'No sense in wasting time on preliminaries.'

The judge looked as though he wanted to come down and give Gardner a kiss.

King just smiled sardonically. 'Glad to see the State's Attorney has come to his senses,' he said.

Gardner smiled back. 'With such a great instructor, how could I lose?'

'Okay, okay.' Danforth took control. 'Now that the love-in is over, maybe we can get on with it.' There were a few snickers, but most people in the courtroom kept quiet. They could clearly see what was going on between the two men, and the judge's sarcasm simply confirmed it.

'Now, Agent Harvey, I direct your attention to the

evening of November twenty-seventh,' Gardner resumed. 'Were you on duty?'

'No, sir, I was at home.'

'Well, did there come a time when something happened to change that?'

'Yes, sir. About two A.M. my beeper went off.'

'And what did that signify?'

'Some kind of emergency. Report to bureau headquarters immediately.'

'And did you respond?'

'Yes, sir. Got there about two-twenty.'

Gardner was back at the rail, posing King-like for the jury.

'When you got to headquarters, what happened?'

'They told me—'

'Sorry, Your Honor,' King said politely. 'Have to object to that. Hearsay.'

Danforth looked at the prosecutor. 'He's about to say what someone told him, Mr. Lawson . . .'

'Not offering it for truth, Judge,' Gardner interposed, 'just to show the information upon which later action was based.'

The judge nodded and turned to the jury. 'The witness can say what someone else told him for the limited purpose of explaining why he acted in a certain way. You are not, repeat not, to take what was said as the truth. Do you all understand that?'

The jurors looked to their foreman. 'Yes, Your Honor, we certainly do,' he said with authority.

'Very well,' Danforth replied, 'the witness may continue.'

Gardner looked at King. He and Justice were whispering. King said something, and T.J. smiled.

'Mr. Lawson, the objection has been overruled. Let's get on with it,' the judge said, suddenly aware of the lull.

'Okay.' Gardner picked up the flow again. 'What happened at headquarters? What information did you receive there?'

'They got the team assembled and briefed us on the murder of the Russian boy . . .'

'Uh-huh . . .' Gardner almost had King's mannerism down pat.

'. . . said there was a suspect out at Hodges and that we were needed to effectuate the arrest.'

'Uh-huh . . .'

'That "uh-huh" is annoying, Your Honor,' King said from his seat.

Gardner looked back and smiled. The judge ignored it.

'After you received the briefing, what did you do?'

'Got in the van and headed out.'

'Uh-huh . . .' Gardner repeated. 'And what armaments were you carrying?' Gardner gave another look to the defense table. The last question was clearly objectionable and he knew it. King had to object, or the jury would be left with the impression Gardner was trying to create: Justice is so dangerous that it takes a squad of men and heavy firepower to bring him down. The facts were true, but the question was not really relevant. If objected to, it would be sustained. Gardner tensed for the interruption, but it did not come. King just sat there, waiting . . .

'Nine-millimeter Beretta automatics. Mac-ten

submachine guns. Smoke canisters, tear gas grenades, and twelve-gauge pump-action shotguns,' the witness said, as the jury sat wide-eyed soaking up every word.

'Agent Harvey.' Twenty-five minutes later, Gardner was still on direct. 'I ask you to look at what has been marked for identification as state's exhibits ten-A and ten-B.' He handed the witness two serrated-edged knives, each tagged with a red sticker. 'Can you tell the jury what these are?'

'Yes, sir. These items were recovered in unit fifteen of the Hide-Away Motel. Found when we conducted the search operation.'

'Where, specifically, in the unit were they located?'

'In the bathroom. On top of the basin.'

'And when you first saw the knives, what was their condition?'

'Wet, like they'd been washed recently.'

'Objection!' King leapt to his feet. 'Conclusion, Your Honor.'

Judge Danforth looked at the jury. 'The witness can tell what he saw, but he may not draw conclusions from his observations. That is a matter of argument, and ultimately, a matter for you and you alone to resolve. Objection sustained.'

Gardner watched the jurors as the judge explained his rationale for sustaining the objection. Their minds were still on the witness's response. 'Wet . . .' Their curiosity had been piqued, and the seed had been planted. No matter that there was an objection. The point had been made. T.J. obviously washed the knives to clean off the blood. 'Thank you, Your Honor,' the prosecutor said. 'Now, you say they were wet when you first saw them?' He emphasized the word 'wet.'

'Yes, sir.'

'How wet?'

'Water droplets on the blades. Underside of the handles still damp.'

'Okay. What did you do with the knives after you found them?'

'Put them into marked evidence containers.'

'Okay. And what was the purpose of that?'

'To preserve them for later forensic examination.'

'And, to the best of your knowledge, was a forensic examination ever performed?' Gardner looked at King. He had just asked a question soliciting hearsay. Objection should be imminent.

King leaned back in his seat and stared at the witness as if to say, 'He asked you a question, dummy. Aren't you going to answer?'

'Yes. The FBI laboratory in Washington, D.C., did the tests.' Gardner was surprised that King let that one go. The next question was sure to bring him up with a bang. 'And what, if any, conclusions was the lab able to come to with respect to the examination?'

The defense side was eerily silent.

'They couldn't find anything,' the agent replied.

Gardner stood and walked to the witness stand. He picked up the knives and scrutinized them carefully, drawing the jury's attention to the focal point of the sharp blades in his hand. King had let him go this far, so why not go all the way?

'You say the lab was unable to find anything. What, under normal circumstances, would they be looking for?'

'Fingerprints. Foreign materials. Bloodstains.'

King was still as mute as a rock formation.

'Nothing on the knives?' Gardner continued.

'No, sir. They were wiped clean.'

At 10:50 it was King's turn with the FBI agent. He rose dramatically from his chair and strolled over to a new spot he had picked out against the jury box railing, intentionally avoiding the old one as if it had been contaminated by the prosecutor.

'Agent Harvey? Good morning.' The tone was sugary.

'Good morning, sir.'

'Now, you say you found some knives at the Hide-Away Motel.'

'Yes, sir.'

'Anything particularly unusual about those knives?'

'Sir?'

'What kind of knives are they?'

'I believe they are steak knives, Mr. King.'

'Steak knives. Ordinary everyday steak knives. The kind that most people have in their homes?'

Gardner saw immediately where King was headed. 'Objection, Judge. Argumentative, and calls for conclusion.'

The defense attorney turned as if to say, 'Hey! I didn't object to your illegal questions,' but Danforth intervened. 'This is cross, Mr. Lawson . . . witness may answer.'

'Uh, I guess they may be pretty common,' the agent

said. 'Can't really say for sure.'

'But you can only say that these particular knives are designed for one and only one purpose, the preparation of food.'

That didn't sound right to Gardner either, but he decided to let it pass. Jennifer pushed over her pad. *No way!* it said.

'Yes. I believe that would be a correct statement.'

King was settling into his recent acquisition of jury rail, arms crossed, back arched, relaxed and casual. 'And would you not also say that the cleaning of such items, which have been used in preparing food, is not at all unusual?'

'Yes. I could say that.'

'Okay. Now, Agent Harvey, when you searched the room, did you happen to find any food-stuffs?'

The witness looked at Gardner apologetically. 'Yes, sir. We did.'

'In fact, the place was a mess. Boxes, cans, and discarded wrappers everywhere. Isn't that right?'

'It was pretty messed up, yes.'

'With the remnants of bygone meals?'

'Yes, sir.'

King had made his point. Now he shifted gears. 'Agent, when you searched unit fifteen, where was my client?'

'I don't know, sir.'

'You don't know?' King's voice pitched up with indignation. 'You mean he was not in the room?'

'No, sir.'

'Well, when did you see him that night?' King turned toward the jury.

'Never, sir. First time I ever saw the gentleman was today.'

When Gardner and Jennifer returned from court, Krysta Collins was sitting in the waiting room. She was immaculately put together, as usual, and stood up when the two prosecutors came through the door.

'Miss Collins . . .' Gardner nodded a polite greeting.

Krysta put out her hand. 'Hello again.'

'Uh, this is Jennifer Munday,' he said, rapidly transferring her hand to his assistant's.

'Hi,' Jennifer said casually.

Krysta paused for the introduction, then seized on Gardner. 'Can I see you?' The look on her face was serious but nonthreatening.

Gardner squinted. 'Uh, we just got out of court . . .'

'Please,' she pleaded. 'It won't take long. I promise.'

Gardner looked at Jennifer. It was obvious that she was not to be included.

'I've gotta run tomorrow's witness schedule,' Jennifer said smoothly, allowing Gardner the option of receiving or dismissing the reporter. Then she smiled a good-bye and turned toward her office.

Gardner hesitated, then extended his arm in a lead-the-way gesture. 'Okay, you can come back, but you'll have to make it quick.'

Gardner piled his case file on the desk and sat down. Krysta took up her former position in Jennifer's chair.

'Now, what's up?' he said.

'Have you reconsidered my previous request?' she asked, managing a halfway-sincere smile.

Gardner frowned. It was the same old story. 'No, not really,' he said solemnly. 'Have you?'

Her expression remained fixed, the smile frozen. She picked up her black leather purse and placed it on her lap. 'Why, yes, I have.' Gardner squinted again, unsure of what was happening. Krysta pulled a videocassette out of her purse and handed it across the desk. 'You were right. T.J. said a lot more in the interview than we put on the air.'

Gardner was speechless. He took the tape and flipped it over in his hand. The interview date and caption were printed on the cover.

'Why are you doing this?' he finally said.

Krysta's smile was still there. 'I believe I have the prerogative—'

'But I'm still not doing the profile for you,' Gardner interrupted.

'I know. I never expected it.'

'Then why—'

Krysta pulled herself up in the seat. 'That's not important.'

Gardner looked at the tape again. 'Did you get authorization to give me this?'

She didn't answer, and the obvious inference was 'no.'

'So your buddy King is going to blow when he finds out.'

Her face drew taut. 'I told you before, there's nothing going on in that department.'

'So I still don't get it,' Gardner said. 'Why the change of heart?'

She stood up. 'Just look at the tape. Maybe you can figure it out.'

Gardner wanted to pursue it, but she was in a hurry to leave, so he didn't stop her.

After she was gone, Gardner remained standing. This was certainly unexpected. A giveaway at a time when he really needed it. But there was something too pat about the way it went down. King not knowing didn't sound right. He always called the shots, and it was not in his character to let something like this slip by. Somehow he was involved. And that fact alone took away any incentive to cheer.

Gardner walked over to his bookcase and removed the dust cover from the office VCR monitor. They used the unit for legal education courses and reviewing police videos of crime scenes. He popped the tape into the cassette carriage and poked the play button, leaning back against his desk as the short scene unfolded. There were questions and answers and an unsolicited comment from Justice. That was it. No startling revelations. No dynamite contradictions he could use on cross-examination. It was standard defendant pap. Self-serving garbage. Gardner sighed, crossed his arms, and waited for the fade-out. He rewound the tape, ejected it, and slipped it into its case. 'I'll say one thing for you, T.J.,' Gardner said as he opened the bottom drawer of his desk. 'You are one hell of a liar!' He threw the tape into a pile of outdated papers and kicked the drawer shut with his foot. Then he hustled out to find Jennifer. They had tomorrow's witness lineup to discuss, and time was short.

*　*　*

Brownie picked up the phone and punched in eleven numbers. 'Listing for Harley Smith, please.' He was on the trail of the alibi witness whose name Gardner had slipped him two weeks ago. The only problem was, there was no address to go with it. 'Can't give what I don't got,' Gardner had said, quoting Kent King's response to the same demand. Then he asked Brownie to root the man out.

A name without an address and accompanying ID numbers made the task almost impossible. Maryland didn't seem to have such a resident. Neither did Virginia, D.C., or Delaware. But Brownie persisted, and finally dug up a reference to the name in an old Martinsburg, West Virginia, phone book. When he tried the number, it was no longer in service. Maybe it had been changed.

'What city?' The male voice on the other end sounded tired.

'Martinsburg.'

'Address?'

'Twenty-two-fourteen East Avenue.'

'Hold on please. Checking.'

The line buzzed as the computer searched. Brownie got his pen ready and yawned. It was after five and fatigue was creeping up on him.

'No such listing.'

'You sure?'

'For the name Charley Smith, twenty-two-fourteen East Avenue, Martinsburg. No listing.'

Browning drew a large capital *H* on his pad, and circled it. 'That's Harley, with an "H" as in "Hungry," ' he said, wishing he had a handful of beef barbecue squeezing through his fingers.

'Harley Smith. Same address?'

'Yes. Same.'

'Hold on, please. Checking . . . No. No such listing.'

'You sure about that?'

'Yes. No listing for the name you gave me.'

Brownie backed off for a moment, trying to hit a new angle.

'Can you do me a favor?' he finally said.

'You have another number request, sir?' The voice was telling him that if he didn't, his time was up.

'Look. I'm a police officer from Maryland. It's very important that I locate this person. We have a murder case going on over here, and Mr. Smith may be a witness . . .'

'I just told you he doesn't have a phone.'

'Look. You got a crisscross directory there, right?'

'We cannot give out that information, sir.'

'I told you, I'm a policeman. Please run the crisscross for the address I just gave you. The phone may be listed to someone else.'

'Sorry. Our rules do not allow us to divulge that information.'

Brownie was getting steamed. 'Fuck the rules!' he yelled. 'I just told you we got a murder case here.'

'No need to use profanity,' the voice replied.

'Sorry,' Brownie said in a quieter voice. 'Please, can you help me?'

There was no answer. The voice had silently severed the connection.

He was trying to save time, but it wasn't to be. Now he was stuck. A call to the cops in West Virginia might come back to haunt him, especially if the chief found out. No . . . Now he had no choice. After duty hours tomorrow, he'd have to take a drive out west.

The court day had ended, and Gardner was alone in his bed. It was past midnight, and he had finally fallen asleep. He was sleeping, but not at rest. The battle in courtroom 1 was taking its toll internally. The hidden war was inflicting wounds that bled into the subdural lining of his brain, and always in the background was the fear . . .

His dream started peacefully, as always. A surface shot, without a hint of trouble. The wind was barely lifting the flag from the short staff on the stern of the *Mindy*. Curling and uncurling with the shifting breeze, it seemed to be sending him a message, a hypnotic call to enter the blue-green expanse that undulated like liquid marble beneath its tattered furl. The sun, above and behind Carole's head, turned her dark curls into a shimmering aurora of auburn, transforming her into the silhouette of an ancient siren, urging him to follow her into the sea.

And then they were in the water, treading at the surface, adjusting hoses and weights, pausing briefly in the transparency of the first ten feet, before upending and kicking downward into the diffused curtains of penetrating light that hung from above and then faded into nothingness thousands of feet below.

Down. Down. The blend of illumination and shadow thickened into total obscurity at one hundred feet, and ate the spearing beam from the lamp that was to guide them into the unknown.

And all the time, the tinny voice of the regulator, like air sucked through clenched teeth, rasping at intake and then exploding at exhaust, sending a silver legion of bubbles racing toward the unseen sky.

And at every click of the depth gauge, every new layer to the blanket of ocean above . . . the deepening terror . . .

The panic usually woke Gardner up. The memory of leaving Carole behind as he blasted upward from the darkness. The shame of his cowardice under fire. The loss of control. The disgrace.

Tonight he couldn't get out. He was trapped in the dream, and the exhaustion of his body and soul wouldn't let him escape. He was caught inside the shipwreck. Swimming frantically in circles, searching for an exit, gulping air like a suffocating fish. Around and around, banging into bulkheads and steel beams . . . Then the flashlight quit, and the terror compounded. Shaking the rubber cylinder like a madman, he tried to get the light back on. Suddenly he felt a soft contact in the darkness, and he recoiled in horror, banging the flashlight against his own hand in a hysterical effort to relight it. The beam flickered, and he stifled a scream as the body of Mikhail Anatov washed against his face plate and draped across his arms in a listless embrace.

At the same time as Gardner struggled in his dream, Bob Hamilton was ensconced at his kitchen table. As usual, his materials were spread out in neat piles. The only difference was, this time his 'personal' T. J. Justice file was larger than the official one.

He was looking at the postmark of the letter that Dean had found in the Foreign Relations Committee archives. The date was very clear: November 16. The posting location wasn't. It had been overstamped several times in an enthusiastic clerk's attempt to cancel. He studied it with a magnifier. The letters were so garbled it was impossible to make out. He turned it around for a different perspective. No use. It wasn't legible. The only letter partially discernible was the first. It looked like an *O*.

Hamilton put down the envelope copy and picked up the other sheet. The numbers were laid out in rows and columns. 'Twenty-one twenty-four,' he said aloud. 'Twenty-one twenty-four,' he repeated. At first he had thought it might be a time reference. In the military, the twenty-four-hour clock reading of 21:24 translates to 9:24 P.M. According to the news reports, the Russian boy was killed sometime between 6:00 P.M. and midnight. That would place 21:24 directly in the middle.

That had been his initial theory, but the more he thought about it, the less it made sense. Why on earth would someone forecast the exact time of a murder? And how could he possibly know that the child would be available to him at that specific hour? The time-number correlation had to be a coincidence, Hamilton finally decided. 21:24 must refer to something else.

He leaned forward and put his face in his hand, repeating 'Twenty-one twenty-four' over and over.

Suddenly he sat upright, as if the chant had cleared his inner vision. He got up and went to a tall multilevel bookcase in the living room, running his finger along the lip of each wooden shelf until he reached the selection he was looking for. Then he walked back to the kitchen and sat down at the table, laying the book open to the first section. He scanned it, then jumped to the next block of text. 'Holy shit,' he said when he saw the inscription under the heading. There were the numbers, and beyond, the meaning of it all. 'Exodus. Chapter twenty-one, verse twenty-four,' he read aloud. ' "Eye for eye, tooth for tooth . . ." '

CHAPTER 14

April 22
2:30 P.M.

The persistent winds of spring had finally warmed enough to make an afternoon in the meadow of Appalachian Park a worthwhile alternative to the shopping mall. Gardner watched as Granville in jeans and a red crew-neck sweater raced to the stream that bisected the lush greenery of the park.

'Could be a few salamanders still hiding in there,' he had told his son, knowing that the boy didn't need any prompting. The slick-skinned lizards had squirted through his small fingers before, and he was hooked.

Gardner measured his own steps with painful strides, keeping sight of the blond head bouncing down the pathway. The weekend had intervened just in time. Gardner was running out of reserves in his comeback arsenal, King kept chipping and chipping away, and at this point it was hard to tell what was sticking with the jury and what was being obscured behind the steam that erupted each time the defense threw water on a state's witness. The prosecutor needed to rest his brain, and on this Saturday afternoon, the promise of peace lay in the lee of a mountain brook.

'Daddy!' Granville had located a possible salamander sanctuary, a set of three black humpbacked rocks bared at a bend in the narrow streambed.

'Lift it up,' Gardner instructed with an approving nod.

'You help me,' the boy answered.

'You can do it, son. Go ahead.'

Granville looked at his father as if to say, 'You always did it before.' He was used to an adult hand finding a notch under the edge of the stone.

'Put your fingers here,' Gardner instructed. 'Now lift!'

The boy followed his father's directions, and the rock sucked out of the mud with a slurp, then clacked over into the rushing water. For a second the hole was cloudy with stirred-up bottom, then it cleared. Two three-inch salamanders clung to the indentation as if they were still sheltered in the safety of darkness under the stone.

Granville looked at Gardner. His eyes were wide with excitement and wonder, as if he had never seen such a creature before.

'Well?' his father prompted.

The boy's hands were in and out in an instant. Giggling with joy, he raised them up so Gardner could see. A tiny bullet head peeked out of each dripping fist, one speckled black, the other orange.

'Neat!' Gardner exclaimed. 'What are you going to do with them?'

Granville looked at the exposed heads, and opened each palm slightly for a close inspection. He then bent down and flattened out his hands all the way, allowing the two captives to slither off his fingers and disappear into the flow. 'Gonna let them go back to their mother,' he said.

Gardner looked at his son standing empty-handed on the banks of the stream. The breeze carried the scent of fruit blossoms, and the sun felt like a down blanket across his shoulders. He opened his arms, and the boy entered, trying as best he could to hug as hard as his daddy. And Gardner felt the old ache of loss tighten in his chest.

Things had been okay after Granville came along. It appeared that their lives would be forever entwined. The three of them, happy in an old house overlooking the most beautiful valley in the state.

But when Carole and Gardner returned to Watson Road after the disaster in the Caribbean, he noticed a change. The sparkling eyes that had signaled her love were gone. There had been times, especially in the pre-Granville days when the pregnancy was so elusive, that the shiny glints of affection had faded. But they had always come back. This time was different.

Gardner hated to let things ride. When harsh words came between them he was anxious to clear the air and put the unpleasantness to rest. Carole was just the opposite. She could nurse a festering dispute for days, weeks, and even months. She could carry it with her like a grenade and, whenever the mood struck, hurl it with all its original explosive fury.

After Cayman, it was different. Gardner tried to get

through the barrier, but she switched her tactics. Suddenly she had errands to run. She had projects outside of the home. She had no time for her husband.

Gardner tried some new approaches of his own. Wit. Attentiveness. Gifts. Flowers.

She still didn't respond.

Then, two months after they had returned, she began going to Baltimore.

At first she took Granville, and spent the day in the city, returning late at night. Gardner usually had to retrieve his son from the car, slumbering deeply in the baby seat, not yet able to talk coherently, incapable of telling his father where they had been. And Carole was tight-lipped about the trips also.

'So, what did you do all day?' Gardner asked.

'Zoo,' she replied.

'All day?'

'Uh-huh.'

'From dawn to dusk at the zoo?'

No answer.

'Did you have lunch?'

'Of course.'

'Where?'

'Zoo.'

It was no use. She wouldn't let Gardner back in, and the harder he tried, the more she stonewalled.

Then her trips to the city became solo. She left Granville with a baby-sitter and blasted down the highway before the sun came up. When she returned fifteen hours later, Gardner did not bother to ask her about her day. He knew she had a new agenda. And he knew that he was not a part of it.

Finally the trips became overnighters. Granville asked for his mommy, and she wasn't there. Gardner rocked his son and soothed his anxiety. 'Mom will be here soon,' he said, but inside he knew that she was never coming back to the life they had before he'd lost her in the silence of the sea.

April 24
10:30 A.M.

'State your name for the record, please,' the clerk said from her post behind the barrier that separated court personnel from the combatants in the pit.

'Dr. Peter Stinson, Assistant Medical Examiner, Maryland State Pathologist's Office.'

'You may examine, Counsel.' Judge Danforth looked fresh and rested, as though he had just gotten in thirty-six holes of golf.

'Thank you, Your Honor,' Gardner replied. The weekend's serenity was suddenly replaced by the reality of a clean-shaven witness in a tan sports jacket.

'Doctor, can you please tell the ladies and gentlemen of the jury your educational background and professional experience?'

The prosecutor glanced at the defense attorney. He had stipulated to the FBI agent's qualifications, maybe he would do the same here.

'Graduated from the University of Virginia with a degree in biochemistry, medical school at Johns Hopkins, internship at Union Memorial Hospital . . .' King was taking detailed notes. No sign of an objection.

'Residency at Union Memorial for two years, then signed on at the ME's office,' the witness continued. 'Been there for the past three years.'

'Okay,' Gardner said, shifting his gaze toward King again. 'Have you been board certified to practice medicine in this state?'

King's head was still down.

'Yes, sir.'

'And, during the course of your tenure at the pathologist's office, how many autopsies have you had the occasion to perform?'

The witness reviewed a gallery of dead faces in his mind. 'About two hundred,' he said solemnly.

'And have you, during the period you worked for the ME's office, ever been qualified as an expert witness in a court of law?'

'Yes, sir. Many times.'

Gardner had completed his qualification patter. 'Move the witness as an expert, Your Honor,' he said.

Judge Danforth turned to King expectantly. 'Stipulation, Counsel?'

'No, Judge, we would request cross-examination on qualifications.'

Danforth didn't bother to get Gardner's approval. 'Very well, Counsel,' he announced, 'that is your right.'

King rose and strutted up to the elevated pulpit that housed the witness chair.

'Mornin', Doc,' he said casually.

Stinson acknowledged him with a slight dip of his head.

'Say you performed hundreds of autopsies?'

'Yes, sir.'

Gardner began to tense. This was not starting out as normal cross on an expert witness's background.

'And how many of those were nonintrusive, Doctor?'

'Objection!'

Gardner's objection caught the judge napping. He had not expected any fireworks on such a tame topic as witness qualification. It usually flew by with little hassle. 'What's the problem, Mr. Lawson?' Danforth demanded when he finally regained his senses.

'May we approach?' the prosecutor asked.

King gave the jury a look that said: 'I'm on the verge of something important here, and he's trying to shut me up.'

'Yes. Come forward.'

King shrugged in mock frustration and marched up to the bench. 'Judge, he's out of line,' Gardner said. 'The man has done two hundred autopsies. He's qualified as an expert before. This is not the time for a general issue cross-examination.'

Danforth looked confused. 'I didn't get the impression that he was off track.'

'He's trying to get into the details of this autopsy,' Gardner persisted. 'He can do that later, if he likes, but not at the qualification stage.'

The response didn't help. The judge still looked confused. 'Is there something about this particular autopsy that makes it an issue?' he asked.

That was King's cue. 'You bet there is, Judge,' he said. 'The man may have done hundreds of autopsies, but he never did one like this.'

Danforth put Gardner back on the hook. 'Is this true? Was some nonstandard procedure used here?'

'Yes. But it is still within the scope of the witness's qualified abilities.' Gardner knew that the case would end here if Danforth found the witness unqualified. Stinson had performed the autopsy. Without his testimony about the child's manner of death, they could never punch T. J. Justice's ticket to the gas chamber. He had finally managed to convince the court that the chain of custody wasn't broken at the breakfast stop. With that hurdle gone, the next step was crucial. Stinson had to attribute the death to homicide.

'Well, I think that the defense is entitled to explore the extent to which this autopsy deviates from the standard and if his expertise covers what was actually done. Objection overruled.'

Gardner's legs felt weak as he walked back to the table.

'Can he knock it out?' Jennifer whispered. The prosecutor looked at King gloating at the witness stand, as though he were just given the right to run a sword through the man seated there. 'Pray,' he whispered back. 'Pray as hard as you can.'

'Now, Doctor,' King resumed. 'Can you answer my previous question? How many of the two hundred autopsies were nonintrusive into the body?'

The jury fixated on the witness, aware vaguely that this was some sort of crucial juncture in the trial.

'Only one.'

King looked at the jury to make sure that the words hit all twelve targets. 'Only one?' he repeated.

'Yes, sir.'

'And the procedures you used in that one,' he emphasized the word 'one', 'were they different from all the others?'

'Somewhat. Yes, sir.'

'Now, Doctor, how many times have you been qualified as an expert in testifying concerning a nonintrusive autopsy?'

The witness looked toward Gardner. 'Never, sir.'

'Never?' King was almost screaming. 'Not even one time?'

'No, sir. Not once.'

Then it was Gardner's turn at redirect, and he had to counter King's insinuation that there was something inherently improper about the autopsy. With painstaking precision, Gardner led Dr. Stinson through all of the procedures he had performed in lieu of actually opening up the body. External measurements and examination. Wound probes. X rays. Toxicological studies on body fluids. At each stage, he forced King to concede that the procedure was an accepted medical technique and that the doctor was qualified to perform it. And when he was finally through, the objection lay in tatters on the floor, cut to pieces by the logic of Gardner's presentation. It was a classic case of witness rehabilitation, and Judge Danforth knew it.

'While the situation is unusual,' he ruled, 'it by no means renders the physician incompetent as a witness. He has demonstrated his familiarity with each and every step in the process. He will be subject to cross-examination, and it will be up to the jury to decide whether or not to believe his conclusions. I rule that the witness is an expert in the field of postmortem examination, and that he may testify accordingly.' Amen. Now, on with the case.

'Doctor, I show you this knife, which has been marked as state's exhibit ten-A, and ask if you've ever seen it before?' Gardner handed the witness one of the steak knives.

'Uh, yes. I believe I have.' Stinson gingerly grasped the weapon by the handle and turned it over.

'Objection!' King was still hot about losing the qualifications skirmish. 'Which of the two knives did he see? They look the same.'

Gardner walked back to his table and picked up the other exhibit. 'I'll clarify, Judge,' he said, bowing to the defense attorney in a forced show of chivalry.

'Doctor, take a look at this also, state's ten-B. Have you seen either of these before?'

The witness examined the second with the same aplomb as the first. 'Yes, I have. A police officer brought them to my office.'

'Thank you. Now can you please relate these knives to your examination of the Anatov child?'

'Objection!' King snarled. 'Ambiguous and confused.'

'Ask another question, Mr. Lawson,' Judge Danforth directed, 'and try to make it more lucid this time.'

'Yes, Judge.' Gardner flashed a cool smile. 'Doctor, please describe the wound dimensions again.'

'Certainly. It was four and a quarter inches in depth and five-eighths inches in width.'

'Thank you. Now, did you have occasion to take

measurements of these knives?' Gardner removed the exhibits from the witness's hand and held them aloft so the jury could see their cold glint in the artificial light.

'Yes, sir, I did.'

Gardner was still lifting the knives, staring at them, pulling on the jury's attention as hard as he could. 'And how did they measure out?'

The witness seemed mesmerized by the sharp blade, as caught up in their deadly allure as the rest of the people in the courtroom. 'Four and one-half inches in length . . . and . . .'

'And?' Gardner held one of the knives poised as if to strike.

'And five-eighths inches wide. Exactly five-eighths inches wide.'

Bob Hamilton stared blankly at his typewriter. A half-eaten tuna sandwich lay to the side. Despite his private obsession with T. J. Justice, he still had to produce a product for the higher-ups at the State Department, and this afternoon they would be expecting his update report. The notes were locked in his safe, and his secret folder was back at the apartment. By now he didn't need them. All of the facts were deeply burned into his brain.

Hamilton looked out of his window. The midday sky was as bright as it had been over the weekend, a summer haze barely muting the clear blue background beyond the monument. He paused to follow two pigeons flying across his field of vision. Then he began to write:

The Soviet government has expressed satisfaction

with the manner in which the Justice case is being handled. They have stated publicly their belief that Justice is guilty, and should be punished for the crime, but have left the door open for acceptance of a not-guilty verdict by announcing that they will abide by the requirements and safeguards of the American criminal justice system. Clearly, the Soviets have placed their relationship with the U.S. government above concerns for the outcome of this case. Reported agent activities, which were at a very high level immediately following the murder, have all but ceased. This may be interpreted as an additional sign that the Soviets would like to see 'nature take its course' and the case concluded without any controversy. The current social and political climate in the Soviet Union makes a continued positive relationship with the U.S. mandatory. It is obvious that they don't want to appear to be critical of, or dissatisfied with, the prosecution. In conclusion, it is logical to assume that this case will not result in any significant change in U.S.–Soviet relations regardless of the outcome.

Hamilton stopped and reread the last line. 'No significant change,' he said aloud, his voice seething with sarcasm. The world would go on as before. A child killed, a man arrested, investigations run, prosecution commenced. And now it would end, and no matter which way it went, nothing would change.

He yanked the paper out and buzzed his secretary for a copy. While waiting for her to return, he went over it

one more time. The Russians lost a diplomat's son.
They kept the father incommunicado. They had been
cryptically warned. They sent top agents into the field.
They went wild behind the scenes, and suddenly they
stopped. Now everything was fine. Now the Russians
were happy. Now the warming trend could continue.
State wanted his lowly input and analysis, but as usual,
it didn't mean a thing. Outside forces controlled everything, and all he could do was watch and report. And
try to figure out what it all meant.

Suddenly a feminine arm whipped around the door-
frame and dropped two pages onto his desk. Hamilton
picked one up and put it in a blue plastic binder. The
other he laid in front of him. On the top he wrote
PERSONAL. On the bottom he wrote: *The assumption here
is that nothing rocks the boat. T. J. takes the heat, and
life goes on. Change the scenario, and . . .* He paused,
then put a final notation: *?*

Gardner and Jennifer grabbed a quick bite at Russel's,
trying to avoid contact with the jurors, who had discovered the secret delicacies of the place. Each wore a
pin labeled JUROR so that no one would attempt to
approach and discuss the case. They were 'off-limits' to
the world, so they tended to huddle together in sub-
groups, ostracized by legal fiat until their verdict was in.

'I think they got the point on the knife testimony,'
Jennifer said softly. The nearest JUROR pin was six seats
down the counter.

Gardner took a bite of his grilled cheese and mumbled
'yep' through his teeth.

341

Jennifer finished her milk shake and placed her napkin over the glass. 'So where does he go from here?'

'Same place he's been going since the beginning of the trial.' The prosecutor stood up and stretched his back. 'Down the road to destruction.'

They were about to leave when something caught Gardner's eye in the second booth. Four 'pins' having lunch. The hard-core cadre of the jury. The foreman and three law-and-order henchmen. They were examining something at the table. Gardner smiled and pushed Jennifer gently out the door. It was one of Russel's other trademarks: a serrated knife they sent with the plate whenever a customer ordered the sirloin strip.

The courtroom filled after the lunch break, and the medical examiner took his seat again in the witness chair.

'Dr. Stinson,' King asked, 'if you didn't do a brain section, how can you be sure that there was not a physical condition that contributed to the boy's death?'

This was cross-examination. Gardner had made all the points he could with the witness, and now the defense had a shot at him.

'The piercing of the heart was the primary cause of death, as I testified,' the pathologist answered. 'Any preexisting physical condition would not have mattered.'

King assumed a reflective 'body-fix,' hand to chin, arm supporting elbow, eyes elevated to the ceiling. 'What about neurological conditions. Epilepsy. Seizure disorders. Things like that?'

'They wouldn't—'

'Let me finish my question, Doctor.'

Gardner stood up. 'It sounded to me like he was through.'

'Gentlemen!' Danforth intervened. 'Ask a question, and let the witness answer. Okay?'

'I was trying to,' King replied.

'Okay, okay,' the judge said impatiently. 'Get on with it.'

'Okay, Doctor, you testified previously that there were marks on the boy's neck and that this was an indication of strangulation.' This time King clearly stopped. He looked at Gardner, the judge, and back at the witness.

'Correct,' Stinson said.

'Now, can you tell the jury whether or not there was a medical condition that might have been triggered when the strangulation occurred?'

The witness took a deep breath. 'I said that the cause of death was—'

'That's not the question, Doctor,' King responded angrily.

Gardner was helpless. The doctor was avoiding the issue, and there were no grounds for objection that could save him.

'I was asking about hidden medical conditions that may have been activated by strangulation, and contributed to the child's death.'

The doctor shifted uncomfortably in his seat. 'I can't really address that,' he said softly.

King picked up the reply and went for the kill. 'Can't address it?' His voice boomed across the courtroom.

'Can't address it? And why not, Doctor? Why can't you address it?'

'Because we didn't do an internal.' The reply was weak and apologetic.

'Didn't do an internal. Didn't do an internal,' King echoed mockingly.

Gardner finally stood up. 'I think everybody gets the point, Your Honor. We don't need it parroted by the defense attorney.'

King was already launching into the next question, so the judge bypassed a reply.

'You can't really rule out some other condition as being in fact responsible for the child's death. Isn't that so?'

'It's unlikely . . .'

'Yes or no, Doctor. A simple yes or no.'

The witness shifted before answering. 'No. Not positively.'

King feigned a yawn and sat down. 'No further questions, Judge,' he said.

By 3:45 King was winding down. He had milked the cross for every possible drop of reasonable doubt, and now he was running out of questions.

'May I have a moment, Your Honor?' he asked, picking up a stack of state's exhibits and walking over to the defense table.

'Don't take too long,' Danforth replied as King settled in next to T. J. and began examining one of the X rays that Gardner had introduced on direct.

The jury was restless. At this time of the afternoon,

their minds were on dinner, and grandchildren, and bed-side novels. Attention waned as the sun approached the mountain ridge, and both sides knew it. Each would soon find a way to conveniently end the session for the day.

King stood up with one of the X rays in his hand. 'Just a few questions, Your Honor.'

The judge signaled okay and the defense attorney approached the witness stand. 'Doctor, you said that these X rays were taken in an effort to determine the wound track. Correct?'

'No,' the witness replied, 'that is not correct.'

'Well, why don't you tell us again what their purpose is.'

'I said that because we were forbidden to section the body, we took X rays to determine the internal con-dition, and to also trace any intrusive wounds.'

'And how many X rays did you take?'

'About forty.'

'Forty? There are only ten that have been introduced into evidence. Where are the others?'

The witness bent down behind the partition and came up with a large brown envelope. 'I have the rest of them here.'

King stepped closer and reached for the shadowy gray negatives that had just been pulled out. 'Mind if I take a look at them?'

Gardner shrugged. He had seen them before, briefly. They were mostly repeats of the ten he had marked for admission.

King took the X rays and, one by one, held them up

to the light. The reverse angle gave his face an eerie pallor, like a skull peeking up from a grave. The courtroom was silent as the frames were lifted into the air. Suddenly he stopped and shifted one to get a better view against the bulb-clustered chandelier. Gardner noticed a slight change in his expression. A hint of recognition. A flash of discovery. King lingered with the raised X ray, then slowly put it down. The look in his eyes sounded an alarm in the prosecutor's head. The defense attorney had seen something.

King leaned against the witness stand and handed the X rays back to the medical examiner. 'You say that you confirmed the probe of the wound track with these. Is that correct, Doctor?'

'Yes, sir.'

'And the pattern was consistent?'

'Yes, sir.'

King picked up the X ray that had caught his attention earlier. Here we go, Gardner thought, he's about to unleash a zinger. King looked at the X ray, then at the doctor. 'No further questions, Your Honor.'

The medical examiner had allowed Gardner to copy the X rays after court. They were not easy to get duplicated on the copy machine, but after dampening the dark/light contrast all the way down, the outlines of the child's body finally came through, and the white incision between the narrow, fragile-looking ribs appeared, looking more like a flaw in the film than a mortal wound to the heart.

Gardner felt uneasy. King's behavior seemed to be swinging from one extreme to the other, an unusual pattern, even for him. He usually kept the pressure on from the opening gun, never letting an opportunity for destruction of the state's case pass him by. He always hammered away at it every chance he got, grinning gleefully as he swung his mallet with shoulder-high strokes, marveling openly as shattered pieces of evidence powdered under the blows and drifted silently to the courtroom floor. But this was different. King was constantly on again, off again with the attack. Start, stop. Start, stop. He was up to something, and that worried Gardner. Battling the 'normal' King was bad enough. The new version was even worse. The prosecutor was starting to lose his timing.

By 5:30 he had returned to his office to study the X ray copies. He picked up one. It was marked LS–2. 'Left front view of the chest cavity, frame two,' Dr. Stinson had told him. 'We ran a complete circumferential series on the body.' He further explained, 'Without an actual dissection, it was the best we could do to get a picture of the internal structure.'

Gardner studied the X ray. It looked like the others. The wound was a straight line. He picked up the next. Same thing. Same with number four. He was reaching for LS–1, when the phone buzzed. Instinctively he picked it up.

'Gardner Lawson.'

'I thought we had an understanding.' It was the police chief, Paul Rawlings.

'What do you mean?'

'Don't bullshit me, Gardner. You know what I'm talking about.'

The prosecutor was still focused on the deadly little

line that entered a child's heart and let out all its life.
'Seriously, Paul, I don't have a clue.'

'There's a rumor going around the department that
you've got some officers on your payroll.'

Gardner tensed. 'According to whom?'

'According to the whole goddamn second squad.
Now, what's going on?'

Gardner decided to play for time. It didn't sound like
the chief had discovered Brownie yet, but he was on his
way. 'Paul, I asked you to give me somebody . . .'

'We did. Larry Gray. At your disposal as long as you
need him.'

'But I told you my needs were different.'

'You're not answering my question. Who you got
snooping for you?'

'Before I respond,' Gardner said coldly, 'let me ask
you a question. Whose fucking side are you on?'

There was silence on the other end, then the chief
spoke again. 'You moonlighting one of my men or not?'

Gardner paused before answering. 'As of this
moment, no,' he said.

'You can't fire me,' Brownie said. 'Can't fire what you
didn't hire.' The two men were alone in Gardner's car
at 10:45 in the parking area of Westbrook Farm, the
sole participants at an emergency meeting the prosecutor
had called two hours earlier.

'You know what I mean,' Gardner replied. 'It's time
for you to take a break. I appreciate your help, but it's
got to stop here.'

The sound of a car passing on the roadway beyond

the orchard stopped the conversation. Gardner followed the light with his eyes as it passed the entrance and kept on going. The last thing he wanted was for someone to catch the two of them together, draw a conclusion, and report back to higher authority. For that reason, Gardner had chosen the deserted pick-your-own produce farm to terminate the unofficial relationship. Out of business for the past two years, its chained entrance warded off intruders. And no one knew that old Mrs. Westbrook had given Gardner the key before she closed the place up and moved to her daughter's house in Florida.

'From now on you're just a lab man,' Gardner continued. 'I can make it from here.'

There was a thin paring of moon visible above the grove of untended trees. It gave off just enough light for Gardner to see Brownie's pained expression. 'That ain't the way it looks to me. The papers make it sound like you in trouble.'

Gardner forced a smile. 'You know the papers. Typical gloom and doom. It's not as bad as they say. We're over the hump, Brownie. On the way to conviction.'

The officer's eyes flashed skeptically. 'You serious?'

Gardner nodded. 'We're gonna win . . .'

'But what about King? All that shit he's layin' on . . .'

Gardner shook his head. 'Smoke. Pure smoke. No way the jury's gonna buy it.'

'You really think you got a lock on it?' Brownie's words sounded more like a statement than a question.

'Justice is goin' down,' Gardner said solemnly. 'One way or another, the fucker is dead.'

'So you don't want my services anymore.'

Gardner looked his friend in the eyes. 'I'm sorry, Brownie, but we can't risk it. If the chief finds out, you're gone, and I'll have to explain to Danforth why your activities haven't been documented and turned over to King under the rules of discovery. We have more to lose than gain . . .'

Brownie took a deep breath. 'I guess you're right, but I still got some problems with this case I'd like to check out.'

Gardner leaned his head back against the seat. 'Such as?'

'Harley Smith, the alibi man, for one,' Brownie answered. 'He said he picked up T. J. at the motel, went drinkin' all day and night, and then delivered the son'bitch all the way to the state line. That's what he told me. Never let Justice out of his sight . . .'

'So?'

'So? There ain't no way T. J. could'a got back 'n' got the kid, took him to the woods, gone back to Hodges, and then made it to where he got picked up . . .'

'That's assuming you believe Mr. Smith,' Gardner said. 'After hearing your rundown on him the other day, I put his testimony at the bottom of my worry list.'

Brownie shifted uncomfortably in his seat. 'You think he's lying?'

'Christ, Brownie!'

'What?'

'The guy's a West Virginia hillbilly! He probably saw T. J. and thought he was lookin' in the mirror. Of course he's lying!'

The two men stared at each other, and Brownie's mind flashed back to the countless times he'd seen Gardner devastate alibi witnesses at trial by exposing their prejudices. Wives lying to protect husbands. Friends lying to protect friends. And now, fellow hillbillies covering for each other.

'You got a problem with that?' Gardner continued.

Brownie tried to smile but couldn't. 'Guy sounded sincere . . .'

'They all do, but juries see right through it, thank God.'

Brownie didn't reply. He was still thinking about the interview with Smith. Gardner was probably right, but this one bothered him. For the first time in years, an alibi had the ring of truth.

'What else?' Gardner broke into his thoughts.

'Got one other angle I'm lookin' into,' Brownie said. 'Got a buddy works air force intelligence. May be able to get some high-resolution aerial shots of the crime scene . . .'

'Brownie, we've already got the state police aerials,' Gardner interrupted. 'We don't need any more. Besides, if your name's on the evidence log, it's back to having to explain your involvement. No. Give it a rest. Let me handle it from here.'

'But—'

'Goddamn it! Did you hear what I said? You're off the case. Go home. Hang up your binoculars. We'll talk when it's done.'

Brownie didn't argue. He could see it was no use. The State's Attorney was now in control of the situation, and his secret operative was being relieved of duty. It was as simple as that. But as he walked to his car, a thought kept repeating in his head. Despite what Gardner had said, the man still needed help. And Brownie had no intention of quitting.

PART IV

Verification

CHAPTER 15

April 25
9:45 A.M.

'Request that the sheriff remove the witness's leg irons, Your Honor,' Gardner said. Dallas Stubbins was standing in the door that led from the back hall to the courtroom. The jury hadn't been brought in yet, and there was still a flap in the gallery as spectators and reporters vied for the few remaining seats.

'Not too fast, Judge,' King interposed, as Danforth signaled the deputy to unlock the ankle cuffs. 'He may be headed back for the detention center sooner than Mr. Lawson thinks.'

'Better hold the jury,' the judge instructed his bailiff. It looked as if there would be some preliminaries this morning that had not been on the schedule.

'Approach, please, Your Honor?' Gardner wanted the discussion out of the hearing of the press. King seemed like his old self today, and whatever he said was not going to be complimentary to the state. They took their customary positions against the dark brown rail of the bench.

'I wish to inform the court that, by calling this witness, Mr. Lawson is knowingly suborning perjury, Your Honor.' King led off with a grenade. 'It has come to my attention that the state has subjected their own witness to a polygraph examination, and that he came up deceptive. Now they appear to be ready to call him as a witness. If they do, they are presenting testimony that they know is false.'

The judge turned to Gardner, and at that moment, the prosecutor cursed the game of golf. He could see Chief Rawlings and Kent King small-talking on the fifth tee at Fair Hills. Simple conversation. A casual chat before the balls were sliced and hooked into the hazards lining the fairway. A simple conversation, but by the time they got to the green, the defense attorney knew that Dallas Stubbins came out as a liar when they put him on the 'box.'

'Well, Mr. Lawson,' Danforth sounded almost accusatory. 'What's this all about?'

'We tested Mr. Stubbins, and he did come up deceptive on some things, Judge,' Gardner answered. 'But the substance of the testimony we are offering today was supported by the exam.'

The judge glared over the lip of the bench. 'You say he did fail part of the polygraph? What part?'

Gardner held steady. 'Some of the control questions. Background inquiries about his prior record. He did show falsehood on three of them, but they had nothing to do with the facts of this case. He came up truthful on all of the questions we're gonna ask him here.'

'A liar is a liar is a liar,' King cut in. His voice was singsong and taunting.

'The issue that Mr. King raised is one of prosecutorial misconduct,' Gardner continued over the defense attorney's heckling refrain. 'Are we putting testimony that we know is perjured? That is the question. The answer is simple. No . . . in fact, we know that what the witness is going to say is the truth. You can't do better than that.'

Danforth looked at King again. 'What are you asking me to do, Counsel? Sanction the prosecutor?'

King seemed surprised that the judge was not more receptive. Even though he had not been a party to conversation on the green, he was a fellow traveler.

'No, Judge. Disqualify the witness.'

Danforth frowned. 'You can cover his veracity on cross. Witness is competent to testify. Objection denied.'

The witness and the defendant were locked in a stare-down that made Justice's previous attempts at intimidation seem almost frivolous. It was obvious that carnage would ensue if they were placed in arm's reach of each other, so the sheriff doubled the guard and stood his reinforcements behind each of them, ready to pounce if the war of the eyeballs escalated.

'Mr. Stubbins, can you tell the jury where you were on the evening of November twenty-nine?' Gardner had moved over to try to block the line of sight.

'Wuz in the detention center.'

'And what caused you to be there?'

'Objection!' King was on his feet. 'He's trying to impeach his own witness.'

'Background, Your Honor,' Gardner announced. 'It's no secret that the man's an inmate.'

Judge Danforth was contemplating this one. The proponent of a witness cannot raise questions about his veracity. That is reserved for a cross-examiner. But in this situation . . . His face took on a 'what the heck' expression. 'Mr. Lawson's right,' the judge said. 'It's going to come out one way or another. Objection overruled. Witness may answer.'

'Did some B and Es.'

'You mean breaking and enterings?'

'Yeah. Broke into a couple of warehouses.'

'And that type of activity is the extent of your criminal record?' Gardner turned to King, expecting another objection. He was trying to show that Stubbins was just a thief, not a violent criminal like the defendant.

'Yup. That's it.' The witness seemed to pick up the drift of the question. 'Never hurt nobody, if that's what you mean.'

King didn't say a word, and Gardner felt a twitch of uneasiness in his stomach.

'Now, did you have occasion to share your accommodations at the detention center with anyone on the twenty-ninth?' Gardner stepped back so the two former cellmates could see each other again.

'Yup. They put that man there in with me.' He pointed a bent finger at T. J., and the jury turned in unison as the identification drove the defendant's face into an even deeper scowl.

'And how many others, aside from the defendant, how many others were in the cell with you?'

'Nobody. Just us two.'

Gardner took a reading from the jury and decided that things were going well. They were serene and receptive looking at Stubbins, but every time they were diverted to T.J. their noses turned up slightly, as if they smelled a foul odor. He decided to make them sniff some more. 'And while the defendant was there, did you have occasion to talk with him?'

'We talked. Yes.'

Gardner faced Justice again. 'And what did you discuss?'

'Talked about what he done . . .'

'Objection!' This time King came through loud and clear.

'To the bench!' Danforth ordered. He knew what was coming.

'The witness is about to characterize a physical movement by my client as *speech*, Judge,' King said angrily. 'He is implying that there was a specific conversation about a specific crime—'

'He can say what he asked and what he saw the defendant do,' Gardner cut in forcefully.

'But we all know that my client had an incident in Kansas. How do we know that he wasn't referring to that in response to the question?'

Judge Danforth looked at King. 'Finally figured it out, have you?'

The defense attorney looked puzzled. 'Say what?' he said flippantly.

'You convinced Judge Simmons at pretrial not to allow the state to bring in the prior crimes of the defendant. Now you have a jury who knows nothing about his history. Do you really want to tell them that your man killed a child in Kansas?'

King's expression changed. 'You know I don't. That's

not the point. This witness should not be allowed to make an ambiguous characterization of my client's actions . . .'

'It's only ambiguous if they know about what he did in Kansas,' Danforth replied.

Gardner kept silent. The judge was doing fine without him.

'So what are you saying?' King asked.

'I'm saying you can't have both. You can't make the ambiguity argument unless they know what he did out west. And they won't know about that unless you withdraw your previous objection to the evidence of prior crimes. It's up to you. What's it going to be?'

King turned to T. J. and whispered something in his ear; then he shifted back to the bench. 'We're going to need a few minutes on this, Judge. Thanks to you, we're gonna have to decide which of the two bullets we have to bite . . .'

'Take a fifteen-minute recess,' Danforth bellowed, standing abruptly and sweeping off the platform.

'Can't believe it,' Gardner said to Jennifer back at the table. 'Dan's found himself some balls.' He smiled, remembering the joke that King had told at the chambers conference.

'What do you think he'll do?' Jennifer asked.

'It doesn't matter,' Gardner replied. 'Either way, we win. For the first time in this trial, we've got King against the wall. He'll probably opt to let in the Kansas history. He can't let the jury think that T. J. confessed to Stubbins that he killed Mika. That's too dangerous. He'll take the lesser of the evils. Write it off as a reference to his past . . .'

Jennifer was taking it all in. 'So we'll get to offer the criminal history after all.'

Gardner smiled. 'Exactly. Let King fuss about Stubbins all he wants. We're getting something better. A chance to show the jury T. J.'s true colors.'

The time was up, and the players came back to the field. King and Justice looked calmer than they had when they left. It seemed that their conference in the small witness room adjacent to the outer doors had cleared the air. They returned to the bench to deliver the verdict. 'My client has authorized me to allow the state to present information concerning the murder in Kansas,' King said.

Gardner flashed Jennifer an 'I told you so' look.

'Very well,' Judge Danforth replied. 'When do you want to do it?'

'Request that the stipulation be entered into the record now, Judge,' King said.

Danforth looked at Gardner. 'That okay with you?'

'No, sir,' the prosecutor said curtly. 'It's our evidence, and we have the option of when to present it.' Delaying the presentation would give the jury some time to toy with the idea that Gardner and Jennifer had discussed earlier: that the exchange with Stubbins was a confession of 'this' crime.

Danforth looked at King. 'We can't force the state to present its evidence in any particular order. You know that.'

The defense attorney smiled and shrugged. 'Whatever you say, Judge.' It was clear that he was not going to argue the point. 'As long as we're given full range of comment on the issue at closing argument, it doesn't really matter what comes in.'

'So when are you planning to offer it?' Danforth asked Gardner.

The prosecutor glanced at King, then returned to the judge. 'At the end of the state's case, Your Honor.'

Walking back to counsel table, Gardner tried to savor the victory, but two nagging thoughts intervened. Why hadn't King foreseen the dilemma? He was usually way ahead on those kinds of issues. And why hadn't he pressed to force the stipulation in earlier? Again, the man was acting out of character. And as much as Gardner wanted to write off King's blunders as mistakes, he could not help considering another interpretation: It was all intentional, part of a diabolical master plan.

The scene played out even more perfectly than Gardner had hoped. 'Asked him what it felt like to kill the kid,' Stubbins began. 'Man smiled at me. Actually smiled. Then he picked up his pillow and squeezed it, chokin' it . . .' The jury was horrified. Several were grimacing openly, and most of the others were shooting cold-eyed glances at T. J. 'Told me there wasn't nuthin' like it, that I ought to try it myself.' That almost brought the entire front row over the rail. They looked like a lynch mob. Stirred-up. Angry. Resolute. The testimony was perfect.

But the best part of all was played by T. J. As if on cue, when Stubbins pointed a crooked finger at him again, and assured the jury that what he was saying was the God's honest truth, Justice let out a scream. 'Liar! Liar! Liar!' The third one was partly muffled, as a six-feet-six deputy slammed him down, keeping him from his tormentor a few steps away in the witness box. And all the time King sat there calmly, letting the drama unfold, making no effort whatsoever to intervene.

'Your witness, Counsel,' Gardner said. After what just went down, what could the defense do?

King rose and walked to the witness stand, putting his face so close that Stubbins tried to lean back to get away. For a moment he just stood there staring, as if the witness were an animal at the zoo.

'You're a liar, aren't you?' he finally said.

The witness didn't know how to answer. 'Uhh . . .' was all he got out.

'Object,' Gardner said, trying to help.

'Overruled,' Danforth responded without hesitation. 'Fair cross.'

The prosecutor sat down.

'Mr. Justice was right. You're a liar.'

Gardner gave it another try. 'That's not a question. It's a statement.'

'Ask questions, please,' the judge replied, flicking a glance in King's direction.

'You are a liar. Yes or no?'

Stubbins was still twitching from the last barrage. 'I told the truth . . .'

'Mr. Stubbins!' King yelled at full volume. 'Answer the question! Are you or are you not a liar?'

'No!' the witness fired back recklessly, his anger rising against the man so persistently up in his face.

'No?' King's sarcasm overflowed. 'Well, why don't you take a look at this?' He stepped back for a moment and ran a piece of paper across Gardner's table. It was the intake report when Stubbins arrived at the jail. The one the prosecutor had asked the warden to keep under wraps. Gardner returned it with a casual snap of his wrist.

King handed the witness the paper and stepped up to read over his shoulder, pointing out the part he wanted to read. 'Okay. Now, Mr. Dallas Stubbins, who did you say you were when you got arrested?'

The witness handed the paper back. 'Johnny Stubbins,' he said sheepishly.

'And who, if you would be so kind, is Johnny Stubbins?'

The witness reddened slightly. 'He's my brother.'

Gardner didn't move a muscle. He didn't want the jury to see that King had scored a point, so he sat at his table and tried to force a smile, but all that appeared was a tight line across his lips.

The scullers were out early that afternoon, rotating their oars in harmonic pulses, cutting a rippling swath in the calm surface of the Potomac. Above, on the rocky bluff, the spires and classical façades of Georgetown overlooked the stirrings on the river and lent an air of permanence to the fleeting brightness of the spring afternoon.

Bob Hamilton watched from the iron railing that protected the bike path he had walked for the past hour, trying to clear his head of the pressure that was squeezing everything out, leaving him unable to complete even the routine functions of his job. He had taken the afternoon off, hoping to reach a decision. Hoping that some-how the silence of a solitary stroll would trigger a subconscious latch, and the answer would pop into his mind.

The Justice project was screwed up from the begin-ning. They wanted him to collect the data, but they prevented him from going to the source. And it was never made clear *why* they wanted the information. Col-lect and report, but don't think, seemed to be the mess-age. But that wasn't the biggest problem. He had started his own private investigation, and the department didn't know about it. And now he had some serious doubts about the project *and* the case.

He turned and looked behind him in the direction of the parkway. A lone man was leaning against the rail about a hundred feet away. Hamilton's heart rate kicked up a notch in a spasm of paranoia. His secret file was against regulations. Maybe they had found out about it and had him under surveillance. He looked at the figure against the rail, trying to make out the face, but it couldn't be done. The distance had erased the man's features and left a faint darkened smear where the eyes, nose, and mouth should have been.

He grabbed the iron railing and squeezed, as if the tactile reality of the metal could bring him back to his senses. He closed his eyes for a moment, then opened them and looked down at the river. A racing shell passed directly below. It was up to full speed, as the sculls loaded and unloaded against the olive water. His mind flew back to college. To Professor Tompkins's philo-sophy course. 'Never compromise truth,' the professor had said. 'You can twist it and turn it, but never break it. You can't tell where the severed ends are going to end up.'

Hamilton smiled as he remembered his classroom reply: 'They'll end up around your neck.' It was an honest reply, delivered with the clear voice of a true believer. But those were the idealistic days, when ethical problems were theoretical. A time when it was easy to spout out a glib answer. He was beyond that now. An experienced State officer in the service of his country. At a place and time when the answers were not so obvious.

At that moment, with the words of his youth still ringing in his mind, he made a decision. Somebody in authority had to know what was happening. It might be a violation of official protocol, and it might even open him up to disciplinary action, but the burden was too much for him to carry alone. The Justice prosecutors were on the wrong track, and someone had to tell them. There were too many anomalies. Too many loose ends writhing like snakes in a pit. He really had no other choice. Despite the consequences, he had to take the wraps off his private file.

Hamilton took a step toward the blurry form still leaning against the rail. For a moment it was stationary; then, as if the two were interconnected by a rigid brace, it began to move off, maintaining the same distance ratio until it reached a curving tree line, where it vanished from sight and did not appear on the other side.

By the time he reached his car, the shadowy outline had faded from his mind. The burden was lighter now, and soon it would be gone. He was a foreign relations man, not a detective. It was time to let someone else worry about the pursuit of Justice.

Gardner and Jennifer sat in the 'State's Attorney's' booth at Paul's. At 7:45, dinner had been ordered, but not served. Gardner was on his second 'special' martini, and Jennifer was still only one-third down on her original drink, an imported sparkling water, soaking a lime.

'It's amazing, isn't it,' the chief prosecutor said. 'One minute you're drifting toward the rocks, and suddenly you get a rope from your opponent.'

His assistant flattened the straw between her teeth. 'How do you figure it?' Her eyes picked up a touch of neon, adding to the sparkle that always danced behind her specs.

'Could be a trap.'

'Trap?' Her head cocked to the side, and the light mixture changed to predominant red.

'He's done it before. Gotten our guys to think he's going one way, so they commit to a strategy . . . then, wham! He comes around the other side and cuts their legs off.'

Jennifer had heard all of the stories, but this time she couldn't see the punch line. 'Boss, what could he possibly gain by letting us get into his history? His best bet was to keep it out, make like T. J. was an innocent bystander swept up in a dragnet.'

Gardner rolled his olive. 'He got caught, finally. Had to choose between that or letting Stubbins finish T. J. off . . .' The prosecutor put his glass down and looked over its bowed rim. 'Jennifer, the guy's definitely going somewhere with this, but I don't have a clue where. His behavior is really starting to baffle me.'

'So what's our plan?' The emphasis on 'our' was not lost on Gardner.

He smiled. 'What do I always say?'

'Try your own case. Don't let the defense make decisions for you.'

'Right.'

'So we don't put in the other crimes as evidence after all?'

'Maybe. And maybe not. Do you remember my other maxim?'

'If the defendant says it's okay, then we don't want it?'

Gardner smiled again and touched her arm. 'Exactly. He seemed too anxious to let it in.' His hand remained on her arm, and she could feel the warmth of his fingers against her skin. She was conscious of her heart beating. 'I'm sure we'll put it in eventually, but I don't want to rush. I think we ought to make King wait.' He removed his hand, and Jennifer picked up her drink in an effort to shield her disappointment.

'So we're going to give him a dose of his own medicine,' Jennifer said, putting her glass gently on the table.

Gardner sneered. 'Yes, my dear, and we're gonna administer it rectally.'

The food arrived. Grilled open-faced steak sandwich for him, tuna melt for her. Gardner ordered another martini and Jennifer passed on a refill. She felt more comfortable not drinking now, after the tequila exhibition in the winter. Gardner had gotten the point and never hassled her again. And she appreciated it, and enjoyed their off-duty time together more than she wanted to admit.

By 9:30 Gardner had reached his drink limit, almost to the irresponsible stage, but not quite. Jennifer volunteered to drive him home, but he refused. She didn't push it, and settled instead for leading him out of the bar.

They passed amid a smattering of 'see ya Gard's and 'later, man's, as townies, former defendants, and off-duty cops paid their respects. Jennifer took his arm when the door closed behind. He didn't resist as she guided him through the maze of pickup trucks and campers that were jackknifed across the parking lot. They were almost to his car, when Gardner pulled up abruptly and stopped.

'Jen?' He rarely used that abbreviation.

'Boss?'

He turned and looked into her eyes. 'Ever get lonely, living by yourself?'

The liquor coated his voice with sadness.

The timing caught Jennifer unprepared. She often thought of calling Gardner at night, just to talk. Or dropping by with a pizza. But she was afraid of rejection and didn't want to spoil the special relationship they had built. 'Uh, sometimes,' she finally said.

He swayed slightly on his feet, and Jennifer noticed a thin film of moisture glistening his pupils.

'I miss my boy,' Gardner blurted suddenly.

Jennifer hesitated, waiting for Gardner to continue, but he had stopped talking.

Instinctively, she put her arms around his back and

nestled her ponytail against his cheek, tapping lightly on his shoulder with her short manicured nails. He did not resist, and neither of them spoke a word.

Just then a car pulled in, but they didn't notice it. The gentle embrace continued, until Elaine yelled, 'Get your hands off him, you bitch!'

Jennifer dropped her arms and stepped back as Elaine punched open her door and stomped over to them in her high-fashion boots.

'Hey!' Gardner yelled. 'It's not what you think!'

Elaine ignored him, choosing to close in on Jennifer instead.

'Miss Four-Eyes lawyer-girl better learn how to keep her hands to herself.'

The Assistant State's Attorney stood her ground. 'It's not what you think,' she said calmly. 'We were just—'

'Don't kid me, bitch.' Elaine cut in. Her hair was a mass of red, corkscrewed into a million ringlets.

Gardner stepped between them, facing Elaine. 'Stop it!'

'Get away from me!' she shrieked.

'He didn't do anything!' Jennifer shouted from behind his back.

Gardner turned to his assistant. 'Maybe you should head out. I'll take care of it . . . Okay?' He gave her a reassuring look.

Jennifer agreed silently. 'Nice seeing you again, Miss Tower,' she said sweetly, before slipping away between a pair of four-wheelers.

Gardner turned back to Elaine. 'Please don't act this way.'

She gave him a cold stare, then ran to her car and jumped in. 'You're a bastard!' she screamed over the roar of the engine as she raced off the lot.

After the sound died away, the prosecutor looked up at the night sky. The wind was from the east and the clouds were backing up on the mountain, a sure sign of rainfall before morning. Just then, Jennifer swung around the corner and shuddered to a stop beside him.

'How about that ride?' she said.

Gardner opened the door and stumbled in.

'Sorry,' he mumbled as he eased his head back against the seat.

Long before they got to the town house he dozed off, so Jennifer let him sleep. 'Home,' she whispered gently when they arrived. A nudge on the arm woke him into a partially functioning state, so she guided him zombie-fashion into the unit and helped him onto his bed. And before she left, she touched his cheek and softly said good night.

Sometime well after midnight the phone rang. The alcohol had worn off and Gardner's head ached, but his mind was alert.

'Hello?'

'It's over between us, isn't it?' Elaine sounded drunk, and her voice cracked.

Gardner didn't answer.

'You and that Jennifer girl. That's what it is . . .'

Again, Gardner stayed silent.

'How could you treat me this way?' Her voice was tuning up to a plaintive wail.

'Elaine—'

'I love you!'

'Elaine, please!' Gardner interrupted. 'We had some fun, but I never promised anything . . .'

Now she went silent, her breathing a substitute for words.

'I'm sorry if you think I did. And I'm sorry that you got hurt.'

'Do you love *her*?' Elaine's voice was back.

Gardner hesitated. That was a subject he'd never faced straight on. Jennifer was a good friend and a super lawyer. He'd never really projected beyond that. He was her boss, and that put her off limits.

'You *do* love her!' Elaine gasped, interpreting his silence as a yes. Then, in characteristic fashion, she slammed down the phone.

Gardner rolled over and tried to go back to sleep, but Elaine's words kept haunting him. His mind drifted to Jennifer, and he tried to understand what had just happened. For some reason, he'd not been able to deny Elaine's accusations.

April 26
9:45 A.M.

'Sorry, Bob, I can't fit you in until Friday at the earliest,' Deputy Director Thomas Quinton said over the phone.

'But sir, this is important,' Hamilton stuttered.

'I have no doubt that it is, but my schedule is packed.

I'm leaving within the hour for Chicago, and I won't be back until late Thursday. Have Cathy set you up for first thing on the twenty-ninth.'

'But I don't think this can wait that long.' There was tension in his voice, which implied he might go elsewhere in the meantime.

'Bob, I think I know what this is about. I promise you it'll keep for two more days. We'll go over everything then.'

Hamilton hesitated. It seemed as though the man was reading his mind. 'How do you know what I'm going to tell you?'

This time the deputy hesitated. 'I know a lot more than you think,' he finally answered. 'See you in a couple of days.'

The feeling that had hit him by the river came rushing back, as if he could now see the face of the shadowy ghost by the iron rail.

'But—'

'Gotta go,' Quinton interrupted. 'We'll talk Friday, and I'm sure you'll feel a lot better about things when we're done. 'Bye.'

Hamilton put down the phone. No sense worrying about it now, he thought. The load would be off his back by the weekend.

He picked up the phone and dialed a number. 'Constance, please, and yes, it's official.'

'Hello?'

'Con, Bob.'

'You calling about that file again?'

Hamilton smiled to himself. 'No, actually. I was

wondering . . . you got any plans for Saturday afternoon? Maybe we could go bike riding.'

At 10:15 Brownie rushed into the post office to pick up the special-delivery letter that the notice slip had listed *To Sgt. Joe Brown from Capt. Alonso Carlton, Langley AFB, Virginia*. On the way through the glass door, he ran into a roadblock.

'Well, if it ain't the black man's answer to Sherlock Holmes,' Bruno Calvano sneered, as he maneuvered his thick body into the pathway.

Brownie hunched his shoulders. 'Out of my way, man.'

'Take it easy, pal. I'm just going about my business.'

The officer laughed. '*Your* business? That ain't what I heard.'

'Yeah? What's it to you? You're just a fuckin' test tube jockey.'

'That ain't all I can do . . . and if you don't get the hell out of my way, you'll get to see a few of my other talents firsthand.'

Calvano turned sideways to let him pass. 'You been hanging around Lawson too long. Turnin' his color . . . same as shit.'

Brownie walked by and jolted Calvano's midsection with an elbow. 'Better than yellow,' he said in a voice that told the big man to get out while he still could.

Calvano glared and postured, but otherwise took his advice and left. Brownie kept moving and didn't look back. He didn't have time to waste, even on a one-punch fight.

He got in line and soon was at the counter. The letter was exchanged for the yellow slip, and Brownie took it with a smiling thanks.

He opened it in the car and read the response to the letter he had sent two weeks earlier to his air force contact, a high school chum who had also opted for a career in a blue uniform.

Dear Brownie:

In answer to your inquiry concerning aerial photos of western Maryland, and more particularly, of the Sessy's Woods section of the county, I have been authorized to release the following information: Overflights are routinely conducted of the Camp David perimeter, whenever the President is in residence there. The information gathered during these flights is classified, but often the pilots make prior test runs on outlying areas, and the photos in those sectors may be released to law enforcement agencies upon request.

Due to seasonal changes affecting vegetation growth, there is considerable variance in the views of the area you were interested in. Not knowing which particular views would be most appropriate for your needs, I have taken the liberty of providing a sample list of dates when aerials were shot. Let me know which set you need, and I'll prepare the paperwork and get them to you asap. Good to hear from you. Keep in touch.

DATES:

JULY 1–3, 1988
JAN 16–18, 1989
APR 10–12, 1989
NOV 25–28, 1989

Brownie stared at the November date in disbelief. He had only wanted reference material, a chance to see hidden nooks and crannies around Sessy's where someone might have tossed a knife. A perspective on the scene more refined than the fuzzy state police helicopter shots that Gardner had. He'd never bought the theory that the steak knife in the cabin was the actual murder weapon. The one T. J. used was probably part of the set, discarded near the scene. If he could find it, the prosecutors would be home free.

But now there was a new angle. Unexpected. Right out of left field. The President had gone to Camp David for the long weekend after Thanksgiving. He remembered that now. At the time it had cleared up the mystery of how the feds jumped in so quickly on the case. They were already in the area. And while they were there, the air force was busy overhead, freezing the landscape on film.

Brownie started the car and gunned the engine. He suddenly had a letter to write and a request to make. Lunch would have to wait.

'Call the next witness, Madame State's Attorney.'

Jennifer stood up. 'The state calls Reena Hodges to the stand, Your Honor.' The assistant prosecutor was dressed in a navy blue suit, and her hair was fluffed and shiny. Her demeanor was calm. There was no question that she was in charge of the case while Gardner was in Baltimore, appearing before an Attorney General's hearing panel to answer questions about the Back River Canyon deal.

'Can't postpone the case while you iron out your personal problems,' Danforth had said when the State's Attorney showed him the subpoena. 'You've got an assistant who hasn't said a word all trial. Why don't you let her have a shot until you get back?'

Gardner didn't have any choice. *Failure to appear will result in your arrest*, the summons warned. Jennifer could handle it while he tried to put out the fire, and if everything went well downtown, things would be back to normal tomorrow.

Mrs. Hodges jerk-stepped down the aisle on unstable legs. Jennifer made a show of helping her get up on the witness stand, a psychological ploy that Gardner often used as a subtle reminder to the jury that his side really 'cared' about people.

After the swear-in, Jennifer stood and approached the stand. 'Mrs. Hodges, my name is—'

'Objection!' King was up, back arched like a growling dog. 'We know who she is,' he said nastily. 'This isn't a social hour, it's a trial.'

Jennifer had expected this. 'He'll hit you hard from the first word,' Gardner told her, 'try to make you lose it before you get going . . .'

'I was attempting to make the witness comfortable, Your Honor,' Jennifer said calmly. 'She's obviously nervous, and I wanted to ease her into the routine.'

'Well, try to do it with some relevant substance, then,' Judge Danforth responded. 'Just keep it moving.'

King grinned and sat down. Out of the corner of her eye, Jennifer picked up Justice giving him an 'atta boy' poke on the arm.

'Yes, Your Honor,' the assistant prosecutor continued. 'Now, Mrs. Hodges, would you be so kind as to tell the ladies and gentlemen where you live—'

'She just gave her address!' King was up again, flashing an annoyed look toward the jury.

'She did just tell us that,' Danforth said. 'Please get to something we don't already know.'

Jennifer took a deep breath. 'Mrs Hodges, do you run a motel in—'

'Your Honor, am I going to have to play law school professor all day? Now she's leading the witness.' King feigned a yawn.

Danforth peered down sternly. 'Miss Munday, I assume that you did get a law degree, or you wouldn't be here. Please show us that you learned something.'

Jennifer looked up at the bench and smiled. 'I did, Your Honor. I learned that it's impossible to be heard over the loud voice of an unreasonable man.'

A sudden silence fell over the room, and then gave way to the twitter of laughter. Every eye turned to the jury. The entire panel was smiling at Jennifer, cheering her on.

While Jennifer was battling King, Gardner was being interrogated by an Assistant Attorney General in Baltimore. It was a hearing, not a trial, conducted by the investigation division of the AG's office in a small room on the tenth floor of their downtown high-rise building. Gardner elected to appear without counsel in answering the allegations.

The hearing room was crowded with spectators and media reps, and Gardner felt the pressure of their eyes on his back as he faced the panel from the witness chair. He had been under questioning for several hours, as the investigators took turns. Now they were finally to the last inquisitor.

'Did you or did you not meet with two members of county licensing on the fifteenth of August?'

'Yes, I did meet with them. Used to see them all the time, before . . .' The prosecutor adjusted his burgundy tie and looked squarely at the interrogator.

'And you had a conversation?'

'We talked, yes.'

'And what did you ask?'

'I asked if they knew how long it would take to get the permits approved.'

'Anything else?'

Gardner didn't like being on the receiving end of a barbed question. 'Like what?' Never volunteer information, he always told his witnesses.

'Like what it would cost to get them through faster.'

'I said that the county always drags its feet on those things, and that it was too bad because it cost the investors a lot of money.'

'Really? That's all?'

'Yes. It was a comment. Only a comment.' Gardner did not even blink.

'And you didn't offer anything to move it along?'

'Absolutely not. I would never do anything like that.'

'Uh-huh.' The hearing examiner sounded like King. 'So you say . . .'

Gardner looked the balding, stoop-shouldered man in the face. 'So help me God.'

'Your witness, Mr. King,' Jennifer said as she turned the questioning rights over to the defense. After the laugh break she was able to get past King's pecking and draw out the old woman's testimony. Yes, that there was the man who stayed at the motel in unit 15. No, no one else shared the room with him. Yes, he had been there up till the twenty-seventh of November, when, for some reason, he decided to leave. The relevant point was made. Justice was in view until the day of the murder, then 'for some reason' he disappeared.

As she walked back to the table, she saw the clock on the wall register 11:45. Until then she hadn't realized how wiped out she was. Thank God they'd break for lunch within the hour.

'Ms. Hodges, how old are you?' the defense attorney began.

'Object, Your Honor! The lady's age is not relevant.' Jennifer arched her back. 'And besides, it's not polite.' The jurors smiled.

'Relevance, Mr. King?' Danforth asked.

'Memory. Reasoning ability . . .'

'There's no automatic correlation between age and senility, Your Honor,' Jennifer shot back.

The judge gave King a chiding look. 'Do you really need to know the lady's age?'

For the first time today, King didn't have a ready retort. 'Okay, Judge, we'll pass on that,' he said, turning to Jennifer. 'Wouldn't want to offend anyone's sensitivities, now would we?'

The prosecutor smiled. 'I certainly hope not,' she said out loud.

9:30 P.M.

Officer Charlie Barnes paced the floor of his small apartment like a cardboard rabbit in a shooting gallery. His uniform top was unbuttoned and shoes were off, but the side arm was still in place, and he nervously jacked it in and out of its holster.

The evening paper was displayed on the coffee table in front of his worn secondhand sofa. The lead article had been ripped out, leaving a hole that jagged into a picture of the pockmarked Berlin Wall. The missing piece lay to the side, inky finger marks along its border, the heading blotched but still legible: JURY STILL OUT ON PROSECUTOR.

The officer's legs gave out as he rounded the course for the twentieth time. He flopped on the couch, kicked his ankles over the sagging armrest, picked up the article, and held it to the light, reading the words one more time:

State's Attorney Gardner Lawson is not out of the woods yet. According to sources close to the investigation, influence-peddling charges may yet be brought despite a day of hearings marked by a lack of any substantial evidence of wrongdoing. 'The case is a study in cause and effect,' the unnamed source told our reporter in Baltimore. 'Things were at a standstill in the development process until Mr. Lawson met with a number of county licensing agents in a series of so-called informal discussions. After that, there was a flurry of activity, as clerks fell over themselves to issue the permits. The public has a right to know what transpired between these people. They have a right to know if a different set of standards applies to elected officials than it does to the average citizen.'

Barnes let his arm drop to his chest, resting before he put it back up to the light. He took two deep breaths, then extended the article again. It continued:

The reaction of county officials has been mixed. Two members of the county council have suggested that Mr. Lawson step down until the investigation is over, another said he should stay on, and the fourth member had no comment. 'I'm in the middle of a crucial trial,' Mr. Lawson said, when asked for his reaction. 'Do they realize that? Or do they just want blood?'

Barnes crumpled the paper and threw it against the wall. Then he swung upright, picked up his phone, and dialed. 'Hello?' The voice sounded tired. 'Mr. Lawson, this is Officer Barnes. Charles Barnes.'

'Yeah, Charlie. What's up?'

'Gotta talk to you. Gotta tell you something. God-damn it, sir, I know what they're trying to do to you . . .'

Gardner could hear the shame in his voice. 'What do you mean, Charlie?'

'They're trying to burn you, sir. And I know you didn't do anything.'

'Thanks for your support,' Gardner said. 'I appreciate it.'

'There's more, sir.' The voice foretold an ominous truth. 'I helped them.'

Gardner went silent.

'Sir? Did you hear that?'

'What did you do, Officer Barnes?' The prosecutor now sounded upset. 'I told you to stay away from them!'

'I'm sorry . . . I'm sorry.' It sounded as though he was crying.

'Okay! Okay!' Gardner yelled. 'Just tell me what happened!'

Barnes confessed his betrayal in a burst of sobs. He told everything from the beginning, leaving nothing out. Calvano and the videotape. His work indiscretions. The notes. The threat. He ended with a choking apology. 'I know you'll hang me for it, but I had to tell you.'

Gardner took it in like a priest in a confessional. He was angry, but held back on recriminations.

'What are you going to do with me, sir?' Barnes asked at the end.

The prosecutor paused, then spoke softly. 'Charlie, would you be willing to tell the grand jury what happened?'

'Yes, sir. You can count on me, Mr. Lawson,' the officer answered, swearing to himself he'd never let the man down again.

'Okay. After we get through with Justice, we'll take on Calvano,' Gardner said before hanging up. He wanted to add another name, but on the evidence so far, it wouldn't fly. As always, King was insulated from direct accusations.

CHAPTER 16

April 27
9:15 A.M.

'Say hello to the new star of the daytime soap, "How to Win Friends and Influence Politicians," ' Kent King said as he and Gardner came face-to-face in the hall beyond the judge's chambers.

'And if it isn't the scriptwriter.' Gardner didn't miss a beat. Both men looked at each other coldly, then splintered into slick, armored, trial-attorney smiles.

'Come back to give your little girl a helping hand?' the defense counsel asked.

Gardner's cheeks bunched. 'No. To give you a break. From what I hear down at the office, she tore you a new one yesterday.'

King's smile slid off his face. 'It's not over yet.'

'No,' Gardner replied, 'it certainly isn't.'

The prosecutor's revulsion for his adversary was reaching its limit. He wanted to deliver an uppercut to the underside of the man's square jaw and drive his fist through the skull and out the top. He wanted to kick him in the stomach. Garrote him. Stab him. But it could never be, not in a 'civilized' society. He had to substitute words for blows, creative strategy for weapons. That was the only way it could be done. The minute he swung his fist, King would win.

'By the way, I think she missed you,' King said in an oily tone.

'Huh?' Gardner was still butchering King in his mind.

'Your girl. I think she has the hots for you.'

Gardner strained for composure. 'Jennifer's not *my* girl.'

'Yeah? So she's free territory?'

The prosecutor smiled thinly. You fucking bastard, he thought. 'Good luck.'

'Thanks. That's what I always seem to have when it comes to your women . . .'

Gardner stepped so close to King their foreheads almost touched. His eyes were bonfires of anger. 'You've reached the end of the line,' he said, shaking with a tremor of rage that threatened to burst him at the seams. The defense attorney had just pushed the attack button too far in for the voice of reason to pull it back out.

'Well, good morning . . .' Jennifer sounded like maple syrup dripping on a pancake.

King had tensed for a blow, and Gardner was coiled to strike.

'Am I interrupting something?'

'Mr. Lawson was about to do his Mike Tyson imitation,' King said in mock horror.

'Well, don't let me stop you,' Jennifer said with strained nonchalance.

Suddenly the crisis was over. 'I usually don't work with an audience,' Gardner said calmly, turning to his assistant. 'Mr. King tried to talk me into it, but as usual, he failed.'

The three entered the courtroom in silence. When they split to their respective corners, Gardner noticed King signaling to him, moving his lips and motioning to Jennifer's back. Gardner deciphered it before he sat down. 'T-H-E H-O-T-S.'

'Agent Cirelli, I show you what's been marked as state's exhibit number fifteen, and ask if you can identify it?' Gardner had saved the best live testimony for last. The blood analyst from the FBI. He looked like a laboratory man. Sixtyish, gray hair, and thick glasses. Deliberate in his actions and his words.

'Yes. This is one of the shirts we received from the Maryland State Police in November.' The arresting officer had testified earlier that it was the shirt T. J. was wearing when he was taken into custody.

'And can you tell the ladies and gentlemen of the jury what, if anything, you did with the shirt after it arrived at your lab?'

'Certainly. It is customary for us to—'

'Objection!' King jerked up from his seat. 'The question was what he did on that occasion, not what he normally does.'

Gardner's inner flame had not yet cooled from the earlier run-in. 'Mr. King's rudeness is exceeded only by his lack of understanding of the rules of evidence,' he said, cocking his head toward the jury. 'There's nothing wrong with the witness saying what he customarily does before he goes into the specifics of what he did here.'

'But the answer was not responsive to the question,' King fired back.

Judge Danforth had finally arrived at a way to deal with the daily grudge match. Let them spar, then cut off the debate. 'Just ask another question, Mr. Lawson,' he said in a tired voice.

'Agent Cirelli, what is your usual procedure when evidence is sent in for processing?' Gardner looked directly at King.

'Visual screening, followed by microscopic examination, and then, if any foreign substances are found, chemical analysis.'

'Did you follow that course of action with state's exhibit fifteen?'

'Yes, we did.'

'And what did you find?'

'Object. Assumes that there were positive results,' King said.

'What, if anything, did you find?' Gardner corrected. King's rantings at this point were just a nuisance, hardly worth a reply.

'Liquid stain on the lower portion of the right sleeve.'

Gardner took the exhibit from the witness and held it up. 'Which sleeve, Agent Cirelli?'

King knew what he was trying to do. 'Your Honor, we all heard the answer, there's no need to repeat it.'

'Which sleeve, Agent?' Gardner persisted over the interruption.

'Your Honor!' King was almost screaming.

'Which sleeve?'

'Okay!' Danforth yelled. 'That's enough!' He then turned to the witness. 'Tell the jury which sleeve the stain was on so we can move ahead with the trial.'

'Object!' King was staring at the judge with a 'how could you!' expression on his face.

'*I* asked the question, Mr. King,' the judge replied, 'and *I* say the witness can answer.'

'Well, *I* object anyway,' King said defiantly.

'And *I* overrule your objection.' He turned to the witness. 'Agent Cirelli, which sleeve of the defendant's shirt contained a stain?'

The witness pointed. 'The right one, Judge. Lower portion of the right arm.'

The prosecutor smiled. Everyone on the jury knew that Justice was right-handed.

Forty-five minutes later Gardner was in the home stretch with the witness. He had finished his explanation of analysis procedures. Now he was coming to the conclusions.

'Mark this please as state's number thirty-five,' Gardner said, handing the clerk a one-page document with the FBI logo on top.

King waved it off when he attempted to run it by. T. J. already had a copy in front of him.

'Now, Agent Cirelli, can you please tell the jury what this is?'

The witness took the paper and scanned it. 'My report.'

'And to whom was the report issued?'

'To the county police department and State's Attorney's office.'

'Now, have you set out your conclusions in this report?'

'Yes, sir.'

Gardner handed the witness the report. 'Now, Agent Cirelli, can you please tell the ladies and gentlemen what conclusions you reached with regard to the stain on the right sleeve of the defendant's shirt?'

The witness adjusted his eyeglasses and perused the paper, then looked up and turned to face the jury.

'The substance on the lower sleeve portion of item Q–6, uh, the shirt, was found to be blood. Human blood.'

'Move to admit it as state's exhibit thirty-five,' Gardner said.

'Defense?' Danforth looked at King.

'Objec – Uh, no objection, Judge,' the defense attorney replied, rising halfway, then dropping down to his chair.

'Very well, the exhibit is in evidence,' the judge announced.

'Request to show it to the jury, Your Honor.'

'Defense?' Another deferral to King.

'Go ahead,' he answered with a shrug.

Gardner made a dramatic show of delivering the report to the foreman. Carrying it gently past the crime scene photo he had placed on the corner of his table, he acted out a message: The blood on T. J.'s sleeve had spurted out of the knife wound in the chest of the little boy. As the jurors read the words, they had to see his pale face, and beyond, the gaunt twisted features of Justice himself.

It was 11:30 when King started to cross-examine. 'Agent Cirelli,' the defense attorney asked, his arms folded across his chest, 'did you have occasion to perform DNA testing on the bloodstain?'

The witness took off his glasses. 'No, sir, we did not.'

'And why, might I ask, was that? Isn't it standard procedure?'

'No. It has to be requested.'

'Uh-huh. And was it requested?'

'No. I don't believe so.'

'Do you know why it was not requested?'

'Objection!' Gardner said. 'Beyond the witness's scope of knowledge.'

'If the witness knows, he may answer.' Danforth looked at the agent. 'Do you know why it was not done, sir?'

'No, Judge, I really don't.'

'Okay, let's move on to something else, Mr. King.'

'Just one more question on that, if Your Honor pleases.'

'Very well.'

A few of the jurors shifted in their seats and glanced down at their watches. It was 11:40, nearing lunchtime.

'For whatever reason, your lab performed no test to determine DNA profiling characteristics. Correct?' King bored on.

The witness adjusted his glasses. 'Correct, but it was not an issue, we couldn't—'

'Thank you, Agent,' King interrupted. 'Now let's look at something . . .'

'Your Honor!' Gardner sprang to his feet. 'The witness was in midsentence, and Mr. King cut him off. He should be allowed to finish his answer.'

Judge Danforth shifted his eyes back to the witness stand. 'Did you have something more to say?'

'Object!' It was obvious that King did not want the man to continue.

'Please be quiet, Mr. King, I would like to hear the agent.' Danforth shot an annoyed glance down at the defense table, then returned to the stand. 'What were you going to tell us, Agent Cirelli?'

'Objection!' King wasn't giving up.

'Overruled!' The annoyance had reached its limit. 'Continue, please, sir.'

'Uh, Your Honor,' the witness said, 'he asked me why the DNA test was not done. First, there was no request, and second—'

'Your Honor!' King was back up. 'I did not ask "why" in the last question. I asked "if." Only "if." '

Danforth put both hands to his cheeks and rubbed them. 'Mr. King, we're beyond that point. The witness has an explanation, and *I*, repeat *I*, want to hear it. You got that clear?'

King exhaled loudly, stared for a moment, mumbled, 'Yeah,' and sat down.

'Finish your sentence while you still can,' the judge said.

'Well, sir,' Cirelli's eyes flew to King and back to the jury, 'we couldn't have done DNA even if we had a request. After the first set of blood grouping tests, there was an accidental spill in the lab. The stain got contaminated, and once that happens a DNA profile analysis is out of the question.'

Gardner and the judge both glared at the defense attorney, but he ignored them. Then he leaned forward, checked off a line on his legal pad, and stood up again.

'Agent Cirelli, please tell the jury whose blood you found on the shirt.' He was back on the attack.

'I cannot do that, sir.'

The defense attorney picked up the agent's report. 'Human blood, it says here. Which human?'

'Don't know, sir.'

'So all you can say about the little brown stain is that it is human blood. And, of the billions of humans on this planet, you cannot tell us which one it came from.'

'Correct. But we could say—'

King put up his index finger. 'Uh, uh, uh. That was a yes-or-no question.'

Gardner jumped up. 'He's doing it again, Judge. Trying to cut off the witness's response.'

Danforth had cooled from the earlier firefight. 'I think Mr. King is entitled to get a yes-or-no answer to a yes-or-no question. Ask it again.'

'But . . .' Gardner mumbled at the judge's sudden reversal.

'Go ahead, Mr. King.'

'Thank you, Your Honor. Agent, you have identified the stain as human blood, but according to your testimony on direct examination, your blood grouping tests were inconclusive, and you were unable to assign a blood type. Is that correct, yes or no?'

'Yes. That is correct.'

'And without assigning it a blood type, you cannot tell us from where, out of whose body, that particular blood came. Again, yes or no?'

'Yes. That is correct.'

King started to move his lips, but stopped. He picked up the report again and stared at it, then walked back to the stand and slid it on the top of the rail. 'Thank you, Agent,' he said with a smile. 'I have no further questions.'

'Does the state have any more witnesses for us this morning?'

Gardner rose and made a quarter turn toward the jury. 'No, Your Honor. All we have remaining is presentation of the background information of the defendant and introduction of the drawings . . .'

When Danforth heard the last word, his eyes seemed to glaze over. 'You'd better come up here!' he boomed.

The lawyers marched to the bench and the judge looked at Gardner. 'What are you trying to pull?'

The prosecutor recoiled. 'Excuse me?'

'I thought that drawings issue had been disposed of at the motions hearing.'

Gardner drew close to the bench, gripping the lip with both hands. 'Judge Simmons reserved that point, Your Honor . . .'

Danforth didn't react.

'He ruled it would be considered when offered at trial, and now we're gonna offer it.'

The judge scoured his face with his hand, as if he had

hoped that the whole thing had somehow gone away. He looked at King. 'You got anything to say?'

The defense attorney smiled. 'Let him put it in. We won't object.' His demeanor said, 'Who cares?'

The judge widened his eyes. 'You don't object?' He was clearly trying to communicate: If you do object, I'll sustain it.

'No objection,' King repeated. 'You're gonna let in the criminal history. Allowing the pictures in too is no big deal. But we would object to any testimony commenting on their significance. Just admit the pictures, without comment.'

Danforth turned to Gardner. 'Well?'

The State's Attorney was so used to King's flip-flopping, he hardly registered surprise. 'We did want to put in some psychological evidence—'

'To lay a foundation for admission?' the judge interrupted. 'Without objection, it's not relevant.' The message to Gardner was clear: Take the offer and shut up.

'Very well, Your Honor,' Gardner replied. 'We'll submit the drawings without additional testimony.'

The judge nodded. 'Good. Now, Mr. Lawson, is there anything else you wish to present?'

Gardner released his hands from the bench. 'No, Your Honor, after admission of the history and the drawings, the state will rest.'

Danforth looked at the clock. 11:55 A.M. 'Should be able to get that done right after lunch.' He turned to King. 'Defense going to be ready to start this afternoon?'

King whispered to T. J., then turned back to the bench. 'No problem, Judge.'

'Very well,' Danforth said. 'We're adjourned until one-thirty.' He peered over his glasses, staring seriously at both sides. 'One-thirty on the dot.'

The prosecutors walked to their counsel tables. 'He caved again,' Jennifer said.

Gardner mumbled, 'Uh-huh,' and stretched his shoulders.

'Why do you think he did it?'

Gardner put his hands on his hips. 'I've given up trying to understand the son of a bitch. Right now I'm thinking about this afternoon.'

'Opening statement?'

'Yeah,' Gardner said. 'He's kept it under wraps till now, but it's time for the unveiling. The secret defense . . . revealed at last.'

The FBI agent was waiting in the hall as Gardner left the courtroom. 'Can I talk to you a minute?' he asked in a low voice as Gardner came alongside. 'Uh, alone?'

Gardner patted an apology on Jennifer's arm and moved ahead of the crowd that was beginning to flow from the courtroom to the marble staircase before cascading down to the street.

'What's up?' the prosecutor asked as they reached the bottom.

'Needed to check something. Your questions kind of took me by surprise.'

Gardner steered him to a bench on the stone walkway behind the courthouse. The sun was washing leaf shadows across its wooden backrest as the high branches of a maple tree were buffeted in the freshening breeze. They sat in time to watch a two-seater child stroller go by, identical twins dozing peacefully, immune to the bustle around them.

Gardner spoke first. 'I have to apologize for rushing you out here like we did. I had something to do in Baltimore, and I couldn't prep you as well as I wanted . . . sorry.'

Cirelli looked confused. 'That's one of the things I wanted to ask. I thought you might not be using me at all, you know, after the phone conversation.'

The confusion jumped to Gardner. 'Phone conversation?'

'Yeah. With your law clerk. Two days ago.'

Gardner frowned. 'I don't know anything about it.'

'That's what I figured, after the questions I got.'

'Who did the caller say she was?'

'Wasn't a she. Was a he. Said he worked for your office and needed to go over the report before I came out.'

Gardner was beginning to worry. He hadn't authorized any such call. 'What did you tell this person?'

'He wanted me to get my notes and go step by step over the analysis. What tests did I do? What were the results? Things like that. Then he says, "Your conclusion states you cannot identify the blood type of the blood in the stain. Can you eliminate any blood types?" Well, at first I said no, but then, when I looked back at my notes, I realized that my first set of tests had been nonreactive to the B and AB blood groups. This would tend to rule out those groups as possible sources—'

Gardner's confusion turned to shock. 'What are you saying? You can eliminate certain groupings?'

'Blood typing requires two separate and distinct tests,' Cirelli answered. 'The first categorizes, but does not identify the specific group involved. If we cannot complete the second, the confirmatory test, the results must be reported as inconclusive.'

Gardner frowned again.

'We did get a nonreactive B group response on the first set of tests, but when the spill contaminated the stain we couldn't proceed with the confirmatory, so we reported: human blood, type unknown.'

'But you did rule out that group,' Gardner said gravely.

'Not entirely, but the probability of B or AB blood being contained in that stain is very, very remote. That's what I told your clerk, and I was trying to explain it in there, but the judge wouldn't let me . . .'

Gardner felt like a time bomb had just gone off under his seat. The bloodstain was supposed to be the final nail in Justice's coffin. The evidence that would shut him down for good. Mikhail Anatov had AB-negative type blood. What Cirelli had just said virtually eliminated the possibility that his blood was on T. J.'s sleeve.

Gardner's mind was whirling. Suddenly it locked on a scene in the jail. The outtakes of the Krysta Collins interview. He'd shrugged it off when he'd reviewed the tape, but now it came roaring back into his head like a force-ten gale.

'What happened when you arrived in the county? How

did the people treat you?' Krysta asked.

The camera centered on T. J.'s craggy features. 'Not too good.'

There was a pause. The prisoner wasn't volunteering information. It had to be dragged out. 'Any specific situations you care to talk about?'

'Got beat up. Local boys busted my nose real good.'

The camera caught Krysta's 'concerned' expression, then switched back to the prisoner.

'Said they didn't need no child molesters 'round here. Said if I stayed I wuz gonna git hurt. Then this big ole boy hit me.'

Another cut to the interviewer. 'Did you report it?'

Back to T. J. 'Whut fer? Ain't nobody gonna do nuthin.'

'So, you never told anyone that you were assaulted.'

'No, ma'am. Not at the time. Only one knows about it is Mr. King.'

There was another pause as Krysta readied a new question. The camera was still on T. J.

'Ruin my shirt,' he said suddenly.

'What?' She didn't follow.

'That was the worst part. Messed up my new shirt.'

Krysta was still lost. 'What do you mean, Mr. Justice?'

His face took on a sad cast he hadn't shown before. 'It was the blood. Got my shirt all bloody. Couldn't git it out . . .'

'Mr. Lawson?'

Gardner snapped back to the present. The blood was not AB negative. Not the boy's blood. It was the lynchpin of the entire case, the only direct evidence that tied Justice to the frail corpse in the woods. And now it looked as though Gardner was wrong. T. J. wasn't lying to cover his ass. He was telling the truth. It *was* his own blood on the shirt, just as he'd said, and the fact could be scientifically proven. And someone else, someone outside the prosecutor's office, knew it.

'The voice,' Gardner said suddenly. 'Can you describe it?'

'Normal midrange-type male voice. Nothing unusual.'

'No deep guttural tone?' He was imagining Calvano.

'No. Nothing like that.'

'How about the words? What type of words did he use?'

'Standard legal-type vocabulary. Just what you might expect from a law clerk.'

'Or a lawyer?'

'Or a lawyer.'

Gardner was homing in. 'Agent Cirelli, you've gotta help me here. None of my people made that call, but I've got to know who did. Think. Was there any unusual phraseology? Any mannerisms? Anything at all that sticks in your mind?'

Cirelli leaned back and took off his glasses. 'Come to think of it, he did seem to repeat something . . .'

'What?' Gardner pressed close to the FBI man's face.

'Well, every time I answered one of his questions, seems like he'd go "uh-huh . . ." You know, the way Mr. King was doing in court this morning.'

CHAPTER 17

Gardner desperately needed to think, so instead of going back to the office, he detoured to his car and began driving west. The words of Agent Cirelli were playing and rewinding on an endless tape inside his head. 'Non-reactive to AB blood group . . . Uh-huh . . . probability very, very remote . . . uh-huh . . . rule out AB group as possible source . . . uh-huh . . . uh-huh . . . uh-huh.'

He pulled onto Mountain Road and accelerated to several klicks above the speed-limit. The wind had whipped up a sudsy line of cirrus clouds high above the ridge, and the car bounced against the sudden gusts that rolled down from the craggy peak like shock waves of thunder. King had to be setting him up. That would explain the phone call, and the fact that there were no questions about eliminating the boy's blood type during cross-examination. He was saving it for the defense. Recall the agent as 'his' witness and devastate the state's case. Son of a bitch. That had to be the plan.

Gardner checked the time and realized that the court was due to start up again in less than an hour. He snapped his blinker down and swerved abruptly into the 'scenic overlook' pull-off carved into solid rock at the midpoint of the angled climb to the summit. The wind was a constant at this level, a solid wall of air pushing against Gardner's door as he tried to open it. With a grunting shove, he overcame the pressure and stepped out.

The town looked like a piece of driftwood in a green sea. A jumble of rectangles and squares encircled by crop fields and orchards. The spire of Saint Michael's Church pointed skyward from the center, and beyond, the smooth domed cupola of the county court-house.

Gardner spent his lunch break alone, pacing the walk-way at the overlook. The sun was warming, despite the slight nip of the wind, and he removed his suit coat and slung it over his shoulder. The turnabout in court had left him reeling, and he needed to shake it out of his nervous system. He thought he'd been prepared for everything, but not for this. This was one stunt that one-upped King at his most devious. A well-laid trap. And Gardner had tumbled right in.

As he tried to rework his trial strategy, another puzzle began to emerge. King had made no effort to cover his tracks on this one. He had maneuvered brilliantly, but exposed his move. There was none of his characteristic sneakiness. Cirelli could ID his voice, and King had to know that. It was almost as if he was trying to telegraph to Gardner exactly what he had done.

The prosecutor looked at his watch and realized that he'd be cutting it close to get back by 1:30. He put on his coat and hustled to the car. On the winding road to town, he considered a number of countermoves, but no sure winner came to mind.

Jennifer was waiting anxiously outside the courtroom when Gardner entered the hall at a full run. She pushed the big door aside and let him through, just as the judge retook the bench. There was no time to confer.

'Gentlemen?' Danforth split his attention between the prosecution and the defense. Jennifer frowned, and Gardner stood up.

'It has been agreed by both parties that the jury will be told that Mr. Justice was charged with, and convicted of, murdering a child in the state of Kansas, Your Honor,' Gardner puffed. Despite his conditioning, he was out of breath. 'And that the drawings are to be admitted without comment.'

'Mr. King?'

'With the added proviso on the history that the conviction was reversed on appeal,' the defense attorney answered. 'We will accept it, and permit Your Honor to submit the evidence to the jury.'

Danforth twisted his neck. 'You want *me* to do it? Why? It's the state's evidence. They should put it on.'

King looked at the prosecutor. 'Mr. Lawson likes to omit things . . .' Gardner kept his cool as he interpreted King's double entendre. 'And we'd feel more comfortable having the court do the honors.'

Gardner turned to the judge. 'If it would make Mr. King feel better, go ahead, be my guest.'

'Okay, okay,' the judge replied. 'I'll do it. Now,

anything else?' The attorneys turned to each other, waiting for a move, staring like reptiles in a desert, steadily engaging eyes in a blinkless glare that radiated pure hate.

'Well?' Danforth broke the spell. 'Any other business?'

'No, Your Honor,' Gardner and King said in one voice. 'Not at this time,' the defense attorney added, pausing to give the prosecutor a final look before he returned to his table and sat down.

When the judge told the jury of Justice's past transgression and used the word 'murder,' only two panel members perked up. The rest sat blankly, as if they had known about it all along. The drawings got a much greater reaction, particularly from the women. They looked at the pages with disgust, and then sneaked clandestine accusatory glances at T. J. The effect was obvious: They were now absolutely certain that the man was guilty.

At precisely 2:05 P.M., the state rested its case, and the jury was asked to return to the jury room. This was the stage where the defense could argue for 'judgment of acquittal.' Whether or not the prosecution had made out a prima facie case against the defendant was the issue. If the judge said yes, it had, then the case could continue, and the defense would have to put their case. If he said no, T. J. Justice would go free.

King argued all of the technical legal points first, then hammered on the fact that the case was circumstantial and that there was no direct conclusive evidence of guilt.

After forty-five grueling minutes, he was finally winding down.

'And, in conclusion, we reiterate the position we have taken from the beginning of this trial,' King said, 'that the state has not proven any connection whatsoever between my client and the murder. All they've offered is speculative reference to his past. They have not put in one single piece of evidence to tie T. J. Justice to the crime scene, or the killing itself. The proof is fatally deficient—'

'What about the blood, Mr. King?' Danforth interrupted.

'Sir?'

'The shirt had blood on it. Human blood. How do you get around that?'

King looked at Gardner, then back at the judge. 'But whose blood is it?' he said with a slight smirk.

'That is the question, Mr. King. The state says it's the boy's.'

The defense attorney arched his back. 'And you agree?'

'No, but the jury is entitled to draw that inference, and at this point, without proof to the contrary, I'd say it's quite reasonable.' Judge Danforth leaned forward. 'Motion for judgment of acquittal denied.'

Danforth called a ten-minute recess and Gardner used it to pull Jennifer aside for a conference. They slipped into a witness room and latched the door. 'What's wrong?' Jennifer asked. 'Since you got back from lunch, you've been acting weird.'

Gardner sat at the small table and kicked out the chair on the other side. 'We're in trouble, real trouble.'

Jennifer sat opposite and maneuvered her head to catch his eye. 'This sounds ominous.'

Gardner's face pulled taut. 'King outdid himself . . . goddamn it! Set us up big time.'

The assistant prosecutor reached across the table and grasped her boss's forearm. 'Take it easy.'

'He's gonna accuse us of withholding evidence, and then lay on the jury the fact that the blood didn't come from the Anatov child.'

'How can he do that? The report doesn't specify the blood type.'

Gardner banged his fist. 'Because he was smart enough to ask Cirelli the right question.'

'But,' Jennifer tried to break in, 'he didn't—'

'Yes, he did! Behind our back. The son of a bitch stuck it to us. Behind our back! And we didn't even feel it! Goddamned . . .' Gardner banged his fist on the table in frustration.

Gardner replayed his conversation with the FBI agent in its entirety. 'Nonreactive to AB blood type. Uh-huh . . . uh-huh . . . uh-huh . . .'

Jennifer looked stunned. 'But that's our whole case!' Her thoughts suddenly jumped to the videotape Gardner had showed her. 'So Justice wasn't lying in the interview . . . he really did bleed on his own shirt.'

'Looks that way.'

'Oh, God . . .' Jennifer's expression shifted from surprise to fear. 'What are we going to do?'

Gardner gave her an assuring look. 'The evidence is

not totally exculpatory. There was minimal blood from the wound. T. J. could have stabbed Mika and never gotten blood on him.'

'But we've already implied to the jury that he did.'

The prosecutor grimaced. 'That's the problem. If we backtrack now, it could kill us.'

'So what are we going to do?' Jennifer repeated.

Gardner was used to the 'we' by now. 'We're gonna figure a way to turn it around. Talk to Cirelli, prep him for our cross-examination after King calls him to testify in his case. He can't rule out AB entirely, and that may save us. Maybe we can get him to come on stronger than that, leave the door open to argue that it's the boy's blood after all.'

'Do you really think that's gonna happen?' Jennifer pushed her glasses back up on the bridge of her nose.

'What other choice is there? Surrender? King wants a fight, and goddamn it, he's gonna get one from me till I gasp my last breath.'

Jennifer's face had a serious mien. 'That's really what this is all about, isn't it?'

'Huh?'

'The war. Who wins the war between you two. That's more important than anything else.'

Gardner said nothing. The image of King burned in his brain even brighter than the one of T. J. Justice. They were almost indistinguishable at times, but the defense attorney always came out on top. He felt the anger and pain of the loss of his family, and the suspicion that King played a part. He despised the man's techniques. His smug assurance. His slick manipulation of men and laws. He felt the competitive fever. The call to combat where only one walks away at the finish.

Gardner looked at Jennifer. 'You really think I've lost my objectivity?'

She was solemn. 'When it comes to King.'

'So what do you suggest?'

'I think you'd better reevaluate why you're pushing so hard, that's all. Is it Justice or King you're really after?'

Gardner didn't answer. He had no ready response to Jennifer's question. But deep down he knew she was probably right. Wearily he pushed back his chair. 'It's time to go back into the ring.'

At 2:30 P.M. the time had finally come for the defense to present its case. Because King had 'reserved' his opening statement, he had saved it for this moment. Now he was at the rail, telling the jury what they could expect from his side.

'. . . so you have been instructed by Judge Danforth that the burden of proof rests entirely on the state. It is their responsibility to prove the defendant guilty beyond a reasonable doubt. Not the responsibility of the defendant to prove himself innocent. So why does the defense get a chance to speak during a trial? Why not let the state put on its proof, and then let the jury decide? I'll tell you why.' He began to pace in front of the jury. 'Because they don't always tell you the truth. Because they put in evidence that isn't—'

'Objection!' Gardner had heard enough. King was making a speech, not outlining facts he expected to prove during his case.

'Let him continue, Mr. Lawson,' Judge Danforth boomed back. 'I'd like to get a few witnesses in before the day is over.'

Gardner sat down, and King put his hands on his hips. 'Some people,' he looked at Gardner, 'would have you believe that they are the guardians of the truth.' He turned and pushed against the railing. 'But they have no right to make that claim. They strut and gesture. And they cloak themselves in righteousness.' He looked at the prosecutor again. 'But they couldn't care less about the truth—'

'Object!' Gardner couldn't believe that Danforth was allowing this.

'Sit down, Mr. Lawson!' the judge said sternly.

'But, Your Honor—'

'You heard me,' he thundered. 'Sit down now! Continue, Mr. King.'

Jennifer touched Gardner's hand when he was back in his seat. 'I think he's trying to tell you something,' she whispered.

'Reasonable doubt!' King had switched objects. 'We talk of reasonable doubt all the time, but do you know what it is?' A couple of front-row jurors seemed to be caught up in the oratory. 'It's the feeling you get in your gut when you make a bad decision. When you wake up in the middle of the night in a cold sweat because you did something that you know is wrong. It's the sour taste in your mouth . . . the burning pain in your stomach . . . the cancer in your brain that eats away your life . . .'

'Your Honor, please!' Gardner had to give it one more try. King was starting to stir up the whole front row.

'Mr. Lawson,' the judge said in a slow, deliberate tone, 'one more peep out of you, and I'll use the 'C' word. Do you really want that?'

Gardner sat down. He couldn't afford to add contempt to his list of alleged offenses.

'Mr. King, please continue,' Danforth said. 'And try to tell us a little of what you expect to prove.'

King turned to the judge. 'I was just getting to that, Your Honor. I wanted to explain the system first. So the jury would understand that we are not required to present any evidence. That the state has the entire burden of proof, and that we don't have to say a thing.'

'Well, just give us a hint about your case,' Danforth said sarcastically.

'That's just it,' King replied. 'We're not presenting any. We rest.'

Gardner and Jennifer spun to face each other, their eyes mirror images of astonishment. 'What the hell . . .?' the prosecutor mumbled, unable to finish the sentence. Another bombshell, and this one was even more explosive than the last.

'Sorry about this, Bob,' Deputy Director Tom Quinton apologized as he motioned Hamilton into his spacious office and indicated a chair. It was almost four o'clock. 'Flight got delayed, and no way I could've been here this morning.'

Hamilton sat down in front of the desk and leaned forward. 'No problem, sir. I'm really glad you're back.' There was a pitch of urgency to his words that said, 'Let's get right to the point.'

'Bob, before I hear from you, there are some things I have to cover.' Quinton rose from his desk and closed his office door, snuffing out the corridor sounds and leaving the room in an eerie hush. Then he pulled down the window shade, obliterating the expansive view of lawn and lettuce-green trees, accentuating the apprehensive mood. 'How long you been in the department now?'

Hamilton suddenly noticed his personnel file on the desk and felt a bolt of fear flash through his innards.

'Uh, six years, sir.'

'And do you like what you're doing?'

The scene was not being played the way Hamilton had imagined it. He was quickly being maneuvered into a defensive position, and he didn't know why.

'Uh, yes, sir. A lot.'

'Good. That's important.' Quinton opened the file and riffled through the first three pages; then he shut it abruptly. 'How would you like to move up?'

The question caught Hamilton by surprise. The initial tone had been dismissal. Now, it switched to promotion.

'Grade advancement, sir?' he asked cautiously.

'Uh-huh. Two steps.'

'That would be fine with me, sir.' He tried to keep his voice level.

'Great. I was sure you would say that. Now, before we get to the details, I need to give you a set of rules . . .' Quinton's voice turned ominous, and Hamilton could see that there was going to be a catch.

'The world as we know it plays by a double standard,' Quinton began, shooting a look that said he did not want to be interrupted. 'We do what is best for us, and everyone else does what's best for them. We spy. They spy. We interfere in their affairs. They interfere in ours. Everyone is madly scrambling behind the scenes. We know it and they know it, and as long as it continues that way, everything is fine. But then' – Quinton's voice shaded deadly serious – 'something goes public, and the rules change. We're outraged. They're up in arms with denials. We retaliate in some half-ass way. They come back at us. And on and on . . .'

Hamilton was trying desperately to see where this speech fit into his personal scheme. He had lived the duality ever since he came to the department, and it had never been a problem.

'Bob, we've got to be sure that you can play by the rules when we let you go upstairs. You're gonna have to make some tough decisions. You won't just be an information man . . . you'll be a policymaker.'

'Excuse me, sir, but why are you telling me this?' Hamilton asked.

In answer, Quinton opened his desk drawer and pulled out a thick file. Before Hamilton looked at the lettering, he knew what it was. A blue CIA standard-issue file with the name ANATOV stenciled on the flap.

Gardner was in shock. Court had adjourned for the weekend, pending closing arguments on Monday, and now at quarter to four he was back at his desk, trying to put the situation into perspective, trying to understand the meaning of the defense attorney's words: 'We rest.' King had a stick of dynamite, and he wasn't going to light it. That was not just out of character, it was insane. In some cases it might be a reasonable strategy to forgo a defense, especially if the state was weak on the evidence, but not here. King had a whole arsenal at his disposal. Alibi witness. Blood type elimination. Psychological evidence. He could give the state a fit. Throw out enough issues to give reasonable doubt a face that even this jury would love. But no. He was hanging up his sword and bowing farewell. Gardner tried to fight a thought that was burrowing through the wall that separated reality from fiction. It couldn't be. Not King. Not in this case. Not against his archenemy. But all the signs were there, and they couldn't be ignored: King was taking a dive.

Gardner opened his trial folder and pulled out the autopsy X ray copies. King's behavior during cross-examination of the ME suddenly took on a new meaning. He had been interrupted the last time he tried to check it out. Now it couldn't wait.

LS–1. LS–2. LS–3. The left-side sequential views fanned out like a deck of cards in a poker hand, each complementing the previous image by adding a variable increment to the track of the wound. One by one the pages dropped into sequence.

When he reached the opposite angle, and right-side view number 8, he stopped. Something didn't look right. He thumbed through the left-side views and selected one, then laid it next to RS–8. They didn't correspond.

Gardner picked up the phone and popped the button for an outside line.

'Medical Examiner's office,' the answering voice said.

'Dr. Stinson, please.'

The operator put him on hold to the tune of a Muzak melody, 'Any day now you're gonna . . .'

'Stinson.'

'Doc, this is Gardner Lawson. Can you do me a favor? Pull the Anatov X rays? I've got a question for you.'

'Hang on a sec.' The pathologist was back in a hurry. 'Got 'em. What's the problem?'

'Take a look at RS–Eight, and then compare that with LS–Eight. Aren't they mirror images of each other?'

There was a short pause. 'Uh-huh. Supposed to be.'

'Well, doesn't it look like there's an extension on RS–Eight that doesn't appear on the other one?'

Another pause. 'Well, yes, there does seem to be a difference.'

'Can you explain it? I mean, is that significant?' There was a longer pause this time, and Gardner could picture the doctor poring over the flimsy negative. 'Doc? What's the word?'

'It's possible that there was a downward pressure on the handle at the time of insertion . . . that would have shifted the point to a higher level and extended the wound . . . or . . .'

Gardner didn't like the tone change in Stinson's voice. 'Or what?'

There was a final pause. 'Or the knife that made the wound had a blade with a slight upward curve at the tip.'

'I know what you're thinking,' Quinton said as he looked

into Hamilton's widened eyes. 'You were held out of the loop.'

The young State Department officer was speechless, unable to come back with an intelligible response.

'We did it for you, Bob. You may not believe that, but it's true.'

Hamilton finally got his voice back. 'So you know about the situation . . . about Justice, and the threat, and . . .'

Quinton held up his hand like a miniature stop sign. 'That's our job.'

'So why did you let me think . . . ?'

The hand came up again. 'We can't move anyone into the policy shop until they're ready. There's a line' – he glanced down at the Anatov file, then looked up – 'that has to be crossed. Once you're on the other side, you cannot come back.'

Hamilton suddenly realized what had happened. 'You were testing me.'

'I wouldn't put it that way. It was more like a warm-up. The test is yet to come.'

Things were clouding up again. 'What do you mean?'

'I mean you have a decision to make. You know about our world. The people live on one side, we live on the other. The people get outraged over secrecy, and subterfuge, and' – his voice went low – 'injustice.' He shifted the file around so that Hamilton had a straight shot at the closed cover. 'We don't. It's not what we're here for. We deal in the realities behind the headlines, not the sensationalist glop that the public feeds on.'

The implication was clear. If Hamilton wanted to go

any higher in the department, he'd have to cross the line, and opening the file was the first step. He pulled it closer, but didn't lift the lid.

Quinton stirred expectantly. 'Remember, Bob, there's no going back.'

Hamilton swallowed hard and, with a jerk of his wrist, leapt across the invisible barrier into the unknown.

It was all there. The 21:24 note. The Justice background chronology. The Anatov personal history. He scanned the detailed résumé, looking for a key to the mystery, upturning page after page until he hit the one labeled MILITARY POSTS. There, in the margin, was a string of dates and next to them the geographical location of the posting. One was circled in red, and as soon as he saw it, he knew why the Anatov child had been killed. He looked up to find Quinton nodding a confirmation to his discovery.

'So that's what's behind this,' Hamilton said.

Quinton nodded again.

'This wasn't any sex crime, it was . . .' Hamilton's voice began to crack.

Quinton held up his hand in a 'halt' signal. 'Bob, take it easy. What did I just get finished telling you? This is not our concern. We have more serious problems to deal with.'

'Like keeping it quiet?' Hamilton's voice had dropped to its normal register.

'Let's just say that the Russians do not want any publicity on certain facts and that our national interest is in accord with that position.'

The young deputy secretary had not expected this. He

had come to Quinton to divulge a secret, not to learn one. 'So we sit back and let things happen?' he asked in a flat tone.

'You know that's the way things are done.'

'But they're going to convict an innocent man!' Hamilton couldn't keep his voice from rising a notch.

Quinton managed a wry smile. 'Innocence is a matter of degree. I suggest you look at the big picture and not concern yourself with the fate of Mr. Justice. We're on the verge of a new relationship with the Russians. The cold war is over. They need us, and we need them. The case is secondary.'

'And what does it matter if someone gets stepped on in the process,' Hamilton interjected.

Quinton's smile vanished. 'I hope you're not serious, Bob.'

'Uh, no, sir,' he replied, putting up a nervous smile of his own, 'just being facetious.'

Quinton's face remained drawn. 'I hope so. You're no good to us if you can't stay with the program.'

Hamilton looked down at the file still spread open before him. 'You can count on me, sir,' he said, pulling the corner of a photograph from the bottom of a thick stack of papers.

'I'm glad,' Quinton said, rising and extending his hand across the desk.

Hamilton didn't notice what his boss had done. He was staring at the picture. It was a night-scope photo taken with a long-range lens, blown up in grainy detail. There were two men talking. One was Zeitzoff, hulking over the shorter figure. The clarity was not good, but the face was familiar. He had seen it in the newspaper next to an artist's rendering of T. J. Justice. It was Defense Attorney Kent King.

'Bob?' The hand was waiting.

Hamilton stood and reciprocated. 'Thank you, sir,' he said. And Quinton could not help noticing that both the voice and handshake were weak.

Miss Cass had just put through a phone call after her boss hung up with the medical examiner, but didn't tell Gardner who it was. He picked up on the first buzz.

'Afternoon, boss . . .'

Gardner laughed out loud at the sound of Brownie's voice. 'What are you doing, man, reading my mind? I was about to call you.'

There was a characteristic chuckle on the other end, then a fade-off to a serious note. 'I just heard the news—'

'Yeah,' Gardner cut in. 'Can you believe it? No alibi. No nothing.'

'What the hell's he doin'?'

Gardner's voice hushed almost to a whisper. 'I've got an idea, but we can't talk about it over the phone. Can you meet me?'

'Just say where and when. I'll be there.'

'How about the orchard. In about an hour?'

'You got it.'

Gardner was about to hang up when he realized that the call had originated on the other end. 'Brownie? Did you really read my mind?'

Another chuckle, then silence. 'I got something to

show you,' the officer finally said. 'I think we may have a snapshot of the killer.'

At five o'clock Bob Hamilton sat at the Wild Goose Tavern in Old Town Alexandria, trying to celebrate his promotion. The bar was decorated with a nautical flair. Nets and buoys suspended above, ship prints on the wall, waterfowl place mats. The clientele was professional, well dressed, and obviously affluent. They pushed in around him, joyously proclaiming the virtues of Friday, but he just wasn't in the mood. On the way over, the news report had come through his car radio like a high-voltage shock. 'In a surprise move that left the entire courthouse buzzing, Defense Attorney Kent King rested his case without presenting any evidence.'

Hamilton looked around as he tried to stomach the scotch and soda he had been sloshing around for the past fifteen minutes. These were the 'people' that Quinton had talked about. The ones who believed that there should be honesty and fair play in the affairs of the world.

He felt isolated and alone. 'You gonna drink that or just play with it?' the bartender said.

Hamilton took a courtesy sip, twitched his mouth in a halfhearted smile, and set his glass down on the bar. This was harder than he had expected. After six years of waiting, his moment had finally arrived, but now all he could think about was Justice. 'The case is being held over until Monday morning, when the attorneys will give their closing arguments. Then it will be turned over to the jury,' the report had said. 'The line, at this point, is

leaning toward the prosecution, with most knowledge-
able court watchers predicting conviction.'

Hamilton writhed with inner torture, looking at the
people around him, back at his drink, and back to the
people again. Over and over his mind kept churning the
same question, and he knew that before the end of the
night he had to decide which side he was really on.

Gardner drove to the orchard via the southern route.
There was less traffic, and less probability that he might
be seen. Lying in the eastern end of the valley, the
orchard was well away from the developments closer to
town. The land was sparsely populated, filled with wide
pastures and fruit-bearing trees.

He pulled up to the entrance and unlocked the chain
just as Brownie arrived with the lab van. Gardner waved
his friend through and followed behind, latching the
rusted links to block any intruders.

They then proceeded down the narrow road to the
barn. On each side the decaying applewood attested to
the tragic end of a once-thriving business. Some trees
had managed to spawn a leaf or two, but most were
dead, drying into gray, barkless forms that made the
entire grove look like a giant field of driftwood
sculptures.

Gardner drove into the barn ahead of Brownie. They
parked in the center of the cavernous shed and together
they closed the big wooden doors. It was 5:30 P.M., and
two smoky poles of sunlight converged in a shimmery
patch of brightness at the juncture of the vehicles. The
prosecutor and the police sergeant faced each other in

the light. Gardner was still in his jury suit, his tie pulled down, his shirt unbuttoned at the collar. Brownie was in uniform, impeccable as always.

'What's this about a photograph?' Gardner asked anxiously.

Brownie pulled back the sliding door to the van and sat on the rail. 'I'll show you in a minute. First, you gotta tell me what this dude is up to.'

Gardner sat next to his friend. 'He's throwing the case.'

'He's what?'

'He's trying to lose . . . wants his man convicted.'

'We talking about King? Mr. Bazooka?'

'Yeah. The king of the courtroom is taking a fall.'

'Now why would the man want to do something like that?'

Gardner's face assumed a look that Brownie had never seen before, a mixture of wonder and panic. 'Because he wants to finish me off, and he's found a way to do it . . .'

'You're losin' me, boss.'

'Goddamn it!' Gardner snapped back. 'He wants me to convict an innocent man!'

Brownie whistled. 'You tellin' me Justice is innocent?'

Gardner grabbed his knees and squeezed. 'There's a chance of it.'

'Slow down,' Brownie interrupted. 'Put it to me straight. What about the evidence?'

'It's all falling apart. Every piece of proof I put in is crumbling in my hands. The blood. The wound. The knife . . . the damn alibi is even starting to make sense now, just like you were saying.'

Brownie took in the words without apparent shock. It was as if he'd suspected it all along, and Gardner simply confirmed his belief. 'So what the hell can King get out'a all this?' he finally asked. 'He's got a way to get his man off. Why would he blow it?'

Gardner ran his hand through his hair. 'Because he's after me! The fucker's got it all figured out. He played tough guy from the beginning. Motions. Arguments. Everything a defense attorney should do. Shit, no higher court reading the record would ever accuse King of lying down on the job. But he knew! He knew where the cracks were all along, and never said anything . . .'

'So what's he tryin' to do?'

'Put me in a no-win situation. If we get the conviction, he'll file posttrial motions, and all of the exculpatory evidence will miraculously appear. Then he'll say that I knew all about it from the beginning, and I'll come across as the liar he always says I am. Add that to my other troubles, and I'll be a sure candidate for disbarment, maybe even criminal prosecution.' Wearily Gardner massaged the back of his neck.

'So why don't you dismiss the case and cut him off at the pass?'

Gardner gave Brownie an angry look. 'I can't! We've got nothing to prove Justice didn't do it, and I'm not totally convinced he's clean. None of this new stuff exonerates him, it only raises doubts. There's still the possibility he's guilty.'

Brownie listened attentively, nodding agreement to the prosecutor's decision not to drop the case.

'But I've got another problem,' Gardner continued. 'The *Brady* rule requires me to report exculpatory information to the defense. One way or another I've got to tell King . . .'

'But he already knows,' Brownie said.

'Yeah. We know that, but the court doesn't. The minute I put this shit on the record, King will scream foul, win the case, look like a hero, and I'll still get the ax for trumping up false charges against Justice. The son of a bitch really outdid himself this time. Got me in a box, and there's no way to get out.'

Brownie reached into the van and pulled out a rectangular brown envelope. 'Maybe we can do something about it,' he chuckled, opening the packet.

'What's that?' Gardner asked as the officer slid a stack of photographs into view.

'What if you could look back to the night of the crime and see who was in and out of Sessy's? And what if there was something in there that you never saw before? And what if you came up with some whole new evidence?'

'You mean to eliminate Justice as a suspect?'

Brownie grinned. 'Or maybe lock him in as the one that done the deed.'

'But I've closed the case,' Gardner said.

'You can open it again, like you did the Candy trial.'

'Okay, so we get some new evidence' – Gardner was searching for the plan – 'and we reopen the case . . .'

'And you prove Justice *did* do it or he *didn't* do it. Either way, you get the job done and ain't nothing King can say.'

Gardner pushed in over the pictures. 'I hope you're right, Brownie,' he said. 'We need a miracle, and you're the only person I know who can make it happen.'

The photographs were aerial reconnaissance views of western Maryland. 'Ordered these when I thought you was in trouble and needed a boost,' Brownie said. 'Now it seems they might come in handy.'

The photos were high-resolution close-ups, night scenes rendered with the most modern equipment in the air force inventory. 'They were runnin' the Camp David perimeter for an update security check,' Brownie said softly. 'They do that whenever the head honcho is up there.' He pulled a photo from the file and handed it to Gardner. 'Routine procedure for them, jackpot for us. Check out the date.'

The prosecutor looked at an inscription on the bottom margin of the photo: November 27, 1989, 1740 hrs. It was the date and time of the murder. 'Jesus!' he said.

'Yeah, we oughta thank Him,' Brownie replied, placing the photo on the floor of the van under the light. 'Now, see this road?'

Gardner nodded, his heart starting to pound with excitement.

'Follow it along here.'

The prosecutor's finger traced the dark line as it wound a familiar path from the town in the lower left corner to the border of Sessy's Woods. Brownie handed him a magnifier he had removed from his crime kit. 'Take a look.'

Gardner lowered the glass over the light area that stood out in the surrounding darkness like an oasis in the desert. In the centre of the path was a tiny white spot.

'That's the boy,' Brownie said with a sigh. 'Still warm, or it wouldn't-a showed up so bright on the heat-sensitive film.'

Gardner wasn't listening. He had located another object near the edge of the woods. Barely visible, it looked like the tail end of a car. 'Brownie?'

'I'd say that's him,' the officer replied.

'Him?'

'Our man. The killer. Just done the deed, now on his way out the road.'

Gardner studied the blurry image. 'What good does that do us?'

'Don't know,' Brownie said. 'Haven't figured that part out yet.'

Gardner patted his friend on the shoulder. 'But you will, right?'

The officer let loose one of his winning smiles. 'If there's a way, Officer Joseph Brown will get it done.'

Gardner added another pat. 'You're the best.'

Brownie took the magnifier from Gardner's hand. Monday morning was just over the hill. He had work to do.

After almost an hour sloshing his scotch around and brooding, Hamilton walked to a pay phone in the corner near the men's room.

'Con?' The background noise in the bar made it difficult to hear.

Hamilton thought there was an answer, but the quick

fade-out made him not so sure.

'Bob?'

'Yeah. It's me . . .'

'Where are you? Sounds like a party.'

Hamilton smiled at the irony. 'Got promoted today.'

'That's wonderful. I know you wanted it.'

'Yeah. Great.'

'What?'

He had been jostled by a passing member of the crowd. 'I said great,' he repeated.

'You don't sound happy.'

'I'm . . . I am. It's just that—' Another jostle interrupted his words.

'I can't hear you.'

'It's just that something has come up, and I don't think I can make it tomorrow.'

The line seemed to go dead.

'Con? Did you hear me?'

'Yes, I did.' Her voice was choked with disappointment.

'I'm really sorry. We'll do it again soon. I promise.'

Another wave was approaching, so Hamilton prepared to hang up. 'Call you next week, okay?'

'Bob?' Her voice sounded different.

'Gotta go. I'll talk to you soon.'

'Bob!' It sounded like the shriek of a mother whose child is about to run into traffic. 'What are you going to do?'

He hesitated. She had never been told anything concerning the case. All she knew was that he had been researching Anatov.

'Uh, nothing.'

'Are you sure?' She now sounded accusatory.

'Con, I gotta go. I'll call you, okay?'

'Please be careful!' she pleaded. 'Please!'

He hung up the phone as another human wave hit and drove him against the wall. When he recovered he felt a new emotion in his stomach. Con's tone had scared him. She was too low in the agency to know about the Russian-Justice connection, but after hearing her voice, he wasn't so sure. It was almost as if she had been told the whole story and knew exactly what he was about to do.

He returned to the bar, sat down, and ordered another drink. The decision was easy, he thought. The tough part was getting up the courage to see it through.

Thomas Quinton pushed a red button on the bottom of his telephone console. The ceiling lights in his office had been extinguished, and except for a gooseneck lamp on his desk casting a greenish glow, the room was dark. The Anatov file still lay open in front of him. He thumbed an index card clipped to the jacket and flipped it over. There was a number on the back. He raised his reading glasses and read as he keyed the phone. There was a whir and an electronic pulse.

'Security.'

'Outside line, please.'

'Authorization code?'

'Two-six-five-Q.'

'Number?'

'Just hook me up. I'll put through the number.'

'Then you don't want this call logged.'

'That is correct.'

'Yes, sir.' The line converted to a subtle hum.

Quinton keyed the set of digits on the card. There was a purr, and a click, but no words. Quinton spoke into the silence on the other end. 'Possible security breach in progress. Subject under surveillance. Full knowledge of all operational aspects. Situation being monitored.'

He waited for an acknowledgment. After several seconds, it came. A guttural voice spat out a single word. '*Sbacebo*.'

Quinton hung up. 'You're welcome,' he said aloud. Then he picked up the file, placed it in his briefcase, and turned off the light.

At 6:20 Gardner and Brownie were still in the lab van at the orchard poring over the photographs, searching for anything that might give them a leg up on the case.

'Look at this, Brownie,' Gardner said in an excited whisper. The sunspot was gone now, and they had turned the internal swivel lamp to illuminate their work space on the floor. Each man had a magnifying glass, and each was busy scouring the set of pictures for a clue.

The recon jet had made three sweeps in a six-hour period. The logic was not clear, but the results left them a staggered chronicle of the activities on the night of the murder. That realization had piqued an idea in the prosecutor. He pulled Charlie Barnes's notes from his file. Maybe there was a correlation between what the plane's camera picked up and what the gung-ho officer had recorded in his effort to be conscientious.

'What you got?' Brownie put his glass aside and moved next to the prosecutor.

Gardner adjusted the height of the magnifier, so the image underneath came into focus. It was a light-colored rectangle with a distinct V-shaped indentation in the lower end. 'Pull the crime scene, and put it next to this one,' he said.

Brownie tore through the pile and produced the 1740 labeled photo. He placed it beside the one Gardner was still studying. 'Now take a look at the car leaving Sessy's and compare it with this,' the prosecutor said in a hushed voice.

Brownie moved in with his own glass. 'Uh-huh . . . uh-huh,' he breathed, moving back and forth between the two glossy sheets of paper. 'I do believe we got the same vehicle here.' Their respective magnifiers now hovered over the parallel pictures. In the fish-eye distortion of the lenses the evidence was clear. The V-shaped impression on the rear bumper was identical.

The glasses were still in place when Gardner spoke. 'Notice anything else about those two?'

Brownie's eyes went right to the target. 'The first one's blurry, and the other one's crystal clear.'

Gardner nodded. 'Significance?'

Brownie put down his glass. 'One's moving, and the other is not.'

Gardner nodded again. 'That's my conclusion, too.'

'So now we got to figure out where he stopped,' Brownie said, tracing the road back from the stationary car toward a landmark they both recognized.

Gardner had picked up the tempo, his finger busy coming down the road on the other side.

They were talking over each other as they traced.

'Okay. Hodges is here . . . and there's West Run . . .'

'That must be the turnoff to the mill . . .'

They hit the jackpot simultaneously.

'Got it!' Brownie exclaimed.

'Me too,' followed Gardner. 'Minecastle Road.'

Brownie whistled. 'Way on out there in the boondocks. Nothin' around for ten miles any direction, and the man want to stop . . .'

'Check the time,' Gardner said.

Brownie picked up the photo and read the notation: 'Twenty-three twenty-eight . . . eleven twenty-eight P.M. So the same car that was at the scene of the crime turns up in the middle of nowhere five hours later.'

Gardner looked at Brownie in the subdued light of the barn. 'What do you think it means?'

Brownie picked up Charlie Barnes's notes. 'I'd say the man know somethin' 'bout the situation, and if supercop was doin' his job that night we jes' may be able to find him.'

Gardner's hand was shaking as he threshed through the stack of decoded notes. The time sequence and location had a familiar ring. Minecastle Road. 11:28 P.M. The prosecutor had heard that phrase before.

When he got to the third page, he remembered. There, in the unique language of Charlie's acronyms, was the car and, beside it, a tag number.

'God bless Charlie Barnes,' Gardner said with a quaking voice.

430

'Make that a double,' Brownie quipped, grabbing the notes and jumping to his feet. 'Gotta make me a long-distance call to Ohio State Police,' he said. 'Need to locate the owner of a car with plate number one-four-three-CAS. Seem like the man done abandoned his vehicle in our county.'

Gardner stood and stretched his legs. 'I think he has some explaining to do.'

Brownie grabbed the prosecutor in a bear hug and shook him. 'Jus' like the announcerman say, it ain't over yet.'

It was 8:45 and Bob Hamilton had deliberated long enough. He managed to sip three more scotches alone in the throng, then got up and walked unsteadily out of the bar. He wasn't paying attention to the people as he left, so it didn't mean anything to him that a couple of other patrons decided to leave at the same time.

Weaving slightly through the dark parking lot, he reached his car and fumbled the key in the lock. He drove the parkway north toward Key Bridge, which would lead him back to the apartment in Georgetown. As he got to the exit, he put on his blinker and slowed down for a turn, but when the lane melded in ahead of the car, he realized he couldn't do it. He couldn't go home. With a sudden swerve, he cut back to the main road. The road that led to the Beltway, then to I–270, then to route 70, and on west until it spliced its way through the mountains into a green valley, and finally to the door of a county courthouse.

Hamilton shuddered. His lane change had been

dangerous, but luckily, the traffic was light. All he could see was one set of headlights to the rear, and that seemed to be keeping a respectable distance. Once he was out of Washington, he knew, it was all over. No more job. No more career. His mind was still fuzzed with alcohol, but his spirit was calm. He crossed the Woodrow Wilson Bridge into Maryland, and realized there was no turning back. Tomorrow he had a rendezvous with Justice.

Brownie knew his brother's Trans-Am could get him to Cincinnati by morning. The Ohio State Police had run the tag number and delivered the information: 'Thomas Ira Crawford, 3245 Dudley Drive, Cincinnati.' That was all they could give over the phone. If Brownie wanted more, they said, he'd have to get it himself.

'Ain't much, but it's a start,' he told Gardner as he prepared to leave. 'Name don't sound too sinister . . .'

Gardner had moved into the van and listened as the communications officer at the station patched Brownie into the ground line. His thoughts were racing. T. J. was hanging over the jaws of the jury on a rope of circumstantial evidence. Even if it unraveled, he was going to drop in. Brownie was right. He had to get a lock on the evidence before he made a move against King. He had to nail Justice, or clear him. There was no middle ground. If he couldn't do it by Monday, he would have hell to pay, and his archenemy would be the first in line to collect.

'Suggestions?' Brownie drew the prosecutor back.

'We can't broadside the guy,' Gardner answered. 'If he's involved, he'll clam up—'

'So we sneak in the back,' Brownie interrupted. 'Find out all we can about him before we strike.'

Gardner nodded agreement. 'Okay. Then what?'

'By that time maybe I got me some stuff I can use against him. Background. Criminal history. Associates . . .'

'You mean, like T. J.?'

'Could be. Or maybe he got some other reason for bein' up Sessy's that night . . . somethin' that don't involve Justice.'

'We don't have much time,' Gardner said.

'If it's there, I'll find it,' the officer replied.

The State's Attorney climbed out of the van. 'If you don't, don't bother to come back.'

Brownie looked at his friend. The mood was somber, but he thought he could detect an approaching smile. 'What? You ain't gonna be here?'

Gardner maintained the mood. 'Not for long,' he said.

A short time later, Brownie had already passed the state line on route to Ohio. He hunkered down in the seat, kicked the accelerator, and pushed the tachometer toward the red zone.

The road rolled past like a conveyor belt, smoothly slipping under the hood in an endless flow of asphalt. He reached into a bag on the passenger side and pulled out his service revolver, carefully storing it in the space under his seat. Then he went into the bag again, removed his leather badge case, flipped it open to the heart-shaped sergeant's emblem, and placed it on the dashboard. Tonight he was on official business.

He couldn't have cared less who knew about it.

'Jennifer?' Gardner had dozed off in his chair, and the phone woke him up. The day's events had drained his energy. The King reversal. The evaporating evidence. Brownie's photos. The new lead. Things were happening too fast, and he was tired. A brief rest after the orchard was all he had in mind when he got back to the town house, but now it was 10:00 P.M.

'What happened to you this afternoon?'

'Whaa?' He still wasn't totally coherent.

'I thought we were going to go over closing arguments, but you left without telling me anything.'

'Sorry. I had to go out.'

Gardner had kept Jennifer clear of the complications that had set in after King rested his case. As far as she knew, it was a strategy move by the defense. The prosecutor didn't tell her his theory about what King was trying to do.

'So when are we going to discuss it? Monday morning?'

Gardner hesitated. 'Maybe late tomorrow, or Sunday . . .'

'There's something you're not telling me, isn't there?'

Another hesitation. 'Can't pull anything over on you, can I?' He chuckled.

Jennifer cleared her throat with a melodic little chirp. 'You're going to have to get over that some day.'

'What?'

'Treating me like a little Barbie doll who needs to be

434

kept on the shelf. Goddamn it, Gard, you've got to let me in!'

The double Gs took the prosecutor by surprise. 'Jennifer? Okay, you're right, we have to talk . . .'

'When?'

'As soon as I get some more information. We'll get together and go over the whole thing.'

'Before Monday?'

'Of course before Monday. After that it will be too late.'

By 11:25 the alcohol was starting to wear off, and Bob Hamilton felt as if a bumblebee had taken up residence behind his eyes. The roadway had become a lot more rustic since he had turned off the interstate. No more four lanes. No more light poles. Now it was only steep rises and sharp turns on a narrow path that zigzagged unpredictably through the dark countryside. The city lights were far behind, and it seemed that the only color ahead was black.

Several times he had to tap the brake and yank the wheel to keep from running off the road, and now he was tracking a solid double line up the highest angled grade yet. There was no traffic to speak of. He had pulled over to let a big-wheeled pickup pass sometime back, and another set of headlights was coming on fast in his rearview mirror. He looked for a post to repeat the courtesy, but there was no shoulder. The road was bordered by a low rail that divided earth and concrete from the nothingness of a thousand-foot free-fall to the valley floor.

The lights had come on so strong that Hamilton had to knock the mirror down to keep from being blinded. Then he noticed they were gone, and realized that the fool was trying to pass.

The crunch of metal against metal gave a sickening screech that lasted only until the cars separated, and Hamilton's car flew over the rail into the night.

CHAPTER 18

April 29
7:05 A.M.

A plane in the approach pattern to the Cincinnati airport made a lazy banking turn over the interstate, and Brownie's car passed directly underneath. He rubbed his right eye with a knuckle and tried to convince himself that he could still keep it going for forty-eight hours at a stretch. The eye wouldn't clear up, no matter how hard he rubbed, so he decided it was time to get some coffee.

Exit 32B had a knife, fork, and spoon sign pointing east, so the officer pulled off on the ramp and followed the highway markers to the O-HY-O Diner, an old-style, silver-skinned restaurant surrounded by trucks. He finally found an empty spot between two eighteen-wheelers, backed the Trans-Am in the narrow chasm, locked the doors, and went in for breakfast.

On the way back to the car after eating, Brownie felt a familiar jolt that snapped him to attention and made his feet brake to a sudden halt. It was his danger signal.

A sudden, unpredictable alarm that came out of nowhere. The last time it hit was when he had walked within ten feet of a drug gang's ambush. Some officers called it a sixth sense, a gift that God gives policemen to keep them out of harm's way. Brownie didn't know what to call it. All he knew was that when the hairs on the back of his neck started stiffening for no apparent reason, he'd better get ready to jump.

Brownie retrieved his jacket, gun, and badge and hustled back to the diner. He had shared a table with a trucker and wanted to catch him before he got away. Instinct said to leave the car and hitch a ride into town, to make a sudden variation in his predictability. That way, until the hairs went down, he'd keep the enemy guessing . . . whoever and wherever they might be.

'Sir!' The newsstand lady at the airport chased the customer down the corridor after he had picked up a newspaper. He had just come off of a 7:00 A.M. flight and probably didn't notice that he had given her a fifty. 'Your change. You didn't get your change.'

The man turned around. He was very tall and had a thick clump of white hair sticking out of his forehead.

'You gave me a fifty. Here's your change.'

The man didn't say anything.

'Well, are you going to take it?' Her hand had been extended for about ten seconds without any response.

The man finally scooped the bills from her hand and left the coins behind. Then he turned and started back down the hall that led to the exit.

'Well, thanks to you too!' the lady said with a sarcastic huff. Then on reflection she took it back. Maybe the guy couldn't understand English.

Deputy Director Tom Quinton sat in the den of his Chevy Chase home. His wall looked like a photo gallery, stocked with the 'insiders' of past administrations posing with a man who seemed to age progressively as the walnut frames ascended. The leather sofas and executive desk gave the room a feel of cozy elegance.

Quinton was on the telephone, his face pale and damp. 'It's confirmed?'

'Yes, sir.' The voice on the other end sounded young and nervous.

'Automobile accident.'

'That is the official word, yes, sir.'

'Where *they* involved?'

'Sir?'

Quinton added aggravation to his expression. 'Any Soviet involvement?'

'Don't know, sir. Local police aren't saying much. They're listing it as a possible hit-and-run. He did have a high blood-alcohol reading . . .'

'Is that all you've got?' There was an implied threat in his voice.

A pause. 'Yes, sir. That's it so far. We're still working on it.'

Quinton rubbed his cheek and closed his eyes. 'Well, cancel it!'

'Sir?'

'I said cancel further inquiry. Do you understand?'

'Yes, sir. Uh, do you want a written report on what we now have?'

'No! And you are to shred your notes immediately.'

'Yes, sir.'

'I'll take it from here. From now on the subject is restricted to deputy level communication only. Is that clear?'

'Yes, sir. Clear.'

Quinton hung up and redialed. 'All previous orders rescinded,' he said to the male voice that answered. 'Proceed to subject's residence and sanitize. Mark all accessible file references for immediate destruction. Operation terminated.'

There was an inquiry on the line.

'That is correct,' Quinton said. 'Terminated and expunged.'

'Look, Dad!' Granville pointed to the TV as Captain Nemo's submarine began its run toward a helpless sailing ship.

'He's going to ram it,' Gardner said, noticing that his own stomach was starting to tighten as the demonic-looking *Nautilus* gathered speed and sprayed a greenish bow-wave over its forward 'eye.'

They were stuck at home all morning because Gardner had to wait by the phone for word from Brownie. He would have preferred tossing a ball at the park, or collecting rocks, or driving up to the overlook, but a call from Ohio was more important, so they had to settle for a stack of video movies starting with *Twenty Thousand Leagues Under the Sea* and ending with *Pinocchio*.

Gardner watched his son absorbed in the action on the screen. He had grown so much in the last year. The white flax hair was beginning to darken. The nose had gained more definition. And his awareness had sharpened. He was still on the small side for his age, but a spunky streak made up for it. Gardner thought about earlier times when the two of them had explored the yard and played hide-and-seek in the garden beyond the Watson Road house. The wonders of the seasons had unfolded anew each year as father explained, and son listened, and a little more knowledge lit up the boy's eyes. And now the absorption rate had increased. And it was time to go out and see new things, to explore new venues. But grown-up problems intervened. A man was seeking answers in another state, and Dad had to stand by and wait for it all to unfold.

'Wow! Look at that!' The knifelike nose of the sub had just pierced the ship's hull and water was rushing in. Then it began to sink, and the passengers and crew were trapped inside. Gardner watched them struggle frantically as the ship went down, but before the scene had ended, he turned away from the screen.

1:30 P.M.

'You sure you don't mind me messin' with your machine?' Brownie asked the attractive, dark-skinned computer operator at the western district substation of the Cincinnati police department.

The young woman unleashed a bright smile. 'You look like you got a soft touch, Sergeant Brown. Something tells me I can trust you.'

Brownie gave one of his award-winners in return. 'We

are talkin' about keyboards, right?'

The woman kept her even white teeth in view. 'Why, Sarge, did you think I meant something else?'

They both laughed as Brownie took over her spot at the console. A half hour's lead-up conversation had gotten him to this position, and there was no doubt as to exactly what the female officer had in mind.

INPUT DATA, the screen prompted. Brownie typed *Thomas Ira Crawford.*

Date of Birth?

Brownie had picked it up over the phone. *06–06–32,* he keyed in.

Last known address?

3245 Dudley Drive, Cincinnati, Ohio 45236.

Please wait . . . Working, the screen flashed back.

Brownie shifted in Officer Moore's narrow chair. When she got up, he had confirmed his original impression. The lady was okay in the physical fitness department.

No Record, the single entry suddenly popped out on the response line.

Delineate: Criminal/Traffic, Brownie typed.

Another *Please wait . . . Working,* then, *No Record.*

Open charges? Brownie tried again.

After the computer told him to wait one more time, the answer came: *None.*

Brownie was still playing the computer fifteen minutes later, trying to come up with something on Crawford other than the fact that the criminal justice system had never even heard of him.

'Clare, can you tap into vital stats on this thing?'

Officer Moore pulled a roller-bottomed chair from under an empty console and scooted in next to Brownie. He got a sharp whiff of perfume as she pressed in close. 'Can't do it,' she replied.

'You're not on shared access with state government?'

'Not officially. Sometimes we can get clearance for special projects.'

'Well, do you have an interrogation code?'

She gave him a quizzical look. 'What good will that do you without an entry key?'

Brownie gave her a knowing smile. 'You just get me in the door. I'll take it from there.'

Officer Moore leaned across his lap and began rattling numbers and letters on the keyboard. After several strokes, a menu of state computer services came up.

'Okay, where do you want to go?'

Brownie scanned the list. 'State tax division.'

'You're crazy. That's one place that even we're not allowed.'

Brownie smiled again. 'Go ahead. Make an inquiry.'

She gave him a skeptical look and hit several keys.

Access Denied. Oh. St. Penal Code SubChapt. 32.7 materialized on the screen.

Officer Moore turned to Brownie. 'I told you so!' beamed from her face, but she didn't say anything.

'Thank you,' the sergeant said. 'Now it's my turn.'

He took over and typed in *IMX EM 25 – 32.7 0>R>*.

Clare's eyes went wide as the screen took the feed and told the operator to wait. 'You're in! How'd you do that?'

Brownie tried not to look too smug. 'There's always

an override switch. Just gotta know where it is.'

Officer Moore watched in awe as Brownie played back the files in Crawford's subdirectory. Social security number. Dependent information. Place of employment. 'There it is,' Brownie said triumphantly as *Lancaster Furniture, 2778 Malburn Avenue* came up on the screen. 'Now all we do is cross-reference their withholding list, and we got us a bunch of employees to talk to.'

Clare was still speechless. She had never seen anyone take on a computer like this. The man was amazing. She just hoped that he didn't finish his investigation before he got a chance to show her the full extent of what he could do.

The knock at the door at three o'clock was so faint that Gardner didn't hear it at first over the blare of the cartoon video. The second time jt was louder, and Gardner lifted Granville off his lap, placed him gently on the sofa, and went to find out who had come for an unannounced visit. He opened the door and was surprised to see Charlie Barnes.

'Sorry to bother you, sir.'

Gardner could see that he was disturbed, so he asked the officer in. 'What's going on, Charlie?'

'Need to talk to you, Mr. Lawson.'

Granville was so absorbed by the show he didn't even notice they had company. Gardner ushered Barnes into the kitchen and gave him a seat at the small round table. 'What's up?'

The officer started to speak, but the call of 'Faaaattttherrrr' interrupted as Pinocchio searched the ocean floor for Geppetto.

Gardner excused himself and went to turn down the volume. Then he returned to the table. 'Sorry. Now, what's up?'

Barnes's face looked pained. 'Had a fatal out on Mountain Road last night.'

Gardner didn't react, and his frown suddenly made the officer feel uncomfortable. 'You gonna file charges?' Gardner finally said.

'Don't know if there was anyone else involved. Car went over the rail. If it wasn't an accident, it was hit-and-run, but . . . that's not why I came over. There was something . . .'

Gardner's attention sharpened.

'Something strange, I thought I should tell you about it.'

'I'm listening.'

'I was first on the scene. It was bad. A real mess. Guy got the steering wheel jammed in his chest . . .'

'Dead?'

'No. Not at first. When I checked on him he was still conscious. Talking. Sir, that was the strange part. What he said . . .'

Gardner waited.

Barnes's face paled. 'Was talking crazy. Said he had to see you . . . said something about the Russians . . . and Kent King . . . and . . . James Bond.'

'James Bond?' Gardner frowned.

'The medics were working on him. Trying to get him unstuck from the wheel. When they pulled him off, the pressure dropped and they lost him. But before he died, he kept repeating, "Double-O seven. Double-O seven . . ." I just assumed that he meant James Bond.'

* * *

Mountain Road bisected the county as it sliced on an east-west heading toward the state border. When it was built almost a century ago, the builders camped in flat indentations they had blasted into the rock. Most of these sites were proximate to the highway, but a few were set back in the hills, away from the road.

Kent King had received his meeting signal an hour earlier, at 3:00 P.M. Two rings and a hang-up, followed by three rings and a hang-up. They needed to see him, and without delay. It was not the ideal time to meet. Daylight. Saturday afternoon. Lots of fishermen hitting the off-beaten trails. But he was summoned, and at least for now he had to obey.

King gunned the Jaguar around the turns that were now mapped in his mind. His hands readied for the next twist before it appeared, then shifted to a gear-down as the road dipped and the bottom dropped out. Soon he was there, at the narrow stone channel that led to a private ledge overlooking Apple Valley. And then he was inside, pulling to a sharp stop next to a familiar black car.

There was only one of them this time, leaning against the door of his vehicle, arms crossed, smoking a cigarette. King walked the short distance and faced the man, who stood erect and tossed his butt over the rim.

'What do you want?' King spoke first.

'We may have a bit of a problem,' the man said. His accent was British. He wore dark pants and a black sweater.

'Yeah, what?' The attorney's tone was flippant.

'You gave us certain assurances . . .' The man's calm

voice was reserved, controlled.

'Yeah . . .' King put his hands on his hips.

'And we wanted to make sure that you intended to perform.'

'What the hell are you talking about?' King's anger surged to the surface.

The man's aplomb remained. 'There may be some new developments before this case is concluded.'

The attorney's eyes flared. 'Lawson?'

The man nodded. 'We have reason to believe he's starting to think, and that's not good.'

The defense attorney turned his back, then spun around. 'He's not going to be a problem.'

The man stayed steady. 'You told us that, but now it appears that he may be.'

'I told you I'd handle Lawson!' King yelled.

'Take it easy,' the man said. 'You know our concerns. If you can't do the job, we will get someone who can.'

King's eyes burned. 'I assure you, I'll handle it.'

'You'd best do that.' The smugness of the words implied that the man held a hammer in his gloved fist.

'I'm gonna need the package,' King said suddenly.

The man lit another cigarette. 'What on earth for?' he said through the smoke. 'Going to use it on *him*?'

King's face looked sinister. 'Something like that,' he said.

The man coughed, then laughed. 'Hate the bugger that much, do you?'

King said nothing. His face showed a resolve that drove the point home without argument.

'All right. You'll have it. It will be at the drop by six

P.M.' Before parting, the man repeated his warning. 'You know what we expect . . .'

King smiled for the first time. 'Not to worry,' he said. 'Everything is gonna turn out just fine!'

On the drive back to town, the defense attorney chuckled to himself. The foreigners were incredible. They entered and exited the scene like ghosts. Providing information. Giving orders. Setting up scenarios for the trial. There was one factor they couldn't predict, and that gave King the advantage. He laughed out loud. 'Do it, Lawson!' he said. 'Just fuckin' do it!' Then he pushed hard on the accelerator and moulded his sleek Jaguar into the banked contour of the road.

At 7:30 P.M., Brownie went to the home of Jonathan Salisbury, a man listed in the computer files as a long-time co-worker of Thomas Ira Crawford. He had called earlier and set up the interview, using the nice-cop routine. Crawford's car had been reported as involved in a hit-and-run, Brownie had told him, but he was sure it was all a big mistake. All he needed was some background information to help clear it up.

'I appreciate your seein' me,' Brownie said as Salisbury cracked his front door open and peeked through to confirm that the face on the ID was the same as its bearer.

'Uh, okay. Anything I can do to help Ira . . .' The man let Brownie enter his dim foyer, then directed him to an equally dim living room. 'Uh, you said he had a problem in Maryland?'

Brownie sat down in a burlap-covered chair. He could

feel a loose spring pressing unevenly against his left buttock. 'Yeah, 'fraid so. Got a motor vehicle situation that we need to get straight.'

'And you think I can assist?' There was a look of incredulity on the fiftyish man's puffy face.

'Well, let me put it to you this way. If I went to him directly, I just might have to file charges . . . and I think you know what that would mean.'

'Probably kill him.'

Brownie nodded. Crawford's history was written in the sequential filings of his tax returns. In six years, he'd lost all of his dependents. Mother. Wife. Son. There was no one left, and the pages of his state document file left little doubt that his life was in pathetic decline. There was nothing in the records to connect the man with the case, but the officer could sense it was there, a hidden passageway between the paper trail and Sessy's Woods. All he had to do was get someone to show him the way.

'Shame about the family,' Brownie said in a tone that implied he knew the full story.

'Uh, tragedy is more like it.' Brownie could see the man heading for the lure. 'Wife and son gone.'

'Just like that . . .'

'They were the best family in town,' the man said, lapsing into a reverie. 'Mary. Lovely lady. And Tommie Junior . . . never forget the day they went out to the airport to pick the little fella up . . . happiest day of his life, Ira told me. Happiest of his life . . .'

'The boy was adopted?' Brownie asked.

'She couldn't have kids. He wanted one so bad . . .

they waited and waited. Finally the papers came through. He showed me a picture. "That's my son," he told me. "That's my new little boy." '

'And then they were taken away,' Brownie said in a somber tone.

The man's face showed pain. 'He had to let the boy go visit his country . . . something about his heritage. Had to meet his own people.' The memory was tearing him apart. 'Ira couldn't go. Mary was sick, and he couldn't leave her . . . had to let the boy travel alone.' His voice dropped to a whisper. 'That's when it happened . . .'

Brownie waited for the final word.

'That's when those sons of bitches killed him.'

Gardner was restless. Brownie still hadn't called, and the Charlie Barnes visit had twisted his mind into a throbbing knot. It was 8:00 P.M. The sky beyond the living room window had turned black, and he hadn't been out all day. Granville was videoed out, asleep on the couch. It was time to look at the puzzle again. If Brownie didn't get back with some information, he'd have to wing it alone.

The file was scattered across the dining room table. He had been picking at it since daybreak. Between videotape changes and feedings, he was unable to get any continuity to his search.

The evidence, he thought, the goddamn evidence. He slid a legal pad across the mahogany surface. He had made some notations earlier, in the left-hand margin. At the top was the word JUSTICE. He had underlined it and written several other words underneath:

SEX
WOUND
KNIFE
BLOOD
SHIRT
ALIBI

Through each word he had drawn a line.

After the Barnes visit, he had returned to the pad and made some new notes on the right-hand side. At the top he wrote RUSSIANS. He underlined it and made some notes below:

GLASNOST
SECRET INVESTIGATION
VICTIM'S FATHER
NO AUTOPSY
NO INFORMATION
STATE DEPARTMENT

Gardner looked at the pad. The words of Charlie Barnes had been eating at him all afternoon. 'James Bond. Double-O seven. James Bond. Double-O seven.' He studied the page, going over each item as he would in the preparation of his final argument to the jury. What the hell did it mean? How did that phrase go with the others? He wrote *007* below the last entry and studied the list. He had seen the proximity of those words before. A long time ago. In newspaper articles and magazines. Then he remembered.

'Holy shit!' he said. Beside the numbers he added two more words: KOREAN AIRLINER.

Gardner kept pen in hand and moved to the space between the two columns. In giant letters he wrote a final word, then circled it and circled it, until the paper was almost perforated.

'I know what that says.'

Gardner jumped with surprise as Granville spoke. His eyes were sleepy, and he had a crease on his cheek from the fabric on the couch.

' "King," ' said the boy as he pointed to the circled word. 'It says "King." '

Gardner grabbed his son and pulled him close. 'You're very smart,' he said.

Granville arched his neck back so he could see his father's face. The eyelids still drooped slightly, but there was a sparkle. 'So are you, Dad,' he replied.

Brownie called after midnight, waking Gardner from yet another permutation of his continuing dream. This time there were two divers in the submerged wreck. Two divers calmly pursuing him as he scoured the bulkhead for a way out. On one panicky sweep, his light caught their faces. One was a scowling T. J., his eyes vacant sockets absorbing the beam, a death's head in the murk. The other was a smiling, arrogant Kent King.

The phone erased the images and yanked Gardner up with a start. 'Uh, hello?'

'Boss?'

'Brownie!' Gardner snapped, now fully awake.

'Apologize for the time, but had some problems . . .' There was a voice in the background that had a female ring to it. 'Doin' just fine now.'

'You with someone?' Gardner asked.

Brownie laughed, then turned serious. 'A friend. Uh, listen, I think we got a track on this thing. Possible connection—'

'The Russians shot down an airliner,' Gardner cut in.

'You know about that?' Brownie sounded shocked. 'How you know 'bout that?'

'Charlie Barnes.'

'Give the man a medal,' Brownie said. 'Suppose he told you 'bout Crawford's son, too.'

Gardner tensed. The follow-up was logical. 'His son was on the plane.'

'You got it. Blown to bits by a Russian missile in 1983.'

They talked for half an hour, comparing notes and theories, piecing together the information that each had come up with independently.

'So Crawford's son was killed by Russians, and his car shows up at the same spot a diplomat's son is murdered,' Gardner said. 'What else do we have?'

'You mean evidence?' Brownie asked.

'Uh-huh.'

'Nothin'. Not a goddamn thing.'

'Then we've gotta get it from Crawford,' Gardner said.

'Get what?'

'A tie-in to the crime. A connector. Maybe he kept something.'

'Search the man's house? What's my probable cause?'

Gardner hesitated. The facts were speculative at best. They couldn't even place Crawford in the car, so a search warrant was impossible.

'Well?' Brownie was waiting for directions.

'You've gotta confront him,' Gardner said. 'Hit him with the accusation, and hope he'll crack.' There was no other choice. The jury was waiting, and they didn't have time for subtle maneuverings.

'What about King?' Brownie moved to the next phase. 'What the hell's he doin' with the damn Russians?'

'I thought it was me,' Gardner said. 'Thought he was trying to turn the thing around on me.'

'But now it seems like he want to let ole T. J. fry after all . . .'

Gardner had never figured King for this. Selling out his own client. Even for him it was too extreme. He was a defense attorney to the core. Doing a fake fall to gain the advantage was one thing, but letting an innocent client burn was another. 'You have to get me something, Brownie. Something solid . . .'

'Something you can turn around on King?'

'Uh-huh. We can't let him win this one.' Gardner winced at the irony of a conviction being a victory for the defense counsel.

'I'll try,' Brownie said. 'You don't need this kinda aggravation . . . and speakin' of aggravation, you best be careful.' His voice turned taut. 'Them Bears play rough.'

Gardner had already thought about that. It was obvious that the Russians wanted to bury the truth with Justice. 'You think they'd take a shot at me?' he asked.

'They done shot down a whole airliner,' Brownie replied. 'Now what do you think?'

Gardner didn't answer. His mind had latched on to the horror of that scene and the eyes of a child confronting the grown-up realities of the world. 'I get your point,' he said.

'Okay,' Brownie answered. 'I'm gonna have to sign off. Me and Mr. Crawford got a date first thing in the morning, and I need some rest.'

Gardner said good-bye and hung up. One more day was all they had to write the finale, and right now, he couldn't think of a single word of the script.

After an all-night get-acquainted session with Officer Moore, Brownie got an hour's sleep. The next morning he started late, and it was 10:15 when he entered the suburban tree-flanked neighborhood that sheltered the brick ranch house of Thomas Ira Crawford. When Brownie turned the corner of Dudley Drive and saw the whirling bubble lights, he knew immediately that Crawford wasn't going to keep his appointment.

'What's goin' on?' Brownie asked, flashing his badge at a young officer guarding the outside perimeter.

The policeman barely brushed the Maryland ID with his eyes. 'Suicide. Old guy offed himself with a shotgun.' He lifted the yellow tape and let Brownie pass. 'Hell of a way to do it.'

The body was in the kitchen, head half blown away by the blast of heavy-gauge buckshot. The pump shotgun lay on the floor, pointing between his open legs like an arrow.

'Can I help you?' A local police lieutenant had noticed that Brownie was not one of their own.

'Sergeant Joe Brown.' He displayed his badge again. 'I was on my way to see him . . .' He motioned to the body.

The officer gave him a skeptical look. 'You're too late.'

'Yeah. I can tell. What's the word? Man leave a note?'

The lieutenant looked over his shoulder, then back to Brownie. 'Looks standard to me. No forced entry. Nothing disturbed. No altercation. No sign of struggle . . . and . . . no note. They tell me the guy's been a candidate for self-destruction a long time.'

'Would you mind if I took a look around?'

'Mind tellin' me what you're looking for?'

Brownie released one of his patented smiles. 'I've done a few of these back where I come from. Maybe I can help you wrap it up.'

The skeptical look was still there. 'Okay. You can look . . . but don't touch anything!'

Brownie smiled again. 'Wouldn't think of it,' he said, moving off into the living room away from the focal point of the scene.

The photos on the wall supplemented the information that Brownie had already gathered. The dark-haired woman was pretty in a Mid-west way. Wide features. Clear skin. Eyes that still radiated warmth from behind the glass. And there was a little boy. Darker complexion and hair a sharp contrast to his adoptive parents, but clearly a part of the family. Clearly happy to be in America, to be loved by two people in the way that the pictures unmistakably showed that they loved him.

Brownie scoured the house on the pretext of assisting his hosts. He looked for a connector. Anything to tie the man to the crime. All it would take is one tiny piece of physical evidence, Gardner had said. One tiny particle that would confirm their belief. Proof to bring into court and smash into King's face . . . but the house was clean, and the objects inside seemed to say that all Ira Crawford did after his loved ones died was live in lonely misery, and then, when he couldn't take the pain any longer, end it all with the sudden finality of a shotgun blast.

CHAPTER 19

11:30 A.M.

Brownie's alert signal had not shut off since it first kicked in at the diner. He had no problem dealing with run-of-the-mill bad guys, but Russian agents were something else. They had skills that homegrown criminals never dreamed of. And it was for that reason that Brownie decided to stay on the move.

The house was too clean. There were no odd letters. No receipts. No weapons, except for the shotgun. Brownie shook his head in disbelief. If this wasn't a genuine suicide, it was as expert a job as he had ever seen, and that fact left his stomach in a cold discomfort that felt a lot like fear.

'Gonna head out now,' he told the lieutenant.

'Seen enough?'

''Bout all there is.'

'Got any conclusions?'

Brownie looked the senior officer directly in the eye. 'It's a closed shop. Nothin' in. Nothin' out. Whatever really happened you'll probably never know.'

The lieutenant's lips peaked at the corners. 'Thank you for those astute observations.'

'Welcome. No charge,' Brownie said, brushing past and hustling out to Clare's car. He had seen something. One thing in the entire house that could possibly keep the search alive. It wasn't much, but it might lead to the confirmation that Gardner needed.

He started the engine and prepared to pull out, then stopped, extracted his revolver, and reloaded with armor-piercing Teflon bullets. He had to go back and see Salisbury again, and the meeting was too important to abide any interruptions.

Gardner called Jennifer at first light and asked her to come to the town house. She wanted a preview on the phone, but he held back. The earliest they could meet was noon, she said. That was okay with Gardner. He had some father-son business to take care of until then.

When she arrived he told her everything he and Brownie had discovered so far.

'Revenge?' Jennifer's face registered Richter-scale surprise.

The chief prosecutor nodded. They were sitting in the living room while Granville munched a pan-fried hot dog in the kitchen. Both wore their sweat suits.

'And King knows the whole story?' Her face wrinkled in disbelief.

'Appears that way.' Gardner shifted position on the couch. 'He's been rat-holing the evidence all along and keeping his mouth shut.'

'Why, for God's sake?' Jennifer asked.

'So his client will burn. The Russians got to King and bought him off.'

'Almost done!' Granville hollered from the other room.

'Stay till you've finished everything,' his father yelled back, 'then go wash up.'

Jennifer smiled at the exchange, then reverted to her previous expression. 'So what happens to T. J.?'

That was a question that had eaten the prosecutor's insides down to the outer membrane. He looked at his assistant. 'Depends on what Brownie can come up with.'

'Aiieeee!' Granville stormed into the room and charged at Jennifer, diving headfirst and ending up in a tangle on her lap.

'Ooof!' she said. 'You are soooo big!'

'Gran, be polite,' Gardner admonished.

Jennifer adjusted her position and the boy slid to the seat.

'Let Dad talk to Miss Jennifer for a while, okay?' Gardner said gently.

Granville nodded and snuggled next to the young assistant.

'Are you gonna pull the case . . . ?' Jennifer asked over the downy head. 'Or finish it?'

Gardner had thought about her question a lot since yesterday. Let the pieces lie where they were. Let someone else worry about the truth. He had a child killer against the wall, and the defense attorney was giving him a free shot. Why not take it? Why not get the bastard off the street for good? He could do it. Just send the case to the jury 'as is.' Forget the other things. They were mere innuendos. T. J. had sinned in the past and escaped punishment. Now he could get his due and no one would care. It could happen, and King would allow it, and never, now or in the future, raise an objection.

'Gard? What are you going to do?' Jennifer was still pressing for an answer.

Gardner looked her in the eye. 'I don't know yet,' he said, his mind wandering as he spoke to a vision of T. J. Justice strapped in the metal restraining chair of the gas chamber.

The deep-creased shadows of the ridge lay across Gardner's route out to Watson Road. It was 6:00 P.M., Sunday. His visitation privilege had expired, and it was time to return Granville to his mother.

Brownie had called two hours ago with an update. The news about Crawford hit Gardner like a rock.

'Homicide?' he asked.

'Can't tell,' Brownie said. 'Slick. Real slick.'

'So that's it, then.' Gardner sounded beaten.

'Not quite.' There was optimism in the officer's voice.

He'd found a lead, Brownie went on, the thing he'd seen in the house. Spent all afternoon following it up, and now he had a photo to show the prosecutor. It was something they were looking for. Something to turn the case around. And it couldn't wait.

'Have to fax it,' Gardner told him. 'I'll be in my office at six-thirty. Get yourself a machine and send it then.'

Now he had to rush to get the boy home and head back to town. The weekend had worn him out, although they hadn't done a thing, and now he faced one final night before King and the Russians forced him into judgment day.

'Not too much fun, huh, Dad?'

Gardner's preoccupation had shortchanged the boy all weekend. 'Uh, what'd you say, son?' He turned, a lump forming in his throat as he took his eyes off the road for a second and looked at the boy strapped in the bucket seat next to him.

'Don't like stayin' inside. Mom makes me do it . . .'

Gardner patted the soft blond head. 'I'm sorry, Gran. Dad told you he had to do some office stuff. We won't do that anymore.'

'Can we go get ice cream?'

'Gotta get you back to Mom. Don't want her to worry.'

The small face drooped. '*Please?*'

Gardner's heart ached to say yes, but the rules that had been set a long time ago had to be obeyed. 'We can't, son. I'm sorry. Next time, I promise.'

The child sat in silence and the father patted his head again. It was hard to describe the feelings that bubbled up when he was with his son. Gardner knew only one thing. If anything ever happened to the boy, he would go crazy.

The turn-back at Carole's was typical. Her cold stare from the doorway. Granville's hug, kiss on the cheek, wave good-bye, and immediate disappearance into the fortress. The emptiness inside as he drove away. It never got any better. And lately, it seemed, it was getting more painful.

He drove out quickly, letting his mind reabsorb the concerns of the case. What had Brownie found? And would it make any difference? Whatever it was had to be decisive. A half-baked theory or inference wasn't going to cut it. The evidence had to lock Crawford in and Justice out, or they would be back where they started. King had to be dealt a death blow. If they missed, he'd come after Gardner with a vengeance.

He arrived at the office at 7:00 P.M. and went to his desk. The room was cool, so he kept his jacket on while he attempted to thumb through the file. His concentration drifted. He was nervous and couldn't keep his eyes on the pages. He stood up and began to pace. 'Come on, Brownie!' he cheered silently as he made round after round on the oriental rug.

Finally, at 8:30 P.M., the call came in.

'Hello? Yeah, I'm here,' Gardner said.

'Okay. I'm gonna feed it through in a minute,' Brownie responded. 'I gotta show these Seven-Eleven people how to use their own damn machine.'

Gardner sat in the quiet gloom of his office, waiting for the proof that Brownie had spent all afternoon tracking down.

He'd seen a dust-covered trophy case in Crawford's house. Empty, but with an indentation in its velvet lining. The Cincinnati cops didn't give it a second glance, but Brownie measured its dimensions and decided it had to be followed up. That led him back to Salisbury, and finally to a photograph of the evidence they desperately needed.

'First one comin' now,' Brownie announced, as the

office fax began its electronic hum and engaged its rollers.

The page seemed forever coming. Finally it began to clear the chute on its way to the plastic tray. 'But that's—' Gardner said.

'Sending the child first. Thought you should see what got this thing started.'

The tray was almost filled now, and the prosecutor found himself staring into the wide brown eyes of a tiny oriental boy.

'Number two on the way . . .'

As the second page ticked in, Gardner looked at the little oval face. His eyes started to close, then jerked open again. For a second the child had changed into Mikhail Anatov.

'It's in your hands now,' Brownie said on the phone line.

Gardner pulled the second faxed photo out of the machine. It was a picture of a middle-aged man with a child on his lap.

'That's Crawford,' Brownie said, 'with little Tommie.'

The prosecutor pulled the page close and looked at the face. No way was the man a killer. At least not then.

'Now look behind,' Brownie continued, 'on the wall.'

Gardner could see a square glass cabinet behind the sofa.

'You got a magnifier?'

'Uh-huh.'

'Take a look at the case. Inside.'

The State's Attorney adjusted the glass over the page the way he had done with the aerial shots.

'Crawford was in the navy,' Brownie narrated as the object under the glass sharpened in clarity, 'picked up this souvenir in North Africa.'

Gardner's heart felt like it was missing every other beat. In the centre of the display was a dagger, and as the focal point ran down the blade, he recalled his conversation with the medical examiner.

'That's it!' he said when he hit the tip. There was a small curving hook at the end.

'Now check out the handle,' Brownie said.

The prosecutor jumped the glass up to the top of the case.

The grip seemed to be studded with jewels.

'Look at the third one . . . seem familiar?' Gardner's mind flew back to the night that he and Brownie had been one step ahead of the Russians at Sessy's Woods. He saw Brownie bending down . . .

'The chip!'

'Could be. If we got a hold of the knife we could tell for sure.'

Gardner heard a commotion on the other end, then, 'Oh shit! Done all I could. Gotta go. See you . . .' Then the line went dead.

'Brownie?' Gardner knew it was no use. 'Brownie?' There was no answer. 'Goddamn it!' he screamed at the dial tone. His friend was a survivor. He knew that. But the forces against them were deadly and unpredictable. Capable of anything. Gardner put the phone back on the hook. 'Keep your head down, Brownie,' he whispered.

At nine o'clock he was still at the office, praying that

Brownie would call back, fear gnawing at his insides. He literally jumped when the phone rang. 'Lawson,' he barked. 'Is that you, Brownie?'

'No,' Jennifer said. 'It's me. Thank God you're there.' Her voice was trembling. 'Did he come through?'

'Yes. I got something, but it's still not enough. There's one more angle . . .'

'I'm coming over.'

'No!' Gardner screamed. 'I want you to stay away. This is dangerous, and the farther you are away from me the better.'

'You can't order me to do that!'

'Jennifer! This isn't moot court! This is the big time! Do you understand that? It's more serious than we thought.'

'I'm coming over, and you can't stop me,' Jennifer said before slamming down the phone.

'Shit!' Gardner said. He didn't want her hurt, and for the first time, he understood why.

Gardner had come to a conclusion the night that he and Brownie looked at the aerial photos. He was sure that the car had stopped on Minecastle Road for a purpose. There was a mysterious logic to the actions of Crawford on the night of the killing. For hours, he stayed in the area. He didn't run back to Ohio. He took his time, and parked in the most remote section of the county, far from the interstate. He had to know the terrain. And he had to have a reason. And Gardner had thought from the beginning that it had something to do with the knife.

'Minecastle Road,' Gardner said aloud. 'He stopped

on Minecastle Road. What the hell's out there?' He spread the aerial photos out on the conference table next to a county map. There was nothing out there. Nothing for ten miles in any direction.

Gardner studied the map, then let his eyes drift down to the margin. Copyright 1984. A recent edition.

He got up and went into the library, hoping that his predecessor had left behind one of his old county treatises after he relinquished the mantle of power and went off to retirement.

'Andy's corner' had been untouched for years. An oak bookcase full of lop-eared law volumes and a straight-backed chair. That's all it was. The current law was on the other side of the room, so this section served as little more than a memorial to forgotten people in a forgotten time.

Gardner poked through the rubble. *Treatise on Property Transfers 1905. Contract Disputes 1920.* The pages were on the brink of disintegration, so the prosecutor carefully returned each book to its rightful slot. Finally, on the bottom row, he saw it: *Western Maryland History 1800–1955.*

Gardner carefully withdrew the book and put it on the table under the brass swing lamp he had accidentally jostled, leaving the light to finish its hypnotically slow cycle of swings. He sat down and took a deep breath. Then he opened to the back, ran the index, and turned to page 208.

It was a map of the western end of the county, decaying and creased, but still legible. As the shadow of the lamp swayed across the page, he looked for a landmark, the way Brownie had showed him. Soon he found West Run and followed the road out toward the second ridge line. When he got to the intersection, he checked the name. Instead of Minecastle, it said Castle Mine.

His finger continued the journey, finally stopping at the point in the road where Crawford's vehicle had been spotted by a supersonic jet almost seventy years after the chart had been drawn.

'Oh my G—' Gardner felt his body fire with adrenaline. He put an X mark where the car parked. The space above looked normal, the same as today. But below, in the hill area, there was a notation that didn't appear on the 1984 map: HERBERT CASTLE MINE. CLOSED PERMANENTLY 1910. SHAFT FLOODED TO SURFACE LEVEL BY UNDERGROUND SPRING.

PART V

Sounding the Verdict

CHAPTER 20

Gardner was just leaving when Jennifer arrived at 9:25. He ushered her down the stairs and around behind the building where his car was parked. The streets were steeped in Sunday-night silence, devoid of motion from either man or machine, and the rear-lot streetlamp was out.

'What are you doing?' Jennifer huffed, trying to catch her breath from the run.

There was a bright glow projecting around the corner of the State's Attorney's office from Court Avenue. It had found its way to Jennifer's glasses and reflected a double image of Gardner in her eyes.

'I've got to follow up one last lead,' he said.

'You never told me about the first one.'

'Brownie located the murder weapon. I've got to get it.'

Jennifer closed in. 'I'm coming with you.'

'You can't,' Gardner said. His voice was a lot more gentle than it had been on the phone. 'This is one thing I have to do on my own.'

'Still pushing me away!' The anger was shot through

with frustration. Gardner took her by the shoulders and pulled her against his chest the way she had done to him the night at Paul's. 'Jen . . .' She gripped his back, then withdrew her head so she could see his face. Neither spoke. They simply exchanged a look that sealed a new understanding. Then there was a slow approach, and their lips met. And as their bodies nestled warmly, the prosecutor felt that, for the first time in years, the match-up was right.

Gardner finally convinced Jennifer that it was best for her to wait for him at the orchard. He gave her the key and told her how to get past the chain, lock it, and hide the car.

'I'll be out when I'm done. It may be late, but stay there.'

Jennifer nodded, gripping his hand tightly with her squared-off nails. 'Shouldn't we tell someone . . .'

Gardner wrinkled his forehead. 'Who? Who in this world can we trust, except Brownie . . . and God knows what's happened to him.'

They hugged again, and Jennifer got into her car. Gardner signaled her to roll down the window. He leaned in and gave her another kiss. This one lingered sweetly, and foretold others.

'One more thing,' he said.

'What's that?'

'You are hereby ordered not to refer to me as "boss" ever again.'

Kent King banged the keys on his telephone for a third time. 'Damn you, Lawson,' he growled to the unanswered ring. 'You're s'posed to be getting ready for tomorrow . . .'

He let the line buzz six more times, then slammed down the receiver. 'Motherfucker isn't making it easy,' he said, getting up and walking to the window. There was no moon to activate the shadow of the mountains. A garage light framed the rancher across the street, casting enough illumination to reach the pavement. The black car was gone. It had pulled in twice for spot checks, then, in its usual routine, blended again with the night.

King laughed and shook his head. 'Fuckin' cowboys!' he said derisively, then walked back to the phone. This time there was an answer on the first ring.

'Yeah?'

'Bruno!' King huffed. 'Where the hell are you?' The road noise came through the cellular line loud and clear.

'Comin' down West Run now.'

'You got Lawson?'

Calvano hesitated. 'No.' The word carried the question: Was I s'posed to?

'What did I tell you?'

Another hesitation as Bruno tried to remember his orders. 'You said to track him as usual and let you know if he does something strange.'

'Well?'

'He didn't do nothin'. Stayed home with his kid. Took him out Watson Road, then went to his office.'

'Where is the son of a bitch now?'

Silence.

'Bruno?'

'Last I saw him, he was goin' in the courthouse.'

'And you left?'

'Got hungry. Slipped up Wako's for a bite.'

'Well, I suggest you get your ass back to town and pray that he hasn't left.'

Calvano knew he had screwed up. 'Okay . . . okay, I'm sorry. I'm goin' now.'

'Report back when you get there. I'll be on my mobile number.'

King slammed down the phone and pulled a key ring from his pocket. He then unlocked the bottom drawer of his desk and withdrew a small rectangular box. 'Got a victory present for you, Gardner,' he muttered aloud.

King grabbed the box in one hand and his coat in the other, and without further ado ran out of the door, jumped into his car, and drove away.

Gardner drove to the ministorage parking lot and parked in front of bin 25. The last time he had been there was to deposit some overflow items from Watson Road after the divorce. A twinge of sadness pinched his heart as he rolled up the garage-type door. It was 10:00 P.M. and very dark. With a flashlight, he searched through the shrouded furniture. The tank was still there. After three and a half years, still propped against the back wall. And next to it was the wooden crate with the rest of his scuba equipment.

He looked in the box, found the pressure gauge, and fitted it over the valve. It started hissing when he turned the knob, but quickly stopped after the seal took hold.

'Fifteen hundred p.s.i.,' Gardner said out loud.

Enough air for about five minutes at depth.

He rifled the box in search of his decompression table, finally finding the plastic card at the bottom. Then he pulled out his mask, fins, regulator, buoyancy compensation vest, and from another box, his wet suit. Everything looked okay. The dampness of the concrete chamber had kept the dry rot to a minimum.

This was it. Decision time. The nights and days stretching back to Cayman logically ended here. Gardner took another stab at justifying inaction. He did not have to go, he told himself. Justice deserved to die for the Kansas case. What did it matter if the retribution was off center? When the ax came down it would be in the name of all the innocents he had hurt, not Mikhail Anatov. So what?

He picked up the tank and slung it under his arm. The go/no-go decision still bounced around in his head. Then he realized the real problem. It didn't concern T. J. It didn't even concern King. His mind was locked in the nightmare wreck, and the thought of diving again, for any reason, had broken him into a cold sweat.

He bunched the other gear into the carrying-bag, steadying himself against the wall as a wave of dizziness swept through him. He imagined Carole's eyes studying him, smugly predicting he would fold. Then he thought of Granville, and Tommie Crawford, and the Russian child. They were watching him. Cheering him on. Counting on him . . .

In an instant he was out of the door, lugging the equipment to the truck. The coolness of the air and the darkness of the sky confirmed the ominous truth. The sunny days and balmy breezes had flown south where vacationers dived for pleasure. On this night Gardner would dive into the core of the unknown. He would do it for a child, and for himself. And he would do it alone.

Kent King was in his Jaguar, on the Post Road to town, when his car phone purred.

'King.'

'It's me,' Bruno said.

'You'd better have good news,' the attorney growled.

There was a brief pause. 'He ain't here,' the investigator replied. 'Came back the route to his place, and didn't see him. Car's not at the court . . .'

King leaned back hard against the seat and gripped the wheel with a grunt.

'What?' Calvano asked.

'Nothin'.' King huffed. He was thinking. Lawson wasn't home, and he wasn't at the office. 'Bruno?'

'Yeah?'

'Try Tower's. If he isn't there, get back to his house and wait till I call you.'

'Okay . . . Uh, what are you gonna do?'

King had already spun a U-turn and reversed his direction. The engine revved as he pushed up the speed. 'I have an idea where he may be,' he said. 'Call you back.'

King popped the phone back into its holder and glanced into his rearview mirror. The view was clear, but that didn't mean much. They always knew where he was, as if he had a beeper. Bruno had swept the car for him with a debugger and didn't find anything, but they still seemed to know his every move.

He made some turns and cutbacks to be sure that he was alone. If his suspicions were correct, he'd find Lawson. And this meeting was definitely private.

The road seemed different at night. Curves came up faster and turned sharper than they did in the daylight. And the speed was hard to keep under control.

It was 11:15 when Gardner stopped at Hodges so he could wedge the tank between his spare tire and the bag of equipment. It had been banging loosely on the turns, and if the valve end hit too hard the bottle could blow.

He looked at the string of shacks dimly illuminated under the trees, trying to see unit 15, but it was not quite visible from his position.

Gardner pictured T. J. pigging out on the pile of food in his cabin, picking at it with his knife, digging into chunks of meat with the blade. His revulsion for T. J. hadn't diminished a bit since he learned the truth. If anything, it had multiplied. Justice killed for pleasure. No agonizing loss had driven him insane and set him up as an avenger. He was programmed to kill, and all the do-gooder shrinks in the world couldn't change that. If he walked, he'd probably kill again – and Gardner could stop it, if he just turned the vehicle around and forgot all about Crawford and his dead child at the bottom of the sea.

His thoughts continued to flow with the undulations of the road. Pros and cons. Rights and wrongs. Lives and deaths. And underneath was the granite base: the sanctity of the law.

Gardner's headlights illuminated a signpost. He

slowed to read it, then flipped his turn signal to blink at a vacant expanse of road trailing behind. JCT. MINECASTLE ROAD, it said. He took a deep breath. It was finally clear. There was no decision to make. Not really. His course through life was plotted by some other force, and now he knew that it had always led here, to the mine. Whatever lay in its depths had been put there for him. And it was up to him to find it.

Jennifer didn't like taking orders anymore. She started for the orchard, but then had second thoughts. Gardner was too important to lose. She needed him. And he needed her. After all their time together as associates before the bar, they had transcended the barriers of courthouse protocol and knit together as one. And tonight she was not going to let him pull away.

Jennifer picked up the stack of case materials that Gardner had dumped in her car before they were interrupted by the kiss. Trial folder. Witness notes. Report file. Then she saw the book, and it didn't take her long to find the map and the X mark above the mine. She recoiled in shock. The Cayman incident had made the rounds on the office grapevine. She knew that Gardner had not been near the water since then. And she knew what he was going to do. Whatever happened, she was going to be there.

CHAPTER 21

12:00 Midnight

Gardner stood on the lip of the flooded mine and stared into its depths. The entrance was a horizontal cut into the hillside that time had covered with a blanket of vines, but which someone had disturbed in the recent past. A section of growth had been chopped and the boards pulled back. All Gardner had to do was yank some new shoots, push the rotting timbers aside, and he was in.

And now he was perched above the plummeting shaft, shining his light into the frigid crystal water that appeared to be as limitless in visibility as the Caribbean . . .

The nightmare suddenly came back in a wave of gut-twisting intensity. And it was joined by the sharp reality of what had happened in the trench. Gardner's life had always been a mixture of bravado and intellect. Whatever he couldn't rationalize, he could always fake, and that got him through, most of the time. Courtroom bluffs, adversary showdowns, ski slopes, jogging trails, police disputes, elections, the media . . . He managed to find a way through those. Only his marriage had been different, and the day it was shattered opened with the sun and the sea, and closed with a dive into endless midnight reruns. And now he was there again. Standing above the water line. It was either 'in' or 'out,' and the only finessing he could do this time would be against himself.

Gardner checked his pressure gauge: 1475 p.s.i. Slow leak in the system, he thought. No more time. He held his breath; closed his eyes, and jumped.

There was a cold shock as the icy liquid entered his wet suit, and water leaked into his mask and mouthpiece. He gagged and choked, kicking his legs to stay on the surface, trying to accommodate the feeling that, despite the dreams, had lost all sense of familiarity.

Finally his breathing was under control, mask and regulator cleared, and the layer of water in his neoprene suit warmed to body temperature. He checked the pressure again: 1400 p.s.i. Time to submerge.

The walls were forty feet across. Jagged, uneven rock faces, pitted with chinks and crevices like geologic acne. On the descent, Gardner played his light off the wall to keep himself oriented. As long as he stayed next to the wall he'd be okay, and he wouldn't have to think about what lay below.

But he knew he had to look down. That was the whole point. Scan for the knife. And to do that, he'd have to leave the safety of the wall and shine his lamp into the dark unknown reaches of the pit.

The light slowly slid away from the rock as Gardner

rotated it downward, ultimately stopping at his flippers. He gasped. The effect was terrifying. There was no up. No down. Only a cone of brightness forming a narrow probe toward the bottom, maintaining its strength for fifty feet, then vanishing into subterranean infinity.

Gardner was suddenly back in Cayman. Carole was entering the wreck, and he was frozen, locked in a panic that was about to explode him to the surface.

Gardner struggled for composure. His breathing rate was accelerating out of control. Every nerve in his body screamed with the realization that he was free-falling into oblivion. He tried to fight it, to pull back from the past. He centered the light on a granite outcropping and stared at it, focusing on the spot, which shook with the trembling of his hand. He clung to the light, suspended in a sense-deprivation chamber beneath an ink-black column of water.

Slowly his breathing rate backed down, the shaky motion of the light spot stabilized, and thoughts radiated from an eye of calm. Gardner shone the light down into the pit again. This time he handled the startling sight of a limitless shaft plunging to the center of the earth itself. The idea of finding the knife seemed absurd. He checked his depth. One hundred feet. Air pressure, 600 p.s.i. . . . Nice try, but it wasn't going to work. He was never going to find anything. Not in this watery hellhole. He'd made a mistake to think that he could. The final piece of the puzzle was beyond his reach.

Gardner kicked his fins and forced a blast of air into the b.c. vest, activating a positive buoyancy that gently boosted him toward the surface. He shone the light upward into the mirrored bubbles that glinted with silver. The ascent rate was smooth, under control, like an elevator ride to the top. His mind fought a few final flickerings of the dream. He saw a snarling face in the shadowy rock. He heard a muffled scream . . . but he wasn't sucked in. He was handling the fear and ascending with dignity, like a god returning to the heavens.

He was almost there. Ten feet to go. The lamp was picking up the juncture of air and water, a bright wall of refracted light. Suddenly Gardner felt an ominous jolt. The dream fragments had not yet cleared. There was a dark figure looming above and beyond the silvery lining. His heart leapt. He blinked, trying to make it go away like the other tormenting visions, but it stayed there, lurking just beyond visual definition.

Gardner took one final breath and kicked upward through the air bubbles, rising into the atmosphere with explosive fury. He ripped off his mask and raised the light to the hulking specter. The beam caught a face, which flinched under the intensity of the glare. It was Kent King.

Gardner pulled himself up on the shelf and yanked off his flippers, keeping his adversary frozen in the light as he moved. Then he dropped the tank and stood up. 'What the hell are you doing here, King?' he finally said.

The attorney shielded his eyes from the light. 'Mind lowering that thing?' he said. 'It's bothering me.'

'Too bad,' Gardner replied, but he adjusted the lamp slightly so the other man could see. 'Now tell me what the hell you're doing out here.'

King smirked. 'I could ask you the same thing, but I

know the answer already.' He opened a small box in his hand. 'You're looking for this.'

Gardner adjusted the flashlight to focus on King's hands. Blue and red sparkles erupted from jewels in the handle that lay across one of King's open palms. It was the knife.

Jennifer had raced the back roads in a desperate effort to catch Gardner, making several wrong turns before she finally reached Minecastle. She saw his truck and she moaned to herself, 'Thank God.' But then she saw the Jaguar.

The batteries on her flashlight were half dead, but they managed to get her to the mine entrance, and now she quietly crept toward the voices echoing from the interior of the tunnel. Along the way she picked up a piece of board. A makeshift weapon. Just in case.

The two men faced off on the far side of the shimmering oval. The light played off the surface and gave their faces a surrealistic glow. Jennifer ducked into a rock alcove and listened.

'You bastard!' Gardner said. 'I thought you'd do just about anything, but never sell out your own client. And now you've got yourself a twofer. Sell out your client *and* your country. Fuckin' unbelievable!'

King had shifted the knife in his hand so it was in the vertical-stab position. 'You really think I would do that?' he said softly. 'Something that reprehensible?'

'You've fucked over so many people you don't even know the difference anymore,' Gardner replied.

'Wanna be specific?' King asked.

'You know what I mean.'

'If you're talkin' about yourself, I'd be glad to see you prove it,' King went on, 'but you know you can't. Never could. Never will.'

Gardner took a step toward his enemy. 'You've gone too far this time. All the way to the end of the line.'

The defense attorney raised the knife in anticipation.

Gardner took another step closer. 'What? You gonna use that on me?'

Jennifer stirred in the darkness, pulling the plank up to her shoulder, getting ready to charge.

'Hold on a minute, bunkie!' King hollered. 'We're gettin' off track here. I did not come to this shit hole to have a fight.'

That stopped Gardner short. 'What did you come here for?'

King lowered the weapon. 'To make sure you got the message.'

Gardner sneered. 'Give me a break! What message?'

'Think, Lawson. Goddamn it, think! You figured out Justice didn't do it, right?'

The prosecutor had to agree. 'Yeah, so what?'

'Well, I'm the one who fed you the hints. All through the trial. Me! The guy you just accused of selling out his client! I let you know you had the wrong man. The blood. The X rays. The videotape. I knew you'd put it all together and do the honorable thing, just like you always do. No way was I ever gonna let my guy go down. No fuckin' way!'

Gardner squinted. King was right. The hints had been there. 'But you obstructed justice!' he said angrily.

'Me? You gotta be kidding! *You're* the one who's prosecuting an innocent man! On bogus evidence at that! *You've* got a duty to get it right. Not me!'

Gardner stood in stunned silence. 'Why didn't you give me the information up front?' he said, his voice rising to an angry pitch again. 'Why the hell go through all that bullshit?'

King laughed. 'And spoil the fun? Let's just say other considerations made it appropriate to proceed the way we did. Anyway, I figured you'd get the picture about T. J. before we went to the jury, and drop the case. I never thought you'd solve the fuckin' thing. You're too much, Lawson. Too damn much!'

That did it for Gardner. He pulled his diving knife and took another step toward King. 'You . . .' His eyes were glazed with rage. The torment of the preceding months roared through his head like a freight train. King could have stopped it all at the beginning, but he made Gardner suffer through the agony of the trial. And for what? Just for 'fun.' Gardner raised the knife and moved closer, his body trembling with uncontrolled anger. 'Bastard!' he screamed, the sound echoing in the mine chamber like a howitzer shot.

King clutched the dagger in his hand and retreated to the wall, but Gardner kept coming. 'Hold it now,' he said shakily, 'hold it!'

Gardner was within striking distance. He had King backed into a corner, and he kept moving forward, positioning himself for the kill.

'Gard—' King muttered. 'I'm sorry . . .'

Gardner raised the knife and looked deep into the

enemy's eyes. Every ounce of prior hatred was concentrated in that single moment. The vicious attacks on his private life. The cynical courtroom theatrics. The diabolic plotting. It was all going to end. Gardner readied the knife. 'Adios, motherfucker . . .'

Jennifer knew it was time to move. 'Wait!' she screamed, circling the pool behind Gardner. 'Don't do it!'

Gardner hesitated, his weapon still poised. Then he looked back at King. Something was different. He was no longer King of the courtroom. The arrogance and bravado were gone. He suddenly looked weak and defenseless, even though he was armed. It was the final showdown, one-on-one in the privacy of an underground tomb. And the mighty King had blinked.

That ended it.

Gardner lowered his knife, and King slumped back against the wall with relief. The fight was over before blows were struck, just like the last time. Only this time, both men knew that Gardner had won.

The prosecutor turned to Jennifer, and she smiled. 'Sorry, but I had to come . . .'

'That's okay,' Gardner answered wearily. 'I'm glad you're here.'

King was silent, embarrassed that his tough-guy image had been tarnished. 'So what do we do now?' he asked, his voice subdued.

Gardner turned. 'I know about the airliner and the cover-up, King. You're in serious trouble . . .'

The defense attorney managed a wan smile. 'I didn't do anything . . .'

'You helped them,' Jennifer said.

King slowly returned to his old self. 'Yeah? I wasn't aware that Justice had been convicted.'

'Not yet,' Gardner said.

'Not ever,' King replied. 'The boys from Borscht-land have their agenda, and I have mine.' He straightened up and arched his back.

'So you're gonna double-cross them too!' Gardner's voice rang out against the stone walls.

'Gard, I don't work for anyone but me! I'm a defense attorney! That's all I am. Fuck 'em if they don't know the system. My man was never gonna take the fall for Crawford. Never!'

'So you're giving me the knife to prove it,' Gardner said.

'Well,' King hedged, 'not exactly.'

Gardner extended his hand. 'Give me the knife, Kent.'

'There's no one left to prosecute in this case,' King said. 'Crawford's dead . . .'

'I know,' Gardner replied.

'And it would be healthier all round if we left the particulars alone . . . like who he was and why he did it . . .'

'If you say so,' Gardner replied, his hand still out.

King held up the knife by the blade. 'Those boys went to a lot of trouble to get this thing. Robot minisub. Deep-diving gear. The works.'

'The knife!' Gardner ordered.

'Let's lay it all to rest, here and now,' King said solemnly. 'You and me, the case, the Russians, everything . . .'

Gardner's hand reached out, but before he could

grasp the dagger King flicked his wrist and tossed it into the center of the pool, where it splashed and sank in a silvery helix that took it all the way down to the bottom of the pit.

CHAPTER 22

The next morning was a five-star rendition of May. Superclear, without a single droplet of moisture to fuzz the brilliance of the ridge line, and a temperature rising rapidly through the sixties on its way to the warmth of an early summer noon.

By 9:45, the courthouse was more crowded than it had been on any day throughout the trial. Reporters. Townspeople. And, for the first time, a delegation of Soviets. The two embassy attachés who had been at the November briefing were there, in the front row. And next to them the giant white-haired Russian man, dominating everyone else with his size.

Gardner and Jennifer entered the courtroom together and walked to the counsel table. King was already seated next to Justice. The two sides ignored each other as they waited for the judge to come in.

'Are we ready to proceed?' Danforth asked. 'Defense?'

King nodded.

'State?'

'Yes, Your Honor.'

'Very well. Go to the jury.'

Gardner stood and walked to the podium. The crowd waited in electric silence. 'Your Honor. Mr. Foreman. Ladies and gentlemen of the jury.' He paused and looked around the room, then back at the twelve attentive faces. 'Do you remember my opening statement? When I told you that we all have duties to perform? Remember I said that it is my duty to present the state's case against the defendant, and it's Mr. King's duty to defend, and the court's duty to referee, and your duty to decide?' He paused.

'Well, the prosecutor has another duty. Two additional duties, actually. One is to himself . . . the other is to the law.' The crowd was beginning to stir. They could tell that something was about to happen.

'A State's Attorney is a human being. Fallible. Subject to pressures. Subject to the ups and downs of life, and subject to the trustworthiness of his evidence . . .'

The stir in the gallery was becoming a murmur. 'Please keep it down!' Danforth huffed. 'Continue, Mr. Lawson.'

'The part about duty to self comes into play when a prosecutor realizes he may have made a mistake.'

Another throaty mumble swept through the room.

'I entered this case with a certainty about things. I thought I knew the truth. I thought that the evidence was inviolate.' He looked at King. 'But now I know that I was wrong.'

Gardner's mind swept back to the night in November when Larry Gray's phone call propelled him from one nightmare into another. He felt the cold air on his face and saw the grandmother's pain, and the soft blue eyes of the dead child. Another senseless crime in the season of the falling leaves. A known killer on the loose. Business as usual in the prosecutor's office. It had all seemed so clear then. But the sight line to the truth was distorted like the bending of a sunray in the sea. And Gardner's vision had not acclimated to the deception of its path.

There were more rumblings from the crowd, but this time Danforth kept quiet. The look on his face registered shock, as if he did not believe what he was hearing.

'We use the term "justice" every day,' Gardner continued, his mind refocused. 'We hear it, and we say it, and we fling it around like an old sock. We demand justice! We ask the courts to do justice! We beg for justice!' He stopped and looked at T. J., then turned back to the jury.

'Can anyone define justice?' Gardner put both hands on the rail and looked up. 'Can I?'

His head lowered suddenly and engaged the eyes of the foreman. 'I thought I could. I thought I had it locked away in here.' His fist banged the rib cage above his heart. 'But somehow it got away from me . . .'

The room dropped into silence. No one dared to move. Even the Russians were frozen, barely breathing.

'We call it justice when things go our way. When our side wins. That's all the word means anymore. It's only a battle cry. A hollow slogan. Anyone can use it, right or wrong. Good or bad. Innocent . . . or guilty. It's "just" if we get what we want. "Unjust" if we don't.'

King and the defendant sat motionless. Staring ahead. Not looking at the State's Attorney. The Russian delegation remained stone-faced in the background.

Gardner swallowed hard and looked at the jury again, as a spectral vision raced through his mind. Ira Crawford. Tommie Junior. Mikhail Anatov. Bob Hamilton. All adrift in the sea. All peaceful and asleep, forming a circular pattern on the bottom. And in the middle, buried under the sand, the knife.

'Ladies and gentlemen,' Gardner continued, 'I'm afraid I never quite thought it through. I believed that my way was the "only" way. That I had to win at all costs. That "my" case was "just" . . . but now I know that I was wrong.'

Gardner caught King's eye and beamed a knowing stare. He stared back, then dropped his attention to the table.

The prosecutor turned again to the jury. 'True justice has nothing to do with a "side," ladies and gentlemen. It simply exists. It's like water. It seeks out its own level. It flows like a tide. It rises and falls, despite our puny efforts to change its course, and when the forces are balanced out, remains at rest for eternity. True justice is the only "real" justice. Not the counterfeit that we bow down to . . . true justice is the ultimate equalizer. Neutral in its allegiance. Unbiased. Unprejudiced. Unstoppable. True justice belongs to no individual man . . . it belongs to us all.'

Gardner walked slowly back to the counsel table. The crowd still remained hushed as he looked up at the judge. 'Your Honor, I wish to inform the court that I cannot in good conscience continue to prosecute this case. I am therefore entering a nol pros to all charges.

The case of *State versus Justice* is hereby withdrawn.'

Gardner and Jennifer walked down the courthouse steps
into the sunlight. The reporters had gathered in two
pools, one encircling the Russians, the other around
Kent King and T. J. The defense attorney was patting
Justice's back as the reporters fired their questions. He
had an 'I told you so' expression on his face. On the
fringe was Krysta Collins. As Gardner passed, she
smiled and nodded. Her look said she wasn't surprised
at what had just happened.

The big Russian was up at a cluster of mikes on the
other side. His translator leaned in and out as the
answers were given. 'Of course we are sad that the killer
of Mikhail Anatov has not been punished,' he said. The
expressions of both men reflected stunned disbelief. 'But
we do not want to see the wrong person put to trial,
either.' Between questions they whispered hurriedly in
their own language.

'So you're not upset with the dismissal?' a voice yelled
from the rear of the pack.

The two foreigners conferred again, and the translation followed. 'No. No. No. As we said many times,
the American criminal system is much respected by our
country. We abide by its decisions. And we do not feel
right to question its results . . .'

One of the newsmen spotted Gardner and broke free
from the gaggle around the Russians. The State's
Attorney and his assistant had almost made it off the
apron when he caught up. 'Mr. Lawson, any further
comment on what happened today?'

Gardner stopped and looked around. 'As I said in my statement, based upon my appraisal of the evidence, I do not believe that it would have been proper to send the case to the jury.'

'So you're not going to explain your reasons?' the reporter persisted.

'As I said,' Gardner repeated. 'I decline to prosecute the case further, based upon a reevaluation of the evidence.'

The reporter was not giving up. 'So you're saying that Justice isn't guilty.'

The prosecutor put his hands on his hips. 'No. That's not what I said. You have my statement. That's the only comment I'm going to make.'

The reporter tried again as Gardner turned to leave. 'So is he guilty or not?'

The prosecutor took three steps.

'Well? . . . Is he?'

Gardner stopped and turned. The two pools were changing subjects on the courthouse steps. He looked at the far group and smiled. 'Why don't you ask Mr. King?' he said. Then he grabbed Jennifer's hand and ran for the truck.

'So Brownie's okay?' Jennifer asked breathlessly.

'Yup,' Gardner replied, unlocking the doors. 'Called in this morning. Told Miss Cass to let me know he'd made it.'

'That's great.'

They were attempting to back out of the lot when another car squealed in and blocked their path. It was a black Trans-Am.

'Speak of the devil,' Gardner said.

He adjusted the wheel and eased around to parallel the driver. Brownie's window was open, his face beaming as though he had just eaten the side out of a steer. 'So how'd we do?' he said.

Gardner glanced at Jennifer, then back at his friend. 'Bull's-eye.'

'King?'

Gardner jerked his head toward the media gaggle.

Brownie smiled and nodded. 'Won another one, huh?'

The prosecutor smiled back. 'Doesn't he always?'

Jennifer slid close. 'Glad you're home,' she said.

There was a moment of silence as the three of them cast knowing looks among themselves. Finally Gardner spoke. 'Brownie, thank—'

The officer held up his hand. 'Don't you be givin' me none of that,' he said with mock anger. 'We do what we can. When we can.'

Gardner smiled again.

'Now I got to get me a shower and an hour of sleep. Afternoon shift comin' up, and I gotta look sharp.' With that, the officer whipped his car around and spun out, leaving a plume of smoke in the air that drifted slowly across the pavement and dissipated in the gentle wind blowing down from the top of the ridge.

EPILOGUE

The July meeting of the county bar association was being held in the back dining room at Paul's. The Justice storm had blown itself out long ago. The media gang had left town, and no one even talked about it anymore. The only ripple had come two weeks prior, when a supermarket tabloid announced in a headline, JUSTICE GETS IT IN THE END. It went on to say that T. J. was diagnosed with AIDS after his release, and that some activist lawyers were urging him to sue the prison authorities in Kansas for letting it happen. More on that story later, it promised. Other than that, there was little else about the episode to break the daily routine. New cases were coming in, and old ones were being closed. Life in the valley went on as usual.

Gardner headed up the State's Attorney's table. The agenda for the meeting included lunch and a discussion of the new civil case rules recently enacted in Annapolis. Jennifer and two assistant prosecutors sat to his left, a new prospect for the District Court section to his right. They buzzed irreverently as Judge Danforth outlined the procedures that now had to be followed in filing tort actions. One of Gardner's veterans even whispered a threat to toss a dinner roll at the speaker if he didn't cut it off soon.

On the far side of the room, the defense bar had assembled a group of their own. A smattering of public defenders, two old-timers, and of course, at the head of the table, Kent King.

'Okay, okay, thank you, Judge, for a very enlightening presentation,' the bar president said, inviting a round of polite applause. 'Now we have only one more item to discuss before we adjourn. The site of the annual commissioner's reception.'

There was a stir in the crowd as the tables yelled out locations.

'Blazers!'

'The Mill House!'

'Ramada Inn!'

'Okay, okay, I'd like to get that in the form of a motion. How about you, Mr. State's Attorney, can we get a formal motion on the floor?'

Gardner stood up. A few good-natured catcalls greeted him, then died out. He smiled, glanced at Jennifer, then put on his 'serious' face. 'Mr. President,' the prosecutor said, 'I hereby nominate Muhly's for this year's fete.'

'Okay. Do we have a second?'

'Second!' Jennifer piped up. She again made eye contact with Gardner, and he flashed her a wordless thank-you.

'Okay. Any discussion on the motion?'

There was a rumble of chairs at the far end of the

room, and a man stood and arched his back.

'Point of order, Mr. President.'

The room suddenly hushed.

'The chair recognizes Mr. King. What is it, Kent?'

The group's attention flicked back and forth between King and the State's Attorney. Except for the bar president, they were the only two standing.

King took aim at the prosecutor with his patented courtroom glare.

Gardner held his ground and silently returned fire.

The hush continued. 'It is the opinion of this counsel that Muhly's serves substandard food,' King said sternly. 'I must pose an objection.'

All eyes swung to Gardner. His face was drawn tight, his brow narrowed into a V. Suddenly he smiled and grabbed a roll from the bread basket. Then he drew back and launched it across the room at King.

ACKNOWLEDGMENTS

I would like to express my sincere gratitude to Larry Kirshbaum, President and CEO of Warner Books, for his guidance in the editing of this book. His wise comments and suggestions, along with those of Mel Parker, Vice-President and Publisher of Warner Paperbacks, were invaluable to me in putting together the final version of the story.

In addition, I wish to thank my agent, Arthur Pine, for the friendship, support, and inspiration he has given me from the beginning, and for the tireless efforts he has made to promote the project. Through Arthur I met Joan Sanger, whose editorial expertise transformed the format of the book, and created a viable entity. To her I express my deepest gratitude.

And finally, to Gerry Hogan, Tom Caplan, David Abrahamson, Marty McDonough, Tim Wolf, Ronnie Clarke, Tom Hunter, EvaMae Chiccehitto, and the members of my family, I wish to say that without your encouragement, love, and support, this book could never have been written. Thank you one and all.

G. W.

A selection of bestsellers from Headline

SEE JANE RUN	Joy Fielding	£4.99 ☐
STUD POKER	John Francome	£4.99 ☐
REASONABLE DOUBT	Philip Friedman	£5.99 ☐
QUILLER BAMBOO	Adam Hall	£4.99 ☐
SIRO	David Ignatius	£4.99 ☐
DAY OF ATONEMENT	Faye Kellerman	£4.99 ☐
THE EYE OF DARKNESS	Dean Koontz	£4.99 ☐
LIE TO ME	David Martin	£4.99 ☐
THE LEAGUE OF NIGHT AND FOG	David Morrell	£4.99 ☐
GAMES OF THE HANGMAN	Victor O'Reilly	£5.99 ☐
HEARTS OF STONE	Mark Timlin	£4.50 ☐
JUDGEMENT CALL	Suzy Wetlaufer	£5.99 ☐

All Headline books are available at your local bookshop or newsagent, or can be ordered direct from the publisher. Just tick the titles you want and fill in the form below. Prices and availability subject to change without notice.

Headline Book Publishing PLC, Cash Sales Department, Bookpoint, 39 Milton Park, Abingdon, OXON, OX14 4TD, UK. If you have a credit card you may order by telephone — 0235 831700.

Please enclose a cheque or postal order to the value of the cover price and allow the following for postage and packing:
UK & BFPO: £1.00 for the first book, 50p for the second book and 30p for each additional book ordered up to a maximum charge of £3.00.
OVERSEAS & EIRE: £2.00 for the first book, £1.00 for the second book and 50p for each additional book.

Name ....

Address ....

....

....

If you would prefer to pay by credit card, please complete:
Please debit my Visa/Access/Diner's Card/American Express (delete as applicable) card no:

Signature ....Expiry Date ....